D

"I expect they _____ _____ _____ _____ hand to spin the _____ _____ _____ _____ loud enough to be heard by the colonists lurking in the trees. His free arm settled Irene more firmly against him, the electro-pistol snug against her ribs. . . . "If anyone even shows themselves nearer than thirty feet—we will open fire upon them."

His com beeped. Irene stopped breathing. "Base to Captain Keene." Irene was close enough to hear the tinny voice in Willard's helmet. "This is safety net, clear there?"

Willard scrolled the volume back down. "This is Keene," he said slowly, scanning the quiet brush. The seconds beating past were a glacial eternity. Gus. . . .

"Everything under control," said Willard, making up his mind. "Continue checks. Keene out."

"Yes, sir." The guard's voice was perfectly calm—not that of someone who'd just received a coded order to shoot a man. Irene's knees weakened. . . .

There had to be some way out of this, there had to—the guard she was following let the lead rope slacken and raised his pistol. . . .

NAVOHAR

Hilari Bell

A ROC BOOK

ROC
Published by New American Library, a division of
Penguin Putnam Inc., 375 Hudson Street,
New York, New York 10014, U.S.A.
Penguin Books Ltd, 27 Wrights Lane,
London W8 5TZ, England
Penguin Books Australia Ltd, Ringwood,
Victoria, Australia
Penguin Books Canada Ltd, 10 Alcorn Avenue,
Toronto, Ontario, Canada M4V 3B2
Penguin Books (N.Z.) Ltd, 182–190 Wairau Road,
Auckland 10, New Zealand

Penguin Books Ltd, Registered Offices:
Harmondsworth, Middlesex, England

First published by Roc, an imprint of New American Library,
a division of Penguin Putnam Inc.

First Printing, June 2000
10 9 8 7 6 5 4 3 2 1

Printed in the United States of America

PUBLISHER'S NOTE
This is a work of fiction. Names, characters, places, and incidents
either are the product of the author's imagination or are used fictitiously,
and any resemblance to actual persons, living or dead, business
establishments, events, or locales is entirely coincidental.

For my brother,
who guessed very close.

Chapter 1

"Be careful," said Willard, clipping and checking the seals that fastened Irene's gloves to her suit. "We don't know what killed those people. It might still be there."

A really masterful statement of the obvious. But Irene managed not to say it aloud. *He's being kind,* she told herself firmly. But she still had to ungrit her teeth and take a deep breath before she could reply casually, "I'm always careful. Well, almost always."

Willard smiled politely and stepped behind her to check the seals on her filter pack as Irene fought down another surge of irritation. *I'm forty-five, damn it. I don't have to be bundled up like a toddler on a snowy day.*

But toddlers didn't play in the snow anymore.

Then she wondered if Mark resented it this much when she helped him into his suit. *That's completely different. He can barely dress himself these days, and . . .* She knew he hated it. But he, at least, was generous enough not to hate her for it, so she worked up a smile when Willard came around to face her.

"I'll be careful. I promise."

"That's my good girl." A genuine smile lit his even features, and he touched the side of her faceplate, his fingers leaving small smudges.

Irene ungritted her teeth again. *I haven't said yes yet, damn it.*

And she probably never would, she reflected,

stumping down the cramped corridor to the shuttle launch bay. Just because your biological clock is ringing its head off is no reason to marry a . . . a perfectly nice man. And one of the few—very few, since Jeff—to be attracted to her drab brown hair and . . . distinguished was the kindest adjective people applied to her beaky nose and prominent chin. *Willard Keene has no sense of humor*, the sane part of her insisted. *He'd drive you stark mad inside a year.* Even ending up alone would be better than that, no matter how many people told her to get a li—

"Preoccupying, Auntie? You're blocking the corridor."

Mark's cheerful voice made her twitch, even though the wash from his hoverchair was buffeting her calves. "I was *thinking*. Though you seem to be unfamiliar with that particular verb."

Mark's wicked grin stretched the skin over his bones. Did he look more hollow today? More fragile? Something vanished beneath Irene's stomach, leaving it floating, even as he said, "Don't miff, Auntie, I'm just slanging. And we're late. Bad enough to be an amateur copilot—the least I can do is punctualize."

He slithered his chair around her and was halfway down the corridor by the time she called, "You're doing that on purpose!" And then smiled because she didn't have to see him laugh to know he had. But he didn't slow down, though they weren't that late. Mark was seventeen, and dying. They'd wait for hours without complaint, and none of the three people assembled in the shuttle—or the other twenty-eight who comprised the rest of the *Henry Stanley*'s crew—would ever tell Willard—their captain—that Mark was the one actually flying them down to the planet. Mark's "pilot" status was supposed to be strictly honorary, even if they had given him the Earth coordinates and computer purge codes—installed in case they met something else as aggressive as the Vrell while they searched for the twenty-two missing colonies.

Irene realized she'd slowed again, and deliberately picked up her pace. That was another reason no one complained about waiting; after finding eighteen colonies full of corpses, no one was looking forward to it anymore.

She saw her own resigned weariness in Dayna's and Thanh's helmet-shielded faces as she climbed into the shuttle's tiny passenger compartment and fastened her safety harness. There was even a shadow of it in Khalil's face as he came back to be sure everyone was buckled in properly. And why didn't she resent the safety checks when he did them?

"Mark's excited about this," Irene told him, as he bent over her deeply cushioned seat and gave the belts and helmet brace a cursory yank. "Thank you."

Khalil's serious, dark face brightened. "You don't have to thank me; he's a fine pilot. A pleasure to co-for. Are you all right, Goodnight?"

Everyone asked after Mark. Khalil was one of the very few who remembered to ask how Irene was doing. She smiled. "I'm fine."

The stock, meaningless reply. Then she saw the concern in his eyes, and fear twisted her heart. He'd seen the same fragility in Mark's face that she had. *No, it's too soon, he's only been sick eighteen months . . .* GED's victims could live for over three years . . . or die in under twelve months, and she knew it. She should. She'd been present at its creation. *The junior, assistant midwife to death, that's me.* The sickening lurch of her stomach as the shuttle left the ship's gravity was almost a relief.

Atmosphere was bumpy, as it always was. And just a bit more so, she had to admit, with Mark flying. Leaning into the bubble window (a violation of safety regs, since she had to lift the helmet brace to do it) she could see the continent they were approaching. Mostly forested, with a wide band of desert along the coastline. As they drew nearer she could make out the drop that separated the forest from the tawny bare strip—a long drop, though it was hard to put it into feet from above. The jets howled into reverse, the bumps got bumpier, and Irene sat back and locked the safety frame over her helmet. As usual, it didn't seem to do much good. They landed with the spine-crushing jar for which "amateur pilots" were notorious, and the passengers stood and stretched while hull coolant steamed up the windows.

The undeniable thrill of stepping onto a new planet displaced, for the moment, the dread of what they'd find.

Khalil released the hatch, and Mark whooped and fired his hoverchair out the opening—a practice that always gave Irene heart failure, though she knew the cursed thing had over twenty feet of lift, and God knew Mark could handle it.

She followed the others backward down the ladder, then turned to look. The colonists all called their planets a paradise at first. It made reading what followed all the more painful. This one was treed—tall, big-leaved things for the most part, with young ones growing back in the space cleared by the mother ship's landing. Irene found it ironic that a thick, saucer shape had proved one of the most effective for space travel after all. Its hull rose beside their tiny shuttle, a hill of dull gray metal—and not a small hill either. It had carried over five hundred colonists, not to mention their equipment, seed stock, and embryonic farm life. And embryonic colonists as well.

There'd been some debate, when they found the first dead colony, about what to do with these tiny possible-future-humans. It was Willard who'd decided to take them back, compromising the *Stanley*'s scant, precious cargo space. "Enough life has been lost already," he said. A moral man. So why couldn't she like him better?

"Navohar," said Mark, hovering up beside her. "It's beautiful."

"You think they're all beautiful," said Irene. "All you can see is trees." Their uppermost branches rustled in the wind, a sound never heard in the domes. Irene felt a moment of overwhelming gratitude for the excellence of the helmet's sound pickup, which even let them hear each other's voices without having to turn on the short-range suit-coms.

She'd forgotten this planet's name. The Vrell database had held so many planets, with copious notations on the atmosphere, gravity, and ecology of each, that human astronomers had run out of names before they'd gone through a fifth of the local star systems— and descriptions of the farther reaches of the galaxy were still being translated. So they'd put together a program to generate names at random and thrown out the ones that were too undignified. After all, who wanted to colonize Grizzelskrink?

"Well, they're gravely trees. Come on, Auntie, let's explore."

She'd been wrong, Irene decided, looking at Mark's eager expression. So what if he was a bit thinner? No one on the verge of dying could look that happy, even if he did wear skulls on his T-shirts.

The Omega cult, which wasn't really a cult anyway, had sprung from the great plagues. With over a quarter of the Earth's population dropping in the streets, it was no wonder people became obsessed with death. The fundamentalist religions had a field day—"the apocalypse is he-yer." But no one knew which of the billions of net-heads first drew that skull on the computer screen and wrote beneath it, Embrace Me. And no one knew, or could prove, who'd first dubbed the symbol Omega, though the name was never written with the drawing. Many people had claimed both, for

a fortune in merchandising rights had been lost when
the courts decreed it a cultural phenomenon, arising
out of the mass subconscious.

Embrace Me.

The songs, the poetry, heralded death as victor,
teacher, lover—the ultimate step into the unknown.
An obscure artist named Alan M. Clark became, to
his utter astonishment, popular, and very rich. Teenagers all over the planet wore Omega's stark image in
their ears and around their throats. Tattooed on their
skin. And on their T-shirts. The one Mark wore under
his suit today was the one Irene thought of as the
"classic," with roses growing through its eyes. If he
owned any shirts without skulls on them, he hadn't
packed them.

The psychologist said it was healthy—that it made
it easier for Mark to come to terms with the terror
and indignity of terminal illness. Actually, Mark had
coped better than most of those around him, especially
his mother, whose grief and hysteria dragged everyone
down. That kind of scene did no one any good, so
when Mark had pleaded to go with Irene—*I want to
do something with what's left of my life*—his parents
talked it over, cried, and agreed to let him go, even
though they knew that with the mission projected to
last two years, there was a good chance he wasn't
coming back. Irene argued with the oversight committee for the next two weeks. In the end, she thought
they gave in more to shut her up than because they
believed it would be easier to test potential cures if
they had a GED victim aboard. Irene loved Mark's
brother and sister, too—her sister was convinced that
maiden aunts were created to baby-sit—but with Mark
it was different. She *liked* Mark.

Mark, who'd still been walking with canes then, had
hugged his weeping parents and wobbled up the
Earth/Station transport aisle to drop shakily into a
seat beside Irene's. "Whew! I mean, I love them and

all that, but . . . Auntie, promise you won't flood me out, OK?"

She had promised, though she'd had to blink back tears as she did it.

"Auntie? You're preoccupying again."

"Sorry. You can take off exploring as soon as you hack us in."

All the kids these days seemed to be born with a talent for hacking. Mark's dream was to be a space pilot, but Irene thought his real talent lay in manipulating lines of electronic code, which he seemed to do as easily as speaking—and a lot more grammatically.

It took Khalil, whose job was to purge and shut down the mother ship's computer, ten minutes to find one of the portals and jack into it, but once he did, Mark had the door open in under three minutes. "It's an old code. They security much better now. Let's get going, OK?"

Which was easy for him to say, Irene reflected sourly half an hour later. He didn't have to hike.

Khalil stayed behind as the others trudged up the hill. He and Mark had spotted the fledgling settlement on the other side of a ridge they both described as "small." The dense trees gave way to lighter woods on the rocky slope, and they'd found the remains of a trail, but it still didn't make for easy walking. The enviro-suits were guaranteed proof against any form of atmospheric contamination, and the filter pack (advertised as a miracle in efficient design) would provide twenty-four hours of water and waste disposal, and purified air for over a week, as long as the batteries were properly charged. But the miraculous filter pack weighed almost eighteen pounds, and by the time they were halfway up the ridge Irene swore her boots weighed the same. Each. And this planet's gravity was slightly *lower* than Earth's.

Could it be that in fourteen months on the *Stanley* she'd gotten out of shape? Or old?

"No. Not possible."

"What's not possible?" said Dayna. Irene was pleased to note that she was puffing, too. "What are we talking about?"

"Old age," said Irene grimly.

"Oh, that. I don't believe in that at all." Dayna was in her late twenties.

"Me either," said Mark, with a sinister overtone that won a laugh from Dayna, who was also of the Omega generation.

"Though I don't understand why they settlemented on the other side of a hill," he went on. "Think of hauling all their equipment and stuff over it. They were stupiding."

No one knew who'd started the new slang, verbing, either, which Irene thought was a great pity. She'd have liked to have been present at his lynching.

"Not at all," said Thanh. "They wanted to be able to lift off again without frying their settlement. Very sensible of them."

The trees vanished as they neared the top. Cleared by the colonists? As Irene and the others crested the ridge, she stopped wondering and gasped.

The land dropped away beneath them in a series of plateaus and rolling hills, layering down to the rippling dunes of the desert. The sky was a vast, blue dome, far larger than the domes Irene was accustomed to. And every cubic inch of it full of alien microbes.

"I know why they chose this site," murmured Thanh, who was a botanist. "I can see four different biomes from here."

Irene didn't care about biomes. Delight, agoraphobia, and a compulsive desire to wash her hands, clashed. She gazed out over space and wished the suit's internal environment dealt better with the sweat that soaked her thick suit liner. It was almost like looking at a holo-surround screen from inside a humid box. Almost. The horizon vanished over the planet's curve in a haze of light. It took an effort to drop her gaze to the clutch of buildings just down the slope.

They weren't very interesting. A series of half cylinders, made of the dark gray plasticine that was so light to ship and easy to weld in a tight seal. Just like most of the other colonies they'd found.

Reluctance tensed Irene's neck and shoulders, but you could only admire the view so long. Sooner or later, you had to go down the hill and do what you'd come for.

They must have treated the ground with no-grow, for only a few, scattered clumps of grass thrust through the mulch of dead leaves. Thanh looked longingly at some of the newer specimens, but they'd long since discovered that the most practical way to learn about a new planet's ecology was to find the notes the colonist's botanist and naturalist had made, and go on from there if there seemed to be something worth pursuing. Just as Irene would seek out any research done by their microbiologist—assuming they even had a microbiologist. In many colonies their medical doctor had filled that role. Or more often, failed to fill it.

Dayna had already taken out her holo-cam and wandered off, providing a complete visual record of the site. Irene looked around. "There. That big building in the center."

In most colonies, the central building, whatever other function it served, was also a meeting hall, and the place they stored their records.

Mark plugged his portapad into the jack by the door and started scrolling code—then he snorted and began to laugh.

"What?" Irene asked.

He twisted the jack and pulled it free. "Watch this." He lifted his hands like a conjurer. "Open sesame!"

The door clicked softly and opened about two inches.

"You're kidding," said Irene, as Thanh began to laugh.

"The actual command was just 'open.' I guess they weren't very paranoid." Mark's smile faded. "Not like the New Diasporans."

The New Diasporans had had five layers of security protecting their "holy records." But neither their paranoia nor their faith had protected them from the virus that attacked their respiratory systems till their lungs flooded with so much blood they could no longer cough it up. "God has forsaken us," their final log entry read.

Irene sighed. "No use putting it off." She pushed open the door. Beyond lay a long, shadowy corridor.

Mark was smiling again. "Let me try. Lights!" The shadows vanished.

Irene snorted. "That was an easy one."

"Well, I did some research about the guy who founded this colony. Nature-nut, though he was an engineer himself. Gustave Sardakowski. He was into Thoreau and those guys. So it wasn't too hard to figure out."

Thanh looked baffled.

"Simplify, simplify, simplify," Irene murmured, and stepped inside.

The first door on the left, which swung open at a touch, led to a room full of silent equipment. The only pieces Irene recognized were the sewing machines—no, that was a programmable pattern cutter. The sun flooding through the windows provided plenty of light, and Irene went in. The others pressed on, the quiet thrum of Mark's hoverchair sounding louder in this empty place than it did on the *Stanley*.

The large feeder bin enabled Irene to identify the weaver, which dominated the interior wall. There was no dust on it nor, Irene suddenly noticed, on any of the floors. The security might be casual, but the person who welded in the door frames and window frames had done a good job. Even the oil on the gearing looked fresh. On a hunch, she went to the catching basket at the machine's far end to see if—yes, a length of cloth lay there, pale tan, made of some sort of animal hair. Irene stepped back and wiped her gloved hands on her thighs. The idea of wearing something not raised in a protected environment next to her *skin* . . .

"Here." Thanh's voice echoed in the stillness.

It might have been a schoolroom, or a library, or both. A dozen desks, each with terminal, printer, and pad ports. Thanh and Mark had activated the core by the time she arrived. A passive core, she was glad to see, designed to retain memory through any power failure. They'd just come out when the colonists were leaving—one of the first human applications of Vrell technology. Two of the colonies they'd found, impelled by thrift, or refusal to touch anything to do with the Vrell, had the older models, their memories long since erased by battery failure. Piecing together the fate of those colonists from the surviving scraps of hard copy had been a nightmare.

Mark didn't even need to hack them in; the system was one Irene had used in college, so she dismissed him to explore. Mark might wear Omega on his shirts, but he was fighting the narrowing of his world to the last ditch.

Irene smiled sadly and settled in beside Thanh to scroll through the index. *Building plans. Equipment roster. Field layout.* Why did everyone have to call their settlement logs something different? Thanh, who just ran a search for the words plant(s) and/or botany, sighed happily and plugged in his pad. They'd copy all the colony's files for record-keeping, but before they left they had to be sure, as sure as they could be, that this world held no cures for the diseases that even now sometimes swept through the protected domes. GED itself was noncontagious, but that hardly mattered since every human being now carried its genetic marker. And it only activated in one in every two hundred or so adolescents, which most thought a fair price to pay for the Vrell's deaths.

We won. But it wasn't only when she looked at Mark's thin face that part of Irene's soul demanded, *At what price?*

Parts catalog. Rainfall and temperature. Records of birth and death. Irene hesitated, but it was the why she needed, not the who, and she hated adding human names and faces to that knowledge. *Satellite data. Settlement log!* Irene snickered. At this point, she should have guessed. The first entry was dated October 4, 2075. So they'd spent what, three months, waiting for a passing gravity wave to spin them out into the galaxy? Not too bad. Some colonies had waited for over a year.

The discovery that gravity waves traveled faster—a lot faster—than the speed of light had actually come before the Vrell, with no practical result except that Fiesal's theory had replaced Einstein's, just as Einstein's had replaced Newton's. It was the Vrell's Phase Field Generator that gave the knowledge practical application.

The PFG had other, blacker, applications, too. Irene, locked in that secure and secret bunker with her father, had had nightmares about the Vrell coming to seize her. About everything around her going hazy and immaterial. The people who loved her impotent to stop them, to do anything to peel away their tentacled grip. Unable even to hear her screaming. It had happened, to others. *We paid the price to stop it.*

Irene keyed up the first entry.

Navohar is beautiful—a paradise. She winced. *We've chosen to place our first settlement at the edge of the great northern woodland, on the larger of the three continents. It's a site that gives us easy access to a variety*

*of bio-zones between it and the desert, so we can make
informed choices about the placements of future settle-
ments. And if nothing else, the view is . . . beyond
words. We are so happy . . .*

Irene went back to the log index. The information
she needed was at the end; reading the beginning only
made it harder to take. *Come on, Goodnight. You're
stalling.*

The final entry was dated 13/18/78. Twenty-two
years ago. Irene skimmed down the date column.
They'd chosen to divide their planet's cycle into fourteen, thirty-two-day months, except for months one
and seven, which were thirty days each. Solstices?
Equinoxes? Who cared?

*13/18/2078. Ray Gutierra died today, which pretty much
ends our hope of finding a cure for this . . . disease
seems too mild a word. Almost two-thirds of us are
infected, and so far not a single recovery. Ray's death
hikes the total to 188. For myself, I'm almost too sick
to care. Those who don't have it are so exhausted caring for the rest of us, that I expect them to come down
with it daily. We seem to have no defense against this
accursed thing.*

Irene blinked, wishing she could rub her stinging
eyes. She refused to cry inside a helmet, for the absorbent pad mounted for nose blowing became utterly
revolting when saturated. This colony had a three-year
run, which was more than most. Two to five years,
they'd found, was the average time it took for some
alien virus to adapt sufficiently to prey on human bodies. And the human immune system, evolved over mil-
lennia to defeat terran viruses and bacteria, could
never adapt fast enough to cope with these alien
invaders.

They'd been almost certain, Irene's colleagues, that
the microfauna of one planet wouldn't affect the crea-

tures of another. It had taken months to *design* a virus that would affect the Vrell. Random nature . . . was a lot smarter than they'd thought. Microbes rule.

> The kongs have left us alone for several weeks now, almost as if they know their work is being done for them. Kongs? *Which they may—we've never been able to figure out how intelligent they really are.* Intelligent? *I was beginning to think we might reach some sort of compromise with them. Or at least a draw. If they attacked now* Attacked! *it'd be the end, I think. In fact, I think it is anyway. And I had such—*

Irene closed the entry and scanned back, looking for kongs. She found plenty of references, most attached to words like "attacked" and "beaten to death," but she had to go back almost two years to get a description. It seemed kongs were large, very strong, apelike creatures, "hexapedal, like all Navohar's wildlife," but with faces more like a bulldog's, or a giant pug's. Which probably meant they were carnivorous. They were also obviously hostile, and Mark—

"Thanh, come on!"

Irene raced out the door and down the hall without waiting for him. "Mark! Can you—" She shot into the sunlight, blinded, and ran right into his chair, which rocked so far it almost dumped them both on their heads before its internal gyros righted it.

"Are you all right?" Mark beat her to it by half a second, probably because he hadn't had the wind knocked out of him. His face was taut with fear. "Auntie, they're—"

"There are creatures here, Mark. Big apelike things. Hostile. Maybe intelligent! Dayna!" She raised her voice to a shout. Eighteen routine missions had made them unbelievably careless. How could they have forgotten to turn their radios on when they separated? Idiots! "Dayna! Get over here, right now!"

"What?" Dayna ran around the corner of a distant building, calling questions, but seeing her safe, Irene tuned her out.

"Did you see them, Mark? The kongs? Big ape—"

"No! Auntie, stop babbling and listen." Mark's freckles stood out like punctuation marks on his bleached skin. Thanh and Dayna had come up to them by then, and he included them in his glance as he went on, "It wasn't an ape, it was a girl. And she—"

"A girl? Are you sure? These are big—"

"I know a girl when I see one, OK? They're *alive* down here. A human girl. And she shot at me!"

Chapter 2

"But if they're still alive, why didn't they answer our hails?" Willard asked reasonably. The clear light in the *Stanley*'s conference room did nothing to disguise the critical gaze he turned to Mark.

"How the hell would he know?" snapped Irene, who didn't feel reasonable.

Willard's brows shot up, then lowered in a disapproving frown, and Irene took a deep, calming breath. In the wake of the plagues, society had become much more conservative—only "old" people, like Irene, used profanity much. *But Willard's my age, damn it, he shouldn't be so easy to shock. . . .*

"I'm sorry. But none of us knows. You're sure . . ." She didn't bother to finish. Of course Willard had used the proper codes when he transmitted.

"Yes. I'm certain I used the proper ID codes. They know we're human. So why they refuse to respond, and why they fired on young Mark here, is a mystery." He steepled his fingers and looked over them thoughtfully, his straight-lined jacket and combed hair a sharp contrast to the others' rumpled, sweat-stained suit liners. Irene fought down another attack of prickly defensiveness, on "young Mark's" behalf, for he liked being called that no better than any teenager.

It was mostly because she was tired. They'd hiked back over the hill even faster than they'd come, their generally forgotten pistols at ready. Then they'd banged on the mother ship's hull for five full minutes before Khalil heard them and responded, and Irene had begun to panic over him as well.

The planet's sun was setting by the time they reached the shuttle, and the steamy buffeting of the *Stanley*'s decon-bath finished the job the hike had started. The tiny fraction of her mind not taken up with the colonists—live colonists!—longed for a shower.

But she'd barely been allowed time to wash her hands and face and repin her sweaty hair at the nape of her neck before Willard hauled them all into a meeting. Not that she blamed him for that. The entire crew had wanted to be there, but Willard had decreed just himself and those who'd been down to the planet, with an open com from the small conference room where they'd gathered, so the others could listen in. He'd wanted some coherence, at least in the initial stages of the meeting.

Now he turned to Mark, and said deliberately, "Let's get a clear account of this. Start at the beginning. You got down to the planet, and then . . ."

"We left Khalil in the mother ship and the rest of us went to the settlement. It was, it appeared to be, deserted, and since that was what we expected, we didn't question it."

Which we should have, Irene thought, remembering the dust-free floors. Even the most tightly sealed buildings have some dust on the floor.

"Dayna went off with the cam, while the rest of us found the central computer core. Once Thanh and my aunt were set up, I went out to poke around."

Despite his formality—Mark was always polite to Willard—enthusiasm crept into his voice. "I found this old trail leading out of the settlement. At least, I thought it was old. It was almost completely overgrown. Anyway, I followed it. My chair makes a lot of noise in bushes and things, so I didn't see any animals, just trees and stuff. But the trees were big—

really big I mean, not like in the parks. I was treeing when—'' He flushed at Willard's raised brows. "I had boosted the chair up into one of the trees, to examine it more closely. It doesn't make as much noise off the ground, you know. I think that's why she didn't know I was there.''

"She," said Willard intently. "You mean the girl?"

Wasn't that obvious?

"Yes, Captain Keene. She came through the woods, and she seemed to be looking for something. And listening, so maybe she did hear my chair. But she was looking on the ground. I was just—"

"Wait. You're certain this was a human you saw? Your aunt says there are apelike creatures—"

Mark was clearly tired of this. "She was about my age, with Asian features, and long black hair braided down her back. She was carrying some sort of long gun, with a big barrel. Wide bore, I mean. It took me—"

"What was she wearing?" Dayna interrupted.

Mark looked blank. "Pants and a shirt. Sort of splotchy brown. Loose. Kind of rough-looking." He shrugged.

"Go on," said Willard. "Why didn't you call to her? Identify yourself?"

"I was about to," said Mark. "But seeing her surprised me. I'd just about got my voice working, when she looked up, saw me, and swung the gun up."

"You didn't call out then?"

"There wasn't time. I spun my chair so the back of it faced her and ducked—the shot hit it before I finished turning."

"The shot *hit* it?"

"Yes, Captain Keene. I heard and felt it. You can probably see . . ." Mark turned, trying to look at the back of his chair, and it turned, too, just as Irene knelt to examine it.

"Stop spinning, Mark. I want to . . . My God!" She

turned the chair gently, showing the others half a dozen fresh scars in the tough plasticine.

Willard frowned. "Go on, Mark."

"Well, I yelled then. Something like 'watch it' though I'm not exactly sure. Then I remembered I had a pistol, too, but by the time I got it out and turned around again, she was gone."

"Gone?"

"Vanished. Disappeared. Not a trace. Gone."

Irene's face felt cold. "You could have been killed."

Mark shrugged. "So? I was going to look for her, but then I thought about the others and realized I'd better go back and warn them."

A wave of frost flowed from Willard's seat at the head of the table. This time Irene felt no desire to defend any of them, least of all herself. They had been criminally foolish not to turn on their radios.

"Well, I suppose I've already said enough on that subject," their captain said coolly.

Yes, indeed he had.

"Thank you, Mark, that's a very clear account, and coming back to report was the right choice. Tomorrow we'll take the *Stanley* down, and make a proper search for these . . . elusive colonists. Perhaps their firing on you was an error. If for some reason they didn't receive our transmission, that girl must have been as startled as you were."

"Or perhaps," said Thanh, "they've declared a jihad against all other humans. This colony has been isolated for twenty-five years. Who knows how their society has evolved. If they have some religious—"

"They shouldn't," said Mark. "When they took off, they were Back-to-nature-nuts, not Fanatics. And Sardakowski's wife was a pacifist—one of those weirds who believed we should try to communicate with the Vrell instead of fighting."

Willard frowned. He was the only one aboard the *Stanley* who didn't divide the colonies by their original reason for fleeing Earth. Biological Paranoid was the third category.

"In any case," said Willard, "our mission is to make contact with them. As I said, we'll land tomorrow and send out ground teams and flitters. We're already broadcasting a constant message, identifying ourselves and stating our purpose, but if they didn't get the first message, who knows if they'll get this one. We will exercise due caution, and we will all"— a final glare— "follow the standard safety procedures. I believe that covers everything for now. Are there any questions?"

It was probably the silliest thing anyone said all evening. Everyone on the *Stanley* had questions, and despite the fact that the answer to ninety percent of them was "how would I know?" they went right on asking them for another two hours.

Irene was exhausted by the time she reached the shower.

The colonists had been there twenty-five years, she reflected as the water pounded her stiff shoulders. That wasn't long, in terms of societal change.

The Vrell had been efficient slave-raiders, but their PFG, advanced as it was compared to anything humans had to offer, had some practical drawbacks in that the phase field it generated had a harmony so narrow it could only mesh with the big waves—one-time gravity fluctuations set off by huge cosmic catastrophes. So the colonists who wanted to leave Earth had simply sent their ships up, thrown them out of phase (or into phase, depending on your point of view), and waited for the next wave to sweep them off, like a bottle in a flood tide. Some of the colonists waited for a wave going in the right general direction, but many had simply grabbed the first wave to hit and chosen a planet in the direction they were going.

Yes, thought Irene, working soapy fingers through her hair, those early colonists had all been nuts, no matter which category they fell into. Hoping slave races might evolve there in the future, the Vrell had charted thousands of planets with compatible atmospheres and gravities, but those eighty-six colony ships had still been playing dice with the universe when they set off.

And their mail-delivery system was equally unwieldy. The only way to contact home was to send up a message buoy, phase it, and trust the autopilot to negotiate the wave shifts—and to self-destruct if anything tried to tamper with it without first sending the proper codes. These days, Earth's coordinates were a closely guarded secret, and humanity cursed the designers of the old Voyager probes on a daily basis.

All the colony ships, even the Paranoids, had carried multiple buoys. And only twenty-two had returned. Hello, we've reached Salassa . . . Morovi . . . Xandarm at galactic coordinates thus and such. Drop in and see us sometime. (Or in the case of the Paranoids, send a sterile buoy with news.) No further messages had come from any of them. And now, sadly, they knew why.

Crazy.

It had taken only twenty-three years for the Yokito team to produce the discriminating phase field, whose adjustable harmonic spectrum enabled a ship to find the weaker, constant, gravitational currents, and to go pretty much where they chose. And mankind's first choice, impelled by Willard's persuasive lobbying, had been to go find those lost colonists, and with them, maybe, the solutions for some of Earth's problems as well. A goal that had seemed doomed . . . until now.

Irene punched the OFF button, and the blower came on, chasing droplets over her skin, and whipping tangles into her hair. By the time she was dry enough to step out, she was pleasantly relaxed, and tired to the bone. Her bed, bolted to the wall, and spaceship-narrow, had never looked better. She could always comb her hair in the morning.

On the other hand . . .

Irene shrugged into a robe, picked up her comb, and went over to her desk terminal to call up everything they had on Gustave Sardakowski's colony.

The *Stanley* thundered down, landing with a gentle bump, flattening its own scorched clearing beside the mother ship's huge one.

Irene had overslept, and had to draft Mark to help in her wild scramble to suit up. Joining the others for the final briefing, she still felt subtly unkempt—a feeling that became more pronounced when she took in Astrid Evenson's shining hair and flawless makeup. But Willard, at whom this civilized mating display was aimed, never even noticed it. He was too busy smiling at Irene, who'd happily have handed him over to Astrid. Lord, what a tangle.

The *Stanley*'s hull-cooling and fire-suppression systems took longer than the shuttle's, so the ground crews gathered in the decon-hatch, suited and uncomfortable, but too excited this time to care. The flitters would lift from the top of the ship as soon as the steam cleared. Their controls were supposed to be so simple that anyone could fly them, but after her one and only lesson, Irene was more than content to leave them to the experts.

Six flitters, each searching a different sector, with radar that could pick up any chunk of metal over thirty pounds, could cover a circle with a three-hundred-kilometer diameter in twelve hours. The ship's noon was two hours later than the planet's; Willard hoped they'd locate the colonists by either one noon or the other. Being an ex–United Earth Force pilot, of course he was in one of the flitters himself, which was a measure of his involvement. Willard disliked leaving the *Stanley*'s pure atmosphere, even in the protective armor of an enviro-suit.

"All right, ground teams." His voice came crisply

over the radio. "You all have your instructions. You should be able to search the settlement in less than an hour, then you can spread out into the forest. You are not to separate into groups of less than four anywhere outside the settlement, and *at no time is* anyone *to be out of radio contact.* Do you understand that?"

A ragged chorus of agreement sounded over the earbug, and Irene turned down the volume before she added her own voice to the babble.

"Very well. Be careful, and good luck. Keene out."

"Not too bad," said Myrna, who was part of Irene's ground team. "In fact, if you kept him away from the radio, you could almost forget he was UEF."

"Well, you have to admit, it'd be hard to shepherd this lot." Irene gestured vaguely, indicating the *Stanley*'s crew, both present and absent. Given the essentially scientific nature of the mission, all but a handful of the *Stanley*'s crew were scientists—most of whom had no intention of joining the military and made no bones about it. After all, it was science, not force of arms, that had defeated the Vrell, and both the politicians and the voters knew it. Under the circumstances, Colonel (ret.) Willard Keene was the perfect compromise to lead the mission. And really . . . "He's done a very good job, especially when you consider some of the egos he has to deal with."

"All right, I admit it." Myrna grinned. She was in her early fifties, with curly salt-and-pepper hair, a long, homely face, and an aversion to marriage which, as she informed anyone who asked, and quite a few who didn't, came from trying it four times too many. Four marriages was something of a scandal these days. "He's done a very good job. But I hope you don't intend to marry him, Goodnight. He'd drive you mad before the honeymoon was over."

Irene sighed. "Don't you have anyone else's business to mind? Like your own?"

"What are friends for? Besides, that's one of the

joys of being single—plenty of time to mind other peoples'—" The doors swished open. "Oh Lord. How beautiful!"

Burned ground and trees. "You and Mark," said Irene resignedly, and then winced as Mark's hoverchair hurtled into space. His war whoop sounded even more exuberant than yesterday's.

It really was rather nice, Irene thought as she hiked up the ridge again. But not nice enough to fling yourself into a stew of alien microbes for. Yes, Dr. Gustave Sardakowski had been crazy.

Given their general disaffection for Earth, many of the colonies hadn't left too much information about themselves. Sardakowski's had been more forthcoming than most, including a complete personnel roster. The picture in his bio—obviously taken before mankind had moved into the domes—showed a vigorous man in his forties, with a bushy beard, and muscular, hairy legs between his shorts and chunky hiking boots. He'd had his family with him in the picture; wife, Lillian, and two young sons, Gustave Jr. and Rudolph. Irene wondered now if any of them were among the 188 dead. They might have survived. Some obviously had. Dr. Sardakowski himself would be only . . . seventy-six by now.

But the backdrop of the photo, a serene lake surrounded by craggy peaks, had attracted Irene even more than the people. Earth had been so . . . tame back then. Irene herself had gone hiking in shorts and chunky boots. But the viruses they'd turned against the Vrell had been designed to affect life-forms other than human, and they had. And the changes in the animal and insect population had affected the plants as well, which in turn affected the climate, which affected the plants, which affected . . . The rapid-breeding, rapidly adapting descendants of Bugs Bunny's mild prototypes became the stuff of nightmares.

This planet looked, well, not like Earth before the

changes, but like a stable ecosystem. Not so threatening. *Until the kongs come out of the woods, Goodnight. Let's see what you think it looks like then.*

Irene checked the clip in her electro-pistol. Again. The energy-storage technology that created electric rail-pistols light enough to carry had been another "gift" from the Vrell.

"Nervousing, Auntie?" Mark hovered up beside her.

Irene grimaced, but she had too much on her mind to rise to the bait. "I'm not sure. I was just thinking how peaceful it looks."

They topped the rise as she spoke, and those who hadn't seen the view before stopped in their tracks, paralyzed. Irene looked out too: no domes, no buildings except for the settlement. What else to look for? No rising columns of smoke, like in the old vids. She turned away from the desert. Trees. Short and twisted on the verges of the forest, but beyond that, a solid wall. She couldn't see into them more than a dozen yards.

Mark had brought along a pair of the seldom-used binoculars, and the whir of the autofocus brought Irene's gaze down to him. He, too, was looking at the woods. His shirt that morning, under his suit, bore a skull with a pirate eye patch and a dagger in its teeth. They were small binoculars, and light, but his hands were already trembling, and soon he lowered them.

"See anything?" Irene asked softly, scanning the forest once more. The others were starting down.

"Nothing. Not a hide nor a hair. But my guess is that you could hide an army in that forest, walk within twenty feet of it, and never see a thing."

"Well, that's what radar is for. Don't worry. They'll find them."

"Or her," said Mark. "That's what bothers me. What if she's all alone down here."

"For twenty years? You said she was your age. No, she's not alone."

Mark's frown lightened. "But there have been cases. Feral children—"

"Don't fire guns at people. You read too much."

"Says the aunt who gave me book chips every Christmas and birthday." But he was smiling now. "Don't fret, Auntie. It's what makes me dangerous."

"Tell me about it," Irene grumbled. But he'd already turned to follow the others.

Yesterday the deserted settlement had been depressing. Today it felt downright creepy, even with sunlight reflecting off the dirty windows.

The others fanned out, in groups of two or three.

"I don't think there's much in the buildings," Irene told Mark. "I want to go back and really read that log. Do you want to come with me, or go with one of the others?" She hoped he'd notice that going off on his own wasn't an option today.

"Actually," said Mark slowly, "I want to go back to the tree I was in. Whatever she shot at me hit my chair. Maybe it hit the tree as well. Maybe we can find it."

Irene frowned. "Why? No one doubts what you saw, Mark."

"Yet. But if the colonists hide better than we find . . ."

"You really do think too much," Irene told him. Still . . . "The log first, OK? You take the odd months, I'll take the evens, and we tell each other as soon as we hit the first reference to kongs or disease."

"Deal." But he looked toward the forest as they entered the central building, and Irene made a mental note to keep an eye on him.

As it happened, the logs proved interesting enough to keep Mark at her side. They were written by old Gustave himself, and even the first months, which were relatively uneventful, were made readable by his passionate enthusiasm. . . . *the first child has been born on Navohar, and we all rejoice. The Ledeouxes have named him Henri. . . .*

Four months after their arrival, they sighted the kongs. Just glimpses at first: big apelike creatures, with carnivores' jaws.

Then they heard something banging in the woods. Not rhythmic, just deep wooden thumps that went on from sunrise to sunset. They had no idea what it was or meant. . . . *there are so many mysteries on this planet. . . .* But this one was solved the next day as half a dozen kongs burst from the forest and attacked two men who were clearing one of the fields. They used weapons, too, of a sort. Long ropy stalks covered with thorns that left long, swollen scratches. The men had left their pistols in the hoversled, with the other unneeded equipment, and were horribly scratched, but not critically injured. . . . *I can't believe they were so careless. To have your pistol with you at all times is a standard safety procedure. . . .* Irene winced.

The kongs also used stones to smash most of the team's equipment. There was some speculation about their intelligence, but several Earth creatures, including birds, used tools without even approaching human intelligence.

The next attack was not for several months, and that time the colonists took the drumming for the warning it was. When the kongs burst out of the trees next morning, they shot and killed three of them, and sent the other four into flight.

It was their first chance to examine a kong body, and they did so in detail, finding muscle attachment similar to an orangutan's, which would give it strength far greater than you'd expect from its size, and a largish brain, though smaller than man's. . . . *for whatever that's worth. It has also lost the third eye* (third eye?) *which means it's a predator—not that its teeth didn't tell us that already. . . .*

The next kong attack, less than a week later, was different. They swept out of the forest without warning, carrying clubs instead of thorn branches, and beat six colonists to death before they could get off a single shot. At least, that was what the people who found the bodies concluded.

They were the first deaths among the colonists.

Someone sniffed loudly and Irene jumped. Myrna, who also knew better than to cry inside a helmet, was reading over Irene's shoulder, and all the terminals were full, several people sharing some of the seats. Irene hadn't even heard them come in.

It was probably time, according to Willard's schedule, to start searching the forest. Screw Willard's schedule. As far as Irene was concerned, no one left this room until they knew all there was to know about these kong things.

It was over a month till the next attack, and they drummed the night before, and used the thorn branches on people, clubs on the equipment. But this time they were wary, and only one kong was killed. Five days later, a woman and her two daughters, who were coming back late from the sewing center, were dragged into the forest. Two were beaten to death, the third whipped with thorns.

This was the sewing center. The back of Irene's neck prickled as her no-longer-existent hackles tried to rise. She spotted the pattern long before the beleaguered colonists figured it out. For every kong they killed, the kongs killed two settlers. If they weren't killed, they attacked only with the thorn whips, painful, but not lethal, and only after giving the ritual warning. And ritual was the right word, too, Irene realized. There had to be intelligence at work there, but how much? Their technology level was obviously primitive.

"Olsen to Keene, please come in." This was something Willard ought to know; the flitters were armed.

He answered promptly and assured Irene that he and his people wouldn't kill any kongs. They hadn't seen anything yet, but they'd flown less than half the pattern. It was clear he didn't think thorn whips and clubs were a serious threat—easy for him to say—he was two hundred feet up in an armored flitter.

"Condescending prick," Irene muttered, and went back to reading.

Once the colonists realized what was going on, they'd been able to work out a solution—something they called fléchette guns, which fired spiked bits of metal designed to pierce the skin and sting like hell, but not to penetrate and kill. The meeting where they'd decided to try these weapons, instead of lethal ones, lasted seven hours, and they'd had to break up two fistfights, but Lillian Sardakowski wasn't the only pacifist among them, and they prevailed.

Finally, they all agreed that a band of volunteers would at least try the new weapons. The next time the kongs' warning sounded they went out . . . *my hands were shaking like an engine with half the bearings gone.* . . . Not a coward, old Gustave, for all his craziness. But the fléchette guns had worked. They drove the kongs back, with only light injury to one woman, and no retaliation had followed. Just another ritual attack, five weeks later, also driven off.

Slowly, the tide of battle turned. The kongs' attacks became fewer and further between, and even when someone was careless enough to be caught without their fléchette gun they weren't killed. By the time the disease hit, they'd learned to follow the kongs' strange rules, and the attacks were regarded as just another hazard of living on Navohar.

The disease was something else. It started with muscle aches and a low fever, like old-fashioned flu. That was what they thought it was, until the sores appeared. They were followed by a fever that climbed ever higher as the body fought to destroy the alien invader—and failed. Death occurred three to seven days after the onset of the first symptoms.

> . . . *if they attacked now, it'd be the end, I think. In fact, I think it is anyway. And I had such hopes for us, here on Navohar. We worked so hard. I know life's not fair, but this seems a bit much. I suppose it always seems like that, when you're the one who's beaten. Gustave Sardakowski, Navohar, 13/18/2078.*

Myrna sniffled again.

"Don't let it get to you," Irene told her. "They didn't die. At least, not all of them."

Mark had pulled up a screenful of code and was scowling at it.

Myrna took a deep breath, since she couldn't wipe her eyes. "You're right, of course. It was a long time ago. But it sounds like they had a tough run down here. I wonder why they called them kongs."

"Better than calling them kings," Mark said, beating Irene to it by a hairbreadth. "Auntie, take a look at this."

Irene peered obediently at the gibberish on the screen. "OK. What am I looking at?"

Mark snorted, but passed up the chance to make his usual crack about illiteracy. "Here, here, here, and here." He pointed. "These are file purge codes. Four log entries were made after this one, but someone erased them."

"Are you sure?"

Mark lifted his brows in silence. With computers he was always sure.

"Sorry. But that's da—that's odd. Can you get them back?"

"No," said Mark regretfully. "Not with that command, on this core. It's not a simple delete, it's the purge code. Specifically designed to make the data unrecoverable."

"Hmm," said Irene. "Makes you wonder what was in those last entries, doesn't it?"

"I," said Myrna, "am never nosy about things like that. And if you two don't stop snickering, I'll make you come thrash through the jungle with me. Well?"

They drafted Ezra Markhov, the ship's psychologist, as the last member of their four-person team, because he came over to ask what was so funny. He'd been a good friend to both Mark and Irene the last few months.

But it wasn't a jungle, exactly, Irene thought as they worked their way down the path Mark had followed the day before. There, on the fringes of the forest, the trees were only about a hundred feet tall, and the canopy wasn't too dense. Glittering coins of sunlight shimmered and vanished, like someone had hung the old disco mirror ball they'd had on prom night—about a million years ago. Of course, all that light just encouraged the bushes to grow. There were clear patches, but in many places the brush rose over Irene's head. She had wondered, reading the log, how the kongs had killed six people before they could fire a shot. Now she knew.

"At least they give warning before they attack," she muttered.

"They used to give warning." Myrna's ears were ridiculously sharp. "Their society may have changed in the last twenty-five years, too."

"Probably not that much," said Ezra. "That they applied their . . . rules of conduct even to aliens—to something they'd never encountered before—to me implies a fairly rigid social system, not likely to change too fast."

A rigid social system. Intelligence. A chill ran down Irene's sweaty spine. The Vrell had taught humanity a lesson about the dangers of alien intelligence they were unlikely to forget—ever. No matter how primitive their technology, she couldn't dismiss—

"We're here," said Mark. "This is the tree. I think."

Irene could see why he'd wanted to explore it; younger than most of the giants around them, it still had some low branches, though it grew more densely fifteen to twenty feet up. Irene had climbed trees as a child; she knew the allure of that world-above-the-world. Trees in the parks all had signs forbidding climbing, but children did it anyway.

Mark applied thrust, and his chair lifted, making surprisingly little noise once he cleared the undergrowth.

Ezra looked up at the leafy obstacle course, then down at his spreading waistline. "I can't resist," he murmured. "And at my age, too." He caught the lowest branch on his second leap and, after a couple of tries, succeeded in hauling himself up, and climbed to join Mark.

"Show-offs," said Myrna.

Irene grinned. "You're just jealous. We also serve who hang out on the ground and watch."

Myrna laughed. "I hope they find something."

"Me too. Myrna, you believe Mark, don't you? What he saw?"

Myrna hesitated. "Yes. And those marks on his chair . . . But you have to admit, it'd be easy to imagine things, if you were alone out here."

Irene gazed through the rustling, swimming light. "I suppose. But you don't think he did?"

"No. But if he didn't, it means they're hiding from us. Someone shot at Mark, so they know we're here. Why haven't they come out to say hello? I mean, it's not like they were at war with Earth when they left, or anything. Why don't they just knock on the door, and say, 'hi'?"

"All together," said Irene, and Myrna chimed in with her: "How should I know?"

They were laughing when Mark's descent buffeted their suits.

"Nothing." He was frowning. "I was sure it would be there."

"We did find scars on the bark," Ezra, panting, observed from the branch above. He lowered himself and dropped. "In fact, we found places where it looked like something hit the tree and lodged."

"But if it lodged in the bark, then where is it now?" asked Myrna reasonably.

"How should I know?" Ezra's eyes danced. His hearing had always been excellent, too. "The only explanation is that someone, or something, went up and pried it out."

They speculated on who, how, and why for a long time, as they struggled through the undergrowth and clambered over fallen trunks. But it wasn't the only possible explanation. And the thought of how others might interpret it kept Mark silent and preoccupied for the rest of the long, futile afternoon.

"So, to sum up all your reports," Willard steepled his fingers, "no one has found any evidence of the colonists' survival."

This time they were gathered in the communal dining room, so everyone could sit in. Owing to Willard's insistence that anyone late to a meeting had to "come as they were," Irene was still in her suit, though she'd removed her helmet and gloves. She'd have resented it, except that Willard, who didn't bend his own rules, was still in his suit, too.

"That's not true." Irene had been prepared for this. "What about the fact that some of the buildings were dusty, and some weren't?"

"So some of the window seals leaked." J.D. looked almost as tired as Irene felt. "It doesn't prove any—"

"We also found fresh scars on the tree where they shot at Mark," Ezra put in patiently. "As I said."

Mark, who'd twice repeated what he had said yesterday, gazed at his hands, his mouth set sullenly. Given the others' growing skepticism, Irene could hardly blame him. He was tired, too. She shouldn't have let him stay out so long, but there was so much he couldn't do; she hated to restrict the few things he could.

"Gentlemen. And ladies." Willard looked straight at Irene as he spoke. "You've all given your reports, and you must admit, the evidence isn't promising. No one would like to find these people alive more than I would."

Which was true, and they all knew it.

"And we're not quitting yet. In fact, tonight we'll link in to the colonists' weather satellite, if it still works, and try to get some night pictures of the planet. Light will show up better than anything else, if there's no cloud cover. And we'll work a broader pattern tomorrow, and the next day, and the next."

Irene flexed her itching back against her sweat-soaked suit liner and wondered if she could get out of search detail by studying the doctor's records, which she'd downloaded to her datapad before returning to the ship. Dr. Gutierra had been too busy trying to fight the disease to make detailed research notes, but the scans of all his samples were there.

"And the next and the next if necessary," Willard went on. "But we have to face the fact that unless we find something, sooner or later, we're going to have to give up."

"And just leave them here?" Mark's eyes blazed. "Without even learning what happened to them? How they survived? *I saw that girl!* We can't—"

Clang. Clang. Clang.

The metallic thumps were muffled by distance, but still clear enough to silence the rising chorus of protest. Irene gazed at the *Stanley*'s crew in astonishment;

after fourteen months, counting heads was the work
of a moment. They were all there. So what—

Clang. Clang. Clang.

"Son of a bitch," said Myrna, and for once no one
frowned at her language. "They're knocking."

Willard leapt up, his whole face alight, ran for the
doorway, and then remembered his helmet and gloves
and had to run back. Willard, the two late flitter pilots
he'd shepherded in, and Irene's ground team were the
only ones still in their enviro-suits.

They ran for the decon-lock—at least you didn't
have to wait through the spray cycle to go out—but
they fidgeted impatiently while Willard, recovering his
usual presence of mind, made them stop and safety
check each other's seals. Irene knew he was right, but
suppose who ever was out there got bored and decided to—

Clang. Clang. Clang.

Suppose it was a kong out there, and what awaited
them was clubs and thorn whips? Though thorns probably wouldn't penetrate the suit's tough, plasticine-
threaded skin. Suppose—

Willard stepped in front of the hatch and drew himself up, putting on dignity like a jacket, and the others
stilled. Better, Irene supposed, to look like reasonable
adults than a bunch of overexcited kids, no matter
who was out—

Willard opened the hatch, and Irene forgot about
dignity and crowded forward to see.

The colonist, who'd just lifted a thick branch to
knock again, blinked and stepped down the ramp,
stumbling as the drop took him by surprise. He was
in his early or mid-fifties, Irene guessed. Stocky and
fit-looking, with thinning, graying hair, cut short. He
was clean-shaven, giving him an unexpectedly civilized
appearance, despite his rough clothes. Rough clothes,
the vest made of the same, close-woven animal hair

Irene had seen in the weaving machine, which admitted every microbe on the planet.

Come on, Goodnight. You knew they weren't wearing suits. But the part of her mind that wasn't rational felt as if he were naked. No, worse than naked, as if his inner body, the muscles, blood, and bone were visible, exposed to the elements. In biological terms, they were. Irene wiped her gloved hands on her thighs.

"Hello," said the colonist. Did their closed, stiff suits look as strange to him as he did to them? He obviously found their stares disconcerting.

"I'm Gus Sardakowski—"

"Then you must be Dr. Sardakowski's older son," said Willard, stepping forward to shake hands.

"Ah, yes. As a matter of fact, I am."

"I'm Willard Keene, United·Earth Force." The joy in his voice was like a fanfare of trumpets. "We've been looking for you."

"We noticed." Wry amusement made Sardakowski's ordinary face impish. "Look, we've got a lot to talk about. Shall we . . ." A gesture down the ramp completed his thought.

"Of course," said Willard, and they all trooped down. Irene spared a second to pity all those stuck on the ship, without their suits on. Mark's face, behind the Plexiglas shield, was a study of triumphant curiosity. His chair drew Sardakowski's gaze; the pity that flashed in his expression was suppressed so quickly that even Mark, who was deeply sensitive to such things, missed it. And the shadow that lingered looked less like pity than . . . guilt? Surely not.

"Before we start, I've a message for you, young sir. Sondi sends her profound apologies. You have to understand, there's nothing that big that climbs trees except kongs, and with them, if you don't shoot fast, it's too late. She didn't see you clearly enough in time.

But she's very sorry, and hopes you weren't hit, or scared, or anything."

He was obviously quoting when he finished, and Mark grinned. "Tell her I'm fine, and I'm sorry I scared *her*. But why did she run? Why were you all hiding?"

He'd asked the number one question, and even Willard waited in expectant silence for the answer.

Sardakowski sighed. "We weren't hiding, though I can see where it would look like that. Let me start at the beginning. You've read the settlement logs?"

"Yes," said Willard, though he hadn't.

"Then you know about both the kongs and the virus." The shadow of old grief flickered over Sardakowski's features. He had an extraordinarily mobile face, Irene thought. He'd be destroyed at a poker table.

"How did you cure yourselves, Mr. Sardakowski?" Irene asked in her best professional tone. "Possible cures for some of our remaining diseases are one of the things we hoped to find on this mission."

"So your message said," Sardakowski admitted. "When we finally got it. And please, call me Gus. We're not exactly formal around here. The population's too small for it. And you are?"

"Irene Olsen," she replied, and waited impatiently through introductions that followed.

"So how big is your population now?" Ezra asked.

"The virus?" Irene prompted.

"What about—" Myrna started, but Sardakowski was laughing.

"I'll try to keep it brief, but let me take if from the beginning, OK? We started with five hundred and fourteen colonists, and an embryo bank of twenty thousand. By the time the kongs and the virus finished, there were only two hundred and ninety two of us left." Sorrow again, on his craggy face. "I'm afraid I won't be able to help you much, in terms of cures.

Some of us recovered, others didn't. That's all I can tell you. But the kongs stepped up their attacks—"

"Still abiding by their rituals?" Ezra cut in.

"Yes." Sardakowski looked disconcerted, though he knew they'd read the logs. "We realized we couldn't fight them off indefinitely, so, to make a very long story short, we moved away from the forest and into the desert, taking up a nomadic lifestyle. You're lucky you caught us. We only stop here twice a year, to resupply, repair equipment, access the embryo bank, that sort of thing."

"Then why didn't we see you in the settlement?" Mark asked. "Yesterday, when we first landed?"

Sardakowski laughed. "Because we've 'gone native,' Mr. Riley. And in the desert that means nocturnal." He gestured to the setting sun. "I had to get up early, to catch you before you went to bed."

"Then why couldn't we locate your camp with the flitters?" asked Willard, frowning.

"You flew over us." Sardakowski shrugged. "Our tents blend in pretty well; we'd be hard to spot from the air."

"But the radar should certainly have picked you up," Willard persisted.

"Not unless someone has found a way to make it detect something other than metal." Which of course they hadn't. "We carry very little metal. It's heavy. Speaking of technology, I don't suppose they've made any significant advances in energy storage? Or comp-air rifles? You read about our fléchette guns? We still use them, but they don't have the best range, or accuracy, and . . . Well, we can talk about that later. Tell me . . ."

"Tell me more about the virus," Irene prompted. "You must have developed some treatment."

"We were too sick to develop anything," said Sardakowski. "As I told you, some recovered, and some didn't."

From an alien virus? Not likely. "Then you won't mind giving me a blood sample, will you?"

"Not at all," said Sardakowski amiably. "Though it's going to be a bit difficult with me out here"—his gesture encompassed the open atmosphere around them—"and you in there."

Irene opened her mouth and shut it. Why hadn't she thought of that? Because it was the first time they'd encountered living colonists, that was why. *So think about it now, Goodnight.*

Willard was frowning. "Where's the problem? Irene brings the sample kit out, draws blood, takes it back though decon—"

"The heat of the decon-bath would cook the sample," Irene told him absently. "And any shielding that would protect the sample would protect contaminants on the container as well. But it has to be possible."

"Anything is possible," said Sardakowski. "When you figure it out, let me know. In the meantime, please, what's happened on Earth? Is it still . . ."

They talked for three solid hours. News, explanations, promises of cooperation.

"Though you must understand, Mr. Sardakowski, that we can't take any of your people home with us. Closely populated as the domes are"—Willard gestured apologetically—"contamination is a major threat."

"I understand. We all accepted that when we left, and frankly, I think there's only one of us who might want to return. But tell me, what happened to the other colony ships?"

They did, and his mobile face showed a deep and sincere sorrow. But watching that face, as the night wore on, and those still aboard the ship put on their suits and brought out battery lamps (superfluous, with multiple moons shining down), Irene began to doubt, and doubt grew to certainty.

Mark, exhausted, gave up and went to bed. Finally,

yawning, they let Sardakowski go, agreeing to meet again the next night. In the settlement, he requested, since the colonists had a lot to accomplish, and they feared the extra activity might rouse the kongs sooner than usual. "Because nice as it is to see some new faces, when they warn us, we're going to leave. We've stopped fighting that war, and I have no desire to start it up again."

"Well," said Willard as they stepped into the lock and stood, arms out, waiting for the steaming chemical bath to drench their suits. "What do you think?"

"I'm not sure." Ezra looked worried. "He seemed perfectly frank. He answered all our questions, readily. But . . ."

"I'm sure," said Irene. "He was hiding something. But I'll be damned if I know what. Or why."

The waterfall of decontamination buried Willard's disapproving scowl.

Chapter 3

They set out for the settlement at sunset, having napped as much as possible during the afternoon. In Irene's case that wasn't much, and she suspected the same was true for Mark. He looked exhausted by evening, and Irene had almost forbidden him to come. But he chattered so eagerly about meeting some of the colonists that she didn't have the heart. Besides, Willard had given him a special assignment. "You're our ace in the hole, Mark. People are less wary of children than adults, so I want you to meet as many colonists as you can—just get them talking. Sooner or later, someone is going to let something slip, and then . . . Well, we'll see."

People were especially likely to be kind to the dying, but at least he hadn't said that aloud. "Children" was condescending enough. Irene's assignment, self-chosen, was to get a blood sample.

"Do you really think they'll be here tonight?" she asked Mark, as they topped the rise. The sun was setting behind the curve of the desert, and all twenty of them stopped, gazing over the orange-tinted, alien landscape, though most had seen it several times by now. Irene wondered if she was the only one who used it as an excuse to catch her breath.

"Yes," said Mark absently, his eyes on the view. "I think the only reason they revealed themselves was because they needed to come back to the settlement. And they were afraid we'd stir up the kongs before they had time. Otherwise, I think they'd have stayed in hiding."

Some of the others, eager to meet "the natives," were already starting down. The Yes-dears, whose real name was Yassir, stood off to the side, holding suited hands. They'd met on the *Stanley*, and Willard, in his capacity as captain, had married them four months ago. Irene supposed it was a romantic view, if you looked at it that way. The Yes-dears, nicknamed by Mark, looked at everything that way.

"Come on, you two," she called, as Mark started down. "We've got work to do."

They came, but they came last.

"Wait till the moons rise," Mark told Myrna. "They'll both be completely useless."

"They're not that bad," said Irene, hoping her envy wasn't apparent in her voice.

Mrs. Yassir stumbled, and Mr. Yassir caught her arm. They clung together, and she put her faceplate against his and made kissing motions. Mark laughed.

"Well, mostly they're not. If you get them apart, they're almost normal."

"How would you know?" Myrna cut in. "No one's been able to get them apart for almost a year. But don't worry, in a few more months the mush will reco-alesce into brain cells, and they'll return to normal. In the first six months of *my* second marriage . . ."

The sky was dark and the moons had brightened by the time they reached the settlement and spread out to find the colonists. They'd brought wrist lights, but even on the ridge trail no one had turned them on, and the clear space around the buildings was covered with a silvery luminescence, and everyone cast three shadows—one for each of the moons currently in the sky.

Mark turned his chair slowly, playing with the multi-shadowed light, and Irene's heart caught—he was so young. He should have all his life ahead, to see the moons of other worlds, to discover—

A long, lumpy shadow fell over Irene, and she spun and found herself face-to-face with a monster. Huge nostrils blew steam over her faceplate, blurring her view of the slope of hair-covered bone topped by deep brown eyes, half-buried in a forest of fur, looking right at her.

She leapt back, clawing for her pistol, not realizing she'd screamed till the echoes rang in her ears.

The beast stepped back too, lifting its misshapen head up and up—it was huge! With *horns* in the tangled mass of hair at its crown. Its nostrils widened again. It stepped farther back, inflated itself, and hissed like a leaky air seal. A big leaky seal. A really, really big . . .

Irene pointed her electro-pistol straight at it—even clutched in both hands it shook visibly. "Don't move." She eased back, never taking her eyes off it. "Don't move a step you . . . you thing. Don't even think—"

"Ahem. Allow me." Gus Sardakowski stepped between her and the monster, laying one bare hand on the beast's nose and the other on Irene's pistol, pushing it gently down. "Kirk, this is Irene Olsen. Irene, this is Kirk. He's my—"

"They're camels!" Mark exclaimed in delight. His chair whipped past Irene. She made a grab for it and missed.

"Mark, get back here!"

But he was already circling the large beast, far too close for Irene's comfort.

"Relax. Please." Sardakowski worked the pistol free of her numb fingers and tucked it back in her holster. "Kirk won't hurt anyone, I promise. He's just a bit upset because you don't smell like a person."

And indeed the beast was shambling around to sniff at Mark, who stopped his chair and held still for it while Irene held her breath.

It was almost as large as she'd first thought it, the top of its shoulder higher than Sardakowski's head, its humps and long neck rising even higher.

"Take it easy, you idiot." Sardakowski strolled up to the great head that seemed to be trying to inhale her nephew, chair and all. "I told you they wore suits." He slapped the beast's neck and it snorted and lifted its head; then it sighed and snuffled Sardakowski's hair, losing all interest in Mark and Irene.

Two humps. There were camels on Earth once, she thought, that had two humps, but she'd only seen pictures of the one-humped kind. This beast was hairier than her vague memories, with . . .

"Six legs!" Mark exclaimed.

"Of course," said Sardakowski. "Just like everything else on Navohar. I thought you read the settlement logs."

"We did," said Mark. "But they didn't say anything about camels."

Sardakowski laughed. "They're desert creatures, so we didn't have much to do with them at first. But they're in our naturalist's database. I suppose you haven't gotten to that yet."

Six legs. A body so narrow it all but vanished from the front or back, and so broad it looked like a battleship from the side. Long, tan fur. The same fur they wove into fabric? And long, knobby legs, and a long, curved neck with a long face, which displayed the same sappy, complaisant expression Irene had seen in cartoon drawings of Earth's version of this beast. Only its tail was short. And curved horns, which Irene didn't remember camels to have had. But of course . . . "They're not really camels; they're native wildlife. What did your naturalist name them?"

"*Camelus hexaped.*" Sardakowski sounded apologetic, but there was a glint in his eyes, and Mark snickered. "Actually, there are a lot of creatures here whose Earth analogues you'd recognize. Similar environments, similar adaptations, just like Berdotti theorized."

"And that's *yours*?" said Irene incredulously. "What do you do with it?"

Mark gestured to the open space between the buildings. "They're travels, Auntie."

Looking away from the monster, Irene saw that the colonists had arrived—riding the camels, some of them still mounted. A few of the beasts wore saddles or loaded pack frames, but many, even those with riders on their backs, were bare. And none had any strapping on their heads, so how did . . .

One of the mounted colonists—they perched between the camels' humps—thumped the hump in front of her and the beast knelt, collapsing first its middle legs, then the rear pair, and finally the front.

Children darted around them with a fearlessness that made Irene wince. "They seem to be very well trained."

"Well, that took a bit of doing," Sardakowski replied. "But they're wonderful creatures. Very curious and friendly."

The colonist swung her leg over the front hump and slid down. She was about Mark's age, with Asian features and black hair braided down her back. A small girl, she should have looked dainty, but the bones of her face were too strong for prettiness, and she moved with the muscular grace of a stalking predator.

She smiled, hesitantly, at Mark, who moved his chair to meet her. Irene's eyes filled, and she blinked resolutely.

"She really was concerned when she saw she'd fired at a person," Sardakowski said softly. "It's GED, isn't it?"

"Yes," said Irene shortly. She didn't like pity any more than Mark did.

Sardakowski's eyes closed—Irene couldn't interpret

the expression on his face. "I'm sorry. Truly sorry. Well, I have to get some work done tonight, so if you'll excuse me . . ." He was turning away as he spoke.

"Not a chance," said Irene, and he blinked in astonishment. "I've figured out a way to get a blood sample."

Sardakowski laughed. "I thought you would. OK, how?"

"All we have to do is put *you* in a suit. You go through decon, come up to my lab, and we put the needle right through the sleeve into your arm. Pull it, slip on a patch seal, and the chances of environmental contamination are so low as to be virtually nonexistent."

Sardakowski winced. "What are the chances of your hitting a vein through that suit sleeve? In less than eighty attempts?"

Irene grinned. "If it's any consolation I was going to let Karima, she's our doctor, do the deed. She did say it might take a couple of tries, even using the bioscanner, but she's confident she can do it."

"Lovely. I'll be sure to mention that when I ask for volunteers." He was turning away again. "Very well, Dr. Olsen, I'll get someone up to your ship before we leave. I don't suppose those suits have gotten any more comfortable over the years?"

"Actually they have. They're very flexible, except for the helmets, and the internal sensors maintain pretty much the temperature you want." Within limits, and they didn't handle perspiration well, but none of the colonists would be in them long enough for that to matter. "What's wrong with right now?"

"I was thinking of the plumbing," Sardakowski said wryly. "And tonight we're all extremely busy."

He moved off as he spoke, heading for an open bundle at the edge of the settlement, where he took out a compact tool kit—probably the task he'd been pulled from by Irene's scream.

"Busy with what?" asked Irene, following. "Maybe I can help, so you'll be finished early."

Sardakowski laughed. "You just don't quit, do you? Know anything about repairing weaving machines? I didn't think so."

"I'll help anyway," Irene told him. She was following him across the clearing to the sewing center when movement on the ridge caught her eye—over half a dozen people, unhelmeted, were crossing the top. Like the *Stanley*'s crew, they all stopped to gaze out.

"What are they doing?"

Sardakowski looked up. "They're heading back to the *Henrietta* to access the embryo banks. Various people, over the years, have suggested we celebrate that sort of thing. But when the time comes, most couples insist it's private, so we don't make a production out of it . . . at least, not in most cases."

His smile turned smug as he went into the sewing center.

"What do you do?" Irene followed him in, as he called up the lights. "Arrange for the bed to collapse? If I'd known they were going up there, I could have gotten samples from them."

"Those suits are an indignity even I wouldn't inflict on them." Sardakowski set down his tools and opened the front panel of the weaving machine. "Especially not on Conception Night." He flipped a power toggle, and the machine hummed for a moment and stalled. "Hmm. This is the problem with only coming back for a few weeks, once or twice a year. All the maintenance has to be done up front. After this, it's the chem-mixer."

The machine's innards gleamed mysteriously. Perhaps she wouldn't help after all. Irene perched on a table instead. "You have a name for it? Conception Night?"

"Had to call it something." Sardakowski began to tinker. "When your population is as small as ours, conception is a big deal. One of the disadvantages of taking to the desert is that we haven't been able to expand faster than our herds and the terrain can support us—and that's not fast. Ah-ha! Wrench please."

Irene handed it to him, and he positioned it and pushed the loosen button, watching the jaws spiral in and then spin till the nut popped off.

"It must have caused some changes in your society," Irene commented. "All the men being sterilized, and none of the children belonging to anyone, genetically."

"Not as much as you'd think." Sardakowski pulled a twisted belt loose and started smoothing out the kinks. "It's something every colony has to accept, if you're going to have enough genetic diversity for a healthy population. Mostly it just makes things a bit"—he wiggled his brows at her lasciviously— "freer."

Irene laughed. "I should warn you, Mr. Sardakowski, that comments like that are considered pretty risqué these days. A younger person would be shocked."

"Then Earth's young people have my sincere sympathy. And please, call me Gus. Every time someone says Mr. Sardakowski I look around for my father, and he's been dead for decades." He stretched the belt back onto its rollers.

"All right, Gus. And I'm Irene. Don't you need a new one of those?"

"I hope not. It'd take hours to make one, and almost as long to go back to *Henrietta* and pull it out of stock. Your name's Irene Olsen—how come everyone last night was calling you Goodnight? Surely your parents weren't that sadistic, even with a middle name."

"No," said Irene. "But Mark was. When he was little, profanity was very much on the way out. His

parents insisted we watch our language in front of
the kids, so I started saying 'good night!' in situations
where . . . well, you have to say something."

Gus laughed. "I see it coming. How old was he
when he heard the song?"

"Five," said Irene. "When Mark called me Auntie
Goodnight it was cute, you know? But then his parents caught it, and then my parents, then all my
friends. I get called Goodnight about half the time
now."

"It suits you." Gus was smiling, and heat crept into
Irene's face. As if she were a teenager. How absurd.
She was grateful for the shadow of her helmet.

"You'd understand about names, I suppose. Did
you get stuck with junior? When your father was alive,
I mean?"

"No, thank goodness." Gus wiggled the belt back
onto its rollers. "My father was called Stavo—and so
is my oldest son, so you see, I have to plead guilty to
naming sadism, too. But alternating the two nick-
names is an old family tradition, and it wasn't *my*
idea."

So he was married. Of course, he would be. "I'd
like to meet your family," said Irene. "Perhaps they'd
be free for a while tonight."

"You don't fool me," Gus replied, and then fell
silent as he tightened the nut.

*And why assume that I want to meet your wife, you
arrogant jerk?* Irene opened her mouth . . .

"You only want their blood." Gus closed the side
panel and went to the power toggle, and Irene was
very glad for the concealment of her helmet. "Stavo
and Rudy are both traveling with other groups this
year. I think I told you we split into smaller groups
in the winter. Easier on the environment."

"What about your wife?" It was a perfectly natural
question, at this point.

"She died. A long time ago."

"I'm sorry." Now she was in the same position so many people found themselves in with her and Mark. It was as awkward as it looked.

"So was I," Gus said simply. He threw the switch, and the machine hummed, then began to clatter.

"Excuse me?"

Irene jumped. The olive-skinned young man had half shouted to be heard over the noise, and she hadn't been aware of his approach.

"Gus, one of the refrigeration units is squealing."

"Has it stopped working?" Gus looked concerned.

"Not yet."

He spoke to Gus, but his gaze, full of shy fascination, flickered to Irene. He looked to be in his early twenties. Was she the first stranger he'd ever seen?

"How do you do, ma'am?" He shook her suited hand with a formality that went oddly with his baggy clothes and scuffed sandals.

"I'm Eric Hoffman." And no genetic relation to his parents at all, Irene realized. He looked more like an Ali than an Eric.

"Irene Olsen. Tell me, could you spare—" over the ridge, into the suit, find a vein, reverse the process. Three hours, most likely. "—an hour, say, to give me a blood sample?"

"Um, I'm not sure, ma'am." His gaze went straight to Gus—*I thought you were supposed to deal with this.*

Gus snorted. "I told her we were too busy tonight, and that I'd send her some volunteers before we left. If you want to do it, that's fine, but not—"

"I'm afraid I am kind of busy tonight, ma'am," he said reluctantly. "Maybe later. Gus, they also wanted me to tell you that monkey-squirrels got into the stored buoys, so we'll have to do something about barring those windows. And the samples—"

"I know, I know. I'll get to it as soon as I can. In fact, if you'll dump those wool bags into the hopper, I'll get to it now. And tell Ravi that he's in business."

Eric said he would, and good-bye, ma'am.

The moonlight was very bright, possibly because yet another moon, this one small and lumpy, was rising over the treetops.

"I see why you asked me to call you Gus," said Irene ruefully. "I haven't been ma'amed that often in years."

Gus grinned. "You're pretty intimidating in that suit. Almost an alien. And female, too. You were asking about the effects of our genetic contract—one of the subtler ones is that, because female fertility is so important, women are . . . highly regarded. Not quite put on a pedestal yet, but it seems to be heading that way."

Irene wrinkled her nose. "Ick."

"I thought you'd say that. Fortunately, most of the women agree with you. It slows the trend down a— Oh, come on, I don't have time for this!"

A camel approached and Irene, despite herself, took a step back before she found her nerve. It sniffed her from helmet to boots, giving her a close-up of its immense shaggy head. Finally, it huffed and turned to Gus.

"Couldn't you find someone else for this?" he complained.

The beast blew in his face and lifted one of its middle feet. It wasn't a hoof, Irene saw, as Gus took it and turned the bottom up: three leathery pads grouped together in a rough oval, almost as big as a dinner plate. For walking on sand? One of the pads had a reddened, inflamed patch toward the heel, with a hard-looking bump in the middle.

"What's wrong with it?"

"Corns." Gus sounded resigned. "Come on, you. We'll pick up a patch at the clinic and start it softening."

"Corns? Like we get?"

"Yeah." Gus started for one of the smaller buildings. Now that she was watching for it, Irene thought the beast was limping, though it was hard to tell with that rippling, six-legged gait. "Just like us. Sometimes I think corn treatment is the only reason they put up with us. And maybe salt. And grooming, and—"

"Why do you keep them? I mean, wouldn't a hover-sled be more efficient?"

"Not when its fuel ran out." He'd asked last night about improvements in energy-storage technology and been very interested when they told him about the new, deep-cell batteries. "That was my priority long-term project—whenever I got a moment off repairing things—trying to design a solar battery that could power our hoverbarge. You actually have spares of those—what did you call them? Deep cells?—in storage? I don't suppose you know how they work?"

"Not a clue. But we'll happily trade you several for . . ."

"Blood." Gus sighed. "I hope we can work that out. If I could fit them into our equipment, we could haul some of this stuff"—his gesture encompassed the utilitarian buildings around them—"to our summer base. If I ever get the time to work on it."

"You do seem busy," Irene admitted. Fortunately, anyone's blood would do. "I thought . . . Last night I got the impression you were the . . . the leader, or whatever you people call it."

"Take me to your council head?" said Gus. "Yes, they dumped it on me this year, for my sins."

"This council is your governing body?"

"That's an optimistic view of it." Gus grimaced. "The council is supposed to work out a consensus, which the other colonists vote to ratify. In reality, everyone who shows up at the meeting argues their case. Coming up with a workable compromise under those conditions is . . . Let's just say that I duck being council head whenever I can. Though that kind of thing only happens when something that affects the whole group comes up. Mostly it's a matter of settling squab-bles people could easily settle themselves, and of being second-guessed—with perfect twenty-twenty hind-sight—every time a decision turns out wrong. But the pay makes it all worthwhile."

Irene laughed. "Nothing?"

"You got it."

In the clinic they found a short, stocky woman, with straight, carrot-red hair and freckles, whom Gus intro-duced as Nola Page. She said she was "a veterinarian, among other things." And she, and her harried ap-prentice, were too busy fabricating medicines to apply a corn patch, sorry, thanks, good-bye.

No blood there. At least, not yet. Maybe they really were as busy as Gus claimed. Maybe.

The camel's smug, contented expression never changed, but it lifted its foot impatiently when they came out of the clinic.

"All right," Gus grumbled, pulling plastic from the back of the patch. "Give me a minute."

"You seem to have a lot to do with the wildlife here—what was it that got into your message buoys? Monkey-squirrels?"

"They get into everything," said Gus gloomily. "They can't hurt the buoys, but they love to push buttons. They're one of the main reasons we kept all the embryo banks on the *Henrietta*, instead of moving at least some down to the settlement."

He pressed the patch firmly over the sore spot. The camel's ears swiveled, but it showed no other sign of discomfort. At least, none that Irene could see.

"Will it stay on when the camel walks on it?"

"About eighty percent do. We invented a special adhesive just for this." He released the beast's foot, slapped its side, and it ambled away. "That's one of the things Nola's doing—making more patches."

"That's not your Kirk, is it?" Though what made

Irene think that, she couldn't tell. They all looked alike.

"Oh, no. She's unclaimed, as a matter of fact, so she doesn't have a name."

"You mean no one rides her? Why keep them around if no one rides them?"

"They're part of the herd." Gus picked up his tools and started for another building. "They carry packs for us, sometimes. And provide wool. They have a vile sense of humor, but they even make good watchdogs. Remember Kirk hissing at you?"

"As if I could forget," said Irene with feeling.

"Well, that's their danger signal. Look, you don't have to spend the whole night with me. Surely there are other people you'd like to pes—meet."

"Thanks, but pestering you suits me fine. If I do it long enough, I figure you'll find me a blood donor just to get rid of me. Why'd you name him Kirk?"

Gus sighed. "Because he had the largest harem. It's short for James—"

"Tiberius." Irene stopped, glaring at him. "Oh God, you're one of them."

"One of what?" Gus asked blankly.

"A trekkie."

Star Trek had run for over a century, on and off, with one white-hat captain succeeding another. It had taken the Vrell invasion to kill the thing—after that, believing in friendly aliens required too great a suspension of disbelief. But it still had a cult following. One of Mark's T-shirts displayed a skeleton in a Star Fleet uniform and the caption, "The *Final* Frontier."

"Mark is a trekkie," she told Gus with loathing. "I hate trekkies."

"I'm sorry." But he was laughing as he turned into the next building, and Irene growled under her breath as she followed.

The refrigeration unit was an extralarge, industrial type, and it was indeed squealing. Irene laid a hand over the sound pickup on her suit, and it was still too loud. Gus, who had two ears and needed both his hands anyway, screwed up his face and set to work, pulling the back off the big freezer in record time.

He must have caught the *Star Trek* bug young, Irene mused, watching him. Old Gustave's sons had been in their teens when they left the planet, which put him in his early forties now. He looked about ten years older, but constant exposure to sun and wind used to age people's skin, Irene remembered. B.D. Before Domes. Now half the human population had no memory of what it was like to go naked through the world, as this man did. She'd gotten used to seeing him so exposed as the night wore on, but thinking about it still started a shiver in her spine.

The squeal stopped abruptly. Irene lifted her hand just in time to hear Gus say, "That's better!" He squirmed farther into the machine, and clanks and clicks began to emerge. "Let's see here . . . I think . . . Shit! I was afraid of that." He hauled himself out and wiped greasy hands on his thighs.

Irene was the only one she knew who still said "shit" like she meant it. She enjoyed hearing him say it immensely.

"What's wrong with it?"

"Broken bearing. That's something I'll have to go back to *Henrietta* for, and even then it's not a quick fix. Which means"—he rose to his feet with a resigned sigh—"that we're going to have to move the samples before they thaw."

A flash of excitement shot through Irene, even though she knew perfectly well it was most unlikely she could figure out anything just from seeing some-one's labeled samples. "Well, that I can help with."

Gus sighed again.

Most of the refrigerators were full, so they had to rearrange the other samples to make space.

"I keep telling them to clean these things out," Gus

grumbled. "But they say they can't throw anything away, because they might need it."

"They're absolutely right." Irene was a pack rat herself when it came to lab work. What the hell was kedigreen pollen that they needed sixteen dishes of it? "You never know when you'll need something again, or when some sample will prove different from the others in a meaningful way." Sherotti? "Maybe we have your—bearing was it?—on the *Stanley*. We'd happily swap it for, say, two hundred cc's of blood?"

Gus just grinned. His hands were full of frosty petri dishes, filled with some dark matter, whose labels held only dates. "Do you have room for these yet? Good. By the way, why '*Stanley*'? It's not very dignified for an exploratory ship."

"On the contrary," Irene told him. "Here, give me those. It's the *Henry Morton Stanley*."

"Henry . . . Oh!" He laughed in delight. "Here I thought the UEF had no sense of humor."

"Someone who comes from the *Henrietta* has no room to complain."

"Well, it was the *Henry David Thoreau*," he said.

Esclopin. Hopper mouse liver, cross sec. "But?" Irene asked absently.

"But it was a *mother* ship."

They spent several hours moving frozen samples, almost half of them the dark, date-labeled goop, and during that time two different kids dashed in to tell Gus that no one could do anything till the chem-mixer was fixed, and a third that the last couple was back from the *Henrietta* and had brought a load of salt tabs. Which couldn't be coated till the chem-mixer . . .

"I *know*. Here, if you don't have anything else to do, you can finish this, and I can get to it."

This time he lucked out—the lanky, hapless-looking boy didn't have fifteen other messages he was supposed to deliver instantly. They left him peering into the crammed refrigerators and muttering in dismay.

"He'll think of something," Gus said callously. "Did you get anything from the samples?"

"Not as much as I'd . . ." Irene stopped, and glared at him.

"Sorry, Goodnight, but you're not exactly subtle. Why don't you just ask?"

All but two moons had now set. Irene was aware of how much of the night had crept past while she chatted with this easygoing man. His shadowed face looked as open as a child's. Candid. Friendly. Once again Irene was certain—he was lying through his teeth. But about what?

"OK. What was in the last four log entries, which were erased?"

It wasn't the question he'd expected, and for just a moment his mask slipped, exposing the wariness beneath. But only for a moment.

"How would I know? It was over twenty years ago. A lot of people were dying. Maybe he put down something personal, and decided not to leave it for posterity."

Shakespeare had it right: the guilty did protest too much. And it was his father's log—he should have some idea what might have been there.

"All right," said Irene innocently. "Then why didn't you keep up the entries—or at least leave a message saying where you'd gone, so people like us would know you hadn't just vanished off the face of the planet?"

Or died of the virus. For that, Irene suddenly realized, was just what they'd been intended to think. And those final entries had proved they didn't . . . and maybe told why they didn't.

"That was because I couldn't be sure it would be people like you who'd find it," Gus answered smoothly. "Tell me you don't have protections around Earth's coordinates in your database, for the same reason?"

Which of course they did. If any encounter with
intelligent aliens looked like going bad, one of the
officers would activate the purge program. And if it
went really bad, the pilots, who had Earth's coordinates memorized, were supposed to commit suicide.
Irene frowned. "You could at least have—"

"Dr. Olsen!" The girl, Sondi, came flying out of the
night, her long braid flapping on her shoulders. "Dr.
Olsen, come with me. There's something wrong with
Mark!"

She turned as she spoke, running back like a chee-
tah, and Irene almost ran her down. Her heart
pounded, not yet, not yet, not yet. She barely heard
Sondi babbling, "He got kind of quiet—I thought he
was just tired. But then he said he needed to lie down,
and killed the chair boosters right there, and then sort
of rolled out of it, and his face was all red so—"

They rounded a corner and there he was, lying in
the shadow between two buildings, his helmet off, his
hands struggling with the front of his suit.

"Mark!"

It opened even as she fell to her knees beside him.
He'd pulled off his helmet; it was too late anyway.
Too late, too—

"I'm hot," he muttered. She could see no color in
the dimness, but his face was darkly flushed, and she
could feel the heat of his fever even through her glove.
Fever, convulsions, and death.

Irene took Mark's hand, and a deep steadying
breath. "Hang on, kiddo, and we'll get you to bed,
OK?"

"Auntie?" He peered at her, blinking. "I'm sorry.
I didn't—"

"Later, love. Bed first. I—"

"I'll take him." Gus knelt, pushing Irene gently
aside, and worked his arms under Mark's shoulders
and knees. "Here we go."

Mark gasped when Gus lifted him, but made no

complaint; Gus started toward the clearing, walking smoothly to keep from jarring his fragile burden.

"We can't go back to the ship." Irene's voice was shaking. Her hands were shaking.

"I know. There are beds in some of the houses. We'll manage."

He seemed to know where he was going. Irene fell in beside him, trying to slow her racing heart. *I only have to be strong for a few more days. Then I can break down and howl. Probably on Willard's shoulder. Then I'll be so wimped out I'll agree to marry him and spend the rest of my life regretting it. God. Get a grip, Goodnight.*

She'd known this was coming for years, but the part of her that shrank from laying her hand on a red-hot burner flinched from it still. *Not now, not yet, not—*

A lumpy mass of hair moved into Gus's path, nostrils flared. He tried to go around it, but it turned again, sniffing the human it could suddenly smell.

Irene ran and slammed against its front shoulder with all her might—"Get!"

The firm muscle under the fur barely yielded. Knocking a six-legged creature off its feet was probably impossible, but it shambled aside and fell in behind them, still sniffing at Mark over Gus's shoulder.

There were others there as well, colonists and crew members, running into the clearing, following Gus, asking questions, but Irene ignored them, even when J.D. laid a hand on her shoulder, said, "I'll tell Willard," and dashed off.

By the time they reached the small house behind the clinic, the red-haired vet, Nola, was laying some sort of pad over the empty bed frame. It rustled when she tucked the sheet around its corners—God only knew what infested whatever it was stuffed with, but in Mark's case, that no longer mattered.

Gus set him down on the only chair in the small, bare room, and stripped his suit down to his waist, unfastening the belt pack, before lifting him onto the bed where he finished the task. Over Mark's suit liner, he wore the T-shirt with fish swimming around a skull, and peering out of one empty eye.

Embrace Me.

"Here." Nola thrust a bowl of water and a soft cloth into Irene's hands. "Start sponging him down while we get him stripped." After some consideration they took off all his clothes, replacing his underwear with an undignified, but practical, plastic-shielded diaper that crinkled when he moved. Irene bathed his sweating skin, soaking the cloth and wringing it out again and again. After a while the flush faded, and he slipped into an uneasy doze.

"I'll bring you more water," said Nola, taking the cloth from Irene's limp grasp. "When he wakes there's a tea we use for fever and pain. It works as well as most drugs, unless they've developed something better in the last—"

"No," said Irene. "There's nothing that will defeat this."

"Well, this won't stop it either," said Nola. "But it'll help. I'll make it now."

She delivered it just half an hour later, then left again, promising to return and check up on them frequently. Irene sat and watched Mark breathing, and despite her resolve tears welled, soaking the absorbent pad, which became every bit as revolting as she'd known it would.

She was trying to stop when another's sniffling caught her attention. The long, horizontal window over Mark's bed was only about eight inches high, so only the beast's big nose could squeeze through. Irene leapt to her feet and slapped it. The camel jerked back, leaving a tuft of wool on the window frame, and six heavy feet stamped in agitation.

Mark's soft laugh froze her in her tracks. "Sorry

Auntie, but you look so fierce. Like a mouse taking on a titan."

"Mouse. Gee, thanks." She knelt and laid a gloved hand on his cheek, hating the barrier between them. "How are you feeling, kiddo?"

"Awful," he said bluntly. "But I sort of expected that." And indeed, the resignation of Omega was in his eyes, serene, despite the lurking fear in their depths. "I'm sorry to do this to you now. I had a headache this morning, but I thought. . . ."

"Never mind," said Irene. "How'd you like to try a genuine native/alien fever cure?"

"I don't know. Do you have to smear me with camel dung or something?"

It surprised her into a genuine laugh. "What have you been reading? No, it's herbal tea."

She fed it to him in small sips, and he was exhausted by the time she finished. The light through the window was brighter; color began to seep into the small, spartan room.

"No," said Mark as she moved to close the window. "Please, I like the air."

Then he lay so still she thought he'd fallen asleep again, till he whispered, "I only wish. . . ."

"What, love?"

"That I could have done more."

"You did fine, kiddo. You've done plenty." But he didn't stir under her stroking hand, and she couldn't tell if he'd heard her.

Morning brought Myrna, who replaced the yawning Nola. "They didn't tell me, or I'd have been here sooner. And Ezra says he'll come whenever you want him, but he'll stay out of your way till then. Are you OK, Goodnight?"

"Fine," said Irene, who had no idea whether it was true, and frankly didn't care.

Mark's fever fluctuated during the day, and her whole world narrowed to bathing his heated skin and giving him tea. It did seem to help, but not enough. Never enough.

Afternoon brought Willard. Judging by the tramping and snorting outside, he had to drive off several camels before he could enter, which irritated Irene immensely because Mark was sleeping. At least he had the sense to keep his voice down when he finally made it in.

"What are those . . . things doing out there? I had to throw rocks to get them to move."

"How should I know?"

Myrna snorted, but Willard's serious expression never cracked.

"My dear." He took her gloved hand in his. "How are you doing?"

"Fine."

"Is there anything you need from the ship? I sent the fever meds down with Myrna, but . . ."

He never even looked at Mark, and fury flashed through Irene's weary nerves. Just because he didn't have his suit on . . . But it probably wasn't that. Willard's own daughter had died of GED. It must have taken a lot of courage to come here. Irene couldn't have done it.

"Thank you, but no. I have everything I need." Except time to get back to Mark. She took Willard's arm and started toward the door. And if that wasn't a sufficient hint, she'd—

Evidently it wasn't. "My dear." He took her hands again. "You're so brave."

"Bullshit," said Irene, taking a thoroughly unworthy satisfaction in the shock on his face as he let her go. "If it would do any good, I'd be throwing a tantrum that'd knock your socks off. But it won't, so if you'll excuse me . . ."

Mark had the first convulsion that evening, and it terrified Irene, even as she tucked the spare blankets

Nola had given her against the wall so he couldn't hurt himself.

Nightfall brought Nola herself, in a domineering mood. Myrna helped Irene empty the waste pockets in her suit and promised to bring another water pack and the sealed nutriwafers that could be inserted though the portal beneath the lip of the faceplate. It was a sloppy, stupid way to eat, and Irene couldn't imagine being hungry, ever again, but she thanked Myrna anyway and sent her, yawning, back to the ship. Now if she'd been offered a bath . . .

As always, yawning proved contagious. Irene was doing it as she pushed past the camel that seemed to have taken up residence on the doorstep, which was a mistake since Nola took one look at her, and said, "Bed."

Irene argued as Nola, pointing out that this could go on for days, hauled in another mattress and spread it against the far wall. She objected when Nola took the damp cloth from her hands. She swore when Gus dragged her over the mattress, set her down, and threatened to pin her there till she went to sleep.

Then she started to cry and lay down, turning away, and felt his hand rubbing her back in slow circles above the suit's battery pack. The inside of her helmet, padded though it was, made a lousy pillow, and Mark needed her. But if she lay still, with her eyes closed, sooner or later Gus would leave. Then she'd get up again, and knock that interfering bitch over the head, if that was what was necessary. All she had to do was wait till he left . . .

When she opened her eyes, sunlight glared off the wall in front of her, and her cramping neck complained bitterly as she blinked in confusion. Then she remembered and rolled over, onto her knees, ignoring the dizziness of the sudden movement, and froze, staring at the empty bed.

Mark was gone.

Chapter 4

"He's not dead, he's *gone*. Aren't you listening? They *took* him!"

Willard had come with Myrna in the morning. They'd found Irene running from building to building, checking every room, peering under tables, into the larger cabinets, even inside the big refrigerators.

"Irene, calm down." Willard laid both hands on her shoulders; his slow deliberate voice dragged like a file over her guilt-ridden urgency. If she hadn't gone to sleep . . . "Hysterics won't help you or Mark, and you know it. Take a deep breath and tell me, slowly and calmly, what happened. Myrna, you take a look around the settlement—see if you can figure out what's going on here."

He was right, damn him. Irene took a breath. "Sardakowski and their veterinarian, Nola, showed up just after sunset . . ."

It didn't take long, but having to organize her thoughts calmed her; her heart still scurried in frantic little circles, but her mind was functioning.

Willard nodded approval. "All right. Assuming they did take him—" Irene opened her mouth to protest and he lifted his hand and went on. "—and I admit that's what it looks like, the first question we have to ask ourselves is, why?"

"I don't care why," Irene snarled. "I just want to know where, and when I find out I'll make them—"

"My dear, I doubt you'll find out where unless you

figure out why. The most likely possibility is that they took him somewhere to attempt to help him."

That had been Irene's first thought. "Oh, yeah? Then why kidnap him? Why not tell us, the moment they set eyes on him in that fucking chair 'hey, we might be able to help'? Why didn't they at least take *me* with them?"

Willard had frowned at her language, and the crease between his brows deepened in thought. He didn't say anything. Irene hadn't been able to come up with an answer either.

Myrna hurried up to them. "He's not in any of the buildings, and there's no trace of the colonists. The things they were working on last night have either been taken, or put into storage, so it looks like they're not planning to come back anytime soon. But I can't believe they'd hurt him. They seemed so . . . so nice."

Irene, too, had a hard time fitting Gus and Nola into her wilder imaginings of human sacrifice and gang rape. And you don't take someone who's dying for a slave: the Vrell had made that point—only the young, healthy, and fertile. But . . .

"I don't give a damn why they took him. I have to find him as soon as possible. And they've got a full night's start. I'll—"

"Not quite a full night," Myrna cut in. "I was in the last group up the hill, and that was about half past one, ship's time."

"Not quite a whole night's start then," Willard repeated thoughtfully. "And their only form of transportation seems to be those . . . those animals, so they can't have gone too far. The flitters should catch them easily."

"Really? The flitters didn't find them before. You were talking about using their weather satellite to find them. Could you do that now? Pictures from orbit—"

"Would do us no good. Oh, if we knew where they were, we could photograph them easily, but to gain a high enough resolution to pick them up, the lens would have to cover so much territory that it would be slower than the flitters. If they used some powerful light source at night, we might be able to spot it, but their tech base seemed rather low even for that—Sardakowski talked about campfires, if you remember."

"OK, then I want to take a hoversled after them. And I want to leave as soon—"

"My dear, the sled's maximum lift is only about ten feet. You couldn't begin to cover as much ground as—"

"I'm not going to cover ground," said Irene through gritted teeth. If he called her "dear" one more time she would slug him. "I'm going to track them. All those camels left a trail a blind man—or a dome dweller—could follow. But I need to leave now, don't you get it? They—"

"But now we know they're here. I'll simply set a tighter search pattern, and we'll locate them within the day. Far sooner than you could by following their trail on the ground. Irene," said Willard gently, "I know this is hard, but I want you to think about the wisdom of dashing off into the wilds, exhausting yourself, for no purpose."

"What do you mean, no purpose? Mark is out—"

"Mark is dying. You have to face the fact that he may be dead by the time we find them. Is it really worth so much effort on your part—"

"Yes!" He was being rational, Irene told herself. Hell, he was probably right. But neither right nor reason had any force against the image of Mark, dying, without her. "Look, I know you mean well, but I have to find him. I have to be there. I just . . . have to."

Willard studied her face, and his own softened. "Very well, my dear. I'll send for the sled." He was humoring her. He thought the flitters would find them in a few hours. He was an idiot. Irene didn't care what he was, as long as he did what she wanted.

While they waited, Myrna forced Irene to stop pacing and eat two nutriwafers. They tasted like sugarcoated sawdust and left crumbs in the bottom of her helmet. Irene paid attention, though, when Willard showed her how to clip a new water pack into her suit without violating the integrity of either seal—this was something she usually did from outside the suit.

Then the sled, a shining, topless oval, roughly the size of an old-fashioned rowboat, rumbled into the clearing, driving a small cloud of dust and dead leaves from beneath its polished rim.

Astrid Evenson pulled back the thruster and smiled at Willard. "Here's the sled you asked for," she said redundantly. "I did the power and safety checks myself. I wanted to do whatever I could."

"Thank you," said Willard with absent courtesy.

Astrid's smile went brittle as he turned away. There was someone who'd be happy to see Irene vanish for several weeks.

The sled was a four-man craft—now the open passenger bay behind the driver held the big crate designed to carry multiple scientific field kits, securely strapped in for travel.

"What do I need that for? I know what Mark has."

"If you should locate the colonists, maybe there'll be something else you'll want to test," said Willard deliberately.

Irene shrugged. The portable microanalyzer was so weak in comparison to the stationary model it was hardly worth carrying, but arguing with Willard when he used that tone was a waste of time, and Irene felt as if every passing second was being drawn from her own blood.

She had checked out on the sled before the voyage began; unlike a flitter, it wasn't much harder to handle than the hoverbikes most people used inside the domes.

Irene tried to quell her impatience as Willard repeated the safety checks Astrid had just assured them she'd already done. Finally, there was nothing left for even Willard to say.

"You're sure about this?"

"Absolutely." Irene scrambled into the seat, maneuvered her battery pack into the depression in the seat back that was designed to accommodate it, and fastened the safety harness.

"Very well then, Dr. Olsen," Willard said formally. "We'll send out the flitters, too, and contact you when we find them. Should this take longer than I think it will, I want to hear from you"—he tapped the radio in the console with one gloved finger—"at 7:00 A.M. and 7:00 P.M. every day. Unlike your suit-com, this has enough power to reach the *Stanley* from anywhere in this hemisphere. If you sight the colonists before we do, the *first* thing you will do"—his finger moved to the sat-comp—"is establish your coordinates and report to us. Is that *absolutely* clear?"

"Yes, of course," said Irene. She wasn't a complete fool. Though you couldn't prove it by last night.

"All right. One more thing. We've seen no real evidence that these people have anything we want, and we have three other colonies to locate. If we should fail to find them, eventually we'll have to leave."

But what about the epidemic they survived, and how they survived it, and what they're hiding, and— "What about Mark?"

"I'll give you three weeks. If we haven't found them by then . . . But don't let it worry you. I have no doubt that the flitters will pick them up shortly. And I'll send a flitter to get you the moment we do. I promise."

His sorrowful smile told her that finding Mark still wouldn't save him. But she knew that already.

"Good-bye, Willard. Thanks."

"Good luck, my dear." He stepped reluctantly off the running board, and Irene shoved the thruster stick forward and slipped away before he could think of something else to lecture about.

The camels' feet had mulched a path about five feet across through the leafy vegetation of the forest floor. It took careful flying, for the hoversled was about five feet wide; Irene often had to lift it up and over some mass of brush the camels had gone around. But the sled's open top, which made decontamination so simple, gave Irene a wide-open field of vision. Once she dropped off the wooded plateau she made pretty good time down the slopes, as the trees thinned and brush gave way to grassland.

The trail wasn't as obvious on the springy grass. Despite the clear flying, Irene had to slow to a crawl to keep from overrunning the trail. They wandered southwest through the grassy hills, slowly losing elevation; the winding trail didn't look like that of people who feared pursuit. Maybe they hadn't realized anyone would think to track them. Or maybe, she thought, pulling the thruster even farther back as her eyes sought the subtly bent grasses, they thought no one would have the patience to follow them at a whole, whopping four klicks per hour. They were probably moving faster than this on the camels!

No, Irene realized with grim satisfaction, they weren't moving at all right now. They were curled up sound asleep in whatever-the-hell they slept in. In the sled she could travel day and night and would surely catch them soon. And if they'd hurt Mark, in any way, she would shred them to bloody rags.

Within a few hours, she began to see why they'd become nocturnal. Her suit's internal cooling system was working overtime, and she was still sweating enough to soak the suit liner under her arms and breasts. She was going through her water faster than usual, too, but becoming dehydrated would be a bad idea. She needed to be in good shape when she found Mark.

It was midafternoon by the time the grass grew sparser and then gave way to the desert. The soft, tawny dunes hadn't looked so big from above. Their graceful curves towered over Irene and her sled. Sunlight struck them like a hammer, and heat rang back. It made Irene sweat just to look at them. But the wide, round dents left by camels' feet tracked over the dune's lower end, like print over a blank screen. Irene's mouth stretched in a predatory grin; she increased her speed to twenty klicks, shot over the top . . . and promptly lost the trail and had to backtrack.

She found it without difficulty, curving abruptly to follow the dune's crest. Turning the sled, she noticed that the hoverthrusters had erased the tracks they passed over, cleanly as a delete key.

She also saw, flying slowly and carefully, that the breeze that barely stirred the long grass was blowing the sand. Not much, just a few grains with the stronger puffs, beating down the ridges and filling the hollows the camels' feet made. Jaw tight with concentration, she found she could maintain about 10 kph and not waste too much time backtracking when the trail turned unexpectedly. A hard wind would destroy those fragile tracks entirely, but there was nothing she could do about that.

It would take a lot of wind to cover the dark splotches of camel dung, but they were too rare to form a trail without the accompanying tracks.

At 7:00 P.M. her watch chirped a reminder—thank goodness she'd set the alarm. She pulled the thruster back to full stop. "Olsen to *Stanley*, anybody there?" Willard had despaired of teaching them proper radio procedures. The moment she stopped her head started to throb. The sun was low on the horizon, throwing the tracks into sharp relief. Irene wasn't sure, but she thought they seemed deeper now than they had earlier in the day, which meant she was catching up with the creatures who made them, right?

"*Stanley* here. How you doing, honey?"

Irene smiled as Kibibe's warm voice conjured up a picture of her concerned, dark face. "I'm OK. I think I'm gaining on the bastards. I don't suppose the flitters . . ."

Kibibe snorted. "They couldn't find their own posteriors, high-and-mighty as they are. They're just too fast to do a visual search. They're trying to recalibrate the radar, but . . ."

Irene sighed, wishing she could rub her burning eyes. "Then I'd better get moving. I'll call again at seven if I haven't caught up with them before that."

"You be sure to do that, honey, or we'll come looking for you. And try to take it easy—you sound dead-tired."

"Yeah. Thanks, Kib. Bye."

"Bye, Goodnight. I'm praying for you."

Just before dusk the wind picked up; Irene spent half an hour in a state of barely contained panic as the trail sifted away before her eyes. But the breeze died again shortly after sunset, and the tracks, the small precious thread that linked her to Mark, were still there. Had his convulsions worsened? Were they taking care of him? Were— For the thousandth time Irene clamped down on futile speculations. *Find him first. The questions will answer themselves.*

Two moons cast eerie, silver light over the dunes' alien curves. Once she found their camp, even if they'd gone, the tracks would be fresh, and she'd be able to go fast—

The sled climbed a small dune, and Irene found herself overlooking a flat plain of rocky, level sand. The trail vanished.

Irene pulled the sled to a stop. Her eyes stung. No! No. She took a deep breath. They couldn't cross this without leaving some trace. Dung, if nothing else. Don't panic yet.

She clambered out of the sled, ignoring her stiff back and wobbly legs. She should probably eat something. Later.

The soft sand dissolved under her boots, and she skidded down the dune to the firm ground at the bottom. Nothing. Nothing at . . . Wait! That was a print, in that softer patch there. And that stone had surely been kicked out of the hole beside it recently.

She followed the unobtrusive signs for a dozen yards, figuring out what she had to do, then she ran back to the sled. It was harder climbing up the shallow slope than coming down, for the sand slithered beneath her like grease. No wonder the colonists thought domesticating camels was worth the trouble, if this was what they traveled over.

The Mylar emergency blanket was folded neatly into the side pocket of the first-aid kit, right where it should be. Irene shook it out; the moonlight reflected off its surface so brightly she followed the tracks till the sled was almost out of sight, then pinned it with one of the bigger stones and ran back to bring the sled up to it.

She'd traveled over the rocky plain for five kilometers according to the sled's odometer. Irene would have sworn it was fifty. She knew she was losing time, but there was no way she could follow the small signs except on foot. Fastening up the sled's safety harness was an incredible nuisance, and it wasn't as if she was going fast enough for it to matter. She should eat something. Soon.

The source of the long plain seemed to be a series of crumbling, rocky ridges, toward which the trail drew ever nearer. It both cut the prevailing, west wind, and provided the chunks of stone that littered the ground. At least the colonists hadn't gone into the ridges. They were so ragged that taking the sled over them would be a monstrous chore.

Irene climbed wearily into the pilot's seat and engaged the thruster, her eyes fixed on the glittering heap in the distance.

Four hard blows struck her back and shoulders, shoving her forward, and something clamped down on the back of her neck. Her helmet crashed into the console. The engine's roar spiraled up. She was leaning on the thrust stick, but she couldn't rise. She tried, twisting sideways, and the clamp gripping her neck shook her, hard, rattling her head inside the helmet. She caught a brief glimpse of a huge, fur-covered paw. Something—

Impact smashed Irene forward and sideways; her shoulder struck the corner of the cockpit. The sled spun in a flashing circle—the second impact was from behind, and it threw her, skidding, over the back of the sled and pitched her to the ground.

Something big and muscular rolled with her, under her, then heaved her over and lit on her back. The grip on her neck was still there.

It was trying to bite through her spine, but the conduit piping was too strong for it. Irene squirmed, and it shook her again. Hard. Disorienting. But not enough to snap the spine and kill. *Yeah, you prick, try to bite through steel-reinforced plasticine tubing!*

But it wasn't shaking her now. Maybe if she lay still . . . played dead . . .

She could see nothing but a small stretch of sand and a few stones—most of her faceplate was pressed into the ground. Was that viselike grip loosening, just a—

The grip vanished, but before Irene could react she was flipped onto her back like a pancake. A snarling, furred face. Big, pointed teeth. Cat—

It lunged for her neck, its teeth scraping on the

helmet's neck cuff, and drew back, yowling with frustration.

Irene shouted and swung her fist—a mistake, for its jaws clamped down on her upper arm, hurting, pinning her again, and its four rear feet began pounding her ribs and abdomen like pistons.

It's clawing my belly out, oh God, oh God— But the pounding went on, and she didn't die.

Its claws can't tear through the suit! It couldn't get at her! Like a turtle, like a tank, she was safe.

Unless it beat her to death. She had to do something. Her left hand, the free one, scrabbled over the ground beside her and closed over a rock. She hit its nose with all her might and heard the yielding crack of bone.

The cat sprang away with a tearing scream. Irene threw the rock at it, groped for another, then remembered her pistol.

Her belt had twisted—the holster was behind her, digging into her side. She rose to her knees and yanked it around, fumbling with the cover. Her hands shook wildly as she raised it and pressed the trigger.

The shot cracked the stillness, echoing off the ridge. Its recoil kicked her hands up, and when she brought them down again the cat was racing into the rocks, a six-legged streak of rippling fur. She squeezed the trigger again before it vanished, but the rail-shot burst on the rocks above it and to the right. It was gone.

Irene lowered the gun. Her whole body shook, and her view of the moonlit rocks began to narrow around a bright center, smaller and smaller. *Perhaps I should lie down.*

She really didn't have a lot of choice—her buckling knees deposited her on the stony ground, and she rolled onto her back, wishing she could elevate her feet. She kept a tight grip on the pistol.

Soon her vision widened again, and the dizziness passed.

Her throat felt raw, and she remembered screaming "fuck you" at the top of her lungs through much of the fight, though she wasn't sure when she'd started. Or stopped.

The whole thing probably hadn't taken two minutes. Her belly and abdomen were tender, and her upper arm throbbed fiercely, but she was alive. Amazing. If she ever managed to marry, and somehow acquire kids, this would be a story to tell her grandchildren.

Irene sat up slowly, wincing as her right arm took her weight. It must be badly bruised—

Something warm ran down her arm, inside her suit sleeve. The liner was wet and warm. Looking down, stomach already shrinking in anticipation, Irene saw that though its claws hadn't been able to penetrate her suit, its teeth had been stronger.

She clapped her hand over the punctures, foolishly, uselessly, for her suit, and probably her bloodstream, were already contaminated. An overwhelming awareness of being unclean shuddered over her skin. But there was nothing she could do about it. And perhaps she'd gotten lucky.

The half dozen blood-smeared holes weren't an insurmountable problem. She had patch seals in the sled. Treating the wounds inside the suit—well, she could but try. At least there was no arterial bleeding, or she'd be pumped dry already. Cat food.

Irene wobbled to her feet and over to the sled. It was canted up against the rocks of the cliff, a ragged, crumpled gash in its front quarter, and the whole rear buckled in. Engine off, thank God. If it had been thrusting at that angle, it would have overturned, and it took a winch to right the things.

The first-aid kit had been knocked from its clamps, and under the seat—it took a while to find it. Inside she selected a tube claiming to be both antiseptic and coagulant. Or would it be better to let the wounds bleed clean? Irene vaguely remembered that animal bites were prone to infection, but it had been a long time since humans had encountered biting animals. What the hell—that was what the antiseptic was for. She unscrewed the tube and squeezed the whole contents into her sleeve through the various holes, trying not to get any on the outside, for it was greasy. Then she slapped on patch seals, hoping that sealing her suit would convince her subconscious that she didn't actually need to crawl out of her skin. She worked the stuff around, trying to manipulate it into the sore spots without aggravating them further. At least the coagulant seemed to work, for the blood stopped trickling down her arm. That was all she could do for herself—there.

Irene pulled a couple of nutriwafers from the jumble in the storage compartment; one of the water cartons had burst, but everything else was sealed, so it hardly mattered. Then she sat down to eat and think. She hadn't been doing enough thinking lately.

Call for help? It wouldn't take them long to get here, but if he learned she was injured, Willard would never let her go on with her search. She wouldn't even be allowed off the ship till she'd been through weeks of quarantine. By the time she was free to follow, the tracks would be long gone. Irene didn't trust anyone else to follow the trail, faint as it was over this stony stuff. She could barely do it, and she'd been practicing all day. Any contaminants in her system were there already—and should take some time to affect her. She wasn't hurt badly. Apply just enough thrust to shift the sled off the rocks, then pull it down. If she found fresher tracks, she could probably travel fast enough to catch them by 7:00 A.M., which was—she checked her watch—a whole four hours away. Well, maybe not by seven. But the first task was to right the sled.

After a few moments' consideration, Irene decided that getting up on the rocks and pushing the sled away from her was a much better idea than standing on the

ground and pulling it toward her. The spine of rock
it had skidded up against was only about six feet high,
though the ridge rose steeply behind it. There was
even some vegetation on those higher reaches, low,
leafy things that looked drab in the moonlight. But
nothing grew amid the rocks she scrambled onto, fortunately perhaps, for her knees still trembled with the
adrenal aftermath, and her boot soles weren't designed for mountaineering.

When she reached the point above the cockpit, the
sled's side was several feet below her, and the ignition
button several feet below that. Irene laid both her
hands on the sled rim and shoved—solid as the rock
she knelt on. Moving carefully, she slid down onto
the battered plasticine. Ignition should produce just
enough thrust to lift the sled an inch or so—with any
luck, it would slip off the rock and dump her gently,
or even not so gently, beside it. If it started to go
over, she would jump. She reached for the button and
pressed it carefully. Nothing. She pressed harder. No
click, no gentle rumble, not even a light on the dark
control panel.

Irene scrambled into the tilting cockpit, her feet on
the side panel, and punched the button. She tried the
radio, even though the lightless indicator told her it
would be useless. She turned on her suit-com and tried
that—just in case one of the flitters was within range.
They weren't. She climbed out of the sled and opened
the back hatch, gazing at the convoluted mass of con-
duits, belts, and unknown things that made the thrusters thrust. She closed the hatch, kicked the sled
several times, and told it that it was a worthless piece
of shit, which at least made her feel better.

Then she sat down to think some more. The sensible
thing to do was to stay with the sled. She was in no
danger, unless the cat wanted a rematch. As soon as
she missed her 7:00 A.M. call the flitters would come
looking for her, and the sled had enough metal in it

to light up their radar like a beacon. She'd be back on the ship and in quarantine by breakfast time.

Her eyes went to the gleaming clump of Mylar that marked the trail. She'd come so far. Surely their camp couldn't be too much farther. Maybe if she found it, if she could show her rescuers clear, fresh tracks . . . She had almost three hours till check-in, probably four before they reached the sled. And it wasn't like she had anything better to do.

Irene set off across the stony plain. Only half an hour later the tracks led her into a gap in the ridge and she found the remains of their campsite. To someone who'd been tracking for almost twenty-four hours, the thick jumble of human and camel prints was clear as a neon sign. She even found several wide ovals of evenly spaced holes—tent pegs? And the tracks leading off into the dunes were sharp and clear—as if they'd been made just hours before. About nine hours, assuming they left the camp an hour or so after sunset. If she walked through the day, she should be able to catch up with them in their next camp. And if the bloody bastards had Mark with them, and he was still alive . . . She should stay with the sled. Sensible.

Irene's gloved hands clenched, the right one sticky with drying blood. The need to wash it hovered constantly in the back of her thoughts, like an itch she couldn't reach. She would kill for a shower.

She would kill or die, to find Mark in time.

Walking briskly back to the sled, she thought about what she'd need. Water, first and foremost. A fresh gallon in her suit pack, and another, carried—weight enough, even without the nutriwafers, and the spare pistol ammo. The Mylar blanket, on the other hand, weighed almost nothing. Standing on top of a tall dune, waving that in full sunlight, she should be easily visible from the top of the ridge between the landing field and the settlement. No, she'd have no trouble letting them know where she was, when she wanted to be found. When Mark . . . When Mark no longer needed her. If finding him now was all she could do for him, then she'd do it.

The sled still leaned against the rock where she had left it. Irene was reaching for the storage hatch when the scratch of claws against plastic sent her leaping back, snatching out her pistol. If that cat was back, she'd blow it to bloody rags, too!

But the cat was nowhere in sight—and it wasn't exactly small enough to hide under the seat. Behind the sled?

Pulse surging, pistol ready, Irene crept around the sled and peered into the shadows beneath it. Nothing. The scratching began again—in the sled! How was that—

A small, six-legged ball of fur scurried from the sled into a crack in the rock, and Irene began to laugh, leaning on the rock till her legs stopped feeling so wobbly. Again. She had to get control of her nerves, or the adrenaline ride would wear her out before she started walking. But it made a lot of noise for such a tiny creature. Another scratching sounded, but Irene declined to panic this time. They could have the sled, for all she cared.

A tool bag, its contents dumped clattering to the ground, made an excellent carryall, and she slung it over her shoulder. Why did water have to be so heavy? It only took a moment to drink her fill and clip a new flask into her suit. Devising a way to leave a message for the search party was harder, but she finally found a grease crayon among the tools she'd discarded and wrote her note on the sled itself—the first place they'd be sure to look. When she was ready, she'd signal from a high point at every even-numbered, daylight hour, and try her suit-com every fifteen minutes, so as soon as the flitters drew near, they could home in on her signal. *Robinson Crusoe's got nothing on you, Goodnight.*

The exhilaration of action, of clear tracks to follow, buoyed her spirits, though she sobered when she passed through the campsite. Where had Mark slept? Or was he now beyond both sleep and waking? Her throat ached. *Just keep walking.*

She had no hope of catching them during the night, she thought, trudging onto the dunes, her tracks mingling with the camels'. But soon, not sheltered in enviro-suits, they'd stop for the day. Make camp, have a meal, and sleep for a long, long time. And while they slept, Irene would travel, and catch them. And find Mark in time to hold his hand, and be with him. And say good-bye.

Lord, this stuff was hard to walk in.

As a child Irene had played on beaches, running up and down sand dunes. As the hours till dawn passed, and the weariness in her calves became an ache, and the ache crept up her thighs, she realized that she'd been smaller and lighter then. Or maybe the alien sand was softer. Or the hordes of alien microbes that were probably taking over her body were consuming her muscles, or her lungs, or— *Stop it. There's nothing you can do about that now.*

The sun rose over the tree-blackened mesa to the east, and shadows, real, sun-produced shadows, flowed from the dunes' sculpted crests.

Irene's watch chimed at 7:00 A.M.; she smiled grimly and silenced it. Willard would be furious with her.

Tough. Mark was out there.

The walking didn't get any easier. Despite her resolve to travel steadily, Irene had to stop and rest several times.

The shadows shrank and vanished—the dunes looked strangely flat without them. And flat they weren't! Even taking the "easy" route over the ridge tops, Irene felt as if she did nothing but climb, and the short downslopes brought little relief.

Around noon she stopped to eat a nutriwafer. Trying to rub some of the kinks out of her leg muscles, she heard a flitter whine past, but when she looked up she didn't see it. Turn on her suit-com? If she could hear its motor, she was probably within range.

No. Irene gazed contentedly at the road of lumpy tracks stretching before her. Then she rose, slinging the carryall over her shoulder again. She'd walk the rest of the day. If she hadn't caught up with them by nightfall, she'd have to give up, and signal for pickup the next morning. And Mark . . .

She left her suit-com off and started walking. But the shifting sand wore at her strength, if not her will, and her occasional rest stops became more frequent.

The sun was sliding toward the western horizon, highlighting the tracks, when the wind began to blow.

At first, Irene wasn't alarmed—it had gusted several times during the day, then died again. When the small grains started hissing over the surface, she just shrugged and concentrated on making it to the top of the dune, where she'd promised herself a rest.

But when she reached the top, the wind was still filing away her path, one sand grain at a time. Only now it was more like fifty grains at a time. Irene frowned. It had always stopped before after a few minutes. Surely it would stop soon.

But she decided to skip the rest—just in case.

Soon the tracks on the ridge tops had all but disappeared. Irene tried to run, but she couldn't—her exhausted legs dumped her to her knees after just a dozen yards and wobbled like an infant's when she forced herself to stand.

The tracks in the hollows were enough to guide her for a while—from one ridge she could see which slope they'd started up, and from the top of that ridge, she could see the next. But the demon wind that rippled the heavy fabric of her suit and sent her staggering when it gusted, slowly reached into the hollows, too, dissolving the tracks, dissolving her link with Mark. Watching them disappear was like watching him die.

She blinked the tears aside, but even so, she could see nothing in the hollows, nothing on the lower slopes of the dunes around her but smooth, blowing sand.

She went down the dune, sliding on the loose surface, and examined the ground, looking for a few ridges, an overturned pebble—she'd have killed for a lump of camel dung—but there was nothing. That was all she had left of him. *Mark.*

By the time she had finished crying and checked her watch, it was ten past six. But they might still be looking. Irene clambered up the dune, stopping several times to rest. When she reached the top and unfolded the Mylar blanket, the wind almost tore it from her grip. She tied a knot in one corner to hang on to and waved her arm slowly. The thin sheet streamed away from her, flashing brighter than a dozen mirrors.

If they were still looking, they'd see it. If they weren't, they'd see it tomorrow. Irene didn't care. Her legs were almost too tired to ache, but her arm, which had felt pretty good during the day, was getting sore. Infected? Even that fear barely pierced her dull grief.

As she hauled in the crackling Mylar and stuffed it into her bag, Irene looked around. About a klick to the west, a clump of dark rocks broke the sand. She frowned. It might be better to stay here. But even if they'd seen her signal, late as it was, it would only give them a general location. Once in the vicinity, they'd start looking around, and probably head for the nearest landmark, which was that rock pile. Another jutted out of the dunes a bit beyond the first—perhaps the remains of a ridge like the one she'd crashed the sled on.

If there was a cat there, it'd be in for a rude surprise if it tried anything. She was in no mood for crap. All she wanted was a chance to rest. And cry. Irene started down the dune toward the rocks.

It was night by the time she reached them, for she was no longer in a hurry. Night, but not dark. Four moons rode the sky, though two, sliver-thin, were going to set soon. The full ones, just risen, would probably last out the night.

Irene added eating to her list of things to do; a full day hiking in the open air had left her famished, though she was beginning to hate those wafers. Then she would sleep for about a year. Lord, her legs would be stiff in the morning. At least there was a high place to signal from right above her, which gave her an idea.

Food and rest supplied a bit of energy. Irene climbed to the top of the rocks—only about thirty feet. After a day on the mushy sand, their firmness beneath her boots felt as strange as it was wonderful.

When she reached the top, staggering from the force of the wind, her final qualm was laid to rest—there were several stubby bushes to tie the blanket to. Their thin, ropy, narrow-leafed stalks all pointed east toward the great plateau, even in the lull between gusts.

Irene tugged on one to be sure it was sturdy enough—it felt like she was pulling on the rock itself. Then she tied the corners of the Mylar sheet securely around its base, tightening the old-fashioned square knot to be certain it would hold.

Mark considered square knots just one step above what he called "girl knots." He had tried to teach her others, but she used them so seldom that she kept forgetting.

Irene's eyes filled. She was too tired—that was the trouble. She climbed back down, to the lee of the rocks, wiggled her hip into the sand, and fell asleep before she could even cry anymore.

When she woke, it was gray—neither dark nor light, but a shadowless in between. Beads of water dotted her faceplate. *Fog.* The predome memory surfaced slowly in her drowsy brain. She sat up, wincing, as her

head throbbed. Yep. Fog. The nearby rocks were mist-
ily visible, but the dunes swelled away and vanished.
The sand looked darker. Damp. Fog, in the desert?

It was there, sensible or not. And Willard and the
flitters weren't here; no one could see a signal through
that stuff. Irene looked at her watch, wincing again,
for her arm had stiffened. Just a bit past eight. Earth's
fog was usually a morning phenomenon. With any luck
this fog would burn off, too. And she'd better be up
on the rocks, waving the Mylar sheet, when it did.

Irene drank thirstily, as warm in her suit as if she'd
slept under too many blankets. In fact, she finished
the flask and had to pull the second from the carryall
and clip it into her suit. At least she wouldn't have to
haul it around anymore. The half dozen nutriwafers
didn't tempt her at all. She was tired, her mind full of
cobwebs from sleeping so late. When she scrambled
up the rocks, the exertion made her head throb again.
The Mylar blanket lay limply, droplets rolling like
mercury in its silver creases. Irene picked her knot
apart, shook the blanket briskly, and folded it, still
damp, into the carryall. Which was also damp.

But if this was a common weather pattern, it
wouldn't be a desert. Looking at the plants (she had
nothing better to do, after all), Irene saw that the
leaves of the low, drab ones were angled to send water
toward the center, and down to its roots. She could
even see the drops roll down if she watched long
enough. A drop every two minutes or so. Not a lot.
But the plants weren't big. Maybe they could be watered, drop by drop, one at a time, ever so slowly. . . .

When Irene woke again it was just before ten, the
fog was still there, and she realized she had a fever.

She could barely remember the last time she'd been
ill. The viruses people used to consider harmless still
appeared occasionally, but now, confined in the
domes, people took them a lot more seriously. Victims

found to be infected with a "harmless" virus were quarantined in their home, with whoever chose to stay and nurse them, until their blood tested completely clear, and for a full month afterward just to be sure. And breaking quarantine, in or out, was a second-degree felony.

By taking those kinds of preemptive measures, the general population wasn't often exposed to minor viral infections. The major ones either killed you or left you quarantined for months. An alien-animal-bite infection—Lord, she'd be quarantined for *years*.

Yes, it had been quite a while since Irene had had a fever. But the recurrent headache, weariness, and light-headed detachment were all typical symptoms.

Oh well, the fog would burn off eventually, and the flitters would come. Meanwhile, she was tired of lying on lumpy rock. There was no reason she couldn't wait for the fog to dissipate on some comfortable dune top.

Irene shouldered the carryall, climbed down, and set off in search of a dune. They were easy to find. She sat on the first one for some time, but then she got impatient with it, for the fog was still there, and there was nothing to do. She went to another, slowly, for she was tired now. Was Mark tired like this, or had Omega come for him?

When the Vrell mastership phased in above Earth, appearing out of nowhere it seemed, at first the authorities tried to keep it secret while they dithered. But since a strong pair of binoculars could pick it up on a clear night, secrecy lasted all of two days. Which was about the amount of time it took the Vrell to decide that the primitives they'd noted several thousand years ago were now technologically educated enough to harvest.

Shadowy, transparent shuttles landed beside hundreds of major cities, and stubby, transparent, tentacled things emerged and went into the streets. Then they snapped solid and real for just long enough to grab healthy humans, in their teens or early twenties, and go transparent again, taking the humans with them.

It was then that all Earth learned about personal phase fields firsthand, as bullets, clubs, bodies, and even cars passed through the phased Vrell and their captives as if they weren't there.

The Vrell needed to be sufficiently in phase to see the environment, in order to find victims and return to their ship, but there was no way to stop them. And the ships, and the slave compounds around them, were impervious to any weapon in humanity's arsenals. They didn't dare try nuclear weapons so close to their own cities, but they tried them on the mastership instead, and watched it phase to let the missiles through. And when they rigged them to detonate on the spot and the explosion cleared, the ship's shadowy outlines were untouched.

The military kept trying. Killed dozens of their own men in the chaos of all-out assaults, which the Vrell ignored. The Vrell never fired a weapon on the planet they invaded. Messages came from the slave compounds, written in pencil, lipstick, and grease, on anything flat that could be hurled or smuggled past the phase field, into the world free humans could touch. In that way, Earth learned the truth.

The Vrell were slavers, who'd preyed on hundreds, maybe thousands of species. They would take a sample of "appropriate subjects," train them properly, and then take the sample back to their fleet. If they proved good servants, the Vrell would come back for the rest.

Attempts not to be good servants were punished fiercely and consistently; the rest of humanity realized it hadn't much time.

Irene's father, along with other microbiologists, epidemiologists, doctors, and biowarfare specialists everywhere started working on weapons that could be smuggled inside the phase field in the one container the Vrell were taking in—human bodies.

Kids with AIDS and other terminal illnesses, still in an early stage, who looked healthy, were asked to volunteer—and in the hundreds, they did. They were the ones who acted as bait, who enabled the desperate scientists to catch a Vrell in those few vulnerable seconds of solidity when it snatched its victim.

Samples of its flesh, cartilage, for it had no bones, and organs (carefully separated from the remains of the boy who'd died with it) went to concealed labs all over the planet.

In the bunker where her father worked, Irene ran dirty petri dishes through the sterilizer, made sandwiches and coffee, even emptied the trash cans and swept the floors without protest. And listened to exhausted, frightened adults trying to breed a weapon that would affect this alien flesh and not humans.

They never realized, any of them, that once you pulled that sword from its stone, you couldn't sheathe it.

They'd listed her as a junior member of the team when they were given their medals, so Irene got one, too. She'd thrown it in the trash compactor on the night Mark was diagnosed. Genetically Engineered Demyelination. Out of multiple sclerosis, sired by desperation. They tried to make it affect only Vrell, and affect them it did, blending with their genetic codes, dormant for weeks, even months, then killing fiercely, horribly, within days.

But by the time the remaining Vrell fled, carrying death, gift-wrapped, to their home fleet, it had coiled itself around human DNA as well. It was designed to be adaptive, after all.

They saved Earth, after a fashion, but it was no longer the Earth they knew.

Most people still thought of those microbiologists as heroes. Irene tried not to blame her father, and the rest of them, too much. How many people, over the years, had assured her that it wasn't her fault? Dozens? Hundreds? *You don't have to be the one to solve* everything, *Goodnight*. Their voices echoed in her memory.

Humanity had been so naive back then, about biowarfare. Even the people who studied it only understood the dangers intellectually, not in their guts, their subconscious, where true belief lies. The Spanish Flu, in 1918, killed more Americans than both World Wars combined, but just over a century and a half later, when the Vrell invaded, it wasn't even listed in the encyclopedia. People had had no legends about the smallest, deadliest assassins.

They did now.

When Irene woke again it was half past four in the afternoon, and the sunlight seared her eyes so painfully that she crawled up the dune with her eyes shut and waved her crackling, Mylar flag without looking for as long as she could, which wasn't long.

She was roasting. She collapsed on the sand, barely remembering to wrap the Mylar around her hand so it wouldn't blow away. She tried to drink, but after the first few gulps, nausea stirred. Vomiting in her helmet would be appalling, and drinking didn't cool her much, anyway. She didn't know if it was fever, or the sun heating her suit, but this was intolerable. Her pulse beat painfully in her temples and the back of her neck. The cat bite throbbed. Where the hell was the suit's internal cooling system? She hoped the designers who'd made it so inadequate went to hell, too. They couldn't get any hotter there than she was. Irene giggled.

Delirious. You're delirious, Goodnight.

There wasn't much she could do about it. But maybe she could find some shade, and later, when it was cooler, she'd go find Mark. Good plan. Now she had to open her eyes.

One painful experiment told her that the sun was to her right. Cupping her hands over her faceplate to block the light, she looked to the left. The steep face of the dune was only a few feet away, and the sun was low enough that the bottom lay in shadow.

Down was good. Easy.

She started for the slope, and the Mylar blanket rustled, reminding her. Flinching at the flickers of reflected sunlight, Irene stuffed it into the carryall, closed the zipper, and pitched the whole thing over the edge. It hit the sand about a third of the way down and slid another third before it stopped.

It was a very steep slope, and seemed to get steeper the longer Irene looked at it. Wasn't it impossible for it to be steeper than forty-five degrees? It looked closer to thirty.

She crawled over the edge sideways, her hands and knees sinking deep in the loose surface. It wasn't as difficult as she feared—being half-buried anchored her to the dune face, and she had only to move a bit to slither down, with hardly any effort on her part.

Some of the sand slid with her. Lots of sand, cascading ripples racing past her, and the dune began to vibrate and rumble.

Avalanche!

Irene froze—the thought of being buried alive set her heart pounding. She slid to a stop. The sand that had been falling with her slithered down another twenty feet, and slowed to a stop. The grumbling tremor died.

It wouldn't bury her alive, Irene decided, after three or four repetitions of the same phenomenon. Once she reached that conclusion, she started to enjoy making the dune groan and quake; she was sorry when she reached the bottom. But not too sorry, for it was cooler out of the sun.

She drank as much as she could and scooped out a

hollow for her hip. Comfortable. When the sun set, when it was cool, she would go after Mark.

The sun had set by the time she awakened, but it wasn't cool. The soft cloth of her suit liner rasped against her skin. The air she dragged into her lungs was thick and stale, without enough oxygen in it. Which was ridiculous, for the batteries on the air filter were good for weeks and weeks. Well, maybe not *weeks* and weeks, but longer than this.

She giggled again, then stopped herself, irritated by the helmet's echo.

All she wanted was to lie there, but Mark was dying and he needed her. By the time she reached the top of the next dune, the heat in her suit was unbearable. She could hardly breathe, and the internal cooling system had broken down completely as far as she could tell. *Fuck it.*

Irene pulled off her gloves, flipped the helmet clasps, and lifted it off. Cool, fresh air sighed into her lungs and flowed over her face. She ran her hands through her hair, lifting it, letting the blessed breeze soothe her heated scalp. She opened the suit's front seal and air poured through her suit liner, over her chest and belly, seeping down her arms and legs. She wiggled out of the suit like a snake from a dead skin, using her feet to push her boots off, feeling the plumbing slither wetly free.

Then she lay there, bathed in open air. The sand under her hands and face was smooth and soft. She curled up and tugged off her socks, so she could wiggle her feet in it. She thought about stripping completely, and just lying there forever, but Mark needed her.

She crawled several feet before remembering the water and had to go back for it. When she pulled the flask free of its clamps, there wasn't much left, so she drank it down, then looked for her carryall. Which wasn't there. Oh, right. It was down at the bottom, where she'd slept out the day. Well, she wasn't going after it.

She felt so much lighter without the suit that she walked for a time, sand squishing between her toes. But she had to stop and rest, and then she was too tired to get to her feet again. Soon after that she was too tired to crawl, and she lay on the sand, watching silver moon shadows slide over the dunes. She would probably die quickly once the sun rose.

Sorry, love. I tried.

She didn't regret it, either. If she hadn't come after him, the thought of Mark dying alone would have haunted her for the rest of her life.

Maybe she'd see him when she was dead. It was a nice thought, though it had always seemed a little too simplistic. But dying didn't seem so bad, now, with the cool breeze washing over her.

A gust of warm air puffed over her neck, and she frowned. When the sun rose, it wouldn't be so pleasant. Perhaps—

Something soft, damp, and alive lipped the back of Irene's neck, and she found she wasn't resigned to dying after all.

Chapter 5

Spinning over, screaming, striking out with her fist (how *could* she have left her pistol behind?), she struck a mass of bone and hair.

The camel's head jerked up, and it snorted, blinking great brown eyes. Irene scrambled back a dozen feet before her strength gave out, and she lay there, panting.

A camel. Just a camel. At least they weren't carnivores . . . as far as she knew. Maybe they were. Maybe that was why the colonists had kidnapped Mark, for camel food.

"Go away," she told it loudly.

Whatever it ate, its language skills were clearly deficient, for it ambled toward her, its huge head lowering again, nostrils wide. It wanted to smell her, just like the ones in the settlement.

"You can't do that from there?" Her voice was a croak—fear, dehydration, disuse, or all of the above. But if all it wanted was to smell her . . . Even if it wanted to eat her, Irene had no way to stop it.

She lay still, and the great head moved up and down her body, breathing in and in, as if she were a bouquet of lilacs. Which at that point, she emphatically wasn't. Irene's lips twitched. If it killed her, it would probably be quicker than the sun. If it just wanted to smell her, it was welcome. She rolled onto her side and closed her eyes.

A big fleshy nose nudged her ribs.

"I told you to go away."

Another nudge, this time her shoulder. Irene glared at the beast and found it had shrunk, having folded its legs to lie on the sand. It was still enormous, and its small, curved horns looked formidable close up. Irene, who had been thinking about kicking it, thought better of it and crawled away. A few feet should do. She sighed and rolled on her side, away from it.

Now that she was listening for it, she could hear the soft rasp of its feet on the sand. Its next nudge, against her buttocks, was hard enough to shift her several inches.

Irene scowled up at it. "You stupid cow, I'm tired of this. Go—"

As soon as it had her attention, the camel lay down again. Middle legs, front and back, just like the ones in the settlement. Fine. Take a load off. Irene's eyelids drifted down.

This time it hooked its chin over her back and dragged her closer, lifting her off the sand. Irene's hands, outflung to catch herself, met coarse hair with flesh beneath.

She sat up, despite the sickening whirl of her inner ear. "Look, you, I've had enough—"

Its head swung around on its long neck, smacking her between the shoulder blades, shoving her into its side.

"Oof." Even the camels in the settlement hadn't been this . . .

A flash of memory, a camel folding its legs, middle, back, front for a rider to dismount. This wasn't a wild camel, it was trained. Tame. It wanted her to get on and ride it.

"No. No way."

So where was the rest of the herd? The colonists? Mark?

Irene looked around, half-expecting them to spring out of the moon-silvered sand, like what's-his-name's army from the serpent's teeth. They didn't.

The camel nudged her shoulder, gently, toward itself. "No way. I told you."

Maybe the others were just out of sight. Irene closed her eyes to listen. Wind whispered over the sand. The camel snorted. Her own breath. Her tired heart pounding in her ears. Nothing. No voices. No Mark.

Tears wet Irene's lashes. She started to slump back to the ground, but the camel's bony nose looped under her, and she fell against its side, jarring her aching head.

"Ow! I told you not to do that. I'm not going . . ." If she got on its back, the camel would go somewhere. It was trained. Domesticated. Maybe it would take her to its herd, where Mark was.

Soft lips nuzzled her cheek.

"OK, OK, no need to get mushy. You got me."

Leaning on its side, Irene came to her knees—the "saddle" between its humps was just above her head. This wasn't going to be easy.

Gripping a handful of its hair, hoping it wouldn't object, Irene hauled herself to her feet. She was panting by the time she made it. Now its humps were about level with the top of her head—the saddle chest high. Not exactly an easy mount. Hell. Go for it.

Irene bent her wobbly legs, leapt at the camel, smashed into its side, and slid down, keeping her feet by clutching its hair.

The camel's side heaved. *"Whouk, whouk, whouk,"* it snorted.

Irene looked at its head, alarmed, but it didn't turn to look at her. So why did she feel like she was being watched? She turned and looked over the dunes.

The camel snorted again. Its huge head looped around, and it shoved its nose into Irene's stomach and boosted her, squeaking, onto its back.

She landed awkwardly, with one leg twisted beneath her. The camel waited as she straightened herself out and acquired a grip on the firm, rubbery hump before her. Its back was narrower than her distant memories of pony rides might lead her to believe, and hard. Like sitting astride the vaulting horse in gym class. Not really comfortable, and going to get wor—

The camel tipped. Irene swore and clutched the hump in front of her as the camel's back slanted up and up, pitching her against hump at her rear. Then its back end heaved, almost flinging her into the sky, and it started forward, its gait as rough as a bike with oval tires, up down, up down.

She moaned, clung to its hump, and thought of Mark. And the fact that if she fell from this height she'd probably break her legs, if not her neck. These things were *big*.

She looked toward the camel's head, which rose far above hers, silhouetted against the moon-bright sky. On this world, you'd never see more than a handful of the brightest stars.

She could see the back curves of the beast's horns, its big ears pricked forward . . . and one eye, gazing out of the back of its head, barely visible in the shaggy fur. It blinked.

Irene blinked, but it didn't disappear. Delirious. Delusional. She was probably hallucinating the whole thing. Irene clutched the hump and closed her eyes.

She actually slept from time to time—she never knew how long, for when she woke it was always the same. She was riding a camel. The bizarre, oval-tire gait was fairly smooth, once she got used to it. That strange eye proved impossible to get used to, sending chills down her spine whenever she saw it. *You're riding an alien, Goodnight.* But there wasn't much she could do, except try to ignore it.

And dozing was easier than keeping her eyes open anyway.

She was vaguely aware that they were climbing, that the sand underfoot gave way to vegetation, but the

camel's gait remained stable, so it didn't seem important. Nothing was important but sleep.

So it took her a moment to rouse when the camel
tipped again, up and up, its rear sinking away.

Irene grabbed for its hump, but its heavy head swat-
ted her and she lost her seat—falling, free fall, splash!

If the cool air had felt like water on her fevered
skin, the water felt like ice, like liquid nitrogen, a sear-
ing cold.

Irene surfaced, sputtering, and shrieked. It wasn't
deep, thank God, for she was in no shape to swim.
Just sitting upright kept her head above the water.
Which was good, for she needed to breathe to yell.
"You stupid, fucking cow! You . . . you animal! You
piece of shit!"

"Whouk, whouk, whouk." The camel ambled out of
the pool. It wasn't a large pool, Irene discovered,
looking around—roughly bean-shaped, with one end
smaller than the other, its ripples leaping and skit-
tering off the grassy banks as that stupid cow of a
camel waded out.

Irene was thirsty. Even the thought of millions of
alien microbes thriving in the water couldn't stop her;
she drank and drank, till her stomach protested.

The cold made every muscle in her body ache; she
crawled to the muddy shallows before she collapsed,
her legs still in the water.

She had to go back into the pond to drink, and she
did so several times. Expecting it, the water wasn't as
shocking, and the coolness of her damp hair and suit
liner felt wonderful as she eased into sleep.

When she finally awakened, her headache was gone.
She sent awareness slowly through her body, like someone probing a sore tooth. Her fever was gone, too.

Something in the water. It had to be.

This was what the colonists were hiding. Something
in the water on this planet had cured their illness, just
as it had cured Irene's infection. And it had to be

something different—better?—than Earth's known antibiotics, or they wouldn't have tried to hide it. But why try to conceal it, even if it was better? Or different? No matter what it was, why hadn't they told the *Stanley*'s crew all about it? It was in the water, for Christ's sake—it wasn't like they could steal the only source!

And she didn't have even a thimble to carry a sample away with her! Irene swore aloud. If it could cure both viral and bacterial infections (assuming the cat bite was a bacterial infection), could it cure GED? She snorted, despite the leap of hope in her heart. GED, in humans, had become a genetic disorder. Miracles indeed. "You're dreaming, Goodnight."

Whatever happened to Mark, she had to get back and report. Moving slowly, for her head felt like it was about to float off her shoulders, Irene sat up and looked around.

It was day, about midday, judging by the bits of sunlight angling through the leaves. The jungle? No, just the edge of it—the trees were small, low, and only dense around the banks.

The pool itself was small enough that branches overarched all but the center. The water, where the sun slanted into it, had a blue-green tinge. All the microbes in the world probably lived there. Irene wiped her hands on her thighs, as years of paranoid—and not so paranoid—conditioning washed over her. But this pool *healed*, she reminded herself; she should be grateful. Besides, she was thirsty, and it was the only source of water.

The bark of the nearest tree was rough under her hands as she pulled herself up on shaky legs. *And what might live in tree bark?* She waded into the pool—midthigh at its deepest. Away from the trees, the sun was hot on her hair and back. Curiosity overcame her fear of contamination, and she cupped some of the water in her palms, peering as closely as she could, but it looked clear to the naked eye, only showing that odd color where the sun sliced through it. The surface was warm. The bottom, where Irene's feet stirred up puffs of mud, was cold. Things lived in the mud, too. Irene had never felt so exposed, not even the first time, cheeks hot with embarrassment, that she'd stripped off her clothes to make love. Who'd have thought she could miss that wretched enviro-suit?

She summoned her nerve and rolled up her sleeve to examine her arm—a deep, ragged-looking puncture and a smaller one beside it. The cat's lower incisors hadn't penetrated, though her underarm was bruised. The flesh around the wounds was red and sore, but not throbbing like it had been. She was healing.

Irene rolled her sleeve down—she had nothing clean to make a bandage with—and waded up to the tiny stream that supplied the pool. She had to drink somewhere. It tasted cold, and very fresh.

She waded out of the water and into the bushes, careful of her bare feet, and found a clear place to squat. It had been over twenty years since her back-packing days, since she'd pissed anywhere except in a toilet. Her subconscious protested, but her bladder won out. At least the Velcro-sealed seam that had admitted the suit's plumbing eliminated the need to drop her pants completely; Irene felt vulnerable enough as it was.

She washed her hands in the stream that flowed out of the pool, then followed it down, away from the woods.

Surely the camel, having brought her here, hadn't abandoned her? It was trained, right?

Though it might be operating on some sort of instinct. She'd read that dolphins, finding drowning swimmers, sometimes carried them to the surface, even to shore. Maybe camels, finding someone dying in the desert, carried them to water. Did humans smell like the camels—at least to them?—like their calves, perhaps? It could account for a lot.

If it had gone, she would follow the edge of the woodlands north till she struck the settlement. With water, she could make it. *You can go a long time without food*, Irene told her complaining stomach firmly.

She passed out of the trees, and the scrubby hills rolled away before her, down and down to the distant sand. Five klicks distant? Ten? It was hard to judge when you'd lived the last twenty years in a dome.

A soft, snuffling sound made her jump, spinning toward a nearby thicket. Brown eyes blinked at her from a nest of tangled hair.

"Well, hello. I thought you'd run out on me."

The camel sniffed deeply, lying with its legs folded, as if expecting someone to mount. Did it sleep in that position? Evidently, for it closed its eyes, breath sighing in and out.

"Lazy cow," Irene muttered. If the camel offered her a ride, should she take it?

Probably not. She should probably hike straight back to the ship and report to Willard. Lord, she'd be in quarantine for years. It would be worth it, if the pond's curative properties worked on other things besides infection. The settlement couldn't be too far, for she hadn't gone more than a day's hike in the sled— and how far could a camel travel in one night?

She should have stayed with the sled in the first place. Irene sighed. No. No regrets. She'd had to try.

Even if Mark was dead, she needed to talk to the colonists. She'd probably have to forgive them for taking him—they'd no doubt hoped their miracle water might help. Would this camel take her to its herd? *Take me to your leader.* She could all but hear Mark's laughing voice saying the words. If it was trained, shouldn't she be able to make it go anywhere she wanted? Irene tried to remember how the riders in the settlement steered their mounts. She didn't remember any kind of bridle. How far away would the colonists be by now?

Irene gazed over the desert, hoping against hope to spot something—though their tents evidently blended in so well the flitter pilots couldn't find them. She saw no sign of an encampment, but a bit to the north, a ragged, darkish line cut across the dunes. The rocks where she'd crashed the sled? Irene picked her way slowly onto the shoulder of one of the ridges that bracketed the stream. Which, she noticed, didn't go far before it flowed into the grassy hills, shrank, and vanished. From the top she stared as hard as she could. It looked like a ridge of rock. The sun made her blink; her eyes watered. She was getting hot again.

Irene decided to follow her camel's example and find a patch of shade. Soon after, she followed it into sleep.

When she woke, stiff from the tree roots poking into her side, the sun was lower and the dunes cast shadows. Definitely a rock ridge.

Of course, there might be more than one. She'd been making a lot of assumptions lately. But assuming this was the one, and assuming she could convince that cow of a camel to take her there, she could find the sled. The sled, which held nutriwafers (her stomach grumbled), *clean* water, and, above all, a portable microanalyzer. More than anything else (except, by some miracle, to find Mark alive) Irene wanted a good look at her own blood. But to reach the sled—Irene had vivid memories of walking on that shifting sand—she needed a camel.

It was still sleeping in the shade where she'd left it, and Irene's tense shoulders relaxed.

"Good cow." Though it might be a bull, for all she knew.

The camel, which she'd approached from behind, opened two eyes, one on the side of its head and one in the back, and blinked at her. Irene suppressed a shudder.

She stayed in its vicinity as the day wore itself out, using the time to look for something—anything—to carry a sample of that water. There was nothing. At dusk the camel rose and began to graze, and Irene was content to let it, for it must be hungry. And she had no way to stop it if she had objected. Her own stomach had flattened itself, begging, against her spine. _You can go for days without food_, she reminded it. Her stomach wasn't convinced.

Finally, the camel walked upstream to the pool and waded in, drinking deep.

Irene decided she should do the same, and skirted the pool to drink out of the incoming stream; though her mind was convinced she had no choice, her subconscious still had reservations about this water. Even ignoring her qualms, she couldn't begin to drink like the camel, who she watched with widening eyes as it sucked and sucked till its stomach was visibly distended under the shaggy fur.

Finally, it lifted its dripping muzzle, heaved a sigh, and defecated into the pool. Then it pissed.

"Ugh! Yuck!" And she'd _drunk_ that water. Irene's stomach heaved. She wanted to wash, not only her hands, but her whole body, inside and out. At least now she knew the camel was female.

Standing in the water it had just dirtied, the camel inflated its lungs and lifted its nose to the sky. "_Nah-woooooooon._"

Irene clapped her hands over her ears. The two notes, one low, one higher, reminded her of the conch shell a guest anthropology speaker had blown for a class of fascinated fourth-graders. But this sound was deeper, more resonant, vibrating the camel's body till its breath ran out.

"_Nah-wooooooooon_," it trumpeted again, louder this

time. A dead branch crashed down beside Irene and she jumped.

"What the . . . ?"

The camel turned, splashed over to Irene, and knelt on the bank for her to mount. They could train it to do this, but they couldn't housebreak it? Wait. Could the camel's fecal matter have something to do with the curative properties of the pool? It could.

"Yeah, but so could half the damned environment," Irene muttered. Half the jungle probably crapped in that pool. She *had* to get back to her analyzer.

"The next order of business, Cow, is steering."

For all her determination, a shudder shook Irene as she touched its no-doubt-filthy fur. But she'd ridden it before. She was already as contaminated as she was likely to get. She managed to mount without help this time. The sloping ridge of the camel's middle hip was too high to step up on, but hooking her bent knee onto it, she was able to lift herself up to the hollow between its humps—if not gracefully, at least without making a total fool of herself.

This time she was expecting the backward/forward sway of the camel's rising. As Cow walked downstream, Irene looked at her shoulders; she moved her feet in two sets of tripods. No wonder she never stumbled: she had three feet on the ground at all times.

When Cow emerged from the trees, Irene looked over the desert. Three moons, full, half, and a sliver pointing to the newly set sun chased each other across the sky. If she hadn't known where it was, she wouldn't have been able to see the jagged, dark ridge.

"There." She pointed at it, all too aware of the bizarre third eye, watching her. "That's where we're going. Go there, Cow. Go there."

It, no *she*, didn't understand of course, but she was heading down toward the desert, which was the right general direction, and her long, sure strides ate ground as if she was as hungry for distance as Irene was for food. *Not too long, at this rate*, she told her stomach. It looked like a camel could go quite a way in one night.

As they descended the grassy hills to the sand, Irene took a final fix on the rock ridge. "OK Cow, veer right. That way."

But Cow had other ideas. She set off straight into the dunes—or as straight as you could go, keeping to the easier walking of the ridges.

Verbal commands and pointing weren't going to work. On to step two—physical signals.

Irene started by pressing on the left side of Cow's hump. When that got no response she thumped on it, with increasing firmness for several minutes, before giving up. A hump was not a steering wheel, it seemed.

"You need a bridle," she told the half-hidden eye. It blinked at her. Her skin crawled. Hadn't she read that skilled horsemen could guide their mounts by pressing with their legs?

She tried pressing. She tried kicking against first one side, then the other. She tried thumping and kicking. She tried thumping, kicking, and swearing.

If this stupid cow didn't turn soon, they'd have to loop back to find the rocks. Maybe if she could push its head in the right direction. That was how a bridle worked, wasn't it? Pulling the horse's head in the direction the rider wanted to go? But she couldn't reach its head. How about pushing its neck?

Irene looked down; she'd become accustomed to the height of the camel's back. Its gait was steady, and if she fell, the sand would make for a soft landing.

Go for it, Goodnight.

Pressing her legs against the sliding muscles and gripping handfuls of hair, Irene scrambled over the hump in front of her and slithered down onto Cow's front shoulders, perched like an old-fashioned jockey. The ride was rougher there, without the security of humps before and behind. She eased down to sit in the curve of Cow's neck and leaned forward to push.

Cow stopped abruptly, planting all six feet, and lowered her head. Irene tumbled facefirst into the sand.
At least it was soft.

"You stupid cow!" She rose to her feet, hands on
hips, glaring. "We're going *that* way." She pointed.
"That way."

"Whouk, whouk, whouk." Cow's moist, grass-
scented breath puffed in Irene's face. She flinched at
the thought of the germs, then sighed.

"All right, I'm sorry. I won't ride there again. But
I need to go that way." She pointed to the rocky ridge,
just visible from the dune slope where they'd stopped.

"You don't understand me, do you?"

Cow came half a step closer and smelled her hair.
Irene signed again. "Not your fault. I guess I'll have
to go it on my own."

She set out toward the rocks, Cow ambling at her
heels, and walked steadily for almost two hundred feet
before she collapsed, panting. "I don't think I'm . . .
ready for this."

"Whoof." Cow's sides heaved with the depth of her
sigh; she knelt beside Irene, ready for mounting.

Irene remained on the sand, for her leg muscles still
quivered like Jell-o. *Get real, Goodnight.* She couldn't
go anywhere on her own, weak as she was. And to be
caught on the sand during the day, without water or
shelter, would be fatal, even without a fever.

"OK, you win." She hauled herself up Cow's tall
flank and climbed aboard. "Take me to your leader."

The camel set off with Irene nestled between the
comforting humps; Cow's rolling gait felt quite secure.
It took several minutes, tracking over the dunes, for
Irene to realize that she'd changed course. She was
making for the rock ridge.

"Son of a bitch," she murmured. Cow's third eye
blinked at her. "Nothing personal." So what had
worked? How had she made it understand the direction she needed to go? By walking that way herself?

"Must have been." No doubt the colonists had a better way of steering that Cow and the others had been trained to respond to, but Irene just didn't know it. At least they were finally heading the right way.

Irene's watch had gone with her suit, but a full moon, which had risen when the sun set, was high above when Cow, who'd followed the rocks obediently when Irene pressed the side of her hump, came up to the sled.

Irene had no idea how to signal for a stop, so she lifted one leg over the camel's front hump and slid off. The drop was about four feet, but the packed, pebble-strewn plain was harder than the dunes; she staggered and swore as the stones bruised her feet. "Ow!"

Cow turned and gazed at her reproachfully, with two front eyes for a change. Though why Irene thought of reproach she couldn't say; complaisant contentment was built into the structure of the camel's face. Anthropomorphizing. But she still sensed reproach.

"Sorry. I didn't know how to tell you to stop."

Evidently her apology was sufficient, for Cow inflated her sides and turned away, poking among the rocks for fodder or something. Irene turned to the sled.

First things first, and the first thing was to open the back hatch and dig a nutriwafer out of the clutter. The plastic clip that fastened into the suit was invulnerable, but the other end of the wrapper tore between Irene's determined teeth.

Each wafer was supposed to provide a light, but balanced meal, though if they were hungry most people ate two. Irene ate three before she even slowed down. She pulled out a water flask before tackling the fourth. The seal that clipped into the suit was molded into the plastic flask, but a screwdriver, fished from the tools she'd dumped in the sand, penetrated it easily.

There were human tracks by the tools, Irene noted, and around the sled. More tracks than she'd have left? It looked like it, but if they found the sled, they hadn't put anything away. They hadn't left a message either, but why should they? They'd be expecting her to signal.

The Mylar blanket was somewhere not too far from here, in her abandoned carryall. Along with her electro-pistol and ammo. Did she have any idea which direction she'd gone when she wandered away from the rocks? None whatsoever.

Not bright, Goodnight. Not bright at all.

Was delirium a good excuse? Hell, who needed a pistol or a signal—she had a camel.

She also had a portable microanalyzer.

Nibbling her fourth wafer, Irene went for the aluminum chest of lab equipment Willard (bless his meticulous little soul) had foisted on her. It had tipped sideways and wedged itself under the lip of the sled's back compartment—Irene just hoped the analyzer hadn't been broken in the crash.

It was both large and heavy, and for all her care it fell to the ground with a thump, upside down, when Irene finally worked it free. She rolled it onto its side, then right side up, punched in the lock combination, and opened the lid.

The microanalyzer, protected by its own padded, plasticine case, took up about a fourth of the chest. The one in Irene's lab was five times that size, and ten times smarter, but you worked with what you had.

It took some digging among the other equipment— why had they imagined she'd need a geologist's field kit?—but she found the biosample kit eventually.

Irene looked around for a flat surface, then closed the chest and opened up the analyzer on its lid. It looked more like a portable vid-viewer than the primitive microscopes it had evolved from, but its soul was the same. Irene had been four when her father first adjusted his microscope to let her peek at the "teeny tiny creatures" he studied for a living; she'd never forgotten it. No matter how many times she peered

into that hidden universe, she still felt a voyeuristic
thrill slip through her nerves. Today, it was intense.

She swabbed her finger carefully—the risk of con-
taminating the sample in this open environment was
high, but all she could do was her best. Ordinarily she
disliked pricking herself, but this time she didn't even
wince as the needle bit, pressing and pressing till the
domed drop of blood was big enough to flood the
slide.

She wiped away the remainder, dropped the slide
into the slot, and hit the ON switch. Light spilled from
the analyzer's seams, like a café table lamp, shockingly
artificial in the moonlit wilderness.

Field-equipment batteries had solar-recharge hook-
ups, and were good for three days' constant use. Slow
as this portable unit was, it shouldn't—

?— the prompt blinked.

Analyze.

Sample?—

Human blood : Olsen 1., she typed carefully. The
keyboards on portable units were half-sized—they
looked efficient, until you tried to work with them.

Scan for?—

Cell count//flag/identify anomalies.

Begin?—

Y.

The light on the chest flared scarlet, the reflection
of her red cells, magnified a thousand times. Irene
sighed. This was going to take a while.

She stared at the analyzer for five minutes, realized
that was going to drive her mad, and approached the
sled again. If nothing else, she should pick up the
tools. And inventorying the equipment would be a
good idea. She might need a lot of this stuff before
she was finished.

Food and water were no problem—over a week's
worth of both remained. Weapons, on the other hand,
were notably absent. You were issued one pistol, and

you were expected to keep track of it. Irene shrugged.
There was an X-Acto knife in the tool kit, but the
idea of using it to fight off the cat was laughable. The
geologist's rock hammer looked like a better bet. Hell,
without her suit, if that cat came back, she was dead.
It was that simple, and she wasn't going to waste time
worrying about it. Much.

Irene went through the sled, sorting out the things
she might need. The water flasks alone made a pretty
good pile. She hoped Cow was in a carrying mood.
And how to get them onto the camel? The one thing
she didn't have was saddlebags. The Mylar sheet had
been the only blanket of any kind, the carryall the
only bag. OK, improvise. What could she—

The analyzer's "finished" chime made her jump.

Analysis complete. Display?—

Irene stabbed the Y key and watched her own blood
flow over the screen in a tide of glowing green print.
She'd seen it hundreds of times—the quickest source
for a baseline sample of healthy blood was usually
herself. Her white count was up—no surprise—and
her blood sugar low. Not enough time to digest
those nutriwafers.

Ah-ha! There was something, flagged in red—*Unidentified bacteria 1. Unidentified bacteria 2. Anomaly 1.*

Irene's brows creased. The bacteria—two of them!
No wonder she'd been sick—were probably the source
of the infection, and she'd known they wouldn't be
listed in the analyzer's database. The microanalyzer in
her lab would have found similarities between them
and other known bacteria, linked them, and speculated on the possible characteristics of these aliens,
even if it couldn't identify them. This portable model
barely had the brains to tell the difference between
viruses and bacteria. But it should be able to identify
anything as one or the other.

The ?— prompt blinked patiently, asking for instructions. Irene typed, *Display Anomaly 1 : Olsen 1.*

The screen blanked for a long moment, as the image processor searched, then flared to display a sea of quiet cells, with something moving among them.

The hair on Irene's neck lifted. *Magnify X 10.*

Christ! No wonder the analyzer couldn't identify it. Anomaly 1 was a single-celled organism—at least, that was Irene's best guess, for she'd never seen anything quite like it. It was big—five times the size of her red cells, its outer membrane covered with busy cilia. Without the equipment to section it, she could only see its organelles dimly, but that had to be a nucleus, didn't it? So why did it have three lobes? Maybe it was dividing. She'd give a year off her life to be able to section and stain it.

Irene watched in fascination as it wiggled among the immobile blood cells. The sample was beginning to dry by that time—the organism showed more interest in the dead cells, but it didn't consume either them or the live ones. So what did it eat? And how fast did it breed? It didn't seem to be dividing at the moment, but if these things—these parasites?—multiplied exponentially, she'd be in real trouble.

Irene wrapped her arms around herself—the night hadn't been this cool before, had it? Maybe because she was sitting still. . . . *Yeah, you're not scared.*

She watched it till the sample died, till the ciliophora struggled, trapped in the mass of drying plasma. It would die, too, shortly.

Irene saved all data, snapped off the analyzer, and rubbed her eyes.

Anomaly 1. Ciliophora hexaped? A parasite, but it seemed to be benign. Beneficial, even. The colonists must be infected constantly, if it lived in the water, but they all seemed healthy.

If it lived in the water. It could have come from a flea bite. Or the cat bite. Or . . . Why the hell hadn't she had some sort of sample container at the pond?

The analyzer in her lab on the *Stanley* could maintain a sample for a long time. Long enough to watch this thing till it ate, reproduced, and did whatever else it did, and then show it to Irene under full magnification, on a big screen. She wanted to see a breakdown of its DNA, too. She had to get to her lab.

Cow had wandered back to check on her several times, like a well-trained, responsible form of transportation. But "take me over there" was easier to convey than "take me to a place I don't even know how to find." Cow's foolish, dreamy face flashed into Irene's mind, and she snorted. Who was she kidding? Cow would take her wherever Cow wanted to go— back to the herd, most likely. Which wasn't a bad thing. She still wanted a sample of the colonists' blood. Hell, after what she'd just seen, she lusted for their blood like Dracula. Older samples of the parasite. Samples that had lived in a human body for . . . for however long it lived there. News of Mark. Again, the painful, foolish flash of hope. Absurd. She had to pack. And she had to figure out something to pack things in, and . . .

It took about an hour to peel the plastic cover off the sled's seats, front and back. The X-Acto knife came in handy after all. The cover of the driver's seat back made a natural sack, but it took over thirty nuts and bolts to fasten the edges of the seat cover from the rear compartment. Even then, it was smaller than the other bag. *So put the heavy stuff in that one.*

The skirt from the front seat looked like it would lie smoothly across Cow's saddle, and Irene bolted the sacks to it, bolt ends pointed carefully away from Cow. Which meant they'd stick into her thighs, but she didn't want Cow to object to this makeshift tack.

She used a stout, Phillips screwdriver to punch holes in the reinforced plastic. Her hands and wrists had begun to ache, and she wasn't quite finished when she noticed that the moons were fading, the sky becoming lighter.

"Rats." But she wouldn't have been able to get far before daybreak, even if she'd started hours ago, and she was far better off spending the day where she was than on the open dunes.

Cow wandered back from wherever she'd been, and came up to smell Irene's handiwork. She was still disconcertingly big.

"You're going to carry this," Irene said hopefully. "See? That's how I'll take the water, and the analyzer, and the other things I need."

Cow went on sniffing the plastic. If they were going to weather the day here, she should probably give Cow some water.

Irene scrambled to her feet. She knew Earth's camels could go a long time without water; having seen Cow drink, Irene thought it was safe to assume some sort of water storage was practiced by Navohar's camels as well. But she had plenty, and offering some of it to Cow might encourage her to stick around and take Irene with her when night fell. As Cow appeared and vanished through the night, Irene had realized that if the camel didn't return, she was in very deep trouble indeed.

She emptied the geologist's kit into the sled to make a smallish, rectangular water trough; remembering Cow's thirst at the pool, she emptied two of the nine remaining gallon flasks into it. The X-Acto knife might not be much of a weapon, but it made a great flask opener.

Cow's nostrils widened as the water gurgled out. She watched Irene, ears pricked forward. Her bony, lumpy face couldn't change expression, but Irene was beginning to be able to read those ears. At the moment, she had Cow's complete attention. "Yes, it's for you." She carried the sloshing tool case over to Cow and set it down, relieved that the colonists had evidently trained their mounts not to rush over and start guzzling from any available source. Which made sense, for they couldn't let something that drank that much get into their own water supply.

The cool breeze was picking up, as it usually did at sunrise and sunset. Blowing grains smacked Irene's ankles, almost hard enough to sting, and she wiggled her feet deeper into the sand. The thought of what might live *there* whispered across her mind, but a full day and night in the open had begun to dull that fear. You couldn't spend all your time panicking that "things" were going to get you, even if they were.

Cow drained the improvised pail in long slurps and raised a dripping muzzle as the sun rose over the dark plateau in the east.

"OK," Irene told her briskly, pushing a strand of windblown hair out of her eyes. "This is the plan. I'm going to sleep under there." She pointed to the sled leaning against the rocks. "You can sleep wherever you want, but we meet back here as soon as the sun goes down, then leave. You got that?"

Cow turned and ambled off without replying. Irene hoped the colonists didn't give their camels water as a signal that their job was done and they could leave. If Cow didn't come back . . . She'd think of something.

She packed a few things, starting with the important items, like the analyzer and the water, taking only the tools she thought she'd need. The chem-synthesizer kit was particularly bulky, but could create too many useful substances to leave behind.

All too soon, the sunlight stopped being comfortably warm and became uncomfortably hot. Irene struggled on for a bit, then gave up, picked up a flask, and retired to the narrow shelter the wrecked sled created.

The sand beneath it was still cool, and Irene, who hadn't thought she was sleepy, dug a hollow for her hip and fell asleep within moments.

When she woke her back and armpits were slippery with sweat. She tried to push off her blankets, but there were no blankets. The discovery woke her enough to remind her where she was and what she was doing. Lord, she was hot! Had the fever returned? She didn't feel ill. Irene wiggled forward and laid a hand on the sunlit rock. Low oven temperature. She laid her hand on the sled's chrome fender and snatched it back, licking scorched fingers.

No, she didn't have a fever; it was roasting out there! Would Cow be all right? The camels must be adapted to this, though how any creature coped with such heat was beyond her. Irene could see only a narrow wedge of rock face and sand, but surely nothing could survive out there without shade. Perhaps that was where Cow had gone, to find shade.

Irene drank, then finger-combed her hair and braided it off her sweaty neck. It helped, a little. She was thinking that she'd never fall asleep in the heat when she dozed off.

The next time she woke, the sun no longer glared on the sand outside her shelter. But it was still day. Of course—the sun was on the other side of the rocks. She was in the shade. Irene crawled to the end of the sled and looked out.

The ridge's shadow stretched about fifteen feet from its base. The sun seemed to have beaten the dunes flat— no shadows, none of the subtle colors they showed at dawn and dusk, just silent, sand-colored sand.

A slobbering snort pulled her farther out of the shelter. Cow lay on the other side of the sled—all the eyes Irene could see were closed. She whuffed again and twitched. Dreaming?

The sand was hot under Irene's bare hands. She smiled, crawled back under the sled, and went back to sleep.

When she woke again the sunset breeze, warm from the solar-heated sand, was playing with her bare feet, and she was incredibly thirsty. Irene climbed out from under the sled, pulling her damp suit liner away from her skin so the breeze could reach her. It felt wonderful.

To split a flask with Cow, eat a nutriwafer, and finish stowing the last of the gear she wanted, was the work of minutes. One of the mid-sized moons was rising, so they should have pretty good light most of the night. Should she leave another message on the sled? She couldn't think of anything new she needed to say. She'd find a way to signal when she wanted them, and not before.

"OK, Cow, time to go," Irene commanded, and watched in stunned delight as Cow lay down obediently. *Maybe this is going to work better tonight.*

She lifted the saddlebags—at least she tried to. She hadn't realized the stuff was that heavy. She finally dragged them, one bag at a time, to the patiently waiting camel. She unloaded the chem-kit and two water flasks from one bag and managed to sling it over Cow's back. She repacked it, and looked at the neatly loaded camel with satisfaction. Not bad. And judging by their weight when she'd dragged them, she'd gotten them pretty well balanced.

Irene put one foot on a knob in the left-hand bag and seated herself between Cow's humps. The bolts were low enough not to poke into her legs too much. All systems go.

"OK, Cow. Move out."

Cow sat placidly, unmoving.

"I'm ready now. We can go." She pushed the hump in front of her forward. The camel's third eye focused on her. What was the beast waiting for?

"Come on! Get it in gear! Go!"

The eye blinked. Cow didn't budge.

"Shit!" Irene scrambled off. If the camel had been a sled, she'd have kicked it, but she wasn't sure that was a good idea with an animal who was so much bigger than she was. Besides, her feet were bare.

Instead she repacked. She sorted through the miscellaneous tools again—the ones whose batteries had no recharge hookup could probably go. The spare bolts, too, for her saddlebags seemed to be holding together. And if she was dumping weight, the chem-synthesizer kit was one of the heaviest . . .

This time she carried the saddlebags over to Cow, and hoisted one side up between her humps without having to unload it, though it was a near thing.

Irene stepped back and wiped her face. "Does that suit your highness? Or do you want me to dump the water, too? You'll drink that up yourself, you know."

The relaxed ears swiveled, but none of Cow's eyes seemed to be watching Irene as she mounted and settled herself. The third eye blinked, and Cow heaved a sigh and surged to her feet. Irene suppressed a cheer.

Cow moved steadily into the desert. Knowing that the high, dark plateau of the jungle lay to the east, Irene fixed their general direction as northwest, both toward the settlement and away. She wished she knew how far south she'd traveled originally, but the odometer was as dead as the rest of the sled's instruments, and before the crash she'd been paying attention to camel tracks, not digital displays. Not that it made much difference, for she'd no way of knowing how fast Cow traveled. Her long strides were unhurried, but the dunes vanished beneath her at a rate that astonished Irene.

The first moon was halfway up the sky, and a second, small, lumpy, and pocked like a misshapen potato, had risen to join them when Cow suddenly stopped and seesawed down to lie on the sand.

"What is it?" Irene looked around and saw nothing. "What's the problem?"

The third eye was focused on her, but Cow's ears were relaxed, one cocked lazily forward, one half-back. Nothing serious, probably. Maybe she just wanted a rest.

Irene dismounted and decided to seize the opportunity to go to the bathroom. There was no point in going very far; who cared what Cow saw? But the close-packed life of the domes encouraged modesty, and she did turn her back.

When she rose and turned around, the saddlebags lay on the sand. "How did you do that?"

Irene hurried back, but they were undamaged. She pulled out a flask and used a little water to wash her hands. It was probably a mistake to waste water, but if Cow didn't take her to a new supply, that small amount would make no difference. And even though her fear of contamination was wearing away as time passed, being able to clean her hands made a big difference to her peace of mind.

Replacing the jug, she lifted the saddlebags. At her first step toward Cow, the camel lurched to her feet.

"Hey! Get back here! You're forgetting something. Wait!"

Cow set off over the dunes, ignoring Irene's shout. She stopped about twenty feet away, and turned back to look at Irene with her front eyes. The message couldn't have been clearer—*are you coming*?

"Fuck you," said Irene distinctly. But she didn't have much choice. She hoisted the saddlebags over her shoulder and began to walk.

Soon she had to stop and fold the wide center strap, for it kept slipping off. The sand was as hard to walk in as she remembered. The bolts dug into her ribs. Her knees bumped against the kits and tools as she walked. And they weighed a fucking ton.

Six dunes later she stopped and dumped the bags to the ground. Cow, who'd slowed her pace to keep about ten feet ahead of Irene, stopped, too, though she didn't bother to turn her head, watching Irene with her third eye. Irene met the creepy gaze squarely. "If you laugh, I'm going to kill you."

One ear flicked back, but that probably wasn't laughter. Good enough.

Irene went through the bags again. The rock hammer was the closest thing she had to a weapon, but it weighed several pounds. She discarded all the remaining tools, except the screwdriver, and the X-Acto knife that had proved so useful. The binoculars. The range finder, with which she'd hoped to determine how far she'd come. The plant sample kit? No, she needed that, damn it!

Irene drank as much as she could—it didn't change the weight of the flask much. But water she had to keep—who knew how long it would take that stupid, stubborn camel to get where she was going? Irene packed up and started walking, Cow pacing deliberately in front of her.

Irene began to wonder what camel steak would taste like.

This time she only made it over four dunes. Her legs were tiring. She abandoned the plant sample kit, the first-aid kit (it probably wouldn't have what she needed anyway), and the screwdriver she used to puncture the flasks. The X-Acto knife was lighter, and it would do. Nothing remained but the microanalyzer, its solar-recharge panels (which were light anyway), the biosample kit, the water, and the nutriwafers.

She sat down to eat one, wiggling her toes in the smooth sand, drinking again. Cow's ears twitched impatiently.

"I don't care," Irene told her. "If you're in such a damned hurry, you can carry some of this."

But Irene rose soon enough and set off again. She was getting tired of looking at Cow's narrow hindquarters. "Camel sausage," she panted as the wide, leathery feet started up yet another slope. "Camel chops."

She had to stop halfway up the next dune. She was gasping. Her leg muscles quivered and cramped. "I hate you," she told the patiently waiting camel.

Cow didn't even flick an ear.

"I'm not leaving any of this."

Cow started walking.

Camel stew. Irene no longer had the breath to voice her thoughts, but she turned them into a mantra—it helped keep her going. *Camel jerky. Camel à la king.*

Sweat poured into her eyes. Her legs shook. She actually walked into Cow's behind before she realized the camel had stopped. And lain down.

"Had enough?" Irene wheezed. She stepped up, threw the saddlebags over Cow's back and scrambled aboard before the vicious beast could change her mind. See if she ever got off to pee again.

The third eye blinked sympathetically, and Cow swayed to her feet and strolled onward.

As the stitch in her side eased, Irene began to take a more lenient view. The saddlebags had been heavy— though most of it was water, and she was sharing that. But she had carried a few unnecessary items.

Camel meat was probably tough, anyway.

A third moon rose, the big one. The light was so bright that colors began to appear. Not that there were many colors to see—just tawny sand and the tawny back of a camel's head and neck. But the dunes Cow wended through curved as exquisitely as a giant's fili- gree—sculpted waves, in whose subtle, asymmetric grace Irene found solace.

Mark had wanted to see places like this.

Cow showed no further signs of wishing to rid her- self of her load, so when the pressure in Irene's blad- der started to build she threw a leg over Cow's hump, ready to slide off, and was pleased, and not too suspi- cious, when Cow rocked down to the sand. And waited for her, though this time Irene only moved a few steps off and watched her tricky mount all the time.

Shortly after they set off again, the wind began to pick up. Irene had noticed Cow sniffing every now and then—now she stopped and inhaled deeply.

"If it's cat you smell, I suggest we run for it," Irene told her.

One pricked ear flicked back to her, but when Cow started walking again, she moved at the same easy, rapid pace. Either it wasn't a cat, or Cow wasn't interested in Irene's advice. Irene sighed.

Judging by the breeze, sunrise was coming soon, and there was nothing in sight that might produce shade. It was too much to expect, that Cow would know she had to bring Irene to shelter before daybreak. On the other hand, Cow preferred to sleep in the shade herself, so perhaps it would work out. Perhaps it was shade she was smelling for.

A fourth moon rose, another small, lumpy one, and Irene wondered idly how many this planet had. The sky was polished pewter, and there wasn't a star to be seen. Was Cow bearing more toward the west, or was this simply the best route over the maze of ridges? Was the sun going to rise in another hour and fry them both? Tune in next week . . .

Cow stopped, head lifted, ears pricked. Her nostrils opened, her sides swelled between Irene's calves.

"What is it?"

Then a sound caught her ears, a far-off wail, like . . . horns?

Cow broke into a trot—and broke, Irene thought with the small part of her mind not concerned with hanging on, was the right word. At a walk, each set of three feet moved together. At a trot it seemed to be every foot for itself; Irene could find no rhythm in the jarring landslide she rode. She was glad she'd emptied her bladder earlier. She wished she'd found some way to cement her teeth into place while she was at it, for if this kept up, she might lose a few.

"Da-amn it, Cow, this is-s rough!"

The camel paid no heed for several minutes, then stopped as suddenly as she'd started, on top of a dune ridge.

"Thank God," Irene sighed, slumping down to rest between the humps. But Cow wasn't listening to her.

The melodious conch calls trumpeted again, closer. Cow's lungs inflated. She raised her nose to the sky. *"Nah-woooooooon."*

Her body vibrated beneath Irene. The water in the saddlebags vibrated. A flask cracked, with a snap Irene felt more than she heard it, for the camel's howl drowned all other sounds.

Cow's breath ran out. Cautiously, Irene peeled her hands from her ears, just in time to hear the horn chorus answer. *"Nah-wooooooon."* There were different voices among them, some higher than a conch, some as deep as if the dunes spoke. It was as wild and splendid as anything Irene had ever heard, and she couldn't have cared less.

"Come on, you lazy twit, let's go find them!"

Cow stepped out even as she spoke. Soon Irene saw the camel chorus, silhouetted against the pale sky, half a kilometer away. They sang them in, with Cow, to Irene's impatient dismay, stopping periodically to answer. The camp took her by surprise—they came over the rise and there it was, sheltered in a long hollow between two dunes.

There were camels, and bundles and bags lying in disorganized piles. No tents up yet, though several were spread ready on the sand. People milled about—quite a few stopped to watch Cow wade down the slope, though most went on with what they were doing.

Hard as she looked, Irene couldn't see anyone lying down. No one kneeling beside a person who might be on a stretcher, or even among the luggage. No Mark.

Something hard and painful swelled in Irene's heart, but she squashed it down. Later.

First she'd learn the truth. Then she'd kill whoever was responsible for this. Then it would be time to hurt.

Cow strolled into the encampment and swayed

down for Irene to dismount. A small crowd of colonists had gathered; Gus Sardakowski was waiting for her. "Dr. Olsen. This is an unexpected . . . um . . ."

"Where is he, you son of a bitch?" Irene barely recognized the low, cold growl as her own voice. Sardakowski froze as if he'd been slapped.

"Behind you, Auntie," said Mark's voice cheerfully. "Give me a minute to get there, huh?"

Prickles raced up Irene's spine. She turned slowly, as if she might shatter something, something precious, if she moved too fast. The crowd parted and Mark was there, coming toward her, braced on two sticks he used like his old canes—it had been *months* since Mark walked with canes, upright, no wonder she hadn't seen him, hadn't known, hadn't . . .

"It works." She didn't recognize this voice either, hollow and raw. It worked on GED, that bizarre ciliophora. It worked on Mark, and it would work on others, and they'd lied, and concealed it, and—

She spun, her heel sinking, destroying her balance— her clenched fist missed Sardakowski's jaw by a fraction of an inch.

"Hey!" He leapt back, more agile on the shifting surface than she was. "Watch it! You don't have to . . ."

She turned away, his voice vanishing from her awareness. The sticks were giving Mark trouble in the sand. His legs weren't too steady, either. He grinned at her, shyly—there was so much she wanted to say to him!—then his expression changed.

"Auntie, you look terrible. What hap—"

He never finished the sentence, for her arms were around him, a hug hard enough to squeeze his breath away.

Chapter 6

"Come on, kiddo, give. What happened? No, first, how do you feel? Really?"

Sunlight reflected off the sand, into the dense shade of the low tent. In the dim light, Mark's hollow face was alive with a delight that nothing could diminish.

The colonists had pitched a tent for the two of them—though it was more like a giant umbrella than the tents Irene had known. The fabric was a heavy, feltlike cloth, woven of camel hair. Fiberglass ribs ran through its seams to form an upside-down, oval bowl, with two-foot-long flaps that could be lowered to the sand around its edges. At its highest point, it was barely tall enough for Mark to sit upright. It was designed for lying down, and the sand beneath Irene was still cool from the night. Long, plasticine stakes, with crosspieces a foot from the top, secured the tent to the ground and held it up so the breeze could flow under and through.

From Irene's angle, the colonists' encampment looked like a convention of giant sand slugs. From the air, they would look like a group of small dunes. There'd been some fuss, getting everyone to orient their tents in the same direction as the larger dunes, and Irene guessed it was something they'd only started doing since the flitters had been looking for them. She'd been too occupied with Mark, with getting her gear off Cow, and with apologizing, stiffly, to Gus Sardakowski for taking a swing at him, to pay much attention.

The colonists had been busy, too, though that didn't stop them from staring at Irene with expressions that ranged from guilt, through appalled consternation, to fury. Which confused her—after all, *they* were the kidnappers.

Getting the tents up before the sun rose was a matter of some importance, it seemed; now everyone was inside (or under) one, except for the camels, who lay in their strange, upright position with their backs to the rising sun, eyes closed, looking contented. They always looked contented. Irene noticed they weren't penned or tied up. Perhaps they stayed because the colonists provided water. In this barren, sun-blasted wilderness, it would be a compelling motive, even for a camel.

"How do I feel?" Mark repeated thoughtfully. "Kind of . . . stunned, I think. I'm going to live to grow up—that takes some getting used to."

Irene's eyes stung. "I'm sure you'll manage," she said drily. But her hand crept out to grasp his arm, and Mark smiled.

"I expect I will. But what happened to you? You look like you've been through a war, Auntie."

"No, you first. Impatience is the prerogative of age."

"Who says? All right, all right, I'm talking. I don't remember much about the first part, though. I was pretty sick."

"I know," said Irene grimly. "Go on."

Mark's face, in the shadows, had sobered. "I wasn't really awake when they carried me out—just sort of aware of being lifted. Of moving. They took me out and put me up on Ent—that's what I named my camel." He sounded strangely tentative.

"Let me guess, short for Enterprise? Because it's a 'travel'?"

Mark grinned. "Good guess, but no. I was thinking

of Tolkien. The tree people, remember? Long, knobby legs. Haroom boom."

"I should never have taught you to read. No, it's a good name. Go on."

"Well, what did you name yours?"

"Cow," said Irene shortly, and watched Mark disintegrate into laughter. "Though I don't suppose she's mine. They belong to the colonists, after all." And why did that make Mark look at her so oddly? Who cared? "Will you get on with it, please?"

He was still smiling. "Why? We've *got* all day. Anyway, they put me up on Ent, who practically broke down the door trying to get to me, they said. Then Gus—he asked me to call him that—he got on behind and held me on, and Ent carried me to a . . . a pond, sort of. It's hard to explain, but—"

"No, I understand better than you might think."

"Oh? Oh! Your friend, Cow, took you to one? But how did you get ill? Is that why your arm's torn up?"

Irene sighed. "I went looking for you. A big cat bit me. The bite got infected. A camel found me, took me to a pool, and threw me in. I got well. The camel took me here. Now go on."

"OK, Ent carried me to a pool. I got well. Then I came here."

"Mark. You are perilously close to annihilation."

"Sorry." He tried to keep his face straight and failed. "I thought we were synopsisizing."

Irene folded her hands and tried to look patient. She didn't think she succeeded.

"Really, that's about all that happened. I remember some of the riding, but I slept through most of it. I was too sick to notice much.

"They took me to this pond. Gus laid me down in it and told me to drink the water, and I did. I was alone when I woke up except for Ent, which was kind of weird, though Gus came back just a little later."

"Weird," said Irene coldly. To wake alone, in a

strange place . . . "I'll weird him, the bastard. How could he pull a stunt like that? To leave you—"

"It wasn't bad," Mark told her. "Ent was there. And I liked the pool. I spent hours under the water-fall, and—"

"Wait. What waterfall?"

"The waterfall. At the end of the . . . Your pool didn't have a waterfall?"

"No. Which confirms that it lives in more than one pool." Excitement leapt in Irene's heart, but Mark shrugged and went on.

"Anyway, Gus wasn't gone long, and you really do need to eat something besides flat bread and dried mystery meat."

"Dried . . ." Irene sat up with a jerk. "You've been eating the native plants and animals!"

"And drinking the water," said Mark calmly. "And breathing the air. So are you. Be calming, Auntie. The worst it'll do is kill me, and we'd be even. No—I'd owe Navohar for all the days I lived before it happened."

Irene's pulse slowed. "Sorry. It's just that after seeing so many disasters on other worlds . . ."

"Yeah, I understand. It sounds like it almost happened here, too. In fact, they lost a lot of people from the original colony. It's still hurting some of them."

"So what saved the rest? I've got a portable ana-lyzer in my bag, Mark." Which was currently lying just past her feet, for Irene didn't intend to let it out of her sight. "I found what I think is the organism in my own blood. A ciliophora, but it's damn complex. What have the colonists learned about it?"

"Not much," said Mark soberly. "Or at least, not much they'd tell me. I asked Nola what it was that had saved me, and she said it was an organism that mimicked its host's immune system. Symbioticizing, I guess. They like living in a healthy environment, so they keep their hosts healthy. It makes sense, sort of."

"Their *hosts*? How many different creatures can these things survive in?"

"She didn't say." Mark yawned. "But one thing you ought to know, it not only cures diseases and stuff, it stops you from aging, too. Or slows it down, anyway."

Irene snorted. "And here I thought the fountain of youth was in Florida. How many years are we talking about? Ten? Twenty?"

A strange, ironic smile lit Mark's tired face. "According to Nola, their best guess is that people who've had the stuff in their bloodstream from childhood on will live somewhere around two hundred years. It's—"

"What? That's impossible!"

"So's recovering from GED. It's hard for them to be sure, because no one here has died from old age yet. Gus Sardakowski—you assumed he was Dr. Sardakowski's son, but he's not. He *is* Dr. Sardakowski. The one who came here from Earth in the first place. The one who wrote the log we read."

"But that would make him over ninety years old!"

"That's right," said Mark sleepily. "At least that's what Nola said. And I believe it."

Irene lay in silence a while, trying to analyze this new information. It sounded fantastic, but there was something about Sardakowski that fit with the man who'd led his people into space to look for a better world, with the man who'd written the log she'd read. And why not? If anomaly 1 mimicked the immune system but was more efficient, efficient enough to stop a genetic disorder like GED . . .

"Dear, holy God."

Mark grinned. "It's a big step from dying young," he agreed.

"So how old are kids like Sondi? A hundred and four?"

A tinge of color showed in Mark's cheeks. "She's nineteen. Children grow at close to a normal rate—it doesn't really start slowing you down till your twenties."

"When the aging process begins," said Irene thoughtfully. "So anyone here who looks older than twenty . . ."

". . . is one of the original colonists," Mark finished. His eyes were drifting closed.

Irene let him sleep, still trying to take in the implications. Two hundred years. More than doubling the human life span. It sounded unbelievable, but really, the degenerative processes of aging were no more complex than the degenerative processes of GED. In the old days, it might have caused problems with over-population, but since humanity had been confined to the domes, birth control was strictly . . .

Her biological clock had stopped. She could let go of that damned, creeping awareness that unless she had children *immediately* it would be too late. She was no longer as old as she'd thought she was, and it would last for as long as anomaly 1 lived in her tissues. Amazing. She'd have to find out how long that was. Not forever, evidently, or the colonists would surely be willing to share it. There must be a limited supply— how limited could it be, if it lived in their water?— and they were afraid an explosion of off-worlders would take it all, or damage the source. So they'd denied its existence, even knowing it might save thousands of kids like Mark. Like Willard's daughter, who'd died. Irene fought down fury. They had saved Mark, in the end. She had to deal with these people, talk them out of their secrets. She could hardly do that while cursing them for the selfish bastards they were. Eventually, she'd figure out the organism's complexities on her own, but being able to start with what they'd already discovered would save lots of time.

And time was something she was short on. Willard had given her several weeks, but she knew that wasn't hard and fast. He'd delay as long as he could, looking for her—but sooner or later they'd assume she'd died in the desert and go on. Though even if the *Stanley* left without her, there were always the colonists' message buoys. But it would take months for a buoy to reach Earth, and months for a ship to return, and in those months more lives would be lost.

The need to get started itched in Irene's nerves. She eyed her sleeping nephew hungrily, but taking someone's blood without consent was extremely rude, and Mark looked like he needed the sleep. No, it would wait till evening, when everyone woke, and she could confront Sardakowski—*ninety* years old?—and get some answers.

Warmth collected under the tent's dense fabric like a blanket, and Irene's thoughts finally drifted into incoherence, and then nothingness.

Around midday the heat woke her, sweaty and uncomfortable. She groped for the water flask the colonists had given them along with the tent—if it was full of anomaly 1, she almost hated to drink it, but there'd be more where that came from.

The sunlight was slipping under the edge of the tent—not far enough to touch her skin, but it might be adding a few degrees. Irene crawled over to let the flap down. The temperature in the upper part of the tent was unbearable, its small vents obviously inadequate to drain off the heat, and she stopped to pull off her tattered shirt—it wasn't as if Mark had never seen her in her bra before. She'd have to do something about clothes if she planned to stay with the colony. The pool had helped, but her clothing was getting . . . ripe was the kindest adjective.

She unsnapped the strap and the tent flap slithered down, blocking the light. Working her way to the front, she pulled the last strap free and stopped, looking out over the camp.

Heat shimmered off the sand, but it was the camels who caught her attention. They'd turned, so their backs confronted the sun, and they seemed to have doubled in size, for their thick coats bristled like a frightened cat's.

"They're haystacking," said Mark's amused voice behind her. "At least, that's what I call it. The colonists say they 'fluff.' "

"Sorry, I didn't mean to wake you. Why are they doing that? Instant tent?"

"Something like that." Mark sat up and peeled off the T-shirt with the skull and fish. "It gets the sun away from their skin, and lets the air flow through. They designed these tents on the same principle."

"It's not enough," said Irene, using her discarded shirt to mop up a trickle of sweat between her breasts.

"They tell me you get used to it," said Mark ruefully. "But there's another trick: if you dig down into the sand six, eight inches, it usually gets damp. Works pretty well, really. I've tried it the last couple of ni—days."

"It's confusing," Irene agreed, helping him scrape a hollow in the sand for his body. It did turn damp and cool when you dug down a bit, and Mark insisted on helping her dig. "It's my legs that have atrophied, not my arms."

Irene lay down again, cool, firmer sand against her chest and stomach. The breeze flowing over her back was still warm, but the worst of the heat was trapped in the sheltering bowl overhead, and the pale tan fabric would reflect the sun almost as well as white. Not too bad.

A chilling breeze woke her again, much later. The sand outside was drenched in cool moonlight. Mark was still asleep.

Irene got up and spent several minutes brushing the clinging sand from her damp skin, taking off her bra to shake it out. When she finally put on her shirt and crawled out, even the need to discover the facts about anomaly 1 had become secondary to a more pressing concern.

Sondi was sitting cross-legged, not far from their tent. Waiting for Mark? She scrambled to her feet as Irene approached.

"Good evening. I hope you slept well. You must have been exhausted—everyone else has been up for hours."

Then where were they? The camp was deserted as far as Irene could see. But first things first.

"I have to go to the bathroom. Do you have customs, or a proper place for that, or something?"

"Sort of," said Sondi. "If you only need to pee, just go behind the nearest dune and rinse your hands when you come back. We don't have any designated places when we're on the move. If you need to do more—" She crossed to one of the bundles and opened a plastic container. The acrid, civilized scent of rubbing alcohol drifted out. "—take one of these and a shovel and bury everything afterward. It's all biodegradable. The wipes are made of some cottony stuff that grows around seeds. We barely had time to get it woven and saturated, what with having to move on so fast. Because of your ship." She didn't sound too upset about it.

"Thank you."

"Um, Dr. Olsen?"

"Yes?"

"Do you mind if I go with you? There's a meeting going on. About you. What to do about you, I mean. They asked me to . . . to steer you in another direction. If you don't mind."

Or even if she did? Probably.

"I'd like to go to that meeting," said Irene firmly. "State my case. You people have a cure for GED for God's sake, and who knows what else! You can't just . . ."

"We understand that." Sondi's voice was cool. "We've talked about this before. Please . . ."

Sondi borrowed a shovel and led her away from the camp. Irene was grateful when the girl moved some distance off and turned her back politely. Returning to camp, the evidence buried behind her, she felt fairly cheerful—that hadn't been nearly as uncivilized as she'd feared. Surely these people wouldn't choose to keep their secret at the cost of so many lives. The meeting was just . . . the meeting was over.

The camp was full of people and camels, most of whom seemed to be getting in each other's way. At least, the camels were—the people chatted with each other, though here and there tents were sighing down. Some of the colonists held cups, and folded white triangles out of which they took bites. A small flock of children jostled them as they raced past, shrieking in some private game.

Irene located Sardakowski, tinkering with a wooden framework, stalked over to him, and thrust the shovel into the sand.

"You lied to me, Sardakowski. From the very start. What happened at this meeting?"

A smile tugged at his lips, lightening his somber expression. "Gus. If we're going to travel together for—"

"The meeting, Gus."

His plain hazel eyes studied her for a long moment; then he sighed and seated himself on the wooden contraption he'd been working on. "Yes, I lied. I thought it would be safer and simpler for everyone, if you learned nothing and went away."

"You were going to leave the settlement as soon as you resupplied. Without giving me a blood sample."

"That's right."

"Without saving Mark."

His resigned expression changed, both harder and sadder. "We didn't make that decision lightly, if that's what you're thinking. We considered Mark, and all the others like him. But the fact is, that organism only lasts about two years in a human host—and only a few weeks in a petri dish. It can't be removed from Navohar, Dr. Olsen, and there isn't enough of it to save the thousands upon thousands with GED and other disorders. Would you want to play God? Choose which few hundred kids a year get to make the journey here and condemn the rest to death?"

"Of course not, but it—"

"And if anyone took on that role, do you really think the parents of the rest of those terminal children would accept that? That there was a cure, but their kid couldn't have it? They'd get hold of a ship somehow, and they'd come. And if they couldn't steal one, or if the black market couldn't meet the demand, they, and their families and friends, would overthrow the government who made the decision. Not to mention those who just want to live longer and could afford to bribe the right people. Sooner or later, Navohar would face an invasion of ignorant, desperate people, and the organism, and its source, would be destroyed. No, Dr. Olsen, we didn't make that decision lightly, but I believe it was the right choice. And now . . ." He shrugged. "Now we've had to make another choice."

"But why are you so certain anomaly—the organism—can't be sustained, and reproduced, under laboratory conditions?"

"Because we tried it," said Gus wearily. "Don't you think we tried? Time and again, over the last forty years; someone'll have a new idea, and we try that too. They always fail."

"But none of you are microbiologists! At least . . . are you?"

"No." He shook his head. "Nola's a naturalist, as well as a vet, but she's bright, well trained, and has worked her guts out on this. She's still trying."

"Well, I'm an expert," said Irene. She paced before

him, too tense for dignified stillness, the sand warm under her bare feet. Two fullish moons had risen, and a sliver was setting. "And my training is forty years more current than anyone you have here. Maybe I can figure out something the others couldn't. But to do that, I'll need access—not only to blood samples, but to the pools, if that's the organism's natural environment. And I'll need to use my lab back on the *Stanley.*"

"No."

"What do you mean, no?"

"I mean we can't let you go. Wait, listen to me for a minute. We've reached a compromise. We're going to allow you to do your own research, right here. There's not a person in this camp who won't give you all the blood samples you need—and if you can find a way to keep the organism viable in a lab, you can take a plentiful supply with you—in your own blood—and we'll let you go with the deepest gratitude. But if you can't . . ." His face was full of pain and resignation. "We have no choice. And I'm afraid we won't be able to give you a choice either."

"What are you going to do? Keep me prisoner? There's no way you can stop me from reporting this, and when I tell Willard . . ." She stopped. It hadn't occurred to her before, but there was a way to keep their secret. If they were ruthless enough to condemn thousands to death, then she and Mark . . .

Gus began to laugh. "I'm sorry, but you should see your face. No, Irene, you're in no danger of being dumped in a sandy grave—you or Mark. As to reporting to Captain Keene . . ." He shook his head.

"Then how do you plan to stop me? Tie me up?" He seemed so civilized, despite the rough clothes. The whole conversation felt surreal. They couldn't actually be planning to hold her prisoner?

"I doubt we'll have to take extraordinary precautions," said Sardakowski. "The desert is five days' walk in any direction."

Suddenly she did believe it, and fear bled through her anger. Without a camel's cooperation . . . So she'd gain their cooperation! All she had to do was figure out the steering. Once the colonists saw her doing her research like a good little scientist and dropped their guard, became just a little less wary . . .

"All right," said Irene abruptly. "I guess I don't have much choice. But I'll need access to all your previous research—there's no point in wasting time trying things that have already failed."

Sardakowski's gaze sharpened. Was she yielding too quickly?

"Sorry," he said, "but that's another no. We're hoping if you come at this from a fresh perspective, without preconceptions, you might be able to see something we missed. Besides, Nola's the one who did most of that research, and she won't share it. She's part of the faction that thinks the risk of letting you do any research is too high."

"Faction?" said Irene slowly. If there was some division among the colonists, perhaps she could exploit it.

"Quite passionate factions, actually. One side of the debate is that the less you know, the less threat you are; smash your analyzer and keep a close watch on you till the *Stanley* leaves. The other faction, mine, thinks that the chance you might succeed outweighs the potential risk. The deciding vote was—" He stopped suddenly, wariness in his expressive eyes.

Real anger flared. "The risk I'll find some private little secret you're hiding? No, don't answer. And don't give me any sociology bullshit; if getting those kids here was what it took to save them, we'd *find* a way. I don't care what you're hiding. And you don't need to guard me, either. I wouldn't leave this place if you tried to kick me out. I'm not leaving till I can take your miracle cure with me."

And if you believe that, I've got this bridge . . .

"I hope so," said Gus soberly. "And I am sorry. This was the best compromise we could reach. We do want you to succeed, Dr. Olsen. Really."

"Then I thank you for your hospitality," said Irene sardonically. "Gus."

The shadow of his evil-imp grin appeared. "Don't mention it, Goodnight."

Irene snorted and turned away. She'd do her research—to hell with their secrets—and escape the moment she had the information she needed. Cow had brought her here, after all. She would take her away. The trick now was to pretend she'd accepted their terms. Act friendly. Calm. *Tact, Goodnight.*

She returned the shovel to its owner, a thin, brown-haired woman who introduced herself as Maureen Greville, a name that rang a vague bell in Irene's memory though she couldn't place it. Perhaps because Maureen's cool, speculative stare made her uncomfortable.

She didn't care if they hated her. Reparation for GED, for everything she and her colleagues had done, was within her grasp.

She started back to the tent to look for Mark, but a scent caught her attention—cooked meat, though she couldn't tell what kind, and vegetables perhaps, and something that might be basil, but wasn't quite. Irene found herself walking toward the scent without having made any conscious decision, but resisting both her feet and her stomach was too much to expect this early in the mor—night. Whatever.

There was a short line by the cookpots, and Irene joined it, ignoring the colonists' curious scrutiny. The chef, a small, dark man, was scooping dippers of thick stew into the colonists' mugs and bowls. The diners helped themselves to the rounds of tortilla-like bread, though they looked thicker than the tortillas Irene was accustomed to, and yellower.

Irene's turn came rapidly. She summoned up a smile. "I'm sorry, I don't have a bowl," she said. "I don't know—"

The chef looked up, his face brightening with the first sincere smile Irene had seen this evening. "Ah! Signorina Goodnight, also known as Dr. Olsen, and Mark's aunt. Do not fret yourself. I am Cicero Chen, and the answers to all questions culinary are mine. Behold!" He pulled a mug and a spoon from one of the many bundles that comprised his "kitchen" and held them out to her with a gallant half bow.

Irene began to laugh. "Thank you."

"Not at all, Signorina Goodnight, not at all." A ladle (at least two cups' worth) of steaming stew plopped into the mug. Irene thought about asking what was in it, but the only long-term alternative to eating the local food was starvation, and she knew better than to risk offending the cook.

"I should tell you," he went on, "that breakfast is our heaviest meal when we travel, for the sun is our cooking fire; take as much of the fry bread as you wish. Lunch will be eaten on camelback, and is in those containers over there, so take one with you. Dinner, when we stop, will be sadly repetitive of lunch. But when we make a more permanent camp, when my Sondi brings in some game, I will prepare feasts to delight the palate!" He beamed at her.

"I'm sure you will, and this smells delicious," said Irene, trying to juggle the flat plastic box that held lunch, several rounds of fry bread, and the large, warm mug. He must be part of the faction who wanted her to succeed. *So maybe he'll answer some questions.* "Just thanking you seems inadequate. Could I help wash the dishes?"

"Signorina, when you know me better, you will learn that I never turn down help with the dishes." His smile was open and friendly, but the black eyes that assessed her were shrewd.

Irene promised to return after breakfast and went back to the tent to find Mark. Somewhat to her surprise, he was there, sitting on the sand eating stew and folded fry bread, with a better appetite than he'd shown in several years. In fact he was eating like a starving wolf—or a normal teenage boy.

"G'morning, Auntie." He swallowed. "Or maybe good night. I haven't quite figured that one out yet."

Irene sat down beside him. "I suppose I have you to thank, that everyone here is going to call me Goodnight, too."

She took a closer look at the stew, fishing up lumps of things with her spoon. It smelled good, but she couldn't identify anything but the meat. Vegetables of some sort. She hoped.

"It's not bad," said Mark. "Though not as good as it smells, either. The pale green things taste a bit like turnips. Watch out, if you come across them raw."

"Not bad. And that's from a person who likes pickle and potato chip sandwiches."

It wasn't bad, though some of the vegetables were a little coarse, and the mystery meat had a musty, gamy taste. The fry bread was oaty and sweet, though it would have been even better with butter and jam.

Three of the younger colonists showed up to help Mark take down the tent, so Irene left them to it and went back to wash dishes. Scrubbing the big kettles with sand was another new experience, but she managed easily enough and was surprised at how clean they looked. Sterile it wasn't, but neither was the food, or the water, or the air. Irene rubbed her hands on her thighs.

The kettles were interesting—made of dark plasticine, with a solid ceramic base, they were designed to fit into solar collectors with small, round mirrors angled to shoot the sun at the kettles' heavy bottoms. Several of the ceramic bases were cracked, and Cicero Chen was gluing them back together. Looking at the one she washed, Irene saw that it, too, had been mended in several places.

"We tried solar collectors that were reflective all over," Cicero Chen told her. "But it boiled too hard. Those little mirrors will maintain a long, slow, simmer, so I can sleep through the day. It would be a perfect system, if not for the blasted camels. He sounded more indulgent than angry, and Irene quirked a curious brow.

"What do the camels have to do with it?"

"They're the reason for the crack. . . . Oh. You heard them sing last night, did you not?"

"Hard to miss," said Irene ruefully.

He grinned. "That which you hear is just, what shall I say, the tip of the iceberg. The subharmonics in their songs can travel over two hundred kilometers. They also"—he gestured to the fractured ceramic—"crack pots. They play hell with electronic equipment, too, which is one reason we carry so little with us."

"Electron— My analyzer!" Irene leapt to her feet, but Cicero waved her down. "Don't worry. Even if it breaks, Gus can fix it. He's a good engineer, you know. He's wasted fixing pack frames. And he wants very badly for you to succeed, Signorina. Even those who think the risk of letting you try is too great would be overjoyed to see you succeed."

Irene sank down slowly. "I'd have a better chance if I knew what you've already discovered about the organism."

Cicero shook his head. "No. That was part of our agreement, that you should not. . . . Well, we're hoping you can solve the problem on your own. I can tell you a bit about us, yes? Things it might be useful to know while you live among us?"

As Irene helped him pack up his kitchen, he told her many practical details of the colonists' daily lives, and also some background on the colony as a whole.

He described their system as "small-town democ-

racy at its worst, Signorina." Any matters that affected
the entire group were put before the council, and any
proposal they came up with had to pass with a two-
thirds majority vote of all adults in the camp.

*Does that mean two-thirds of these people are on my
side?* Irene wondered.

Cicero cooked for about eighty people "in this
group" and there were five other groups, something
Gus hadn't seen fit to reveal—about four hundred colonists in all then? After forty years, it didn't seem like
a lot. He told her that he was a mechanic, as well as
a chef, the only one besides Gus, though he seldom
used that skill except on their rare visits to the settlement. He and his wife, Yvonne, were Sondi's parents.
"And Sondi can't boil an egg! French, Chinese, and
Italian—the greatest cuisines in the world! Her grand-
mothers would die of the shame. Ah, well, children
are what they are. And someone must provide meat
for the pot. My Sondi, she can track a hopper mouse
through gravel. She is a huntress to make Diana pale
with envy!"

He seemed completely unaware that Sondi, only
nineteen years old, could not be genetically related to
either of her parents. Irene thought about that, going
back to the tent to check on her microanalyzer. If you
bore a child in your body, nursed it, steadied its wobbling steps, would it be any less yours because its
genes were from some other source?

The tent was down. Down, folded, and packed onto
Mark's camel, and a tall, older man, whose hair was
entirely gray, was loading her saddlebags, her analyzer, onto a camel!

Irene broke into a run. "Hey, what—"

The man turned, startled by her shout, and the
camel turned too, to look with its front eyes. Something about it, the shape of its lumpy features, identi-
fied Cow. The stranger was packing for her, that was

all. Heat crept into Irene's face. "Sorry, I thought . . .
I'm . . ."

"You needn't apologize." The lined face held an
immense dignity. He was dark-skinned—Indian or
Middle Eastern perhaps, though his English was ac-
centless and effortless. "After this morning, it's a wonder you're not standing guard over this"—he patted
the analyzer—"with a club. But you needn't," he
added gently. "We've agreed that you should be allowed to do your own research without interference."

"Actually, I wanted to check it over anyway. Cicero
Chen was just telling me that the camel song is hard
on electronic equipment."

"So it is," he said with feeling. "But even if it
breaks, Gus will almost certainly be able to repair it.
Except perhaps if the lenses . . ."

A worried frown disturbed the serenity of his expression, and he took the analyzer down and laid it
on the sand. Was he in the faction that wanted her to
succeed? Perhaps, but Irene still bent over the lock
pad to hide the combination as she punched it in. To
think she'd considered the lock a foolish precaution,
in the small, tight-knit community on the *Stanley*. To
open the case and set up the analyzer was the work
of seconds—it took longer to pull off the cover and
reach the gleaming lenses, but they were all intact.
Irene sighed with relief, and Ravi nodded.

"They don't usually break anything as sturdy as
thick glass. But you may find, when you actually come
to use it, that you need to make some adjustments."

"The lenses are the important part," said Irene,
closing the analyzer back into its protective shell. "Unless those subharmonics will affect software? I didn't
think so. Well, thank you Mr. . . . ?"

"I am Ravi," he said, reaching into his pocket.
"And I should tell you that I also took the liberty of
removing these"—he handed her a pile of nuts and

bolts—"and substituting something a little more comfortable for both you and your friend here."

The bolts in her makeshift saddlebags had been replaced by neat stitches. There was also a thick pad between Cow's back and the plastic.

"Thank you," said Irene. "I appreciate all the support I can get."

"You're welcome. Many of us support you, Dr. Olsen. One thing you may not have learned was that we also discussed how hard it would be on you, having Mark snatched away without a word. We felt, and feel, quite guilty about it." His lips twitched. "Play your cards right, and you could live off guilt alone for several months."

Irene smiled. "Thanks, but no thanks. When I'm not doing my research, I'd rather work for my supper, since, believe me—"

"You don't want to hear her sing for it," Mark chimed in.

"Is there something I could do around here, Mr. Ravi?" Irene went on. "Do you people have any . . . any job openings?"

"Just Ravi," he corrected her. "Most of us have invented a job that suits us, and in truth, your research is all we ask of you. But if you choose to, you can easily earn your keep by pitching in whenever extra hands are needed, as Mark does."

She turned to Mark, brows lifted, for he seemed too weak to work at much of anything.

He grinned. "Who do you think peeled all the vegetables in that stew?"

Irene's heart swelled. He'd hated his helplessness, his dependence so much; she should have known he'd start asserting independence as soon as he could. Some of her pride must have showed in her smile, for Mark's cheeks darkened.

"It's just vegetabling." He clambered aboard his

kneeling camel, leaned forward, and patted its hump, and the beast surged to its feet and walked off.

"He's a fine, young man," said Ravi quietly. "Don't work too hard. We owe you some atonement."

"I'd rather have information," said Irene. "If you're feeling that guilty."

The ancient eyes sparkled. "Not quite *that* guilty, I'm afraid. No one will give you any information—that was part of the compromise that allowed you to do your research. A community as small, as interdependent, as ours cannot afford revolutionaries—or saboteurs. I wish you a pleasant night's journey, Irene." He pulled a pair of sandals from his capacious pockets, gave them to her, and turned away, acknowledging her final thanks with a brief wave.

It was good to know she had friends who would help her. With everything but the one thing that mattered.

The sandal straps were made of soft leather, with ankle ties like the old Romans wore. The soles were braided-leather thongs, stitched tight together and topped with a smooth inner sole that seemed to have been glued on with something rubbery. They were soft, flexible, and would protect her feet from the stones if they encountered another gravel plain, but there was no need for them on the smooth sand. Irene had already observed that the colonists went barefoot.

Except when they went on camel foot.

Throughout the encampment—or the place where the encampment had been—laden camels were swaying to their feet and moving out. Irene mounted Cow and tried Mark's trick, leaning forward and patting Cow's hump. To her delight, it worked like a charm—Cow lurched upright and set off after the others, like the well-trained beast she no doubt was. Now all Irene had to do was figure out the brakes and the steering.

The largest moon was rising as they departed, huge and benign, with a smaller companion preceding it.

Scattered over the swelling dunes, the colonists and their mounts looked like something from Earth's romantic past, except for the small matter of a few extra camel legs. And a spare eye, which was watching her.

"Valentino you're not," she told the camel drily. "But you can make up for it by finding Nola for me."

The eye blinked and focused elsewhere. Irene sighed.

She and Cow wandered among the loosely shifting groups of colonists for some time. Few were willing to talk to her, and even those few seemed awkward and unhappy. Afraid of even seeming to defy their precious council? Irene finally spotted Nola and, leaning, patting, thumping, and cajoling, persuaded Cow to walk beside the red-haired vet's camel.

"I think my steering is broken," she complained, ignoring the vet's cool stare. "I don't suppose you can tell me how to get this . . . this leggy sand sled to go where I want."

Nola snorted. "Sorry, most of us work out our own set of signals. You're doing fine."

"That's what everyone else has been telling me," said Irene. "But the person who trained Cow in the first place must have done something."

Nola shook her head. "Your camel—Cow?—was unclaimed. Like those others." She gestured to three riderless camels, wandering placidly among the rest. The reserve in her expression warred with something else, and Irene, curious, let the silence stretch.

Nola sighed. "I'm sorry for what we did to you, taking Mark that way, with you asleep. I felt like hell doing it, but . . ."

"You saved him," said Irene. "And I'm here now, anyway."

"One of the reasons I didn't want to take him was to *keep* you from coming here."

Irene fought to keep the anger out of her voice, and failed. "Even though he would have died?"

"Yes," said Nola, and the bleak defeat in that one

word shook even Irene's righteous outrage. Whatever it was that motivated Nola, it wasn't indifference.

"If you feel that way, surely you can give me some information about the organism—at least tell me what you call it?"

"Just say 'the organism,' everyone will know what you're talking about. With that stuff in your bloodstream, you don't have to care about any others." Nola's expression was wary, but at least she'd answered. "What have you been calling it?"

"Anomaly 1," said Irene. "That's how it came up on the analyzer's printout."

"Ah." Nola looked at Irene's saddlebags with longing. "Time was, I'd have killed for a portable microanalyzer. Ramon was our microbiologist, as well as our doctor. When he died, I . . . well, a lot of us took on some extra responsibilities then. I had to make all my observations in the lab back at the settlement. At six-to eight-month intervals, in between thawing and implanting embryos, manufacturing the few meds we still need, and—"

"You can use it," said Irene invitingly. "If you'll let me in on your research."

"No," Nola replied instantly. "If it was up to me, I'd dump it down a deep well and keep you tied hand and foot till your ship takes off. You've already learned too damn much."

Granite determination sat oddly on her round, freckled face. The soft creak of overstuffed saddlebags and the softer plod of camel steps were audible in the stillness. What the hell could be so important that this woman was willing to let children die for it? But Irene already knew that asking that question would get her nowhere.

"All right, could you at least give me some background on the biota of this world? Just general information?"

Nola hesitated. "What kind of information?"

"Well, to start with, why does everything have six legs?"

It was the most innocuous question Irene could think of, but the vet still hesitated before she replied.

"All the lower life-forms on this planet have trilateral symmetry. The change, in the upper forms, to mostly bilateral . . ."

Irene learned a great deal over the next several hours. Though none of it was immediately relevant to anomaly 1, all organisms existed in an environment, and the successful replication of that environment in the lab was part of her final task.

She learned about some of the adaptations of various animals to the desert, of mice who manufactured water in their bodies from the seeds they ate. That there were no birds here, but batlike mammals with two feet—opposable thumbs—and four wings who could hover in the air as if they had antigrav.

She also learned something about the cat that had attacked her.

"We call them dire cats," said Nola. "Though they aren't anywhere near as big as the prehistoric dire cats back on Earth. But they're the only large predator in the desert, and when you're looking at one close-up, they're plenty big enough."

"Does that happen a lot?" Irene asked warily. Her arm, which was healing so well she'd all but forgotten about it, throbbed at the reminder.

"No," said Nola instantly. "Almost never. We shoot them with fléchettes, you see. It doesn't kill, but it stings like crazy. After that happens once or twice, they avoid humans. I doubt you'd have been attacked if you hadn't been wearing that suit; it couldn't smell you, so it didn't know what you were. Once the suit was torn, it left you alone, didn't it?"

"Yes," Irene admitted. "I'm surprised you just sting them, instead of killing."

Nola grimaced. "The issue was . . . debated. But

even us nonpacifists had to admit that they're hard to
kill with a load of shot, and if you just wound them,
you're likely to end up dead before you can pump up
a second load. Stinging them with fléchettes from a
distance works, and it's a lot safer; for creatures that
aren't intelligent, they learn pretty quick. If you ever
go far from camp, take a fléchette gun with you. And
before you do that, have someone teach you to
shoot."

"I'll be allowed to leave the camp then?" Irene
asked drily.

"I don't know," said Nola slowly. "As long as
you're on foot, I don't see why not. While we're on
the subject, I want to take a look at your arm tonight.
It looks like it's healing OK—a dip in a life pool works
wonders on infections, but your skin might mend better with a stitch or two."

"Life pools?"

Nola had relaxed enough to smile. "What would
you call them?"

Miracle came to mind, but it sounded overly dramatic. "Why do the camels take people there?" Irene
asked. "Do we smell like their calves when we're sick,
or something?"

"That's one of our best guesses," said Nola.
"Though we don't know for sure."

She told Irene about some of the other guesses—a
few of the wilder ones made her laugh so hard Cow's
third eye blinked at her.

*She doesn't mind me knowing about the pools. But
if that's not what they're protecting, then what . . .*

Irene learned that most of the planet's predators
had lost their third eye, though many still had vestigial
traces, and most prey animals had kept it.

"That's one of the things we do for the camels—
the dire cats hunt them, but with us around they're a
lot safer." Yet there were still many herds of unclaimed camels, Nola told her. The colonists tried to

lure them to join their herds, but they seldom succeeded.

She went on to talk about the great trees they called stilties, whose roots reached down farther than the colonists had ever been able to dig, and which nurtured their own, distinct ecosystem in their branches. Irene learned of the rocky ridges, and the animals who lived only there, including the small, fast-breeding, goatlike creatures, who were the dire cat's favored prey.

They'd eaten lunch, and the big moon had crossed the sky and set, when Irene finally had to plead, "enough," for her mind was clogged with information.

Cow moved away from Nola's camel willingly, and Irene rode alone, thinking. After a while she noticed several colonists pulling their camels aside, and becoming curious, urged Cow after them.

When they reached the hollow between a couple of dunes, the others were pulling out shovels. Irene recognized Maureen Greville among them, and the young man, Eric, whom she'd met at the settlement.

He was the only one who smiled at her, so when Cow knelt for her dismount Irene went over to him, trying to ignore the others' stony stares.

"What's going on?"

"We're gleaning, ma'am. Gathering food on the move." He gestured with his shovel at half a dozen scrawny, skeletal bushes. They had only a handful of leaves between them—to Irene's park- and hydroponic-accustomed eyes, they looked like plants in their death throes.

"Those are edible?"

"The roots are. If you like turnips. You can have a slice when we bring one up." A spark of mischief lurked in the respectful eyes. Good. Irene had no desire to perch on a pedestal.

"Can I help?"

They had only one shovel apiece, but a middle-aged

(or middle-aged-looking) man named Burt admitted that he had a spare shovel head to lend her, and even the damp sand beneath the surface yielded easily to the tough plasticine.

Which was good, for they had to dig down over four feet to reach the misshapen, brown globes that decorated the plant's roots.

The colonists' wariness eased as Irene worked beside them. Perhaps after a while she wouldn't have to face icy hostility from half the people she met.

They took only a few of the many, cantaloupe-sized "turnips" each plant produced, and filled in the holes, assuring Irene (who really didn't care) that the plants would survive their depredations. Then, as promised, they peeled the tough outer skin from one of the largest, sliced it, and shared it out.

"I'm not that hungry." Irene's piece was as large as a small pie, its flesh a bright, acid-green.

"But it's good for you," a young woman who'd introduced herself as Nokomis assured her, dark eyes sparkling in her grave face.

"It's good for you," Burt admitted. "But it's, ah, a bit strong for most, raw like this. Your camel'll appreciate it, though."

Sure enough, most of the diggers were feeding their pieces to the camels, who chewed them happily.

Irene had never fed Cow before. She approached the task with some caution, for the camel's teeth were as big as the rest of her, but Cow showed no desire for "finger food" and bit neatly into the greenish root, her whiskers tickling Irene's hand.

Curiosity got the better of her and Irene took a cautious bite. Turnip. Not too bad. A little strong. She chewed. A bit stronger. A lot stronger. Saliva flooded her mouth, but couldn't combat the overwhelming, acrid taste.

Irene gave up and spit it out, then spit again and again, trying to rid her mouth of the bitter residue.

"Whouk, whouk, whouk," Cow puffed. *She* was ready for another bite. The colonists chuckled.

"You might have warned me," Irene told her mount. "Not that I'd have paid more attention to you than I did to Mark, but it would have been polite of you."

Cow chomped off a big bite of root, chewing steadily. Irene fought down another rush of saliva, though her stinging tongue and gums had begun to ease.

"You're talking to the wrong people," said Maureen Greville. Her voice was pitched low—too low for the others to hear.

Irene jumped and turned. "What do you mean? About anom—about the organism? Who should I talk to?"

Maureen shook her head, leaning casually on her shovel. *Nothing of importance being said.* "I have to live here. But you'll never get anywhere, unless you talk to the right people."

She turned and walked off, mounting up behind Eric. Didn't she have her own camel? And what the devil did she mean? As far as Irene could tell there wasn't a soul in the entire camp who'd give her even a hint, much less any meaningful information. But Maureen implied that someone would. She had to figure out who.

Chapter 7

It took the rest of the day to catch up with the other colonists, and Irene spent that time talking to each of her companions in turn, trying to make her questions sound casual. Who in the group knows the most about this planet? Its biology? Its ecosystem? Its weather? She rapidly realized that she not only didn't know who to talk to, she didn't know what questions to ask.

At camp that morning, dinner was indeed a repeat of lunch—pan bread, camel cheese (hard, and surprisingly good) and dried fruit with a yellow skin and reddish flesh that was mild, sweet, and tasted nothing like turnips. Though judging by the vegetables she helped Mark peel, tomorrow's breakfast stew would contain turnips in abundance.

She had only half an hour before the sun rose to set up her analyzer and take samples. She had to tighten four screws and readjust a clamp, but the camel's song had done no real damage.

Mark's blood also contained the creature she now instructed her analzyer to list permanently as anomaly 1.

The slanting light carved shadows over the dunes. Mark, stretched out under the tent, was already dozing. The camels had turned their backs to the sun, folding down to sleep. Irene rubbed the back of her neck wearily. Time for one more sample, and she knew just who she wanted to take it from.

"Cow? Don't worry, this won't hurt a bit. . . ."

She dragged her analyzer into the tent once she'd filled the hollow slide, for the sun already beat down with appalling force. Cow's blood also held the organism—no surprise, since Nola had spoken to Mark about its "hosts," but still . . .

She watched the organism squirming among Cow's blood cells till the sample died. Heat and concentration had given her a fierce headache. She needed more time. And an air conditioner. And her lab back on the *Stanley*. Irene locked down the analyzer, wet her shirt with water from her drinking flask, wrapped it around her head, and went to sleep.

During the next night's ride she talked to Ayanna Ngazi, a tall, black-skinned woman, who seemed to know all there was to know about the plants of Navohar's desert. Unlike most of the colonists, she'd signed on as a botanist and it was still her primary job. She answered all Irene's questions without hesitation, for she'd never done any work on the organism and knew little about it, though she wished Irene well.

She was a member of Gus's faction, and her manner was pleasant, even friendly, but for all that she was hard to talk to, for she had a tendency to fall silent after answering and Irene had to work to keep the conversation going. She wasn't being obstructive; it was as if silence was her natural state, and she couldn't quite hide her relief when Irene finally gave up and left her alone.

Sondi, the colonist's huntress, didn't approve of what Irene was doing; the only reason she spoke to Irene at all was because she didn't want to offend Mark's aunt. She thought before answering any question, to be certain she wasn't giving too much away, but she was willing to tell Irene about the planet's larger life-forms, their tracks and habits, what they ate, and where they could be found at different times of the night. She had no idea which of them might carry the organism. At least, that was what she said.

Unlike the other colonists, Sondi demanded an exchange of information—for each question Irene asked she asked one of her own, and most of them led back to Mark. Soon Irene, who liked talking about her nephew, was telling Sondi more than Sondi told her. Then they got onto the subject of fléchette guns, which was one of Sondi's passions.

Irene learned that the light, long-barrelled air guns had a maximum effective range of about a hundred feet with fléchettes, and two hundred feet with shot. They were mostly made of plasticine, as were the loads they fired, though their rifled barrels were lined with steel. When Sondi began to lecture her on how many times you needed to pump the gun to kill such and such a creature, at such and such a range, Irene called a halt, but she did let Sondi talk her into a shooting lesson.

"When we get there," Sondi said. And Irene realized for the first time that she had no idea where they were going.

"Get where?"

Sondi blinked. "A grassy place, of cour—oh, I see. The camels find them, so I'm afraid I can't tell you when we'll reach one. The dune grass can live under the sand for years, then the wind exposes it, a little water hits and bang—grass fields. They run for kilometers, sometimes. When we find one, we stop there till the camels graze it off. Dig a well. That's when I'll teach you to shoot."

And that would be when Irene got a chance to do some serious work on anomaly 1. Impatience itched.

As they slept that day, small, trilateral, multilegged beetles dug up through the sand and took some blood samples of their own—or so the colonists told Mark and Irene the next evening when they exhibited the itching welts.

They were referred to Nola for salve, and found they weren't the only victims. In fact, there was a line.

"I can't believe this didn't wake me up." Mark was pale with revulsion under his freckles. But, Irene noticed with satisfaction, he wasn't leaning on his canes as heavily as he had a few days ago.

"The bite probably didn't hurt much," she told him. "Just like mosquitos back on Earth."

Mark, dome-born, had never been bitten by mosquitos. "It's just too weirding. It creeps me."

Lined-up colonists, six deep in either direction, snickered.

"You'll get used to it, kid," said an older woman in front of him. The expression on her weathered face was more sympathetic than her brisk words. "If we move camp just a few klicks, we can usually get out of their range, so it's not so bad. Mosquitos could fly."

"That's all you can do?" Dismay filled Mark's voice. "Move camp after you've been bitten?"

"Well, there's the salve."

"How well does it work?" Irene asked.

Nola, now only four colonists away, looked up indignantly. "It works very well."

The old woman in front of Mark smiled. "Fair to middling," she murmured.

As they left the vet, astringent grease already soothing their wounds, Maureen Greville fell into step beside Irene. She had a swollen welt on her neck—perhaps that was why she looked so aggrieved.

"I told you, you'll never figure it out if you don't ask the right people." She murmured. She was trying to sound mysterious, but it came out waspish.

"Tell me who to talk to, and I'll be happy to try to accommodate you," she said politely.

Maureen got the point—her lips snapped into a tight line, and she stalked away, an impressive feat in the shifting sand.

"That is one unhappy lady." Mark gazed after her,

his bites forgotten. "I wonder what she means. Sondi says no one in camp will break the agreement. They wouldn't tell me anything either, not even before you came."

"Hmm. I'm beginning to wonder if she's trying to pull something, though I can't imagine what. Or why."

Mark shrugged. "Who knows? You have to feel sorry for her, though."

"You do?"

"Don't you remember?" Mark's brows lifted. "Auntie, you read that log. *Greville*. She's the one whose husband and sons were killed by the kong."

"But that was . . ." Forty years ago. When she'd read that story, her mind had filed it under ancient history, participants either very old or dead. But on this world, forty years wasn't so long; the people in that log were all around her. It was hard for her subconscious to keep up with these things. She was still yawning through the nights.

That night Irene noted that Maureen was mounted behind a different colonist. Why didn't she ride her own camel? As far as Irene could tell, only the youngest children rode with their parents; everyone over the age of about ten rode by themselves, except Maureen. Her new doubts about the woman's sincerity itched like . . . like blood-beetle bites. She needed confirmation.

Since their first quarrel she'd been avoiding Gus Sardakowski, so the startled suspicion that swept over his face as she urged Cow over to walk beside his Kirk was probably natural. He smoothed out his expression and smiled at her.

"Hello, Goodnight. You seem to be settling in very well. Can I help you with something?"

He sounded like a well-trained clerk, facing an unreasonable customer. Irene's temper flared. "Not at all," she said with sweet insincerity. "Everyone's been very kind, for jailers."

Gus's lips tightened, but Irene spoke before he could. "No, I'm sorry, I don't mean that. They really have been kind." Why did she always want to snarl at this man? *Tact, Goodnight, remember?* But she already knew that friendly smiles wouldn't work on Gus. So how about a surprise assault?

"You're making a good impression, too," Gus told her. "People who're willing to work are appreciated here."

Irene shrugged. "By the way, I've been told that I'm asking the wrong people about the organism—any idea who the right ones are?"

She didn't expect an answer; the shocked alarm on Gus's face told her all she needed to know. He controlled his expression quickly, but not quickly enough, and one look at her smug grin revealed it.

"Who the hell told you that?"

"It doesn't matter." Irene was beginning to enjoy herself. "Tell me, do you ever play poker?"

She talked to Gus for some time, once he stopped badgering her to name her "source," and she'd promised not to spring any more traps on him. He told her about a spring by some cliffs, deep in the desert, Oasis, where all the colonists summered together, and that the groups they traveled with during the winter changed each year. "If I could get hold of one of your deep-cell batteries and rig it into our hoverbarge, we'd move the settlement there, and some of us could stay year-round. Make a start at actually settling this planet, instead of drifting across it."

But he loved the nomadic life, too, and in forty years of it had collected enough stories to leave Irene's ribs aching with laughter. He tried several times to turn the conversation to her, but she answered shortly and finally left him. A lifetime spent in microbiology labs didn't produce many humorous anecdotes.

But it did give you something to do. Irene spent the next few nights talking to other colonists without learning a thing about anomaly 1. She scraped together enough time when they made camp in the evenings to take a dozen more blood samples and confirm that all the colonists and camels she tested carried anomaly 1. Gus had told the truth about peoples' willingness to give blood samples. Even Nola, who Irene gathered was a ringleader of the opposing faction, rolled up her sleeve without hesitation.

But if she learned little more about anomaly 1, she did find out that Ravi, as well as an astronavigator and a tailor, was a practicing Yogi. "We make the best tailors," he told her, looking remarkably comfortable for a man whose legs were twisted into a pretzel, "because we already have the position down pat."

He made her a soft, loose, cottony shirt and a pair of trousers to replace her torn and dirty suit liner. And he made Mark a shirt, embroidered with an intricate frieze of dancing skeletons. Disco dancing.

"It doesn't freak Sondi," Mark told Irene when she protested. "She thinks it's gravely."

As a kitchen assistant she talked to Cicero Chen a lot, learning about the edible flora and fauna of the planet—none of which carried anomaly 1 as far as she could determine. Cicero too had been attacked by a dire cat, and had the scars to prove it. "Which is why I now carry a fléchette gun when I go gleaning, as well as my harvesting knife. It was the most terrifying thing ever to happen to me, but at the time . . . I was too scared to take time to be scared, if that makes any sense."

Irene, remembering her own white-out terror, began to look forward to her shooting lesson.

That day they camped by a rock ridge. Lower and older than the one Irene had crashed the sled on, it only rose a dozen feet from the sand at its tallest. The scattered stones made Ravi's sandals very welcome, though wearing anything on her feet felt strange, after even those few barefoot days.

It wasn't until evening, packed and ready to leave, that Irene spotted the streak of dark green that marked a water source.

A water source that might contain a sample of anomaly 1? Possibly. A sample not contaminated by her blood. Gus had said she could do any research she wanted to.

Mark and Ent had already gone, to ride with Sondi, probably. Irene went over to where Cow crouched, saddlebagged and ready for mounting. "Sorry, girl. We're not going anywhere yet."

She extracted the heavy microanalyzer from one bag and the biosample kit from the other and went over to the water source. She understood why the colonists had ignored it—just a trickle, creeping from a crack low in the rocks to vanish in the sand. One, perhaps two cups an hour. Not worth gathering, even though the big water bags were getting soft and shapeless. The camels had to be getting thirsty, too—Cow's humps were beginning to get flabby—but no one else seemed worried, so Irene had decided she wasn't either.

It was the work of seconds to fill a slide. She trudged back to Cow, waving to several of the colonists who were on their way out. She was setting up the analyzer when Kirk and Gus plodded up.

"Trouble packing, Goodnight?"

"Not at all. I've decided to seize the opportunity and do a little research," Irene said airily. "Since I know for a fact that camels can be several hours behind, and still catch up with the rest."

Kirk sniffed at Cow, and *whoof*ed. Gus was silent.

Irene put her hands on her hips. "Look, you said I

could do any research I wanted. If you think you're going to maroon me in a camp where there's no fresh water source and keep me from finding it that way, then think twice, Sardakowski, because—"

"Oh, the seep. No, I don't care if you check it out. As long as you don't care if someone stays with you. Just to be certain you find your way back to us."

"I wasn't even thinking about that!" said Irene indignantly. And she wasn't—she needed a lot more information before she escaped.

"Then you won't mind if someone stays, will you?"

Irene scowled. "Actually, I do mind. I hate people looking over my shoulder while I'm working."

"I'll tell them to keep out of your way until it's time to leave. But when that time comes, I do want you to leave; you could survive a day on the sand, with just Cow for shade, but you wouldn't enjoy it."

Which was probably true. "All right," said Irene grudgingly. "Bring on your guard. I won't stay too long."

Gus snorted. "If you got involved, you'd forget the time till the sun got in your eyes. And then you'd only turn around. You need to leave before Pipsqueak is at the top of the sky, or you won't catch up with us before daybreak."

"Pipsqueak?"

"The smallest moon." Gus pointed. It was about thirty degrees above the horizon, sharing sky with one of the mid-sized moons. A long-forgotten question stirred.

"How many moons does this planet have?" Irene asked.

Gus's brows lifted. "Five. The smallest is Pipsqueak. It moves faster than any of the others. Closest orbit."

Which meant she only had a few hours. But still . . . "OK, finish up before Pipsqueak reaches the top of the sky."

Gus grinned. "If you're looking for—what are you

calling it? Anomaly 1?—in that water seep, you'll be leaving a lot sooner than that."

He clucked to Kirk, who ambled off, leaving Irene frowning after him. So maybe it wasn't in the water after all. She'd wondered, when she found so many camels carried it, if it might be contagious. But if it was, what were the life pools for? To hell with Gus, she had work to do.

Her guard arrived in a few minutes, a dark-skinned boy about Mark's age, who Irene had assumed was of the opposition since he'd always refused to speak to her and glared whenever he saw her. He was glaring now, but he did it from a distance, so she ignored him.

She spread her suit-liner shirt and set up the analyzer, its sterile, artificial light flooding over the dirty cloth and the sand beyond. It looked brighter than before, on a night lit by just two of the smaller moons.

?— prompted the screen.

Scan for Anomaly 1.

Sample?—

Desert Water 1.

Begin?—

Y., Irene typed. Then she settled down to wait. The night was still, almost windless. She suddenly realized that she didn't have a fléchette gun; she hoped her guard did. He probably did, to use on her if necessary, but he'd intervene if she were attacked, and dire cats weren't supposed to attack people they could smell anyway. They could probably smell Irene twenty klicks away at that point. She'd been braiding her greasy hair into a plait down her back in the evenings, and then trying to forget about it; everyone else in the camp was in the same shape, but Lord, she'd love a bath.

The cursor blinked patiently. The guard kid scowled. Cow chuffed impatiently, and Irene wandered over and scratched beneath her narrow jaw, as she'd seen other colonists do. "Not much longer, my friend."

And it shouldn't be; even this pygmy-brained analyzer should be able to find a sample of a single organism, already in its files, quite quickly. Quicker than
this, in fact.

Long before the print scrawled across the screen,
Irene knew what it would say.

Anomaly 1 not found.

Irene checked another sample, and even looked herself to be sure. There were a few things swimming
around under the slide, but none she saw approached
anomaly 1's monstrous complexity, not even in a lar-
val stage.

Rats.

So it didn't live in fresh water, which probably
meant its origin was something that got into the pools.
And only into some pools; otherwise, all the original
colonists would have survived. Or had they sterilized
their water, and only stopped when the disease wore
them down too much to bother? Possibly. She'd have
to ask. She kept forgetting that the people around her
were the original colonists. She wondered if they'd tell
her the truth.

Irene packed up again. At least the small moon,
Pipsqueak, hadn't reached its apogee. Her guard
hadn't bothered her. And she hadn't been eaten by a
dire cat. *Look at the bright side, Goodnight.*

Irene finished storing the sample kit and put her
knee on Cow's middle shoulder to mount, but the moment she did, Cow heaved herself up, pitching Irene
to the sand.

"What? You stupid brute, give me a chance to get
on! You're too tall—"

Cow turned away from Irene and shambled off into
the dunes.

"You think I'm going to run after you?" Irene
yelled. "No way. Get back here, you stupid cow!"

But Cow didn't turn, not even her head, though
Irene sensed that hair-buried, third eye watching her.

She spun and called to the guard kid. "I don't suppose you want to do something useful for a change?"

His scowl had been banished by a wide grin. "Can't say that I do, ma'am." His camel trotted off, its wide feet kicking up spurts of sand, passing the slowly plodding Cow with ease.

Irene looked after Cow and folded her arms, not budging, hoping Cow could read her body language, since she wasn't responding to verbal commands.

Either she couldn't, or she didn't care, for her narrow rump kept right on receding. And with the guard kid's departure, Cow was Irene's only transportation. And she carried the precious microanalyzer.

Irene unfolded her arms and started walking. "Barbecued camel ribs," she muttered. "Camel burger."

At least her guard kept an eye on her . . . from a distance.

The small moon was sliding down the sky when Cow finally relented and knelt for Irene to mount. Irene was tired enough not even to consider kicking Cow in the ribs, or plucking her bald.

"But don't think this is over," she announced, settling between the comfortable humps. "Someday, somewhere, when you least expect it . . ."

Only that would be bad training. It had been a long time since Irene had a dog, but she knew that punishment had to follow bad behavior immediately, for animals weren't smart enough to connect current sensations with past events. And if she tried to discipline Cow now, she might end up back on foot. Irene sighed.

"OK, you win. This time." She'd ask the some of the supportive colonists how they handled it when their camels acted up.

It took most of the night for Cow to catch up to the others, and Irene was still tired, sore, and out of temper.

"Don't leave her sitting, loaded, so long," Gus told her, amusement lighting his mobile face. "She was probably angry with you."

Beneath him, Kirk began to puff, "*Whouk, whouk, whouk.*"

"She's not the only one," said Irene icily. But she got no better response from any of the other colonists. Even Mark, the traitor, only said, "Well, you could have taken the saddlebags off, couldn't you?"

"I didn't think about it," Irene admitted. "But that's not the point, damn it."

"It is to her," said Mark.

And Cow had succeeded in making it. The next evening, Irene threw the saddlebags over her back and scrambled up after them before Cow could even twitch. The furry sides between her legs heaved in a single *whouk*, and Cow rocked gracefully to her feet and ambled docilely after the others.

That night as she rode, Irene asked if the colonists had sterilized their water when they first settled the planet.

"But of course we did," Cicero Chen told her cheerfully. "And cooked our food well, too. Not that we believed then that alien bacteria could adapt to humans, but better safe than sorry. It was only after"—he stopped suddenly, looking remarkably guilty—"after we took to the desert that we lost that luxury." It was a smooth recovery, but Irene wished to God she knew what he'd been going to say.

She also asked about the moons. The next largest, bean-shaped, was called Grandfather, because it was bent over and had the longest cycle of the five. The round, mid-sized one was Seer, because one of its land features looked like an eye. The oval, mid-sized one was Rosebud, though to Irene's eye it looked more like an egg than a flower. And the largest was Big Ben, for obvious reasons.

Rosebud set, leaving only Seer and Grandfather, so

the ride was darker than usual; Cow's constant sniffing was all that warned Irene that they were finally approaching the grassy place.

In truth, it wasn't very impressive. Beginning with a few clumps of thin-stemmed grass, scattered over the dunes' gradual slopes and growing thicker in the hollows—it wasn't enough, she'd have thought, to set the colonists cheering.

The camels lifted their noses and bugled, almost as one. As soon as Cow's breath ran out, she broke into her bumpy trot, but stopped at Irene's yell of protest and swayed down to the sand.

Irene took the hint and dismounted, pulling off her saddlebags as well. Cow rose and joined the other camels, who were shedding riders and bundles as rapidly as they could, great teeth ripping through the wispy grass. So now what?

Ayanna Ngazi watched the grazing beasts, a huge smile creasing her calm, dark face. Irene approached her.

"Now what?"

The smile widened. "Now we get our shovels out."

"I don't need to, now," said Irene, and raised her brows as the botanist began to laugh.

"Sorry. You can't know. You can't *know*." Big Ben was rising, flooding the world with light, even half-full. Ayanna lifted her smile to the sky. "But you will. The shovels are to dig a well, and we'll start as soon as the camels show us where."

Irene, still incredulous, was assigned to the group Gus whimsically designated Camel Squad Fourteen. Whimsically, because the number before it was six, and the one before that, twenty-nine. Everyone seemed to be in a very good mood, though Mark, gazing around in astonishment, was as baffled as she was.

Camel Squad Fourteen's job was to "watch the cam-

els and yell if they started digging." No one else
seemed to find this odd, so Irene, who didn't think
Cow looked at all like a burrower, kept her mouth
shut and wondered why people weren't putting up
their tents. All the bundles were on the ground, but
except for a few shovels, no one took anything out.

She and the others assigned to camel squads spread
out over the dune tops. From the height where Irene
was told to watch, she could see that the grass field
was larger than she'd thought, stretching out of her
sight to the north and east. The handful of camels in
the hollows around her dune grazed steadily. Irene
wished she knew what she was looking for.

Then someone shouted, and the watchers on the
other dunes began to whistle and point toward the
young woman who was waving her arms, half a dozen
ridges from Irene. The others abandoned their dunes
and started toward her, and Irene, intensely curious,
broke into a jog.

Deep sand isn't designed for jogging, and Irene soon
had to drop to a walk—but not as soon as she'd have
had to when she first reached Navohar. Not so old
after all. She came around the last dune, cutting over
its lowest point, and found the camels, digging.

There were half a dozen in all, gathered close in the
hollow, and they stood on their front and back legs,
while their middle feet scraped away the sand almost as
efficiently as shovels. They'd already dug a respectable
depression, and seemed to be quite determined about
it.

But when the colonists arrived, carrying shovels and
meter-wide panels of curving plasticine, the camels
gave way to the colonists and went back to grazing.

"I'll bet they dig where the water is close to the
surface." It was Mark's voice, behind her, bright with
the excitement of figuring it out. "They dig their
own wells!"

"That's right." A young woman, passing with a shovel, grinned at him. "But we can do it better."

And they did. Thin, rigid plasticine bands were clipped into a wide circle, then the diggers stepped inside and scooped the sand from beneath it till the upper rim was only a foot above ground level. Another plasticine circle, just small enough to fit inside the first, was constructed, carried over, and laid in place, and the digging team started on the second meter of sand. This layer had cords attached to the rim, so it could be pulled up from the surface when the time came.

They drafted Irene to help move saddlebags from the edge of the grassy place to the long band of connected hollows where they were setting up "a real camp, for a while."

Carrying gear over the soft sand was probably as hard as digging, but Irene found enough breath to question her fellow sherpas.

"How do they know where to dig?"

"Smell the water, probably." The man she spoke to wasn't breathing nearly as hard as she was. "We used to double-check it with the seismocord. Set off charges. Big mess. And they were always right, anyway, so now we leave the seismocord back at the settlement. With any luck, we'll be bathing tomorrow."

A bath? Irene stopped in her tracks at the thought and had to jog to catch up. By the time she'd made four trips, she was feeling very grateful to Cow.

They set up camp with more care than usual, people spreading out a bit farther, placing their tents with consideration. Irene, who'd mastered tent setup over the last few days, helped Mark with their tent, then went to lend others a hand.

When she finished with Ravi's tent he told her to wait a moment, and burrowed into one of his bundles, emerging with two pair of loose trousers and two new shirts. The bottom shirt had a pattern of leaves embroidered around the open collar and loose cuffs. The top one had three plasticine buttons, which had been delicately carved into tiny skulls.

Irene's eyes filled—her throat was tight.

Ravi smiled. "If you think you're grateful now, wait till tomorrow—you'll *want* clean clothes then. Truly, it's no trouble for me. Sewing is one of the few tasks you can perform while riding a camel, and these simple patterns don't take long."

Irene stepped forward, leaning over the bundle of cloth between them, and stood on tiptoe to kiss his cheek—awkwardly, for it wasn't a gesture she often made, but she couldn't find the right words.

The sun was creeping over the horizon by the time they hauled the last diggers up from the bottom of the well. They looked tired, but pleased, and their trousers were wet.

"Up to our knees, already!"

Irene cheered along with the others—if water up to the knees would get her a bath tomorrow, that was plenty of reason to cheer. The colonists filled their own water flasks from the limp bags, then they dumped the remainder into one of Cicero Chen's big kettles for the camels to finish off.

The sun was hot on Irene's back, and her eyelids kept sinking. It felt like being up late, to be awake in the sunlight. How odd. She collected her yawning nephew and went to bed.

Whoops and shrieks of laughter awakened Irene the next evening. And a sound she hadn't heard for a while. Splashing.

"Come on." She nudged Mark's limp shoulder. "Bath time."

Irene had placed their tent over a low ridge, away from the well. Even slowing her pace for Mark's difficult steps, it didn't take long to skirt the small dune. Rosebud was high, half-full, and Seer, just a sliver, setting. Only Pipsqueak was rising full, but there was plenty of light to see the colonists, over half the camp, gathered around the wide, shimmering well, with their buckets, pans, and bundles of clean clothes set off to one side. They were naked.

Well, they're not going to bathe with their clothes on, are they? said a logical voice in the back of Irene's mind. The rest of her was frozen in her tracks.

She looked over at Mark, child of the new prudishness. His eyes were wide, his mouth round as a gasping fish's. Then color flooded his cheeks, and his gaze dropped to his feet.

The sight restored Irene's perspective, and she laughed. "Come on. I'll pour for you, if you'll pour for me."

"You're not serious." Mark's voice cracked, for the first time in four years.

"Oh yes, I am. When in Rome, you do like the Romans. Come on, kiddo. Into the valley of . . . whatever."

Life, her mind sang. *Life.*

It still felt strange at first, to see the faces she knew attached to bodies she didn't. Nola, washing with the smiling, quiet man Irene knew to be her husband, had the kind of figure women called plump and men described as "pocket venus." Ravi, who had already washed and was over by the clean clothes, dressing, had the slim, lithe form of a man half his apparent age, much less his real one. All that yoga, no doubt. Gus Sardakowski looked the most like himself, his body stocky, but firm, with a bit of a paunch and love handles over his hips. Irene realized she was staring; her face grew hot.

"Come on." She drew Mark around the edge of the crowd, to the rise where the clean clothes were stacked.

The small flock of children swarmed, shrieking through the crowd, throwing cups of water at each other and racing back to the well to reload, running carelessly around, and even under, the feet of the camels who came in twos and threes to drink from the trough the colonists had filled. It looked dangerous to Irene, but if neither their parents nor the camels objected, it was no business of hers.

Mark thanked Ravi for the new clothes. He looked grateful to have someone dressed to rest his eyes on.

Irene added her thanks, especially for the three pair of soft underpants, with drawstring waists, she'd discovered when she got back to her tent.

Ravi smiled away their thanks and left, which was fine with Irene. For all her brave talk, she really didn't want an audience when she undressed. On the other hand, she hadn't been kidding about what she'd do to get clean. She took a deep breath and pulled off her shirt, then unfastened her bra. It was far too dirty to put back on; she'd have to go without till she could wash it.

Mark's eyes were on his feet again. "Can't we wait till later?"

"Mark, this well won't be deserted till after sunrise. And . . ." she dropped her voice considerably ". . . I used to change your diapers, so there's nothing you've got—"

"Auntie! Do you mind?" But it brought his indignant, embarrassed gaze up to her face.

"I *don't* mind," said Irene. "And neither will anyone else. That's the point."

"You're track switching," Mark grumbled, but his gaze finally shifted to the others' naked bodies, and lingered. Until he saw Sondi, who was washing her long, dark hair—then he stopped being aware of Irene at all.

She was *washing her hair*. Mark could take care of himself—though if he watched Sondi much longer, he'd really be embarrassed to strip. It wasn't Irene's problem. She pushed off her trousers and underpants and stepped into the crowd. The air, still warm from the day's sun, grew cool and damp as she drew nearer to the well; she almost forgot her own nakedness, and the other nude bodies around her, as she gazed at the lapping water, only a dozen feet below the rim.

"Amazing," she murmured.

"Isn't it?" It was Gus's voice, beside her. "I've seen it hundreds, maybe thousands of times, but it always amazes me. The water table is very high under most of the dune mass; that's why they're stable. In the places where the water table's too low, the dunes will move fifty, sixty feet a year." He looked Irene over as he spoke, candid and casual. No big deal. The heat in her cheeks began to subside.

"Do you put any restrictions on its use?"

Gus shrugged. "Not when it's this high. Some commonsense stuff. It's drinking water so you don't dump anything into the well, or climb down to swim, but you can take out all you want and use it for anything you choose. Need a bucket?"

"Yes," said Irene, taking it gratefully. It was yellow plastic, like a child's beach toy, with a long, soft rope attached. "What do I use for—"

The children rocketed past, and a misaimed cup of water hit Gus squarely amidships. He raced after the squealing offenders, the dirty shirt he'd been using as a towel snapping fiercely, but never quite hitting anyone.

Irene watched, grinning, and then realized she was staring again. And at this point she was really more interested in finding some shampoo.

Mark finally worked up his courage and wobbled over to pour for her, though he still grumbled about "Romanizing." His ribs were stark under his skin, but he seemed to be putting on some muscle, Irene thought hopefully.

The stinking goo the colonists used for soap, shampoo, and laundry soap, they told her, made no suds and was acrid enough to make Irene's eyes water even though she didn't get any in them. However ghastly it smelled, it worked as advertised, the second rinse leaving her hair squeaking beneath her scrubbing fingers.

She would have washed it again, just for the pleasure of doing it, but Mark's knees were getting shaky, and he hadn't even had a chance to get clean yet.

Irene lowered the bucket into the luminous water and poured it over him again and again, though one bucket to wet and two to rinse were all he really needed. Watching Mark and Sondi pretending not to notice each other was worth the extra effort.

And Sondi was worth watching. *Face it, Goodnight, at forty-five, you just plain start to sag.*

Well, she had other virtues. Like intelligence, persistence, and a problem to solve. And time, thank God, to work on it at last.

Life in the settled camp was different from traveling. Cicero Chen hadn't been kidding about preparing more elaborate meals. And Ravi loaned her a small, multitiered rake he called a camel-comb and taught her how to brush Cow, and then separate the soft undercoat from the longer, coarser hair for his eventual weaving. Like the camels, it smelled vaguely musky and spicy, a scent Irene was beginning to like. But . . .

"Why, in a climate this hot, do they need all this hair?" After the first few days Irene had started combing some of the other, unclaimed, camels as well, those who carried loads for the colonists but had no steady rider. They adored being groomed, sometimes following her when she'd finished with them, nibbling her shoulder, begging for more.

"You won't ask that after your first ice storm," Ravi told her. "They're mostly a spring phenomenon, but we get them year-round, even in the summer. The temperature can drop from seventy or eighty to below zero in half an hour, and the windchill is unbelievable. Trust me, they need that hair."

But if there were other chores, including learning to treat the camels' corns, there was also far more leisure time—and Irene spent it working on anomaly 1. It took a lot of time, for even after Mark programmed her analyzer to locate the organism with some shortcut he called "quicking," she still had to make the observations herself.

It wasn't in the well water either—no surprise, for she'd already realized the life pools were somehow special. But she wasn't short of samples, since her own blood held an alarmingly plentiful supply of the things.

Or it would be alarming if Irene, observing hour after hour, hadn't seen what they did. They *ate* the bacteria she cultured from some spoiled cheese. They destroyed mutated cells that could lead to cancer. They . . .

"They really do mimic our immune systems," she told Mark one early morning, rubbing her weary eyes. Her neck and back ached too—she wasn't used to working with equipment on the ground. She couldn't have cared less. "They think they're Mr. Fix-it. They might even be *repairing* some of the cells that aren't too badly damaged, but I couldn't be sure. Mark, this thing, potentially, could cure almost any disease, even most birth defects, if you could get it to the fetus in the right stage. It's . . . it's the fucking holy grail of microbiology, and these people are sitting on it!"

Mark had spent most of the night out in the desert with Sondi, and some of the quiet calm that was so much a part of Ayanna Ngazi lingered in his eyes. "Why?"

"The ten-thousand-dollar question. And I think," Irene's weary eyes narrowed, "that I may know part of the answer."

"Which is?"

"Sex."
Mark began to laugh.

She was serious, though it took a long time to confirm it and not all her time was her own. That night, some of the small, six-legged mice gnawed through one of the plastic food chests, destroying the last of the pan bread Cicero had made at the settlement.

"Not that it would have lasted much longer," he said philosophically. "But now the rest will be *encouraged*."

So Mark grated turnip roots to pulp, and Irene and Cicero rubbed the juice liberally over all the chests that held food, including those in which he buried the camel cheese during the heat of the day. Irene also rubbed some over the microanalyzer's case—even though it didn't contain food. "The camel song is bad enough. If I have to cope with mice as well . . ."

They'd sung last night for over an an hour—it had taken Irene almost that long to readjust and retune all the things that had shaken loose, and she'd had to ask Gus to weld two severed electronic connections.

"Don't I know this? I had to discard two kettle bases afterward," said Cicero. "Cracked beyond repair. Thank goodness the plasticine of the kettles is too thick to crack."

"Can they really break plasticine?" Mark asked curiously. "Just by singing?"

"If it's thin, yes," Cicero told him. "That's why our tent poles are made of fiberglass. We used to use hollow plasticine rods, but when the camels started singing they snapped like . . . like goblets during a diva's aria."

Irene also learned to make several herbal teas over her very own cook fire, fueled, to her consternation, with dried camel dung.

Cicero laughed at her qualms. "Though I know how you feel; it was the same for all of us, at first. But their dung isn't nearly as moist as ours—it takes only a day in the sun to dry it completely, and it burns very clean. Truly, it does no harm."

Gathering the crumbling discs, Irene had to admit she didn't find them as offensive as she'd expected.

Sondi kept her promise to teach Irene to shoot. The mechanics of the fléchette guns were simple: rack one of the eight loads into the chamber, pump once for every eight yards you want to sting at, aim, and shoot. The explosive pop of air wasn't overly loud, and the recoil was tolerable. At the end of half a dozen lessons . . .

"I could hit a camel, broadside, at ten paces," Irene told her. "If it held still. I'd be better off with a club."

Sondi was still young enough to giggle. "You're not doing as badly as you think, it's just that the fléchettes scatter so wide. No aerodynamics. You'd do better with shot."

But shot was a hunting load and Irene wasn't interested in hunting, just warning off dire cats. So Sondi pretended to be a dire cat, creeping toward her till she ran out of cover, and then charging, yelling for Irene to fire her empty gun at sixty feet, three pumps—just a warning shot. Forty feet, two pumps—sting if you hit, but dispersal pattern too wide to be effective unless you're lucky. Twenty feet, just one pump, and sting like hell, but be sure you hit it because you probably won't get another chance.

To kill with fléchettes your best bet was to wait till the beast was less than ten feet away, and pump as often as you could—but not more than ten times, for ten was the maximum pressure, and if you tried to pump again, the lever would jam open and the gun refuse to fire.

"You're sure you don't have a spare club?"

"Don't worry about it," Sondi told her. "Most likely, any dire cat that gets a whiff of you will run in the opposite direction."

"How flattering."

Sondi giggled again.

In her free time Irene went right on observing anomaly 1—it took a lot of time, for the event she was watching for didn't happen often, and even Mark couldn't program her portable unit to recognize a particular behavior and record it. So Irene watched, and the longer she observed it, the more certain she became. The problem was sex. Or more accurately, reproduction.

There were two distinct varieties of anomaly 1—the type with the three-lobed nucleus, which she'd first seen, and another, with a two-lobed nucleus. Both types aggregated to breed—not a rare phenomenon, some Earth organisms did it as well. But when the three-lobed types gathered into a breeding cluster, they produced the two-lobed types. And when the two-lobed types aggregated, they produced nothing at all.

"Which is flat-out impossible," she complained to Mark. "Because if the primes—that's what I'm calling the three-lobed ones—produce only sterile offspring, then where the hell did they come from?"

"Four-lobes?"

"I thought of that. Oh, not four-lobed anomaly, but some sort of setup like bees have, with one fertile queen, and the rest male or sterile. But I don't think it would work for single-celled organisms; they aren't mobile enough for that kind of social order, and it doesn't take much to kill them—sometimes just a small change in the chemistry or temperature of their environment will do it. They have to be extremely fertile to survive."

"But if the . . . the queens lived in the life pools, that would explain why the pools were so special, wouldn't it?"

Such a bright kid. And all his intelligence, his laughter, his Mark-ness had nearly been wiped out. And other kids, as bright, as special, were dying by inches because Irene was stumped by a damn parasite.

"I considered that, too, but an open pool's an awfully precarious environment for microscopic organisms. They'd be far better off doing their breeding in a host, and then spreading into pools or whatever. So why don't they?"

"Maybe they do. Have you checked the camels' blood?"

"Yes," said Irene. "And it breeds the same way in their blood as it does in ours." She tried not to show how deeply that discovery had disappointed her.

Mark's gaze was thoughtful. "Have you considered that the colonists might be right? I know if there's an answer, you'll find it. But what if there is no answer?"

"I won't accept that," said Irene. "I can't accept that."

"No." Mark's smile didn't reach his eyes. "No, I don't suppose you can."

She asked Nola about it, though she didn't expect a reply, and was astonished when the vet smiled wryly. "If it only has to form a committee for sex . . ."

Does that mean it's smarter than we are? the old lab joke finished.

"I'm sorry," she went on. "I was beginning to hope you'd do better than I did. I'm still hoping, but I still won't help you."

She asked Maureen, who'd been a bit less aggravating since Mark helped her clean up the file system on her minicomp. Maureen called herself an archivist, but her real job, in this settled camp, was teaching the restless kid flock. Irene wasn't sure whom she pitied more, Maureen or the kids. Now she scowled at Irene.

"I told you, you aren't talking to the right ones. Until you do, you'll never figure it out." Her refusal to name these mysterious people left Irene gritting her teeth in frustration.

So she sought out other creatures to test. Some of

the burrowing creatures Sondi brought back for the pot had anomaly 1 in their blood, and some didn't. Sondi taught her to set snares for the scaly, hexapedal lizards that lived on and around the small rock ridge, about a kilometer south of camp. None of the reptiles, with their triangular heads and three bright eyes, carried either form of anomaly 1 in their blood, and the organism died when Irene tried to introduce it, though she couldn't tell why.

Nola's husband, who seemed to be a member of the supporting faction, had transformed a plastic crate into a lizard cage, on the condition that Irene killed them mercifully if she had to, and returned them to the rocks if she didn't.

Irene had no need to kill and was glad of it, for the lizards' bright-patterned scales were beautiful, and the third eye looked right on them. Irene had even begun to adjust to it in the camels.

She lured Cow in with a combing, then mounted, with the lizard she'd been working with in a sack across her lap, like people used to carry snakes. According to Nola and Sondi, there were no snakes on Navohar. She directed Cow out to the rocks without much trouble, though the camel paused to seize a bite or two. Her humps had plumped out again; Irene wondered how much longer she'd have before the ravenous camels grazed down the last of the grass, and they had to leave.

"You eat too much," Irene told the lazily watching third eye. "Not that I blame you. I suppose a life pool is the next step, but I have a feeling there's still something I'm missing. Something that's right here, if only I could see it. I hate that."

Cow blinked. Lizard claws pricked Irene's thighs through two layers of fabric. A man with a fléchette gun slung over his back, mounted on his own camel, followed her. Irene was getting used to being followed when she took Cow out of the camp—as long as they didn't stop her she didn't care, though it might throw a crimp in her escape plans. Assuming she ever learned enough to want to escape.

When they reached the rocks, Irene let Cow go— she'd walk back. It would give her a chance to think.

The lizard scurried out of the sack and ran a dozen yards. When Irene didn't move, it decided it was safe and settled down on the sun-warmed rocks to heat its body.

Irene sat too, trying to figure out why anomaly 1 didn't survive in reptiles—too much fluctuation in temperature? But it survived greater variations in the slides. She tried to think further, but the quiet of the night, bright-lit with all the moons but Grandfather in the sky, crept into her mind and drained it, till she just sat, even when she heard the plod of approaching camel feet.

"What are you doing, Goodnight? I—we expected you back half an hour ago." It was Gus. She felt too lazy even to look around.

"My watcher reported in, I see. I decided to walk back."

"So what are you doing?"

Irene's lips twitched. "Lizarding."

"As Mark would say." She could hear the laughter in his voice. "It is contagious, isn't it? Shall I leave you to your lizarding, then?"

"No, stay and frustrate me. That's what everything else is doing." She looked up at last, smiling to take the sting out of it.

Gus slid off Kirk's back without waiting for the camel to kneel and slapped his shoulder in dismissal. "Don't be frustrated. You've learned as much in a few weeks as Nola did in years."

"That's because I have a portable analyzer, and she doesn't. Have I learned anything she didn't? I thought not. In fact, I haven't learned anything a first-year grad student couldn't have figured out. Gus, I *need* my lab back on the *Stanley*. This half-assed 'let her work but don't tell her anything' approach is ridiculous."

"It's a compromise," said Gus ruefully. "And I'm afraid it's proving as successful as most compromises."

"Pleasing no one?" Irene snorted. "Wonderful."

Gus laughed. "Cicero calls it small-town democracy at its worst. We wanted, at first, to give everyone the maximum possible amount of individual liberty—freedom of conscience. But in an interdependent group like this we *have* to cooperate on matters that affect us all if we're going to survive. That involves a lot of compromises, I'm afraid. But there's no rush. Your Willard hasn't given up yet."

Irene scowled, for she, too, had heard the flitters hum by, in the sleepy heat of her tent.

"He's not my Willard, and I can't believe no one but Nola has researched this thing," she grumbled. Like the mysterious "right people" Maureen kept hinting about. *Come on Sardakowski, take the bait for once.*

Gus smiled. "If it's heavy, you can't take it. If it's fragile, it's broken. If it's small, it's lost. Most lab equipment falls into one of those categories."

"Huh?"

"It's a Bedouin proverb. Wait till a gust of wind blows sand into your analyzer—you'll figure it out fast."

"I already have," said Irene grimly. "It was worse than camel song."

Grandfather crept over the horizon, and was instantly greeted by a dozen melodious *nah-woooons*. More voices took it up, the night echoing with the multistranded chorus. The camels were howling.

"Oh no," Irene moaned. She could see them in the distance, leggy clumps, decorating the dune tops. "Do they do that whenever all five moons are up?"

"And sometimes on other nights, if it's very bright.

Or to call someone in, like they did when Cow brought you back. Or when a calf is born—they'll howl all night then, and we do major repairs the next night. But we don't grudge it. They only give the moons half an hour or so."

A fresh wave of song swelled, and Irene's heart rose with it. "It's beautiful."

Gus smiled at the largest moon, then threw back his head and added a high, yipping howl of his own. His smile stretched to a grin at Irene's astonishment. "It's something of a tradition at this point, to howl with the camels."

Listening for it, Irene could hear other human calls coming from the camp, a fragile lacework, hemming the camel's rich chorus.

"You're mad," she said with conviction. "The whole lot of you."

"Why? You said you liked it. Why not join in?"

"Thank you, but I don't think so," said Irene. "My mother raised me as a human child, not a wolf cub."

But even the human's attenuated voices couldn't detract from the camels' feral song. The resonant conch calls fell away and added themselves as harmoniously as the dunes curved into each other. Irene watched the night, unaware of Gus watching her. When they walked back to camp, the camels sang them in.

Even after the camel song faded, Irene carried its memory. She skirted the others' tents, in no mood for conversation. She still had time to look at one more sample before lunch. Perhaps if—

"I can't believe you haven't figured it out yet." Maureen Greville stood squarely in her path, her thin face pinched with annoyance and some other emotion Irene couldn't identify.

"A child could have figured it out by now, and at least tried to deal with the right ones, but not you. Not the expert—"

"If you'll tell me whom to speak to," said Irene politely. "I'll do so. If you don't intend to tell me, then you're wasting both our time." In about two seconds she was going to stop being polite.

Maureen looked around, shifty, furtive. There was no one within earshot, for they'd both kept their voices low, but there was no such thing as a really private conversation, unless you went into the desert.

Irene's heart began to pound. Maybe Gus was wrong about the degree of cooperation his council exacted.

"You were talking to the right ones earlier tonight. I saw you."

"You mean Gus?" Irene tried to sound casual—luring. Was someone finally going to tell her something that mattered? "But he won't say any—"

"Not Gus, you overeducated idiot!" Maureen's voice dropped even lower, shivering with frustrated fury. "The *camels*."

"What?" The statement made no sense at all.

Maureen's breath hissed through clenched teeth. She took Irene's arm and pulled her along—just two women, having a casual chat. As long as no one caught a glimpse of their faces.

"Think about it, genius. Who took you to the life pool?"

"Well, Cow, but—"

"Who took Mark there? Who was all but battering down the clinic door to get to him?"

"But . . ." Irene fell silent.

"Who's been bossing you around ever since the two of you met? You can't possibly have deluded yourself that you control that beast?"

"But the camels aren't intel—Wait a minute." Irene dragged her to a stop, not giving a damn who saw. "Are you trying to tell me you think the *camels* are intelligent?"

"Finally," Maureen's eyes rolled, "the message gets

through. Not only are they intelligent, but they control
the life pools. They're the only ones who know where
they are. The only ones who know how they work. So
unless you find a way to talk to them, genius, you're
shit out of luck."

Chapter 8

Gus was sitting cross-legged, in front of his tent. Something that looked like a circuit diagram was drawn in the smooth patch of sand before him, but he stared into space, the stick in his hand motionless.

Irene stopped just in front of the drawing, so fast her heels sank into the sand, and he smiled up at her.

"So we meet again. What is it? You look—"

"I've just been told that the camels are . . . are . . ." She couldn't even say it aloud, ingrained paranoia about intelligent aliens warring with utter disbelief— this was *Cow* they were talking about!

Gus sighed. "I suppose it was inevitable. Maureen, I take it? Oh yes, we've noticed her stalking you. You don't need to answer. She hasn't been able to think of anything but getting off this world since we first learned about your ship. She thinks if you can get the organism to survive off planet, she could go back with you without having to spend the next decade in quarantine. From what you told me, I'd guess she's dream—"

Irene didn't care about Maureen Greville. "Intelligent?"

"Yes. They are."

"You don't mean like a bright dog, you mean intelligent intelligent?"

"Yes. Intelligent. More or less like we are."

"What kind of IQ are you talking about?"

Gus's lips twitched. "That's . . . difficult to determine. They—"

"Then what proof do you have that they're intelligent. I mean, intelligent—"

"Intelligent," Gus finished. "We've lived with them, and among them, for almost forty years. We've observed their behavior. But if you want stand-up-in-court proof, we don't have any. That's part of the problem."

"So they might not be any smarter than a bright dog. Or a dolphin. You can't prove otherwise."

"No, we can't."

"So you're not really certain—"

"Yes, we are."

Irene scowled, baffled by his determination. He wasn't an irrational man. Or a fool. His reasons might not be susceptible to proof, but they had to be strong, or he wouldn't hold to them so strongly. "Do you need this drawing?"

"No."

Irene dropped to sit in front of him, and tried logic. "Intelligence only evolves in tool-using species. It evolves to *enable* them to use tools."

"Nothing moves faster than the speed of light."

"Huh?"

"What goes up must come down. The sun revolves around the earth. Yet another scientific theory encounters reality, and bites the dust."

"So why would creatures that can't use tools evolve intelligence? What advantage would it give them?"

"Maybe the ability to communicate more clearly? Handy for a prey species to be able to say, 'I think I smell a dire cat behind the third rock left of that bramble bush. How about you, Charlie?' "

"You think they communicate? Clearly? With a language?"

"With a degree of precision that would require a language, or some equivalent, yes, they do."

"But they only sing about once a week! Maybe less."

"Their song probably is one type of communication. The subharmonics travel far enough to reach other herds. But you're right, they don't seem to have any form of speech for close-range conversation."

"So how do they—"

"We don't know."

Irene clutched her hair. "This is impossible!"

"Anything's possible, Goodnight. Haven't you learned that yet?"

Irene snorted. "You have no idea how they communicate, but you're certain they do?"

"We have theories. Short-range telepathy is a popular one."

"Yeah, right."

"I know, I know, the oldest science-fiction cliché. Maybe it's not that. Maybe they secrete pheromones. They have a very keen sense of smell. Maybe they wave their eyelashes in flag signals. We've never figured out how they communicate—and believe me, we've tried. But we know that they do."

"By observing their behavior."

"It's an accepted method."

"It isn't proof."

"We don't need proof," said Gus placidly.

It stopped Irene cold for several seconds. "OK, if they're so smart why do they carry us, and our stuff, around all the time? What's in it for them?"

"Grooming? Corn cures? All right, how about a reliable, plentiful water supply? We can dig wells deeper and better than they can. And we do help protect them from the dire cats. But frankly, I think it's both simpler and more complex than that. I think they like us."

Irene rubbed her temples. "And you know this by observing their behavior?"

"No, that's just a guess. And it may be based on

wishful thinking at that. Nola thinks they keep us as pets."

Irene's head spun. For a moment she saw humans through the eyes, the mind, of an intelligent camel—puny, naked, jabbering creatures, *but my dear, their little antics are ever so amusing*.

"No!"

Gus began to laugh. "How would we know? But if it's any consolation, I think it's a more equal relationship. They carry us to new hunting and harvesting, provide milk and wool, and take care of us. We protect them, provide medical care and water, and take care of them. And we like them. And they act as if they like us. It sounds like friendship to me."

"At least we don't have to worry about *them* conquering Earth," said Irene grimly.

All the wry amusement slid out of Gus's expression. "No. That's not what we worry about."

It really didn't matter, except for anomaly 1. If the camels were the only ones who could locate the life pools—whether by scent or by . . . other methods—then Irene had to convince Cow to take her to one.

"This is a very simple test, Cow," said Irene clearly. She felt ridiculous, and the colonists who gathered in the vicinity, carefully pretending not to watch, only made it worse.

Maureen wasn't among them; she'd been placed under twenty-four-hour watch, and forbidden to go near either Irene or Mark. Which made Irene wonder what *else* Maureen hadn't told her, but the other colonists' anger that Maureen had broken their pact was so deep, even among Irene's supporters, that she didn't dare challenge their decree. At least they didn't seem to blame her; Irene had enough to worry about.

Cow's big, front eyes regarded her lazily. Her smug expression, as always, never changed—her teeth ground the bitter turnip root Irene had given her. It had taken the rest of the night before to dig up a plentiful supply and borrow three colorful, plastic tubs.

Nola, amusement momentarily overpowering her anger, had assured Irene that the camels saw in color. Various families had donated the tubs, and Ravi provided cloth scraps of the same, or nearly the same, colors. Cicero had given her three opaque, airtight, plastic containers. It was a simple, sensible experiment. So why was everyone she spoke to struggling not to laugh?

Even Mark bought into the idea of camel intelligence without requiring proof.

"I've been wondering," was all he said, but glowing satisfaction transformed his thin face, and Irene hadn't had the heart to argue.

"OK, Cow, here's the other half of the turnip root." She held it up, like a stage magician.

Cow's ears swiveled forward.

"Good, watch closely. I'm putting it into one of these containers." The lid snapped down. "Now I'm going to mix them up, so you can't tell which is which."

Irene knelt with her back to Cow, not so much mixing them up—it wasn't a shell game—but handling each one, so her own scent on the container wouldn't give it away. She'd thought a lot about this while gathering the things she'd need. Cow's sense of smell would be her best way around this experiment; thwarting it was a secondary benefit of filling the tubs with water.

She stopped suddenly, realizing one of the drawbacks as well, and then went to the nearest tub and reopened the containers, dipping each one in, filling them so they wouldn't float.

Scattered chuckles rose from the crowd, who'd given up any pretense of not watching. A few curious camels had joined them. Let them laugh. Irene knew, even if they didn't, that all experiments had to be fine-tuned. They almost never worked smoothly the first time.

She closed the lids again and shuffled the containers. They were heavy in her arms when she turned back to Cow, and her shirt and sleeves were damp.

"Listen up, Cow; I'm going to put one of these in each tub. Only one has the root in it."

They splashed softly, and wobbled down to the bottom. That should thwart even the keenest sense of smell. Cow watched intently, nostrils widening with each breath, but she wasn't sniffing deep. Irene would have to watch for that, when she went to the tubs. If she went to the tubs.

"OK, this is it." Irene pulled the blue fabric scrap from her belt and held it out. The moons were bright enough to see the color—dimmer than in daylight, but clearly different from the other two. "The root is in the blue tub. The one that looks like this cloth. The same color. You can have it, if you just choose the right one. But only if you choose it. Come on, Cow, the blue tub. Blue. Like this."

Actually, Irene expected Cow to go and investigate all the tubs, but she was pretty certain she wouldn't dunk for the containers. That was the main reason she'd filled the tubs—and why she'd chosen big, deep ones. The only way for Cow to get the rest of the root was to single out the right tub, from Irene's color signal.

She was prepared to repeat the experiment several times, but if they really were intelligent it shouldn't take long for Cow to figure it out.

Cow swallowed the root she'd been chewing on and started forward. Irene's heart pounded, but Cow approached her, not the tubs.

"Blue, Cow. The tub that's the same color as this. Just go there and nudge it, and you get the root. Do you understand? The blue tub." She expected nothing, really, but hope . . . that was something else. You were never too old, it seemed, to wish for miracles.

Cow's nostrils widened and she sniffed the blue cloth. *No help there, my friend. Figure it out.* Her brown gaze fixed on Irene's, holding it. Were those eyes intelligent? Irene had to make an effort to release her breath. "The blue tub," she whispered. "Are you going to do this? Can you really—"

A soft nose brushed her neck and her shirt collar pulled tight, tugging her off-balance. Irene yelped and would have fallen, but for the grip of the strange camel who dragged her backward, staggering, away from Cow.

"What? Let me go, you demented animal! You're tearing my shirt. Let go!"

But it pulled her, an awkward, stumbling, backwards dance, across a dozen feet of sand, then lifted her half off her feet and released her.

Irene landed with a splash. The tubs weren't that deep, and it wasn't that cold, but she hadn't intended to wash her clothes. Or her hair. Or to listen to the whole damn camp whooping with laughter.

She tried to fight her way out of the tub, but one of her arms was down inside, and the leverage was bad.

Gus came up to her, holding out his hands. "Let me help you. I'm sorry. Really. I am." It would have been more convincing if he'd been able to stop laughing while he said it.

"Go to hell." Irene flung her weight to one side and the tub tipped, the wash of water sweeping her out onto the sand. She rose to her knees and scraped wet hair out of her eyes. She struggled to her feet and kicked the tub.

The blue tub. The blue tub, which had been the farthest from where she stood, so that fiend of a camel who'd . . . who'd *ambushed* her had to pass two others to reach it. Who'd ambushed her while she'd been distracted by . . .

"You bitch!" Irene yelled.

"Whouk, whouk, whouk." Cow's sides puffed in and out. Irene picked up the container and threw it at her, wildly, missing by feet. "You fink, you . . . you fiend. I'm going to make camel chops, do you hear me? Camel cho—"

A roar of laughter from the colonists interrupted her. Irene spun in the direction they were looking, just in time to see her ambusher trotting into the dunes, carrying the sack that held her whole supply of turnip roots. He was already too far away to chase, but his accomplice wasn't. She spun and ran at Cow, fists clenched.

The *whouk*ing camel pranced away, then turned and loped off. Irene couldn't possibly run her down.

She looked around. It was evidently the best joke in years. Mark laughed so hard he had to hold on to Sondi to stand, and Gus had fallen to his knees.

"Sorry," he gasped at her thunderous approach. "Don't kill me, I'm defenseless. Oh God, you should have seen your face when you saw it was the blue . . ." He doubled over, whooping.

Irene's lips twitched. Her belly quivered. She laughed so hard she ended up on the sand beside Gus, clutching her ribs, crying. It took her a long time to wind down and start thinking.

The blue tub.

Measure that, Goodnight.

"They are intelligent." Awe washed away the remnants of her laughter. "They do communicate."

"I warned you," Gus said, "about their sense of humor."

"Don't mind him." Nola's voice quivered, but she wasn't actually laughing. She held out one of the empty, cottonlike sacks the colonists used as towels when they weren't traveling. She had Irene's other set of clothes under her arm. "I'm just glad to have them laughing at someone besides me for a change. *I* tried a dozen different intelligence tests before I gave up."

"The maze was the funniest," said Gus reminiscently.

"You," said Nola with dignity, "weren't the one who had to wash honey out of your hair."

"They always do this?" Irene pulled her soaked braid loose and began patting her hair dry. Her diaphragm still ached.

"Sometimes," said Nola. "Sometimes they just ignore you, or get bored and wander off. The sad fact is, they're just not interested in taking intelligence tests. Their jokes, on the other hand . . ."

"Communication," Irene murmured, still trying to grasp all the little plot had required. "Teamwork. Planning. Cow *deliberately* distracted me. Irony."

A chorus of distant *whouks* drifted to her ears. The story was spreading. "They're laughing at me!"

And they continued to do so every time they set eyes on her for the next few days—but Irene, gathering the equipment and supplies she'd need, no longer cared who laughed at her.

She tackled Gus the next evening. "You said I could do any research I wanted to, right?"

Amusement lurked beneath the wariness in his eyes. "Maybe. Depends on what you want to do. Not another intelligence test though, please. My ribs can't take it."

Irene grinned at the memory. "No, I want to check out one of the life pools. I told you at the start I'd need to. Now that Maureen has confirmed that's where the anomaly comes from, I have to go there."

"Ah yes, Maureen." Laughter faded out of Gus's face. He sighed. "I suppose you do have to go if you're going to make any progress. But you'll go under guard, and if you so much as look in the direction of the *Stanley,* he'll stop you by any means necessary. I mean that."

"Fine," said Irene impatiently. "Just tell whoever it is to keep out of my way. We'll leave tomorrow evening, first thing."

"You're sure of that?" Gus's lips twitched.

"Why not? If the guard has tonight to pack, he can take me—"

"You've missed a point, Goodnight. It's a camel who has to take you. Oh, we know some of the past sites, of course, but they aren't always active. To find a working life pool requires the assistance of a camel . . . and they don't always cooperate."

"Hmm," said Irene grimly. "We'll see about that."

"OK, smart stuff," she told Cow the next night, raking the comb through her long, coarse coat. "I know you understand me. Or at least, I can get you to understand. You're going to take me to a life pool, and you're going to show me everything you know about how they work. Have you got that?"

Cow looked stupid and complaisant, as usual. One ear flicked lazily back to Irene, and then away.

The black guard-kid, whose name, she'd learned, was Rafe, snorted. But he was there and packed, with his own camel—that was all Irene cared about.

"No kibitzing from the bystanders."

"Wouldn't dream of it, ma'am."

When her grooming had reduced Cow (she hoped) to a state of imbecilic bliss, Irene put an arm over her neck and pulled. "Come down, there's a good girl. Let me on."

To her considerable surprise, Cow folded her legs and knelt. Irene held her breath, scrambling for her saddlebags, but Cow played fair, waiting while Irene arranged the lumpy, modified seat covers between her humps. Despite Ravi's stitching they were beginning to show wear, but they'd last for a while.

Irene mounted. "OK, my friend, to the life pool. Take me to a life pool."

Cow's upward surge made her want to cheer. Rafe, looking surly, followed at a distance. Irene was glad, for she didn't want to chat.

She planned her research as Cow headed toward the east, where the forest was, where the life pools were. Anomaly 1's nursery.

A series of tests. It might take several days to see an aggregate form and produce fertile offspring. She also needed to check the creek that fed the pool; perhaps anomaly 1's source was somewhere upstream. That would make sense—Earth's forests produced a vast variety of life-forms, and the streams that fed the pools ran through the forest. Tracing the stream, testing things along its path, she should be able to find the prime breeders eventually. Speculating on what the source might be, what form it might take (animal, vegetable, or mineral?) occupied her mind for hours. So thoroughly, that it was only a few hours before dawn when she realized . . .

"Wait a minute. If Rosebud's setting over there . . . You're going the wrong way! You need to head east, you stupid cow. The life pools. Life pools!"

Twenty minutes later Cow strolled into camp and knelt for Irene to dismount. Swearing.

Gus came up, suppressed laughter crinkling his eyelids.

"Don't say it," Irene snapped. "Not one word. I don't want to hear it."

"I wouldn't dream of it," said Gus. "I value my skin. Want to have dinner with me? Café Cicero is serving groundhog pot roast with sourmint sauce. A specialty."

True to his word, he didn't tease her—though she could see it cost him. It was Mark who said, "Well, that didn't take long. Cow must have winged." It was Cicero who said, "Eat well, Signorina Goodnight—riding in circles always makes one hungry." It was Jake who said . . .

By the time she finished dinner, Irene was beginning to laugh about it herself—bruised, rueful laughter, but laughter nonetheless.

"I was too busy planning to watch where she went," Irene confessed to Gus. "Next time I'll keep an eye on the devious beast."

"Well, Rafe's willing to go again—he says this is the best farce he's seen in years."

Irene sighed.

The next evening, Cow knelt for her, mounting as docilely as before.

"I should have been suspicious then, shouldn't I?" said Irene, settling her legs over the saddlebags. "All right, Machiavelli, this time I'm ready for you."

She was aware of it when Cow started to swerve to the south, though she did it so gradually she might just have been choosing a better route through the dunes. Or perhaps the nearest pool lay a bit to the south. But when she started to veer west Irene corrected her, pushing her hump, leaning, kicking.

All it accomplished was to make Cow realize that Irene was on to her. The camel headed straight back to camp, with Rafe and his mount snickering behind them.

"Maybe I'm just not communicating," Irene told Nola. " 'Take me to a life pool' is a pretty abstract concept for something that probably doesn't understand English, no matter how bright they are."

"Maybe," said Nola. "We've never been certain how much of our speech they understand."

"Then I'll try something else," said Irene.

There was no paper. There was no paint, or crayons, or markers. "I dye my fabric at the settlement," Ravi apologized. "Large amounts of pigment are far too bulky to carry around." But he had glue. He had sheets of plain, white, cottony cloth, and a scrap of blue that wasn't quite the soft blue-green of the life pools, but close enough.

Irene walked out to the rock ridge to gather leaves, and a few dry twigs that she thrust into Cicero's cook fire to make charcoal. She had to burn the tips over and over to draw tree trunks and branches. She glued on leaves to make trees and bushes, and last the blue cloth, cut in a vaguely pool shape, the stream trickling in and out. When she finished, it didn't look half-bad.

"Signorina Goodnight! But you never said you had talent. An abstract in the collage—the green and black, it is the primordial chaos of the galaxy, yes? And the blue, the first thought of life in the mind of God. Or perhaps it is the womb? Never have I seen—"

He dodged the hurled handful of sand, laughing. "All right, no, stop, it is quite good. But where you and I see a life pool, what will a camel see?"

The night was half-gone, but Irene wasn't sure how her leaf "jungle" would stand up to the heat of the day.

She had to hike into the grass fields to find Cow. Strange. She could pick "her" camel out of the herd without difficulty now, and was beginning to recognize some of the others. Kirk and Ent. The unclaimed ones she groomed. They were very individual, for creatures who looked so much alike.

Cow's ears swiveled toward Irene when she saw her, and she ambled over, curious. At least Irene hoped it was curiosity—she might have been plotting something.

"Cow, this is the life pool." She spread the cloth on the sand as she spoke, and Cow looked at it, ears forward, intent.

"This is the forest, see. Trees. Leaves. Lots of trees and leaves. This is the water." Even as she spoke, Irene's heart sank. This was ridiculous. Almost as abstract as words. If only she could reproduce the scent, she'd be sure to get through.

But Cow was looking at the picture . . . and kept on looking at the picture. Irene's heart beat faster.

"Look familiar to you? The woods. The pool. Come on, get the message. This is where . . ."

Cow's long neck bent down. Irene held her breath. The camel's soft lips brushed the pool, the leaves of the forest, then she picked up a corner of the cloth and began to chew it.

Irene was almost too depressed to swear. "OK, scratch that idea. You know, I think you understand perfectly well what I want, you're just being stubborn. Care to confirm that?"

Cow chewed the cloth, looking as stupid as a camel could look—and that was saying something. No, there was a mind in there, and a sharp one, but Irene didn't know how to reach it. Or she'd reached it already, and Cow just didn't want to take her to the pool. And if so, why? Her temples began to throb.

"OK, you've made your point. Give that back. Ravi wants—"

Cow dropped the cloth, but Irene didn't flatter herself it was because of her commands. The camel's attention was fixed to the west, her muscles tense, ears forward as far as they could go. All the camels were staring to the west.

"What is it?" Irene looked and listened, but they were down in a hollow. She saw nothing but the sand slopes. Heard nothing but the soft rustle of grass in the breeze.

The camels hissed, all at once, like a pride of furious cats. The hair on Irene's neck lifted, even before she remembered Gus telling her it was their danger signal.

Cow knelt and Irene scrambled aboard. The others were already loping back toward camp. It was a terrible gait to ride, but Irene clenched her fists in Cow's coat and hung on, gritting her teeth as the sand sped away beneath the camel's wide feet.

When she reached the camp, Irene slid down without waiting for Cow to kneel. The colonists worked frantically, pulling down their tents, bundling possessions into sacks and crates, stacking them together.

"What is it?" She grabbed a man's arm as he ran by. "What's going on?"

"Ice storm. Help Mark get your tent down, we haven't got long."

Irene looked around—clear, moonlit sky, as far as she could see. But the camels definitely sensed something. Irene hurried over to help Mark, who was struggling with the thick wool cloth. They folded the jointed ribs and tied them into a bundle with the stakes. They'd started to fold the cloth when Gus, Sondi, and Ayanna dashed up. Gus carried one of Cicero's big leather carryall sacks, in which he loaded half his traveling kitchen. Their camels strode at their heels, like hunting dogs.

"Don't bother with that," Gus called. "You'll just have to unfold it. I don't know if anyone's told you, but there's—"

Moving as one, the camel's heads turned to the west. Then they all pivoted, facing east, and lay down, their bodies as precisely parallel as if they'd been aligned with rulers.

"What in the—"

"No time," said Gus briskly. "We've only got a few minutes. This is a blizzard sack." He opened the carryall in front of Cow's narrow breast, between her front legs. All her legs, usually tucked neatly beneath her, were spread wide like a series of W's.

"What about my analyzer," Irene protested. "I can't—"

"Will freezing break it?"

"It shouldn't, but—"

"Then forget it. There's nothing you could do about

it anyway." Gus handed Irene three nested camelwool bags, long and thin, like hooded sleeping bags. "Step into the carryall and into these, pull them up and sit down. I'll fasten the flaps."

Irene hastened to obey. Willard had complained that scientists never followed orders without questioning them, and in fact they'd taken some pride in doing so. But an emergency, which this seemed to be, was a different matter. But what was so urgent? "It's only a storm," said Irene. "What's so—"

"You won't say that tomorrow," said Gus.

"Tomorrow! How long wi—"

"Four hours to four days," Gus put a hand on her shoulder, pushing her down to sit in the carryall, then laced it up around her. "Here's a water flask and here's a bottle to pee in. Don't mix them up."

"What if I have to do more?" Irene asked. "Four *days*—"

"Rolling your dirty underwear into a ball and throwing it outside is a popular solution," said Gus. "But feel free to improvise. Don't, under any circumstances, get out of the sacks. If the wind catches the bag wrong and pushes you away from Cow, just let it roll you. You'll end in a hollow and we'll find you when it's over. You'll have to do some wiggling to keep on top of the sand, but that'll make you warmer, and you can survive it. You can't survive—"

"I get the picture," said Irene. "What about Mark?" The side of the sack blocked her view, and she craned her neck.

"Sondi and Ayanna are rolling him up in your tent. He'll be warmer than you are."

Gus pulled the leather top flap over her head, paused a moment, and lifted one hand, his fingers split into pairs. "Lie long, and prosper." His flashing, imp grin was the last thing Irene saw before the flap came down. The leather jerked as he laced it closed.

"I hate trekkies," she called—the bags muffled her voice.

A couple of brisk pats, softened by thick leather and wool, lit on her left shoulder; then there was nothing but the quiet dark. She was on her own. Well, not completely on her own.

Cow's chest made a lumpy backrest, but it was better than sitting unsupported. Irene settled herself more comfortably, wondering how long the storm would really last—surely four days was the outside estimate. Though from what the other colonists had told her, twenty-four hours wasn't unusual. They said mostly it was boring.

Irene was getting hot, and she needed to pee. She told herself that was psychosomatic—she'd done so just a few hours ago, while she tracked Cow down in the grass fields. She still wished she'd had a few more minutes, but Gus had seemed to be in quite a hurry. She hoped he'd have time to wrap himself up properly.

The long, dull moments passed. Irene was bored already. How was she going to—"

There was almost no warning. A gust sharp enough to tug at the thick leather. A whispered growl, barely loud enough to reach her, in her swaddled cocoon. Then a shrieking demon slammed into the bag, buffeting, tearing at the flaps Gus had sealed. The air that sliced through the crevices was cold as a razor's edge; Irene pulled thick wool around her and huddled into Cow.

She could feel the camel's muscles tense as she braced herself, and knew that if Cow didn't shelter her, the wind would pick her up and roll her away like a tumbleweed.

Thunder crashed, right on top of her, deafening, annihilating. Irene ducked, compulsively, though she knew it was useless. If lightning struck, she was dead, and that was that. At least she hadn't felt the electric-

ity on her skin; if it had been close enough to strike
Mark, she should've felt it. The thunder cracked again,
not so close this time, though she still winced. Then
again, close enough that Irene found she'd wrapped
herself into a ball when it faded. She started to unwind
her limbs, but decided not to bother—she'd only do
it again in a minute or so. At least she wasn't bored
anymore.

The lightning was a phenomenon of the storm's
leading edge, passing into the distance after about ten
minutes. But the wind, if anything, intensified. For the
most part it blew straight past Cow, but the occasional,
angled gusts, shaking the firmly braced camel and slap-
ping the carryall like a punching bag, were enough to
keep Irene interested.

The first time Cow shifted, to slide a foot beneath
her body, Irene almost had a heart attack. But since
the foot came to rest against her rump, it was easy to
figure out what had happened.

For a while Irene timed the storm by the intervals
between Cow's foot shuffling, but soon she gave it up.
Cow's chest was lumpy, but warm, the only heat
source besides Irene herself. The thick wool wrappers
kept her comfortable, but barely, and she tucked the
extra folds around and under her feet.

Ravi was right—she understood why the camels
needed every inch of their thick coats.

After a while her feet grew warm. It was day outside; eerie, gray-brown light crept under the jerking
flaps, along with fresh, icy air. Irene got up her nerve
once, and pried open a peephole. She saw nothing
but a curtain of blowing sand—blowing one hundred
percent horizontally, as far as she could tell. The cold
burned her exposed fingers. She tugged the peephole
closed, and didn't try it again.

Eventually she grew accustomed to the buffeting,
howling wind. She was warm enough. She was safe.
Soon she was asleep.

It was dark when she woke, and the wind still blew. Her leg muscles were cramping, and she needed to pee.

Maneuvering the bottle made for an interesting few minutes, but once she'd sealed it, and propped her feet on it to take advantage of the warmth, there was nothing to do but sit . . . and sit . . .

Irene planned her study of anomaly 1 in minute detail, with contingency plans for any possible discovery.

She did isometrics to ease her muscle spasms, and discovered every position the human body can possibly achieve tied up in a sack.

She composed a letter to her sister, detailing Mark's recovery.

She wished to God she had a book, or a vid player—anything to pass the time.

She finally fell into a blank-minded fugue, her thoughts congealing like a frozen reptile's, the gaps filled only with the cry of the wind.

The earthquake of Cow's rising woke her, tipping her onto her face. But the wind didn't catch the sack, didn't send it tumbling away. The storm was over.

"Thank God." Irene straightened cramped limbs as far as they'd go, not caring that the cold air slithered in. She pushed at the flap, trying to free an opening wide enough to get her head out, and couldn't. She was yelling and punching the inside of the bag from sheer frustration when Gus came to release her.

"It took you long enough! Next time I want the knots on the *inside*." Irene squirmed free of the sack. The sun, gloriously bright, was half-up the sky, but the air, in the storm's aftermath, still chilled her.

Gus snickered. "My God, you're a mess. What were you doing in there, wrestling?"

"Go on." Irene stepped out of the sacks. "Laugh. You don't . . . What in the world?"

The sand under her bare feet was hard as concrete, and freezing cold. She started toward her packs and stopped, staring. A mound of sand had grown over them—only on the lee could the edges of the plastic be seen at all. It would take some work to dig them out, and her toes were icy. She hurried back to the sacks and stood on them, grateful again for their wooly warmth.

Mark, a dozen feet away, was wiggling out of the tent; then he stopped, looking around with astonishment.

Irene knelt and felt the ground. "It's frozen solid."

"Down to about four inches," Gus told her. "And wet below that. Those storms have an amazing amount of moisture in them, and with the sand blowing like it does . . . Look, I've got things to do. Once it starts steaming, wait twenty minutes or so and you'll be able to dig your packs out. Then you should get your tent back up. It's cool now, but that won't last." He paused, looking like a man who needs to be elsewhere but doesn't want to go. "What did you think of your first storm, Goodnight?"

"It was boring," said Irene. "It was terrifying. Am I really a mess?" She reached up, smoothing her hair. It had escaped its tie; her braid was coming apart.

"Yes." Gus's smile was softer than his usual grin. "You look all tousled. Like a little kid, first thing in the morning." He reached out, pulling the last of her braid loose, tucking a wisp of hair behind her ear.

Irene's heartbeat quickened. Ridiculous. She had no interest . . . Well, no intention . . .

"Incredible," Mark murmured. "The dunes are sharpening."

Gus's hand fell away. "I really do have to go. But if I don't see you before the heat drives us in, I will later." Then he stopped, looking flustered. "Of course I'll see you later. I mean . . . never mind. Good night, Goodnight."

"If you'd call her Irene you could sing it," Mark told him smartly. His eyes, now fixed on his aunt, were bright with speculation.

Gus gave him a friendly slap on the shoulder in passing. Irene decided to start the conversation before Mark took it in a direction she didn't want to go.

"What do you mean, the dunes are . . ." She looked around and fell silent. The dune ridges, carved by wind and ice, had risen, thin and sharp as knife blades, their color darkened to a deep, mauve-brown. A five-foot-high, U-shaped dune curved around the hollow where Ent's body had lain, and there was another behind Irene. As she watched, a wisp of steam ghosted out of the sand and flickered away. She looked around for Cow, but the camel had long since plodded off. To go to the bathroom, no doubt.

Sondi had had the forethought to give Mark his sandals when she wrapped him up, so he went and dug Irene's out of their packs—which took some doing, for they were near the bottom and he couldn't pull the bag out of the icy mound.

Warm-shod (sort of) she hurried off to follow Cow's example, with more privacy than usual. Steam flowed in gauzy curtains and the colonists and camels moved through them like primordial memories. The grass field had vanished without a trace. Buried? Frozen and blown away?

The sun grew hotter. Putting up the tent was like working in a sauna. One of Cicero Chen's young assistants came around, passing out dried fruit and hard cheese.

Irene and Mark pulled the wool bags from the blizzard sack apart and lay on them, for the wet sand was still cold, and in the shade it wouldn't dry quickly.

"How did you like the sandstorm?" Irene asked Mark. The dune's high sculpted ridges were crumbling away, like wet cookies.

"It was boring," Mark admitted. "And terrifying too. But . . . I don't know . . ."

Irene nodded; she, too, had felt the primitive exhilaration, the satisfaction of being safe and warm in the midst of cold and chaos. Having slept away the better part of twenty-four hours, she wasn't in the least sleepy. "I wonder how often they get those storms."

"Depends on the season, Sondi says." Mark colored slightly when he said her name, but Irene was in no position to tease. "In the summer, very rarely, sometimes not at all. Fall and winter, about one a month averaging. Spring, which we're approaching, they come more and more often—five to eight days, for a few months, then they spread out and stop. She says it's the desert's main source of water. That and the fogs, and she says fog is rare except in the summer, though there was one just a few weeks ago."

"I remember," said Irene. A feverish, aching memory of mist wetting the rocks, beading on her faceplate. Only a few weeks ago? Her friends on the *Stanley* must be frantic. Except for Astrid, who'd probably started flirting with Willard the moment Irene left. They might even have given her up for dead. How long would they linger, searching for her, for the colonists? Given the mystery of the colony's survival, quite a while. No, she needn't fear Willard would get impatient and take off on her—not while there was even a remote chance they'd find the cure, the miracle they'd looked for on so many planets. And it *was* there. Irene had only to unlock its secrets.

She spent the rest of the day sweating over her microanalyzer while Mark dozed.

That night the colony ate, bathed, and packed up the camp. Irene, and even Mark, stripped and joined the others at the well without a second thought.

It was Cicero who warned her to pack up some

dried dung to take with her, "for Ravi tells me there will be a Dark in the next few days."

"A Dark?"

"But yes. A night when there are no moons in the sky. We often have them, a week or so after the Howling Moons. The camels won't travel on such nights, unless they're very thirsty. So we kindle fires, tell stories, sing—like a big party. You'll enjoy it. But a round of dried dung is the traditional price to join someone's fire. You should take at least two dozen, you and Mark between you."

Yesterday they had to break four inches of ice in the well, she was told. Now they pulled up the concentric plastic rings one at a time, with the cords Irene had noticed, and disassembled and packed them. By the time they pulled the last hoop, the sand had begun to cave in. Within an hour the well was a murky puddle, just a few feet deep. In two days it would be gone.

The entire camp was picked up, packed, and ready to move in three hours.

It felt right to be on Cow's back, to be traveling once more. Which seemed stranger, when Irene thought about it, than if it had felt strange.

Irene smiled at the sight of her fellow riders—they really did look like something out of an old vid. Then she saw that someone wasn't riding. Maureen Greville was on foot, her face set with resentment.

"Why isn't Maureen riding?" Irene asked Nola, who'd come up earlier to ask how she'd weathered her first storm.

Nola's face went hard. "She walks till we've forgiven her. And if it's up to me, that's going to be a long time."

"Because she talked to me?" A breath of cold that had nothing to do with the aftermath of the ice storm chilled Irene's flesh. It was so easy to forget that these people were the enemy. Even Nola, who opposed her, might have been a friend under other circumstances.

"She can't keep up. What happens when the sun comes out?"

"Oh, we'll send someone back to pick her up before daybreak. We'd send her on to another camp, if she had her own camel, but as it is . . ."

Maureen plodded up one of the dunes, pointedly ignored by the riders around her.

"This is ridiculous; I'll give her a ride." Irene's heart sank at the thought of a whole night in Maureen's company, but she couldn't let the woman suffer for trying help her.

"No, you won't," said Nola. "And Mark won't either."

"But I can't let her—"

"No." Nola's expression was implacable. "She broke our agreement, this is how she pays. It won't kill her to walk a few nights. I only wish I thought it would teach her something."

"Excuse me," said Irene shortly. "There's someone I need to talk to."

Nola smiled grimly. "Gus will say the same thing."

"We'll see." Irene nudged Cow away.

But Nola was right.

"This is an internal, Navoharan legal matter, Dr. Olsen," said Gus. "As an outsider, it's not your business at all."

"What do you mean, not my business—she's being punished for talking to *me*."

"She's being punished for breaking the agreement that lets you do your research here," said Gus. "We allow everyone a hand in hammering out a consensus, but once we've reached it, we expect it to be respected. Our survival as a society depends on that. And what she did endangers your research as much as . . . anything else. If she had a camel, we'd send her packing. As it is, someone will take pity on her in a few days. And she'll quit when she gets tired. She probably won't walk as far as Cow made you."

Irene thought this over. "You're sure?"

"No, we're going to leave her to roast. Of course I'm sure. Be reasonable, Goodnight."

"Reasonable isn't my best thing," said Irene absently, and lifted her brows as Gus burst out laughing.

"I suppose it would be tactless to agree with you?"

"Yes, it would. Why doesn't Maureen have her own camel? Everyone else seems to."

Gus shrugged. "None has claimed her. I can understand it; she doesn't like the camels, so it makes sense that they don't like her. She usually rides with one of her ex-students. Or a current student's parent. It's hard on her, I suppose, living like we do." He sounded like someone who knew he should be sympathetic but found it uphill work.

"So how do people usually get claimed?" Irene asked. "Do you have to need a life pool?"

"Sometimes," said Gus. "But not often. Kids are generally claimed by one camel or another when they're about, oh, eleven or so. Sooner if they get sick, but with the adult community so healthy, that doesn't happen as much as you'd think. That's why we keep our population so small—we don't want to produce more kids than there are camels to claim them, plus a generous margin just in case."

"How do they know they've been claimed?"

Gus's imp grin dawned. "Sometimes the camels will follow them around for a day or so, smelling them, and making up their minds. When they're sure, they kneel for the kid to mount. Sometimes they lick them all over, like newborn calves. It's great to watch, because the kids are trying to be very adult and dignified, but it tickles. And sometimes . . . well, there's more than one way to scent mark something that belongs to you."

"Scent mark?" It had been a long time since Irene had dealt with animals herself, but the old nature programs had been extremely popular with her nieces and nephews—and their baby-sitting aunt liked them better than cartoons. "*Scent mark?* You mean they piss on them?"

"Copiously," said Gus. "The beginning of a beautiful friendship."

Irene laughed so hard people riding ten yards away grinned in sympathy. "I owe Cow more than I thought. All she did was kidnap me and toss me into a pond. I'm not sure it's worth two days of delirium, but at lea—"

The idea struck all at once, blinding, consuming. But it might work. It was a cue they understood, responded to. It—

"Goodnight?" Gus leaned over to wave a hand in front of Irene's eyes. "You still in there?"

"Huh? Oh, sorry, I just had a thought."

"I could tell. I don't think I've ever seen anyone's jaw drop before. What was it?"

"Gus, what if I . . . No, I want to think about this a while. Tell me, what are those things that look like little clumps of leaves? I've been seeing them all over the dunes for the last few hours."

"They're little clumps of leaves." Gus's sharp gaze recognized the deliberate change of subject, but he accepted it. "We call them storm flowers, for the obvious reason. They'll sprout, flower, and seed themselves in just five days. You'll see a lot of them over the next few nights."

The conversation became general, and Irene left as soon as she could, for her whole mind was taken up with the question, *What would Cow do if I got sick?*

During the next night's travel, the storm flowers grew to a height of about four inches and budded. A few opened—six-sided stars in white and yellow, though you had to look closely to make out the color by the dim light of the two smallest moons. Some of the younger girls pinned them into their hair and clothing. The next night was the Dark—and dark it was.

Irene hadn't really seen the stars since she came to Navohar, but there they were, spread over the sky in glittering glory.

She had to dress by feel in the tent's deep shadow. Outside, eyes fully adapted, she could see well enough not to run into things, but her depth perception was off, and the dune slopes surprised her with their steepness.

The storm flowers' scent was the strongest indication of their presence, almost too sweet in the clean desert air. She picked one and tucked it into her shirt collar on the way back to camp—why not? She was going to a party.

When she came over the last dune, she saw that they'd started the fires; low, for dung fires never burned high, but very bright, the intense orange light coating bundles, tents, and people for twenty feet around them.

Irene hesitated. Even though she'd only known these people for a few weeks, several had become her friends. But many more hadn't, and facing the frozen wariness most of the opposition still showed her, in a social setting . . .

Couldn't I just spend the night in my lab, looking at samples? It was what she usually did, faced with a party.

Mark came out of the darkness to stand beside her, accompanied by a wave of the sweet, familiar scent; his hands were full of storm flowers. Not to wear, Irene realized, but to give.

"What are you waiting for?" he asked. "It sounds like the party's getting started."

A fact easily deduced by the distant ring of voices and laughter. A harmonica wailed, bright and mournful. But Mark was hesitating, too. Irene couldn't see his face in the dimness, but something in his voice . . . Mark hadn't been to a party since the first, awkward tremors of GED set his hands shaking. Looking at them now, rock-steady and full of flowers, Irene suddenly felt up to fighting dragons.

"Lead on, Macduff. And damned be he who whatever, whatever." Shakespeare, taken as a required course and forgotten as rapidly as she could, but a few lines had stuck. "You bring the flowers and I'll bring the shit."

"Auntie!"

"Not that kind of shit. You're too young to understand about bringing shit to a party. Thank God." Maybe there was something to be said for the new prudishness.

Mark's smile was too smug for her comfort. "I wish the camels would sing the Darks, too—that was gravely."

"Did you howl with them?" Irene asked curiously.

"Sure."

Irene grimaced. "Your mother didn't bring *you* up to be a wolf cub, either. And you know who she's going to blame."

The first fire they came up to was the Myersons'. They were opposition, but polite about it, so Mark and Irene stayed awhile, getting a feel for things. The main topic of conversation was a passionate philosophical debate about the ethics of forced choice. If someone held a gun to your head and threatened to kill you, were you still responsible. . . .

Mark grimaced at Irene, and she shrugged. They stopped at the cook fire, which drew a big crowd, and picked up mugs of thick stew and sandwiches before moving on. The next fire held a group who seemed to be telling favorite fairy tales to the wide-eyed kid flock. The next held the harmonica player, who turned out to be Nola's quiet husband, and Sondi, singing along with the others, high, clear, and truer than most amateur voices. Several camels were also present, listening. Irene wondered if they might sing along, but they didn't.

Irene left Mark there and wandered on. The group of colonists swapping "remember when" stories about their landing and the original settlement fell silent, and then changed the topic when they noticed Irene's presence. She smiled stiffly and moved on again.

The fire in front of the Kobiches' tent was banked down and deserted—perhaps they'd gone to get some food. Irene sank down beside it, gazing at the dance of flame in contented silence.

These colonists were the same as any other group of people—different personalities, different abilities, goals, and dreams. So why did she like them so well? Even some of those who'd rejected her, like Nola, had become friends. And Maureen, who'd helped her, was the one person she disliked.

She had to do something for Maureen. A rider had looped back on both of the last few nights and brought her into camp, tired and bedraggled, just before sunrise. And she wasn't at any of the fire circles tonight, either. Irene frowned. Mild as it sounded, shunning could be a devastatingly effective punishment in a small community, and—

"Mind if I join you?" said Gus softly. "Or do you want to go on scowling by yourself."

"You can join me if you want to. I was thinking about Maureen."

"Ah." The Kobiches had piled their packs around the fire to make backrests; the one Irene leaned on was large enough to accommodate two or three people, but Gus could have chosen to lean against one of the others. "Maureen's by her own tent. She wouldn't be welcome at most of these fires tonight."

"I'd like to speak with her," said Irene abruptly. She wasn't used to asking for permission, and it grated on her pride. "Under guard if necessary. I don't want information, I just need to—"

"OK," said Gus.

"OK?"

"Yes, I'll take you to talk to her, as soon as you like. I have to be there, but if a short conversation will reassure you, you can talk to her."

"Oh," said Irene. That had been much easier than she'd expected. "Thanks."

"No problem. I see you've discovered the proper use for storm flowers." He unpinned the one he'd fastened to his shirt and tucked it casually behind Irene's ear. It promptly fell, and they both smiled.

"Allow me." Irene pushed the stem securely into her braid. "Mark gave Sondi a handful. I hope they don't have a deep symbolic meaning to you people—he's a bit young to get married without even knowing it, for instance."

Gus laughed. "No. They're just flowers. Gather ye rosebuds while ye may, and all that."

"Whoever wrote that had too much time on his hands," said Irene. "Idle. I'm beginning to feel like a kept woman around here."

"You certainly don't seem idle to me."

Irene shrugged, restlessly. "Oh, I'm busy enough, but aside from my research, all I can do is help Cicero and groom a few camels. Things the older kids do before they find a worthwhile job." She'd realized that, over the last few weeks.

"So? It all needs to be done, and you're in the same position as the kids."

"Everyone else had a real job."

"And most have another job they pursue on the side, to produce luxury goods for trade," Gus told her. "Though they usually do that kind of work when we're settled in Oasis for the summer. That's when we make everything we don't need the settlement's equipment for. If we could get that equipment from the settlement to Oasis, it'd be invaluable."

"Yes, but . . . How do people get real jobs around here?"

Gus shrugged in turn. "Some kept their old jobs, or

modified them, like Nola and Ayanna. And me, for that matter. Some created jobs out of what used to be their hobbies, like Cicero and Ravi."

"I thought Ravi's hobby was yoga."

"That's one of his hobbies. Another was sewing. Another was opera. What are your hobbies, Goodnight?"

Irene felt her cheeks heat. "I don't have any. And you needn't tell me that I ought to get a life, because I've already heard it. Microbiology is the fastest-growing scientific field—just keeping up with the journals is—"

"You kept up with the journals? All of them?"

"A scientist is supposed to keep—"

"Yeah, but I've never known one who actually did it."

"That," said Irene, "is because they had hobbies." Lives too, probably. "And I don't want to hear cracks about obsessive-compulsives either, because I've heard all of them, too."

Gus was silent for a moment. "In the bad old days, that kind of behavior was described as 'dedicated,' and it was a highly respected trait."

"No one thinks that way anymore." Irene wiggled her toes in the soft, cool sand, her eyes on her feet. "You know . . ."

"What?"

"I found the cure for bioengineered intractable smallpox. Over two thousand people, carriers, were able to come out of quarantine, rejoin their families, take up their lives, because I spent my spare time in the lab, instead of knitting, or watching *Star Trek* reruns. I know some people who think work is a dirty word, but it can be more rewarding than anything else."

"I can see that," said Gus. "Though you might leave some of it for the rest of the world, you know."

"What do you mean?" But Irene already knew. "Have you been talking to Mark?"

"No, but I'm not surprised that he agrees with me. Don't prickle up; I think you're wonderful. But you don't have to do it all yourself, Irene. Let other people solve some of the universe's problems."

Irene snorted. "Do any of them know about anomaly 1?"

"No," Gus admitted. "They don't."

"Then this problem is pretty much mine, all mine, isn't it?"

"I suppose it is, but one thing living with another sentient species has taught us, is that not every problem is ours to solve. Taking it all on yourself seems . . . a little vain?" His voice was amazingly gentle, but it still stung.

"Almost as vain as hauling five hundred people into space on a wild gamble," said Irene sharply.

Gus laughed. "You've got me there. In fact, vain is too mild. Starting a colony like this was downright arrogant."

"So why did you do it?" Irene asked curiously. He wasn't an arrogant man. "The record didn't say much about your motives, except that you were one of the nature-nuts."

"Nature-nuts?"

"As opposed to religious fanatics, or biological paranoids."

"That's accurate, I suppose. You see, my hobby was backpacking. The thought of living out my life inside a dome, never getting into the wilderness again, was intolerable. Since I couldn't have Earth's wilderness anymore, I went to look for another. Everyone said we were crazy. That it was impossible for creatures that evolved in one environment to survive in another." His eyes sought the darkness beyond the fires, and he smiled as if he could see his wilderness there. "I told them anything was possible."

"You really believe that, don't you?" Irene asked softly.

"Why not? It's proven true so far. And someone who's devoted her life to finding impossible cures has no room to criticize . . ."

They talked for hours, until the Kobiches returned with a party of friends, and Gus and Irene rose and strolled off.

"Maureen now?" he asked.

"Yes," said Irene. She preferred to get unpleasant things over with.

They'd pitched Maureen's tent some distance from the others, though Irene supposed it was close enough that a call for help would be heard. Maureen, too, had built a fire before her tent; the small blaze looked pathetic compared to the others' companionable bonfires. Her face was inscrutable as she watched Irene and Gus approach.

Gus stopped about five feet away and folded his arms, clearly ready to listen to anything they said. Irene sat down on the opposite side of the fire.

"I'm sorry about what's happening to you," she began, trying to put some warmth into her voice. The apology, at least, was sincere. "If there's anything I can do . . . anything they'll let me do, then I'll—"

"Good," said Maureen, "then find some way to get me off this barbaric dirt ball and back home. My blood is full of the organism. When your ship takes the cure home, I'll be happy to supply the human samples."

"Enough," said Gus sharply.

Irene blinked, wondering what clue she'd missed. The *human* samples?

The corners of Maureen's mouth turned down. "Oh, all right." But satisfaction gleamed in her gaze.

"We'd better go," said Gus.

"All right." Irene rose willingly. Maureen didn't seem too badly abused, for all her obvious anger. "But I am grateful. I wanted you to know that."

"Don't bother. I didn't do it for you."

The sudden insight froze Irene in her tracks. "You didn't do it for them, either, did you?"

Embarrassed guilt flashed across Maureen's face. "Well, of course I . . ."

Irene turned away. Gus was right—Maureen could look out for herself. She was probably an expert at it.

Irene would have gone back to her tent then, disillusioned and disgusted, but Gus wrapped an arm around her shoulders and led her to a fire where they played word games. Then to one where scientific topics were discussed. Then one where they were telling a circlestory, each speaker trying to be more outrageous than the last.

In Gus's presence, even the chilliest members of the opposition were polite.

When the sky finally lightened, Irene had learned more about the colonists than she had in all the days she'd traveled with them. And she liked what she'd learned. It was a very good party.

The next night Seer, Rosebud, and Grandfather rode the sky, and the colonists moved on. The storm flowers formed six-sided green pods. By the following night there was nothing left of them but shriveled leaves, and the pods rolled across the dunes in the light breeze, scattering seed in all directions. The next night they reached a new grass field, which had sprouted near the strangest sight Irene had seen on Navohar. "*That's* a stiltie grove? Those are *trees*?"

Riding closer she could see that they were indeed trees, with thick, knotted trunks, and branches that grew out, then turned straight up. Their leaves were narrow and scant. The strange part was that each tree began thirty feet above the sand, held aloft by the long, thick pillars of its roots.

"They start to grow, and then the sand blows out from under them," Ayanna told her. "And back again. We could come back next year, and find those trees on top of a dune. If they're lucky. If they're buried completely, they'll die."

Walking through the grove was like being in a giant's zoo, not sure if you were spectator or specimen. And Irene had to pick her way around bushes, real, thick-growing bushes. It was the most vegetation she'd seen in one place since she left the life pool.

"Heli-bats nest in the trees," Cicero told her. "Their droppings put nutrients into the soil, and there is shade, of sorts. I just wish we were here a few months from now; we could do some harvesting then. Cotton bushes, stiltie fruit, sweet star berries—but now, nothing is ripe."

Ayanna had already told her that in the desert most plants went dormant in the summer and did their growing, blooming, and fruiting over the winter months.

"This place is completely backwarding," Mark complained. "Winter is summer; night is day."

"And the women are forward and immodest," Sondi quipped smartly.

Mark grinned. "That I can live with."

A chill touched Irene's heart. *Mark is going to stay here.* The thought had been creeping around the subcellars of her consciousness for some time—now she turned on the light and looked at it. Mark was going to stay on Navohar, where he would always be well—where he would be with Ent and Sondi. He might fall out of love with Sondi—they were both young. But he had attached himself to Navohar with bonds even Irene could see.

On the other hand, if Navohar became the source of the cure for three-quarters of Earth's diseases, there'd be a lot of travel back and forth. If Irene could find a way to make anomaly 1 breed viably in a lab, take it off planet, he could come home for visits. And she wouldn't have to tell his mother that she'd taken him into space and marooned him in an alien wilderness. As if she wasn't motivated enough already.

The site the camels chose for the well was only a few hundred feet from the grove, and the water table was only twenty feet down. The heli-bats that roosted in the stilties were fascinated by the cook fire, and showed an annoying predilection for snatching small, shiny objects. Turning on the analyzer there would be impossible—but Irene had other plans.

The next night, she went to Ayanna. "Are there any plants around here that would make me sick enough to show symptoms, but not kill me?"

"Lots," said Ayanna. "Though the not-killing part narrows the field some. You think if you get sick, Cow will take you to a life pool?"

"Why not?" Irene shrugged. "Don't they do that, when people are sick?"

"Sometimes," Ayanna admitted. "But sometimes they just wait till their person gets well."

"Do you have a better idea?"

Ayanna frowned. "Did Nola approve of this?"

"She's not my mother," said Irene. "I don't need her permission."

Ayanna snorted. "She may not be your mother, but she's damn sure your doctor, and if you want my help, you do this under her supervision. And you need someone's help, Goodnight; there are plants here that can kill you if you just chew a leaf, and the organism can't do much about poisons. You talk to Nola."

"You're nuts. You're out of your mind. You *want* to get sick?"

"Just enough to convince Cow to take me to a life pool," Irene repeated patiently. "Do you have a better idea?"

Nola scowled. "You could wait for one of the kids to come down with something, and go along with them. Or . . . No, I don't suppose you could. But Irene, this may not work. Usually when someone gets food poisoning or something, the camels just wait till they get better. I don't know how they know the difference—scent maybe—but they're pretty good at diagnosing the things the pools will cure and the things they won't."

"Then you'll just have to help me set up a really good fake," said Irene. "What can I do that would produce visible, scentable symptoms. Especially a fever."

"Hmm." Nola still didn't look convinced.

"*Do* you have a better idea? Nola, you know what's at stake. I need to work with a life pool to solve this."

"I suppose you do." Nola sighed. "Poisoning people is against my principles, but if I don't help you, you'll just go ahead on your own, won't you? And get into God only knows what kind of mess."

Irene said nothing.

"Oh, all right." Nola gave in. "If you can make those stubborn wigglers reproduce, it will be worth almost any risk. Probably the best, least harmful thing would be soap berries. Toddlers eat them sometimes, despite the fact that they taste terrible. They often run a low grade fever, but mostly, it's a powerful emetic."

"Wonderful," said Irene drily. "Soap berries. How do I find them and how many do I take?"

"Anyone can point them out to you," said Nola. "They're what we use to make soap. At your weight . . . two will make you nauseous, three will make you sick, and four will make you sorry you had this idea. Not more than four—you'd be too sick to ride."

"Got it," said Irene. "Thanks Nola. You won't regret this."

"No, but you might."

Irene had already turned away. She still had most of the night remaining, and she wanted to get this over with while there was still time to set out for a life pool. Say it took several hours to convince someone to show her the berries, and for them to start working. And it had to be someone who wouldn't tell Mark or

Gus what she planned, or they'd waste even more time arguing. . . . Wait a minute. If they made soap from the berries, why not just use the soap? She already had that.

Irene packed her saddlebags with everything she might need to spend at least a week at a life pool, and warned Rafe to be ready. Cicero was happy to provide her with food, since she was carefully vague about how she intended to convince Cow to take her there. And Cow usually showed up for grooming in the early part of the night, so she'd be there to witness the symptoms if Irene got busy. There'd never be a better chance.

Stomach churning in anticipation, Irene pulled out the small tub of gelatinous goop she and Mark shared. How much was four berries' worth? Not strawberry sized, surely; desert berries tended to be small. Blueberry sized? Pea sized? And it might be somewhat concentrated—safer to err on the small side, than to overdo it. After all, she could always take more.

Irene scooped about a quarter teaspoon of the stuff onto her finger. Lord, it stank. She uncapped her water flask, swallowed the goo, and drank before her awareness of the taste had time to reach her brain.

"Bleach!" As vile as she'd expected, but a few more swallows of water washed it away. She wondered how long it would take to work. Her stomach's current queasy tossing was probably due to the taste—so why was it getting worse?

Five minutes later a rush of nausea sent her scrambling out of the tent. She made it about fifteen feet before vomiting, helplessly, for far longer than she considered necessary.

Even in the midst of her paroxysms she was aware of voices above her, of legs, both human and camel, in a loose circle around her, but her heaving stomach demanded all her attention.

Only when the desperate spasms eased, and she

crawled a few feet from the stinking mess and collapsed, did the words begin to register.

"I can't believe you let her do this." Mark's voice, indignant. The hand patting her back with awkward gentleness probably belonged to him, too, but Irene was too tired to open her eyes and confirm it.

"She'd have done something even stupider on her own." Nola sounded defensive. "And I didn't expect her to do it tonight, without telling anyone."

"You should have," Mark grumbled. "Headfirst, right now, no brakes—it's her style."

"No, it's not," said Irene. "I analyze things." At least she thought she said it, but Nola went right on.

"Well, done is done. If she followed my dosage recommendation, the next hour should see her over the worst of it. I'll get a nice, low basin and come back and take care of her. She'll be OK. I promise."

"An hour?" Irene moaned.

" 'Fraid so," said Nola heartlessly.

"I'll take care of her," said Mark. "Though I'd appreciate that basin."

"No," said Irene. "You shouldn't have to—"

"How many years have you been nursing me? Don't be such a worry. I'll take care of it."

And he did, holding her head when she vomited, propping her up to ease her bubbling, liquid bowels. Irene was too exhausted to feel anything but gratitude. She'd lost all sense of the passage of time, but Nola's voice roused her from her weary doze.

"Irene, wake up a minute." The vet's firm hand gripped her shoulder, but she had the decency not to shake it. Irene's insides were wobbly enough. Wobbling, stirring and starting to rise. . . .

Mark carried the basin away to bury the contents—again—and Irene let her eyes drift closed. But Nola was still there.

"No, you don't—wake up and tell me how many of those berries you ate. This should have stopped hours ago. I swear I thought you had more—never mind. Come on, Goodnight, how many?"

"Hardly any—only about a quarter teaspoon," Irene mumbled.

"A quarter teaspoon? But that'd only be about one berry. It shouldn't have this. . . . Wait a minute. You didn't eat soap, did you?"

"I had it." She wished Nola would go away and let her die in peace. Omega as lover. She could see it.

"You idiot! That soap is *highly* concentrated."

"Thought so. Why I didn't take much."

"Will she be all right?" Mark sounded scared. Irene wanted to reach out and pat him, reassure him, but she was too tired to open her eyes.

"Don't worry, honey, this stuff can't kill you no matter how stupid you are with it. That's why I picked it. A quarter teaspoon . . . about six berries' worth, maybe. Even so, the worst effects should let up soon. Fairly soon," she amended, as Irene moaned and reached urgently for the basin.

And it did begin to let up shortly after that, the intestinal cramps easing, the dry heaves growing gentler and further between.

In the early hours of the morning, Cicero wrapped himself up in a long-sleeved, hooded robe and braved the sun to brew her a pot of sourmint tea.

Mark got half a cup into her, a small sip every few minutes; her stomach settled even more, and she finally fell deeply asleep.

When she woke the sun was gone. The sounds of the waking camp crept into the tent—colonists' voices, the distant clatter of Cicero's pans, a camel's snort, the war whoops of the kid flock.

"Auntie? You've stopped snoring, so you're either awake, or you've died."

"I don't snore," said Irene.

"It's actually more a snort," said Mark. "How could you be so stupid?"

Irene thought this over. "I was in a hurry," she said at last. "Did Cow come by?"

"Yes," said Mark.

Irene tried to sit up, winced and fell back. "Did she try to take me to a life pool? You should have let—"

"*She* had better sense than to try to take you anywhere. She just sniffed you and snorted and went away. How do you feel?"

"Like I went ten rounds with that guy from Dallas Dome, what's-his-name, the boxer."

"Grego Alvarez," said Mark. "You look like it, too."

"I hate flattery."

Mark laughed.

Irene spent the rest of the night resting, and eating the bland, cooked grain and dried fruit mush that was all her abused stomach could handle.

Nola checked up on her several times, pronounced her on the mend, and even won the heroic inner struggle not to say "I told you so," though it looked like a near thing.

Gus came and chatted with her—making her laugh, which hurt her tender stomach muscles, but not too much. After he left, Mark told her that Gus had come to help when Irene was at her worst, and she was horrified.

Several other friends came to see how she was, but they didn't tax her strength by staying long. Cow didn't come at all.

By sunset next evening, Irene had slept herself out, and though she was still weak enough to enjoy the day's heat, she felt human again.

She had to put on her sandals and take the woolen blizzard bags to sit on, for the sand was scorching. But the diffuse, angled rays felt good on her face and hands, and she peeled off her shirt to feel them on her chest and stomach. In the sleeping silence, the

plod of camel's feet was almost loud. Irene knew who
it was. She didn't even open her eyes when Cow's
moist breath puffed over her face. She smelled like
grass and hot camelwool.

"Took you long enough," said Irene, opening her
eyes. Cow looked like she always looked, but she
sniffed Irene with a thoroughness that might indicate
concern. Or it might not.

"I suppose you think this proves you can't be
fooled, and I'll have to give up." Irene grasped one
of the short, smooth horns and tried to turn Cow's
eyes to hers. It was like trying to bend a boulder.
"Well, I haven't and I'm not going to. Sooner or later,
camel, you're taking me to a life pool, and—"

Cow finished her inspection and knelt for mounting.

Irene's jaw dropped. "Do you mean it?" The sunset
glowed in Cow's shaggy coat, creating a most inappropriate halo. "You better mean it, because I'm in no
mood for jokes."

Cow blinked her front eyes patiently, waiting. Irene
hauled herself onto her shaky legs and went to get
her saddlebags.

Chapter 9

"What are you going to do without a tent when the sun comes up?" Mark asked. Irene had known she'd get an argument from Mark.

"If there's no other shade, I can sleep in Cow's shadow. I'm told it's warm, but survivable," said Irene patiently. Several of the colonists who'd gathered to watch nodded, but Gus didn't. His mobile face was sober, but he said nothing.

The colonists hadn't really believed she could talk Cow into taking her, but Gus was holding them to their agreement. Rafe's furious protests had been audible all over the camp. Now he sulked on his camel, his fléchette gun prominently displayed. One of the reasons the opposition agreed to let her go was that they trusted Rafe to stop her if she tried anything.

"What if it ice storms?" Mark continued. "Then what?"

"Then I'll scrape a shallow hole beneath Cow and wiggle under her," said Irene. "Cold, but survivable. If a dire cat or the kongs turn up, Rafe will shoot them. I asked all those questions already. I've packed everything I need."

"But you've been sick." Mark's face, no longer quite so thin, was filled with concern. "You're not strong enough to go off on your own."

"Cow thinks I am," said Irene, and was astonished to see her nod.

"Give it up, Mark." Gus laid a hand on his shoulder. "She's not going to back down—nor should she. This is her job."

"Thank you," said Irene sincerely.

"I still wish you'd let me come with you," said Mark. "Or Sondi, or Ayanna, or Ravi."

"Dragging Rafe with me is bad enough," said Irene. It's only a few weeks' research, not a journey over the rim of the universe. And I've got Cow to look out for me and bring me back when I finish. Don't be such a worry."

Mark grinned, reluctantly. "If you've made up your mind, I'm not going to change it. But be careful, OK?"

"That," said Irene, "I can promise."

One of Cicero's assistants trudged up carrying a pair of the smaller water bags and slung them between Cow's humps, positioning them behind Irene's well-stuffed saddlebags. She hoped Cow wouldn't object to the extra weight—four gallons altogether, though the others figured the forest was only a few nights' ride away. Irene hoped she could handle them when it came time to unload; she didn't think Rafe would be much help. She stepped up to Mark and hugged him. A year ago he'd have squirmed with embarrassment at being publicly embraced—now he hugged her back, hard.

"You promise to be careful, right?"

"You got it." When had he grown up? Irene swore she hadn't turned her back for a second. Her eyes were misty when she turned to Gus and held out her hand.

"Thank you, for letting me do this," she said.

"You're welcome." Gus swept her outstretched hand aside—his arms closed around her, warm and disconcerting. Irene was far too old to be embarrassed at being hugged, she told herself firmly. And felt her cheeks heat, anyway.

"Good luck, Goodnight." Gus let her go and stepped

back, his imp grin appearing when he saw her flushed face. It drew an answering grin from Irene.

She smiled at the others and scrambled onto Cow's back, rejoicing in the familiar, rocking-horse sway of the camel's rising. She was on her way, at last.

Rafe showed his displeasure by hanging back even farther than usual, but Irene didn't mind. It felt good to be alone. The desert's silence, the grace of the dunes, were easier to appreciate when you weren't surrounded by people. Irene hadn't had time, these last few weeks, to realize how much she missed having time to herself.

"Not that you're not here." She met Cow's third eye comfortably. "But you don't crowd me. Maybe it's because you don't talk."

The camel didn't even blink, and Irene realized that she'd become completely accustomed to Cow having three eyes. In fact, she'd probably find a two-eyed camel odd-looking.

About two hours before dawn Cow found a rock ridge, and Irene unpacked without quibbling. Shade during the day was more important than a few more hours' travel. The colonists had told her that Cow could go many days without water, and Irene had seen her do it, but the more she drank, the guiltier, the more churlish, she felt. Finally, she offered Cow a couple of quarts, in the bucket she'd brought to catch any larger life-forms that might live in the pools. It was no more than a token, for a beast as big as Cow, but it made Irene feel better.

Rafe and his camel had disappeared, but Irene knew he was keeping an eye on her, for he took his job seriously. He also had the typical teenage fascination for playing spy. He was good at it, too, she had to admit. The soft clack of a falling rock was the only sign of his presence, and it might have been dislodged by his camel.

A bit of exploring located a deep crevice in the ridge, where Irene would be protected from the sun all day. She already knew that Cow would start off on one side of the rocks and move to the other side as the shadows shifted, and there was enough sand in the rocky cleft to make a soft bed.

She woke in the evening with Cow's warm breath on her neck. Rafe and his camel, already packed, were out on the sand, waiting. Impatiently, she hoped.

The night stretched on, the colonists' camp drawing farther away with each of Cow's long strides. The alien desert felt comforting—as benign as her own lab, and far more beautiful.

Though she did find herself talking to Cow more often.

"Pretty soon, I'll be wishing you could talk back. What am I saying? I do wish you could talk—then you could just tell me about the life pools, and anomaly 1."

But of course, Cow couldn't.

Toward the middle of the night the terrain began to rise. The foothills that marked the base of the forest's plateau were rocky and treacherous beneath Cow's feet—good thing she had six of them. Irene had to shift her legs among the saddlebags, leaning forward as Cow scrambled up some of the steeper slopes.

Bushes, green, leafy bushes appeared and grew thicker and taller as they climbed. Irene found herself trying to see through them, as if some danger lurked there, and told herself not to be silly. There were no large predators in the forests. Nola's guess was that the kong had hunted them to extinction.

The sun came up before they reached the top of the plateau, but they'd gained thousands of feet in altitude, and the air was cooler. The sun was just the sun, not the blazing nuclear hammer of the desert's forge. Its light still seemed too bright to Irene's eyes.

The life pool lay on the forest's edge—not the one Irene had been to, and with no waterfall, so not Mark's either. How many of these things were there? It was a bit larger than the one she'd seen before, long and narrow, but the branch-slivered sunlight woke familiar blue-green lights in its depths.

Cow knelt for Irene to dismount and pull off the saddlebags before wading in to drink, and Irene bit back a yelp of protest. Cow wasn't polluting the sample, she told herself, any more than it had already been polluted by hundreds of other creatures. Hell, for all she knew anomaly 1's breeding primes lived in a special fluid secreted only by wet camel feet.

She unpacked the saddlebags and set up her camp, such as it was. She folded the woolen blizzard bag the colonists had told her she'd need if the nights turned cold and set it on top of the food chest to keep it dry. Then she double-checked the food chest's lock—even in the desert, you couldn't leave your food open without some clever creature getting to it. The hopper mice stole food from the kitchen chests while Cicero was right there, cooking.

Rafe had vanished, just as a good commando guard should. She should eat, then get some sleep, and start fresh the next night. Irene eyed her microanalyzer, set out by itself on a nearly flat rock that made a decent table if you were willing to kneel beside it. She'd never be able to sleep until she did just a few tests.

Anomaly 1 wasn't in the stream. Irene checked samples from three different sites, then hurried back to the pool. Could Cow have led her to an ordinary pond, after all?

No. Anomaly 1 lived in the pool, though its concentration was fairly low. And its concentration of primes in relation to secondaries was bafflingly low.

Cow watched Irene work for a while, then plodded back down the slope. Irene remembered that Cow had chosen to sleep in a sandy, open place before. She hoped, vaguely, that the camel didn't know something she didn't. But most of the her attention was taken up with the hunt for anomaly 1.

If it didn't come down the stream from the forest, then its source was right here—somewhere.

By the time she went to sleep, it was two hours to sunset, the microanalyzer had cataloged 418 new forms of microbiological life, and she'd observed three aggregates of breeding primes. They bred only secondaries. So where was the nursery?

That same thought flashed into her head when she woke in the midst of the night, but her stomach was cramping with hunger, for she hadn't bothered with dinner and had worked very late indeed.

I swore I'd never make myself ill with overwork again. The day she'd spent in the hospital, and the two weeks the doctors had forbidden her to work after she collapsed in the lab, had delayed the cure for bioengineered intractable smallpox by two weeks and one day. Longer than if she'd taken proper care of herself in the first place. Now, already weak from soap poisoning, it wouldn't take much. *No hospital, no exasperated sister to take care of you here, Goodnight.* The thought was sobering, and she resolved to eat, sleep, and work at a moderate pace.

But the complex, interactive microecology of the life pool taxed her resolve to the breaking point. Most of the organisms on Navohar reproduced by *tri*nary fission. She found two sets of organisms, Iota 3 and Gamma 7, which interbred and produced a whole new species, Rho 1, which could reproduce itself—something never seen in Earth's microbiology. *There's a whole paper right there.* But she never found any organism that would breed an anomaly 1 prime—including anomaly 1 primes.

She made time to eat, but forcing herself to sleep more than the bare minimum was a lost cause. Besides, she didn't quite trust the forest. It *rustled* all the time, making her turn from the analyzer's screen to look over her shoulder even though she knew she couldn't see anything in the thick undergrowth. Assuming there was anything there, except Rafe. She'd called to him once or twice, but he hadn't responded.

She found several larger life-forms in the pool— small, darting, dun-striped fish, which were damned hard to capture in her bucket, though she managed in the end. There was also a six-inch-long cross between a salamander and a fish, which ate the darters. It had dappled tan-and-black skin that blended with the leafy bottom, lungs *and* gills, and six short legs, each of which ended in a . . . a foot-fin? For normal fins didn't have a foot's skeletal structure, flesh, and small claws at the tips of the toes—and even webbed feet didn't spread into delicately veined, leaf-shaped fins. It was an efficient combination; the thing flowed through the water like camouflaged lightning, and could turn on the proverbial dime.

Irene had seen people tickling for fish in old vids, but it proved a lot harder than they'd made it look. Or maybe the salamanders were trickier.

Her first, drenching attempt surprised a gust of human laughter out of the nearby forest.

"Care to try it yourself?" Irene called. "I bet you wouldn't do any better." She tried to look scornful and provoking, which was hard with her hair dripping into her eyes. Actually, she was relieved to have Rafe's presence in the underbrush confirmed. Her imagination had been getting out of hand.

He came out, looking sheepish at having given himself away. "I'm not interested in helping you. How much longer is this going to take? It's really boring just hanging around watching you mess with stuff."

Irene shrugged. "It takes as long as it takes. I could use an assistant."

"No way." Was that regret in his eyes? "Not if I was bored to death."

"Tough luck, then." Irene went back to work. The next time she looked up, he was gone.

She continued her tickling for over an hour, providing the watching Cow with considerable amusement—the *whouk*ing was definitely laughter. Then she got smarter and improvised a net out of her blizzard bag. Propping the mouth open with sticks, she was able to herd the salamanders into it and snatch it up before they found their way out. She also captured a couple of larger, flat, mud-brown fish whose existence she hadn't even suspected, and dozens of tiny, transparent, squidlike creatures. They all had anomaly 1 in their systems, and in none of them did the primes breed primes. Rats. She'd been betting on the salamander—large enough to survive small changes in its environment, mobile and adaptable enough to go from one pond to another—it would be the perfect host. . . . But it wasn't.

So maybe the source was in one of the plants around the pond, or in the insects that lived in them, or one of the animals that visited—in the days she'd spent there, Irene had seen several species of shy, leggy, deerlike creatures, and found tracks that looked like those of the desert foxes Sondi had shown her, though these were larger. And there were tree bats, smaller than the heli-bats in the stiltie grove, who hovered in clouds when she turned on her analyzer at night and swooped down to snatch up her slides when the light flashed on them. And innumerable small mammals that scurried and climbed and drank at the pond—washed food in the pond in one case. For all she knew something bore its young in the pond, delivering millions of anomaly primes in the amniotic fluid. Or maybe they droppeth like the gentle rain from heaven, upon the place beneath. Irene rubbed her eyes.

She had an entire, complex, living, alien ecosystem to search—far too big a job for one person, and yet . . .

The answer was there. Irene flexed her stiff shoulders and decided to go out for lunch. It was about an hour before sunrise; she took dried meat, flat bread, and dried fruit from the food chest—relocking it carefully—and wandered out to sit on a rock that gave her a view over the desert. She'd been here six days; her food supplies were about half-gone.

Cow, who'd formed the habit of checking in on her several times a night, and usually grazed fairly close to the pond, had left half an hour ago to find an appropriate place to sleep. Irene's gaze searched the plateau's rugged shoulders, but she couldn't see her, even with Big Ben over half-full, and Rosebud and Pipsqueak helping out.

She wished Cow were here, or Gus, or Mark, or Nola—someone she could talk to about this irrational conviction that the key to the maze was in her hands already, if she could only see it.

"Or it could be that I'm just deluding myself because I want to be the one to find the answer, and not have to share credit with the *Stanley*'s crew. Ego, Goodnight."

But it wasn't ego. Did she feel that guilty for a crime she hadn't committed, which wasn't even really a crime?

No, damn it, it wasn't either of those things. Not entirely. She didn't want the *Stanley*'s crew around because . . . because they wouldn't understand. There was something about this puzzle, a fragile mystery that someone isolated in an enviro-suit's armor could never hope to touch.

And if that isn't a ridiculous flight of fancy for a scientist.

Irene snorted. But the bone-deep conviction remained—if she called in the *Stanley*'s crew they would . . . break something. Destroy some friable link in the chain of evidence. But what? As far as Irene could tell she hadn't managed to hook two links together, much less form a chain.

She finished eating, and the beauty of sunlight rolling over the desert distracted even her circling thoughts. The problem returned to her as she walked back to camp . . . and found a tribe of monkey-squirrels playing with the analyzer.

"Hey! Get out of here, you little skunks!" They scattered at her charge, chittering saucily as they swung into the trees. The colonists' logs had described them—squirrel heads, tails and pelts, attached to a six-limbed monkey's body, with *six* curious, clever hands. The colonists considered them a nuisance, but cute. The colonists hadn't seen them tampering with the only portable microanalyzer on the planet.

Irene rushed over—they'd twirled the dials in every direction, the keypad, which she'd folded closed, lay open, and one of the adjustment knobs had been pulled off and tossed several yards away. But wonder of wonders, they hadn't managed to turn it on, which limited the damage they could do considerably.

"Next time I'll close it up. I defy you to work the lock pad." Though maybe she shouldn't. They'd watched her do it often enough. . . .

Irene picked up the knob, and was twisting it back onto its shaft, when the pounding began.

Something beating on wood, irregular, but loud—it echoed off the trees, directionless, as if the forest itself was warning her off. Her heartbeat was almost as loud, and a lot faster.

Where the hell was Rafe? Irene took a deep breath, forcing her shoulders to relax. *Think, Goodnight!* What had the logs said? The kong gave their ritual warning from sunrise to sunset, and then gave the trespasser till the next dawn at least before attacking— and sometimes waited five or six days before they came. She had one full day; she couldn't go tearing off into the desert in the daylight, anyway. When Cow came tonight she'd—

"Do you hear that?" Rafe burst out of the scrub, panting as if he'd run some distance. Or was as scared as she was.

"No," said Irene sardonically. "I can't hear a thing. Of course I do. It's the kongs, isn't it?"

"Pack up, lady. We're leaving."

"But if it is the kongs, we have twenty-four hours before they attack." She had to raise her voice to be heard over the vibrant thuds.

Rafe's eyes widened. "You're going to *stay* here? With that going on? You're nuts!"

If they left this pool, how long would it take to convince Cow to bring her to another? Willard wouldn't wait forever. She *had* to figure out how the primes bred.

"Look, we have a minimum—*minimum*—of twenty-four hours after the warning begins, right? We certainly don't have to leave before . . . Where are you going?"

"To pack." Rafe flung the words over his shoulder. "And you will, too, if you have any sense."

"Wait a minute. Wait! You have the gun, damn it!"

He didn't stop.

It took Irene several minutes to find the analyzer knob—she'd dropped it when the pounding started. She was disgusted to see that her fingers shook when she picked it up and jammed it back on. *Don't be so cowardly. As long as they're pounding, they're not attacking.*

Unless, of course, their rules had changed.

Irene's knees quivered, and she sat on the rock and swore. *Pull yourself together, Goodnight. You've got one full day left.*

One day to find the elusive nursery. Sooner or later she'd get Cow to take her to another pool, but at another pool she'd have to start from scratch. Who knew what subtle differences in water chemistry, algae mix, and biostructuring she'd . . . differences. *Changes*.

What if it was some *change* in the pool, chemistry, temperature, algae mix, atmospheric pressure, amount of light, that *triggered* the anomaly primes to breed primes? She had just one day to test it.

The pounding went on, but Irene ignored it, and eventually got used to it.

If it was a long-term change that triggered the different breeding pattern, she was out of luck, but if it worked rapidly . . .

She set a bucket of pool water in the direct sunlight, to see if more light would do the trick. She strained another pail though a filter from the biosample kit, to see if a higher concentration of life in a small space would trigger the change. She made the water more alkaline, she made the water more acidic, she made the water more . . .

She didn't even realize night had fallen until Cow's soft lips nibbled her hair and she jumped a full six inches.

"Shit! Don't *do* that, OK?"

Cow blew down her collar, and Irene realized that the pounding had stopped without her noticing. The silence was even creepier, and a chill passed down her spine.

Rafe stood in the shadows at the edge of the clearing. She had no idea how long he'd been there.

"Nuts. Lady, you are deathly insane."

"But I think I'm onto something! I've found that they form breeding clusters more frequently if the water is around ninety-five degrees. That's a body temperature, which implies a host-nursery again, or maybe that they breed in the summer, but they're still just producing secondaries and until I can find the factor that induces them to breed primes . . ."

"That could take days. Weeks! You want to kill yourself, that's fine with me. In fact, I think it's the best idea anyone's had since you arrived. But if Gus finds out I left you defenseless, he'll kill me. So if you want to stay here . . ." He thrust the fléchette gun into her hands. Irene almost dropped it. She'd forgotten how heavy they were.

"I know Sondi taught you to shoot. Keep it right by you, and the moment you see a kong, use it. I'll wait for you out in the desert. They won't go there."

Irene snorted. "Some guard. You're not afraid I'll run off?"

Rafe's expression held a wry, bitter respect. "If you're not running now, you won't leave for anything. Hell, I ought to be glad you're doing this." He didn't look glad. "You really should go."

"I will," Irene promised. "Very soon. Really. I have till dawn at the earliest."

Rafe shook his head, turned away, and vanished into the trees.

"I'll meet you," Irene called after him.

He didn't stop.

Cow stepped carefully over the food chest and knelt beside the empty saddlebags. Irene looked from her to the glowing analyzer and back again.

"You're both right, I know. I swear I'll pack in just a few hours."

Cow chuffed disapprovingly, but she got out of the way when Irene pushed her.

Whether they bred in the pond, or in a host, the trigger was probably chemical. Irene tested sample after sample, noting the changes that took place as the temperature climbed. It might also be a linked interaction—as the water temperature rose in the summer, some forms of algae might die, or new forms grow, or some new element in the pond's surrounding flora might enter the picture. . . .

Cow stayed close to the pool that night, never grazing farther than a dozen yards, and often just standing around in Irene's way. She lay down several times, to be loaded and mounted, but there was always some test in progress, and the kong certainly wouldn't come till dawn, and possibly not for days. It wasn't as if they couldn't travel for a while in the daylight. Just down the slope, say. Just out of the kong's territory.

Irene grew accustomed to Cow's intrusive presence as she had to the kong's pounding. She was startled half out of her skin when the camel hissed, loud and long, like a leaky pressure tank.

"What the . . ."

Irene's temples throbbed as she lifted her gaze from the screen. Tattered spangles of pale, new sunlight shot through the leafy canopy. Cow's gaze was fixed on the forest, her coat fluffed out to twice its normal size. She hissed again, and this time the hair on Irene's neck lifted.

She'd run out of time.

She snapped off the microanalyzer, closing all its panels, locking it tight. Then she lifted the heavy case and hurled it into the life pool; it flew farther than she'd hoped, and sank like a stone. The manufacturer claimed that all field equipment was waterproof and shock resistant, and they'd better be right, because the pond was the closest thing to a hiding place she had, and no analyzer could survive a determined attempt to beat it to pieces. She hoped the kong didn't swim.

There were other biologists on the planet, but only one portable microanalyzer.

That didn't mean the biologist wasn't scared. She'd ignored Rafe's advice; the fléchette gun lay on the food chest, just a dozen feet away. Irene hesitated, looking around. Nothing. Even Cow had vanished. But the silence was a watching silence. Irene leapt for the gun, springing like a deer. She thought she was going to make it but something wrapped around her ankle, sent her crashing, facefirst, to the ground.

Her ankle stung. Irene turned and looked down at

the thorn-studded bramble encircling it, and then looked up and saw the kong.

The colonists had described them as apelike, but the face that regarded her wasn't the gentle, simian face of Earth's primates. Deeply jowled, with a carnivore's short, fanged muzzle, it resembled a bulldog more than anything else. A bulldog's face, mounted upright on its neck like a human head, with pricked wolf-ears, and small, piggy eyes that met Irene's with an intelligence, a consciousness, that took her breath away.

"Please, I'll go right now if you—"

The next lash came from behind, raking across her back, shredding shirt and skin alike.

She pulled her ankle free, tearing her flesh more deeply, and tried to run, but they were all around her, in front of her, driving her back to the clearing and the pool.

She tried to fight, throwing herself at them, kicking, striking out with her fists, but they thrust her off with contemptuous ease, far stronger than she, terrifyingly strong. Her own blood on their skin was the only mark she left on them.

Finally, she curled into the side of her lab-table rock, where a small overhang gave her a bit of protection for her stomach, legs, and the parts of her arms not exposed in protecting the back of her head and neck.

Her back, of course, was fully exposed, but she couldn't do anything about that, except scream.

They left, eventually. There was no warning. The blows simply ceased to come. Irene stayed where she was, locked, shuddering, into a tight, fetal ball. She might have stayed there for hours if she hadn't felt the familiar touch of Cow's moist breath on her torn skin.

Her muscles relaxed all at once, and she slid away from the rock to collapse, jellylike, at Cow's feet.

"Fat lot of help you were." But she reached up as

she said it, to hug Cow's bony head. The camel permitted it for a moment, then she chuffed softly and shook free of Irene's arms to continue sniffing her with the intensity of a concerned friend.

"All right." Irene wiped her eyes and tried to stop crying, but the tears kept coming, and who cared, anyway. "It's not your fault. You tried to warn me, and I didn't listen, and there was nothing you could have done, but *damn* that hurt."

She started to cry in earnest then and Cow lay down beside her. Irene leaned into her coarse, warm coat and cried for a long time.

When she finished she was calmer, and even the wounds on her back had stopped bleeding. She had never been so tired in her life, but before she slept she half crawled, half swam into the life pool and pulled up the microanalyzer. She washed in the pool, cringing when the water around her turned red, but now she could assess her injuries more calmly—the thorn-inflicted cuts were only scratches, though some were deep, and no one whose bloodstream was full of anomaly 1 had to worry about infection. She *had* to crack this thing. But not today.

She salvaged what she could from the battered food chest—they'd torn the lid off, breaking the hinges and twisting off the hasp that held the lock, but there wasn't much they could do to harm the tough, flexible plastic of the chest. A few stones on the top should protect the remains of her food till night fell, and Irene fetched them, wincing, for any movement hurt.

The more complex, brittle fléchette gun had been smashed beyond repair, but some things might be salvaged from the biosample kit. They'd ignored the saddlebags, and any other item made of cloth. When she finally lay down beside Cow to sleep, she placed the blizzard bag beneath her to cushion her tender skin, but she laid one arm over the microanalyzer's hard case and never let go, not even in her sleep.

She woke after nightfall, stiffer than she'd been the day before, but all the cuts had closed and scabbed over.

She was able to retrieve quite a few of the biosample kit's myriad small pieces—enough to go on with—and did a few more tests, but the sting of healing scratches made it difficult to concentrate.

The interactions of the hundreds of life-forms in the pond were incredibly complex—change one and you set off a chain reaction in dozens of others. Which was just as it usually was with life. So why didn't anomaly 1, which *throve* as a parasite, reproduce itself in the stable environment of a host's body?

The pounding began again next morning, and she slept fitfully, even with Cow beside her. She rose to pack in the early evening. Cow's deep *Nah-woooooooon* made her jump, and then swear. The camel had waded into the pool again, but it didn't matter. Irene was finished here. She loaded her gear, mounted, and set off before the sun vanished, before the warning even stopped.

She couldn't blame the kong—not too much, anyway—they were just defending their territory, as humanity had defended Earth from the Vrell. And they played fair, by their own standards.

If the taste of defeat was bitter, well, the cost of victory could be even worse. The Vrell had taught her that. But as Cow's long, soft strides carried her down to the desert, Irene still felt the pull of the life pool, of its gentle, urgent mystery. She didn't look back.

Chapter 10

The journey back to camp wasn't as bad as it could have been. Rafe's guilt over her injuries kept him close to her side; he made camp for the two of them, and assisted her in every way she would let him.

Irene was so sunk in gloom she hardly noticed. She'd been so close! She could feel the answer, just outside her grasp. Why couldn't she find it?

Cow brought them into camp toward the end of the second night. The moons were bright enough for Irene to spot the stiltie grove several klicks away. She thumped on Cow's hump to protest when the camel raised her nose to trumpet their arrival, and, wonder of wonders, Cow fell silent, releasing her pent-up breath in a deep sigh. Irene persuaded Cow to circle and approach her tent from the rear; after the desert's open silence she found herself reluctant to ride through the center of camp, to face the commotion of greeting. Her injuries would cause enough commotion as it was. Rafe cut away, preferring, he said, to put off facing Gus as long as possible. Irene and Cow crept up on the camp like marauders, but even so both Mark and Gus were waiting by her tent. Were the camels really telepaths? Surely not.

Unfortunately, no one needed telepathy to understand what had happened to her. Gus took one look and flinched in sympathy. Mark, however, had never seen the aftermath of a kong attack before.

"Auntie! What the, ah, what in the world hap—"

"Kongs," said Irene shortly. Cow came to a stop, but didn't kneel at once, and Irene was grateful. Maybe the dignity of height would save her from a lecture about how stupid she'd been.

"But I thought . . . Didn't they warn you?"

"Yes," said Irene. "So did Rafe. It wasn't his fault." Which left only one person whose fault it could be, didn't it?

Gus and Mark stared up at her silently. Looming over them wasn't going to save her, so she patted Cow's hump, and the camel tipped down. She started to dismount, trying to conceal her stiffness, but Gus's gentle hand slipped under her elbow, easing the painful jar as her feet hit the ground.

"You just don't know when to quit, do you?" His soft voice held an unwieldy mix of anger, amusement, and resignation.

"It's worse than that." Mark's brows pulled together in the frown Irene so seldom saw. "I don't think she knows *how* to quit. And that's *not* a good thing."

But he stepped forward, hugging her with gentle care. Irene suppressed a wince at even that soft pressure on her back, and hugged him in return.

"OK." Mark released her. "I'll be back in a minute." He turned and walked away. He was only using one cane now, and his steps were steady, if a bit slow. Irene was smiling when she turned to Gus.

"Have I thanked you, properly, for what you did for Mark?"

"No," said Gus. "But to thank me *properly,* your back would have to be in better shape."

It took Irene a second to get it, despite his teasing tone, and her cheeks grew hot with embarrassed indignation. "That's not what I meant, and you know—"

"Of course," Gus cut in, "Ent's the one you really ought to thank, but I'm not sure that would be possible. Or at least, advisable. Or even appreciated, whereas I would *really* appreciate . . ."

Irene began to laugh.

"That's better." He laid a hand softly on the right side of her face. "I'm afraid to touch you anywhere else. Why didn't you leave when they warned you?"

"I thought I might be onto something." The warmth of his skin was more distracting than it should have been. The air seemed thinner, fragile, and inadequate. Irene had to take an extra breath to go on. "I was working on something interesting, and I hoped they'd give me a little more time. The logs said they often didn't attack immediately. Though both Cow and Rafe told me to get out. I was surprised Cow didn't try to help me when . . . when they came."

Gus shook his head. "The camels never fight the kong, and the kong never attack them. We've encountered the same situation in the settlement; they always leave when they're warned. We think they established some sort of truce, before humanity ever arrived here, but maybe they're just smarter than we are."

He softened the insult by clasping the other side of her face. There were scratches there, but Irene didn't mind. She was about to be kissed. She'd only been kissed a few times in the years since Jeffery's death; casual dates that had gone nowhere, and even those had stopped long ago. She was confident, however, that she would remember how. And quite eager, suddenly, to prove it. She moved forward, just half a step, her face turning up—

"Irene!" Nola called.

"Shit," Gus whispered. Then his eyes crinkled with resigned amusement, and his hands fell away.

Irene turned to Nola, who didn't even notice her scowl, for her appalled gaze was fixed on the marks on Irene's face and arms—she broke into a jog, leaving Mark, who must have fetched her, behind.

Thanks a lot, nephew.

"Good God, Irene, you're a mess." With a doctor's unerring instinct, she circled behind Irene, staring at her back as if she could see right through the cloth of her shirt. "What happened? Didn't they warn you?"

Irene sighed.

Nola, whose salve had eased the painful scratches significantly, ordered her to rest till they healed. But a new theory had occurred to Irene—one that didn't require a life pool to test.

"All right, Cow, I've got samples in the analyzer right now. I want you to sing."

Cow chewed placidly on a chunk of turnip root. Moonlight illuminated the fine fur at the tips of her ears as she flipped them forward. She swallowed and stretched out her nose for the next piece, but Irene put it behind her back.

"No, you have to sing for this snack. Come on, Cow, *nah-woooooon.*"

Cow's head jerked up, her ears flattening against her skull. She stepped back and shook her head, like a horse tormented by flies.

"All right," said Irene, nettled. "You don't like my singing, then you take over. *Nah-woo*—"

"What in the world are you doing?" Gus demanded. "I could hear you on the other side of the camp."

In fact, Irene was attracting an audience. A large one.

"I noticed that Cow sang at both life pools," she said, with all the dignity she could muster. "It occurred to me that camel song might be the factor that triggers the primes to reproduce themselves."

"Camel *song*?"

"It breaks kettle bases. It shakes screws loose. Why shouldn't it have other effects? I've seen reactions to stranger stimuli." She hoped no one would ask what they were.

"Was that what you wanted the turnips for, Signorina?" Cicero looked appalled. "I just got the last of

the new bases fired and attached. If you succeed, my
work will be undone."

"It will be undone anyway, the next bright night,"
said Gus. "I thought you weren't raised to be a wolf
cub."

"I'm not howling," said Irene firmly. "This is science."

"Ah. That accounts for it."

"Well, I think you've got a problem." Mark's eyes
were bright with amusement. And he was holding
Sondi's hand. Irene decided she didn't want to know
what they'd been doing.

"Cow doesn't seem to like your singing," Mark
went on cheerfully. "No surprise, since—"

"No one else does, either," Irene finished with him.
Her nieces and nephews had been teasing her about
her singing ever since she first croaked out "Happy
Birthday." "I don't care if anyone likes it, as long as
I can convince her to sing for me."

"Then I'll help," said Mark. "*Nah-woooooooon.*" His
voice wobbled with suppressed laughter, and Sondi
giggled.

Soon they were all laughing, and Irene had acquired
a chorus of willing teenagers who warbled away for
almost twenty minutes. They attracted several camels,
who watched with interest and happily accepted the
remnants of Irene's turnip root, but they refused to
join in.

Irene wasn't too disappointed. The colonists' lack
of resistance to her idea had already told her that the
camels' song wasn't the catalyst.

So what was?

Irene never knew what awakened her from her
heat-sodden sleep. She turned to Mark—he looked
ridiculously young, with his heat-flushed cheeks. His
breathing was even and easy. She looked down, past
her feet.

Rafe was shrouded like a monk in the light robes

the colonists wore when they had to brave the sun.
His expression held misery, apology, and a determination Irene found terrifying. One hand was locked, be-
trayingly, on the analyzer's handle—it was already half
out of the tent. A thick club lay on the sand behind
him.

Irene drew a breath and screamed.

The sunlit stillness shattered. Rafe scrambled away,
reaching for the club, but Irene rolled out of the tent
and leapt after him, bringing him down on top of it.
An elbow in her ribs made her grunt, but she didn't
let go.

Then he twisted around and broke her grip with
humiliating ease. She hadn't realized he was so strong.
She struggled up again, and dived, barely catching his
sleeve. He whirled and lifted the club, just as Mark
tackled him and the two of them went down in a
churning mass of fists and knees.

Irene snatched up the club, prepared to bring it
down the moment she got a clear shot. Then the club
was tugged from her hand. She spun to face Ravi—
for once, he didn't look serene.

"Let us handle this. Please."

He and Nola's husband separated the two boys.
Mark dropped to the sand, panting, but Rafe went on
struggling in Ravi's firm grasp.

Half the camp had joined them by then—questions
and exclamations spattered like fléchette shot. The
light hurt Irene's eyes. She was shaking.

"He was stealing the analyzer." Her voice quivered
with frightened anger. "He had a club, the fucking
son of a bitch. He was going to smash it!"

"Take it easy." Gus's arm went around her. "It
didn't happen."

Irene pulled away, facing him. "It would have, if I
hadn't waked up. This is all your fault, with your stupid, paranoid compromise. If I was back on the *Stanley,* I'd have the *answer* by now. I'd—"

"She would, too," Rafe's venomous voice broke in. "What's wrong with you people? Can't you see how dangerous she is? She won't quit! You know, you *know,* what that means."

A brooding silence fell. Irene looked at the encircling faces. Anger, fear, compassion. Nola's face was stark with despair.

"What?" Irene was pleading, openly. "What does it mean?"

Gus stirred. "It means, evidently, that Rafe can't be trusted to keep to our agreement any more than Maureen can." Irene would never have believed his mild voice could hold that tone of command. "Owen, Cicero, you keep an eye on him today. He leaves as soon after sunset as he can get his camel packed. If there's any further discussion, it can take place at night."

"Gus, Rafe is right." Nola's voice was hoarse. "Sooner or later, she's going to find out—"

"What can she do about it, as long as we hold her here?" Gus demanded wearily. "*I* think we should have told her the truth from the start, but we reached an agreement, and until we agree to alter it, that deal stands! We'll discuss it when the sun's down."

Nola nodded slowly. The other colonists were already beginning to scatter, and Irene could see the point—the sun's burning touch penetrated the skin on her arms and face.

Several of the men helped pull Rafe away.

"Gus, for God's sake, tell me—"

"After sunset." He turned away, shielding his eyes with his hand.

Mark had already crawled under the tent, dragging her precious analyzer into shelter as well. There was nothing left to do, but follow. It was a long time before Irene slept.

The next night was a strange one. If there had been a meeting, Irene never heard about it. Most of the colonists seemed willing to let matters return to the status quo, but Irene sensed that the opposition had hardened. Nola turned away, refusing to speak with her at all. And even her supporters had trouble meeting her eyes.

It hardly mattered.

There was nothing left in camp to test that she hadn't already tested, and the same instinct that told her she already had the pieces of the puzzle in her grasp told her that now she needed to think, not work. To let her mind settle, let the details she'd learned shift about till she could see the pattern that was eluding her.

"Which just goes to show you that instinct is bunk."

"What?" said Sondi.

Irene, who'd almost forgotten her presence and hadn't intended to say it aloud anyway, grimaced. "Skip it. I'm just frustrated because I'm not getting anywhere."

Sondi shifted the strap of the dung bag on her shoulder, and turned to lead them around the moonsilvered dune into the next grassy hollow. Irene had chosen dried-dung collection as an excuse to get out of camp for a while, though it was generally the kid flock's chore. She'd been pleased, however, when Sondi volunteered to come with her, for she knew she should get to know Sondi better—and Sondi appeared to be bent on the same errand, for the same reasons. Though she was probably acting as Irene's guard as well.

It might have been awkward, but Sondi had the rare quality of being at home with silence, and Irene's preoccupation with anomaly 1 had crept back to ambush her again.

"Don't dismiss your hunches," Sondi told her soberly. "Nola says there are lots of parts of the brain that people don't use, but if we're not using them somehow, then why did they evolve? I think instinct is just another part of the brain speaking up. Though I have to admit my first instinct was to shoot at Mark, so the forebrain ought to come into play, too."

Her eyes turned into sparkling crescents when she laughed. And what she said made excellent sense. No wonder Mark was fascinated.

"My instincts aren't getting me any further than my forebrain," Irene grumbled. "In fact, my whole mind seems to be on the fritz these days."

It must be love. The sardonic thought swam up out of nowhere, and Irene grimaced and reached down for an oval of dung to throw into the bag's open mouth.

Innocuous as it was after a day's sun had dried it, there was a time when the mere thought of handling camel dung with her bare hands would have sent Irene rushing to the nearest sink. Now, anomaly 1 served as her armor—it was a hell of a lot more comfortable than an enviro-suit, too. But there was more to it than that.

"I don't think your brain is fritzing," said Sondi solemnly. "It's like . . . like draining a marsh. Once you've dug the trench for the water to drain off, and the reflective surface is gone, the shape of the land beneath it emerges. I'm not saying that very well, I guess." She picked up another round of dung and dropped it in the sack.

"No, it's fine. Except for the way Mark's corrupting your vocabulary. But how do you know about marshes?" Irene gestured to the sandy dune slopes, to the dry entirety of the desert beyond.

"We've drained wetlands," said Sondi. "It was about . . . eleven years ago? Something like that. We decided to try building a settlement on the coast."

Irene summoned up her vague memory of the continent she'd seen from the shuttle window. "The desert runs into the coast, doesn't it? West of here?"

"That's right. That's where our weather, the fogs and ice storms, come from. That's what forms the desert, for that matter—there's a really cold current running just offshore. We don't know how far out it goes, but the surf is icy." She shivered, even in the warm night. "And the wind is *fierce*. On the coast it can knock you off your feet on a brisk day. And *it's* cold, too." She bent to pick up another round of dung.

"So why settle there?"

"We thought we could stay year-round. It was cold, but the ice storms tend to skip over it. Plants grow there all year, and when we drained a marsh the soil was good—at least for plants with a high salt tolerance. And you can fish anytime, no matter what the plants do."

"So what went wrong?"

"There was another species already occupying that territory—they didn't want to share."

"Another *intelligent* species? What is it with this planet?"

Sondi grinned, then sobered. "We were never sure they were intelligent, not like the kong. They looked sort of like seals or sea lions—mammals, but amphibious, with small arms and hands for their front set of limbs, like hexa-otters, but more . . . more carnivorous-looking. They were slow on land, but in the water they were faster than a dire cat. And smarter, too." The bones of her face stood out as her expression tightened—this was how she would look in twenty years, or thirty. Or a hundred and thirty, given the life span anomaly 1 granted its hosts.

"They never attacked on land, and once your boat overturned, or sank, you were helpless. And without being able to fish, there wasn't enough food to support a colony, so it didn't work out. But it was worth a try. Though the camels didn't like it either."

"Any life pools there?" Maybe anomaly 1's nursery was in another ecosystem altogether, and—

"No," said Sondi, dashing that possibility. "That was one of the drawbacks, but we figured we could go back to them when our organisms started to die off. A booster shot, Nola called it."

"How often do you have to renew the organism, to keep it in your bloodstream?" Irene tried to sound casual—this was one of the questions Nola wouldn't answer.

She must have failed, for Sondi gave her a wary look and didn't reply.

Irene sighed. "You know, I'm at a standstill here. If you people won't tell me what you're hiding, I'll never get anywhere. And if you didn't want me to solve it, then you should have let Mark die and sent the *Stanley* on."

Sondi flinched. "We thought about it," she admitted. "But we wanted . . . We hoped you'd be able to . . ."

"To make the primes reproduce in the lab without learning where they come from? Well, I'm stuck, so it looks like you're going to have to make another choice."

Sondi's face was sad. "Nola was right. We should have faked your deaths and sent your ship away."

"What?"

"That was the other plan. Splash some blood around your wrecked sled, and tell Captain Keene and the others that a dire cat had killed you, and that Mark had died of GED. Tell them we cremated the bodies for sanitation. If they couldn't find you, they'd have accepted it. They'd be gone by now. But we 'compromised' instead. And now . . ."

She fell silent. She loved Mark, damn it. She wasn't so callous as to condemn others to die without some overwhelming reason. Irene was just beginning to realize how much the colonists felt they were risking. So what—

"Three to five years," said Sondi abruptly. "That's how long it lives in humans. Some people wait till they get sick before going to renew it, but most go to a pool every three years or so."

Irene gazed at her in astonishment. Had she converted a member of the opposition?

Sondi smiled shyly. "Parents take their kids. Couples . . ." Her smooth cheeks darkened. "Couples make love in them, I've heard. Especially newlyweds. For luck."

Irene remembered the velvety mud of the pool floor, the warm light arrowing through the water. She imagined the mud against her back, a man's body, Gus's stocky body, pushing her deeper into the mud, and her own cheeks heated.

She was growing uncomfortably aroused, and she tucked the fantasy away—she could make good use of it later. How long had it been since she'd fantasized about sex with someone real, someone she knew? Too damn long.

"I can see the appeal," she admitted to Sondi, reaching for another round of dung to hide her expression. How long could she keep the girl talking? "But I'd think it'd put you off a bit, when your camel waded in and shit in the . . ."

Cow, shitting deliberately into the pool. Cow— *They control the life pools,* Maureen's furious voice echoed in her memory. *They're the only ones who know where they are. The only ones who know how they work. So unless you find a way to talk to them, genius, you're shit out of luck.*

Shit.

Irene began to laugh. Her hands clenched on the chip of dung, shredding it. Dried, it was worthless. She needed fresh dung.

Sondi was staring at her, alarm on her open, young face, as if Irene had turned into Dr. Frankenstein before her eyes. Not good for Mark's courtship, perhaps, but Irene didn't care.

She turned and ran back to camp—light-footed for

once, on the shifting sand. She plunged into the shadows of her tent and fumbled for the biosample kit, an empty vial.

Fresh camel dung was ridiculously easy to come by, though the grazing herd looked curiously at her as she knelt to gather it into the plastic container. One of them snorted.

"Same to you," Irene muttered absently.

The camel bent its long neck and goosed her.

Irene raced back to her tent. Adrenaline danced through her blood, and her heart drummed for it, but now was the time for caution. For science. By the numbers, by the book, because if she blew it, she'd just have to do it over.

Irene set up the microanalyzer, step by methodical step, took a small sample of dung and stirred it briskly into a cup of well water. It might not work outside a life pool, of course. There might be dozens of other elements involved. She might be completely wrong. Her hand shook as she poured a few milliliters of the sample into her slide and dropped it in the waiting slot. A circle of light bloomed on the sand around the analyzer.

?—

Locate., Irene typed.

Sample?—

Camel dung 1.

Scan for?—

Anomaly 1.

Begin?—

Y.

The cursor blinked, and she settled in to watch. At least Mark's programming enabled the analyzer do the searching for her. Anomaly after anomaly flashed on the screen; Irene clicked through them. It would take a while to locate a breeding aggregate.

She'd run off on Sondi without a word, laughing like a madwoman. She'd have to apologize, and Mark would start telling his "crazy aunt" stories. If he hadn't told them already. He probably had, and to Gus as well as Son— There!

The aggregate was just forming, dozens of anomaly 1 wiggling into position, their cilia blending and clinging, walling off her view of what happened inside.

It would take a while. Irene shifted restlessly. She needed the patience of a hunter, a stalker, for this. The minutes crawled past, and she sat and dithered, her fingers fidgeting in the loose sand. In her lab on the *Stanley* she could have set the analyzer to record the whole event, mark the offspring as it escaped, and gone for a cup of coffee. As it was, she didn't dare take her eyes off the writhing mass of microbes as they pulsed and twisted in an effort to aid the fragile fission going on in their midst.

In the end it always happened fast. The cluster elongated, and began to contract, not quite rhythmically, beating to its own, essential imperative. Irene backed the range off, blessing the hours she'd spent watching this event—they allowed her to spot the new anomaly as it shot out of the cluster, like something expelled from a syringe. Had she not backed off, it would have spurted out of the lens's field and been lost in the sea of cells.

As it was, she quickly moved the vertical and horizontal tracking lines to mark it, then she moved the focus down and looked.

Its nucleus had three lobes.

The *camels* were the nursery, the host in which anomaly primes would reproduce themselves. Not in their blood, but in their intestines. They made the pools and maintained them. By shitting in them.

Irene fought down an inappropriate giggle. But this was an aspect of science that never made it into the textbooks, this giddy delight that seized the heart when some tiny portion of the universe revealed itself. The cup of life lay in her hands, brimming with light, a light that would overflow to heal kids like Mark, and Willard's daughter.

Irene gazed at the squirming, newborn ciliophora and laughed.

She spent the rest of that night confirming her hypothesis; she tested other camels' feces, she tested their urine, which didn't contain anomaly 1 but did provide an incredible number of chemicals, some of which they might need to survive. Cow had pissed in the pool, too, she remembered. And she found her guess was right—in pure water all the anomaly 1 died within hours. There were other interactions involved, probably chemical, that the samples would need to maintain themselves, but she would isolate them eventually. By the time she finished, the only thing she didn't understand was . . . "Why just the camels? Why not hexamoles, or heli-bats? Why not us?"

"Why not us what?" Mark demanded. "Auntie, what's going on? You've worked half the night, and you haven't eaten breakfast *or* lunch. All you do is sit in front of that . . . that damn screen and mutter and cackle. You're beginning to worry me."

"Hmm? I'm sorry Mark, did you say something?" Why was he gritting his teeth that way?

"Yes." Mark's voice was full of strained patience. "I asked you what was going on."

"Mark, I've got it. I've finally got it. It's the camels. . . ."

By the time she finished, Mark's eyes were alight with excitement. "That fits, doesn't it? I can even guess why they make the pools. Sondi told me that when a calf is born, the camels take it and immerse it in a life pool. That stuff, the anomaly, it must not be able to pass through the . . . what do you call it?"

"Placental barrier," said Irene.

"Yeah, that's it. They had to find a way to pass it to their young outside their bodies, so they invented the life pools. And that's how they knew to take the colonists there when *they* got sick."

"That was a pretty big risk," said Irene. "There are creatures, the reptiles I've tested for instance, in which anomaly 1 can't live at all. It might not have survived in humans."

"Not much risk," said Mark. "If they were dying anyway. Besides, it worked. It *works*."

"So it does." Even her weariness couldn't dim that satisfaction.

But Mark was frowning. "Why didn't they tell you this in the first place? Why keep it a secret?"

It took Irene a moment to switch from microbiological behavior to human, then she frowned, too.

"I don't know. But I know who can tell me—and now, they have no reason to keep anything back."

She stopped by Cicero's kitchen to scrounge a meal from the remains of lunch. Cicero asked no questions, but the way he looked at her hair induced Irene to shake out her braid, comb, and redo it. It was bad enough she was acting like a wild woman—she didn't have to go around looking like one.

She found Gus repairing a camel's pack frame; stiltie wood was both light and flexible, ideal for many tasks, but it looked odd strapped in among the plasticine struts that made up the rest of the frame.

Gus was running some kind of tool over it, shaving off long slivers, his square hands working with a competence Irene found appealing. Sexy in fact. Which she would rather not have felt just then, about this secretive son of a bitch.

"I've figured it out," she announced.

"So I'm told." Gus smiled, but for the first time in Irene's memory, it didn't reach his eyes. "Sondi said you looked like someone hit you on the head with a rock. She half expected you to tear off your clothes and run through the camp yelling 'eureka.' I must say, I wish you had."

Irene refused to be distracted. "Why didn't you just tell me in the first place? Why keep me prisoner?"

Gus hesitated for a long moment, then he sighed. "Because if we'd told you, you'd have gone straight to Keene and told him all about it. Wouldn't you?"

"Damn straight I would! Gus, this cures *GED,* and God only knows what else! It could save thousands—"

"And how do you propose to get it back to Earth?" Gus's voice was pleasant and reasonable, but his eyes were very sharp.

"I'll . . . There must be someplace it will survive, reproduce itself, outside of a camel."

"That's what we hoped you could find," said Gus. "Preferably without ever discovering that the camels were involved. Because in forty years of trying, none of our doctors or biologists has found one. It won't even survive outside a life pool for more than a few days, no matter how exactly we try to reproduce the environment."

"But Sondi said it lives in the human body for years. We could—"

"It dies when you transfer it from one host to another," said Gus. "We've tried. When it leaves the pool for a host, it adapts itself to that one person's immune system, and it can't deal with any other. Nola can show you her research on that now. It's been her project for—"

"Why not before? Why couldn't she tell me all this before?"

"If she had, what would Willard Keene have done? Because once he finds out about this, he's going to want to take the breeding primes back to Earth, and there's only one vessel that will keep it alive to do that—a camel."

"But you don't—"

"He'll put as many as he can into any room on his ship where he can set up biocontainment. Someone told me that you had a conference room, half of which was designed as a sealed biochamber, so you could talk to colonists without anyone having to wear enviro-suits. How many camels could he cram into that space, Goodnight? Two? Six? What kind of lives do you think they'd lead? And not only on the ship, what about on Earth? How much space would they be granted in those crowded domes—a pen? The freedom of a few acres of park? They're nomadic! They range almost eight hundred kilometers a year."

"I know that, but—"

"And the organism might not survive in their bodies away from Navohar—native grasses, native water, who knows what goes into maintaining the balance that—"

"All right!" Irene yelled.

Gus stepped back, blinking in astonishment. "Sorry, I didn't mean to—"

"Fine, forget it. I know all you've said. But even if you assume that Willard, and I, and the *Stanley*'s entire crew are the kind of . . . of sadistic thugs who'd kidnap and imprison a sentient race for our own purposes, you're still going to have to deal with them sometime. When the flitters find you—"

"They won't," said Gus.

"You think they're just going to quit? Willard *knows* that you people survived a plague that should have killed you. He suspects that you took Mark to try to cure him. His own daughter *died* of GED, other kids are dying back on Earth right now, and this is the only planet we've found that offers even a hope of a cure. Those flitters cover a lot of territory— sooner or later they'll spot you, maybe even today, and—"

"Not likely. They're almost to the coas—" He stopped himself, but it was too late; his face was full of guilt and mischief.

It took Irene a second to get her voice working. "You *know* where they are?"

"Pretty much. They've been flying a very regular

search pattern, right from the start—it makes it easy to be where they're not. We sheltered in the outskirts of the forest till they moved outside our range. The only time they deviated from the pattern was when they went looking for you—we had a couple of close calls then, but they never actually overflew us, and we blend in pretty well. Since then they've been working steadily outward and—"

"How do you know what they're doing?"

"The weather satellite is tracking them," said Gus. "It's really quite sophis—"

"You're in contact with the satellite?"

"Why not? A portable sat-link is both light and sturdy, though I must admit the camel song gives it fits. Having some warning when an ice storm's coming in can make a big difference."

"Then you could use it to contact the *Stanley,* couldn't you? They could come get me."

Gus's expression set like iron. "We could, but we won't. I'm not going to let you tell Keene about the camels. For God's sake, Goodnight, you'd lived with them, with Cow, for weeks when Maureen told you they were intelligent, and *you* didn't believe it. You had to test them, and—"

"Yes, but—"

"People usually empathize with people who resemble them—speak the same language, worship the same god. Who's going to empathize with people who look like *that*!" He waved wildly at the nearest camel, who happened to be Nola's husband's mount, Bambi.

Irene's face was hot. "You think I don't know that? You think *I'd* enslave them?"

"No, but I think the only reason you wouldn't is because we took the time to let you learn they were intelligent—and we practically had to ram it through your teeth! And you're not—"

"No, I'm not," said Irene. "I'm not a fool, but I'm not about to let your bloody paranoia and . . . and arrogance get in the way of saving thousands of lives. You think you're the only ones who can care about someone who doesn't happen to be human, then fine, but I'm not going to let—"

"No." Gus's face were red with anger, and he took a step toward her. If he were taller he'd have loomed, but he was almost the same height as Irene, so it didn't have much effect. "You're not leaving this camp unless you can find a way to make the organism breed *outside* a camel, because I'm not going to let your damned, self-righteous crusade endanger the lives of a gentle, generous people whose only crime is their willingness to save all the people they find who need saving. You think that makes me a callous son of a bitch, then fine, but—"

"You self-centered bastard," Irene hissed. "What makes you think—"

Gus grabbed her arms as if to shake her, but instead he brought his mouth down on hers. It was so unexpected, Irene didn't have time to react before he'd done it. His grasp was firm, but his lips were amazingly gentle, considering the fury that must be singing through his veins. For one wild moment Irene wanted to respond. To kiss him back, and let elemental anger transform into another, even more elemental drive. And that instant of humiliating weakness was the final straw.

She pulled away; his grip on her arms was too strong to break, but she gained enough distance to kick his shin, as hard as she could.

It probably hurt her bare foot as much as his leg—not very much—but he let go of her arms, his eyes widening in dismay.

Irene shoved him backwards, onto his ass.

"You arrogant, egotistical . . . bastard." She couldn't think of anything bad enough to call him, and frustration put the final edge on her temper. This was useless! She turned and stalked away, ignoring the stares of the colonists who'd lingered in the vicinity. He'd never listen! If he thought she was the sort of mindless zealot who'd trample over anything and anyone to get her way, then fine. She whirled to look back.

Gus still sat in the sand, and the anger on his face matched her own. He opened his mouth, but Irene beat him to it.

"FINE!" Her shout cracked the desert silence like a china plate, and half a dozen nearby camels shied and snorted in protest.

She spent the rest of the night muttering and pacing—not even Mark dared to approach her. She spent most of the long, hot day tossing in the shade of her tent, but eventually the heat, and her own growing weariness, drove her into sleep.

When she woke she was calmer. Calm enough to go to Nola and ask, in a reasonably polite tone, if she'd share her research. At least, Irene hoped it was reasonably polite.

If it wasn't, Nola didn't take offense. She brought out a lightweight, portable datacorder that Irene had never suspected she possessed, and its contents kept Irene busy for the next two nights. Nola had spent much of the last forty years trying to figure out a way to take anomaly 1 off-planet.

"It's the weirdest stuff," she told Irene, the relief of being able to talk freely brightening her face. "If you freeze fresh dung, it lasts forever. I've got freezers full of it back in the settlement. And pool water, too."

Irene remembered the numbered containers of dark matter she'd helped move. No wonder Nola hadn't bothered to put names on the labels.

But the vet went on, "You can thaw and combine the two, and it breeds just fine—for a few days. And even in those few days it only transfers to a host about twenty percent of the time. You know, your idea about the camel song being a catalyst might not be as crazy as it sounds. I swear to God, I've tried everything else."

"In my lab," said Irene, "I could subject it to a whole spectrum of subharmonics. I could analyze the content of working pond water down to the last molecule. I can *solve* this with the right equipment."

"Maybe," said Nola. "But if you fail, you're not the one who'll pay. All the camels on this planet couldn't produce enough dung to inoculate every human who'd like to live two hundred years. We hoped that if you started from scratch, you might be able to see something the rest of us missed. Maybe even find a way to make the primes reproduce without learning about the camels' role in the process. That was why we were willing to give you blood samples and help you get to a life pool, but not . . ."

"But not tell me the one thing that mattered," said Irene wearily. "Never mind. I understand that, now."

"Do you?" Nola looked at her searchingly. "We're taking a terrible risk on you. We wouldn't have done it, if we hadn't known we could keep you here, no matter what you discovered."

"I understand," said Irene.

That didn't mean she agreed.

Most of Nola's notes were scientific, but the subtext made it clear that she shared Gus's concern about what might happen to the camels if other humans found Navohar. They'd been preparing for this, for her, Irene realized, for decades. The thought was sobering. Even more sobering was Nola's failure to find any environment except a camel in which the anomaly primes would reproduce themselves. Eight days was the longest she'd succeeded in keeping them alive outside a life pool. But the only chance Nola had had to work with anything like proper equipment had been on her rare visits to the settlement, and her analyzer there wasn't much better than Irene's portable analyzer. She had to get back to the *Stanley*.

And the colonists wouldn't let her go. She'd hardly been aware of being guarded before. Now there was always someone following her, unobtrusive, at a distance, but there.

Ravi willingly showed her the sat-link that let him contact the weather satellite that hovered over this continent, and showed her Willard's flitters, searching over an obvious grid with meticulous predictability. No wonder Gus wasn't worried about being found. And he was also right that if they found no trace of the colonists, sooner or later Willard would have to give up and leave. The other groups of colonists had been warned to avoid him as well; they used the satellite to pass messages from one group to another.

They'd looked so primitive, seen through the faceplate of an enviro-suit—it had been easy to underestimate their tech base. They'd deliberately created that innocuous impression.

Gus was right, it would be hard to convince Willard and the others that the camels were intelligent—but not impossible. The Vrell had taught humans that they couldn't ignore the possibility of alien intelligence. And that the price of victory could be too high.

Even if she failed, they already had the samples they needed, right there in the settlement's refrigerators. The camels wouldn't suffer. She'd make sure of it. The cure for GED was within her grasp; she couldn't let it go because Gus might not forgive her. Because Nola, Cicero, Ravi, and the rest of her friends would feel betrayed. As for Mark . . . Mark no longer needed her. He wouldn't have needed her for the last several years if he hadn't been ill. Sondi would be there for him, and the others as well.

It was time to escape. But to escape she had to have cooperation, from Gus, from the colonists, and most of all, from Cow. The camels had better not be telepathic.

* * *

"I've been thinking about what you said," she told Gus without preamble.

He looked up from the cracked, plasticine shovel blade he was welding. It was the first time Irene had spoken to him in three days.

"I don't agree with everything you said" (she would have, if it wouldn't have looked suspicious) "but you were right that I had to see the camels' intelligence for myself, or I wouldn't have believed it. So you're probably right about the others on the *Stanley* as well."

Gus's shoulders sagged with relief; keeping the surge of guilt off her face was one of the hardest things Irene had ever done.

"I'm glad. More than glad. You're so stub—determined, I was beginning to be afraid it would have to be a sandy grave for you after all."

Irene remembered their conversation when she first found the camp, and her grin was almost sincere. "Of course you did. I hoped you were done insulting my intelligence."

Gus blushed. "I'm sorry about that. I didn't mean it as an insult to your intelligence. Exactly."

"Kiss her and she'll melt into your arms and forget all her principles? You think that's not—"

"It wasn't deliberate." Gus rose to face her, still flushed. "It just sort of happened. Besides, it works in the vids."

Irene snorted.

"Anyway, I'm sorry." He held out his hand and Irene shook it gravely. "Pax?"

"Pax." She fought down another wave of guilt. "Gus, I need to talk to you. I've been looking at Nola's research . . ."

Gus wasn't so easily lulled. It took her two more days to convince him that she needed to go to back to the life pool, now that she knew what to look for. He finally agreed, but insisted that she take both Nola and the lanky boy who had replaced Rafe as her chief guard. All of this contingent on Cow's willingness to take her.

Irene's calm acceptance convinced him, and all the others, of her sincerity. They might have been harder to convince if they had watched a beloved nephew dying of GED. They'd certainly have been harder to convince if they'd known that her biosample kit contained tranquilizer darts.

Irene spent the better part of that first night wondering how she could poison two people without at least one of them noticing. But in the end it was riduculously easy—she simply made the tea.

She added a few odd spices to mask the taste, and told Nola she was experimenting. She thought that might make them suspicious, but Nola, and even the guard kid, took their cups without hesitation. It told Irene, more than anything else, how much trust she'd earned among the colonists. How angry would they be to find that trust betrayed?

Sipping the plain water with which she'd surreptitiously filled her cup loosened her tight throat, but nothing could quell the surge of guilt that hit her when Nola started to yawn.

It will only make them sleepy, Irene told herself firmly. *It probably won't even knock them out.*

The guard kid slept several dozen yards away, which kept him and Nola from observing each other's behavior. Irene waited for several minutes after Nola's breathing assumed a light, slow rhythm before going to check on the boy. She packed with quiet care, then checked them again, but neither showed any sign of an anaphylactic reaction. They had made camp in a deep cleft that would be shaded all day. And they had their camels to take care of them.

Irene had considered drugging the camels instead, but she didn't know enough about their physiology to feel safe giving them alien drugs. As their placid gaze followed her and Cow out of camp, she was glad she hadn't tried.

"I won't betray you," she told Cow's third eye. "I'll convince them, and between us we'll save all those kids."

Cow didn't even twitch an ear, so she probably couldn't read Irene's mind.

Irene sighed. She'd swathed herself in robes, stolen from Nola's pack, for travel in the sun, and she thought they could reach the cool plateau by mid-morning, but even so she'd underestimated the heat. It rose off the sand in shimmering waves, burning her slitted eyes. Her robes were drenched with sweat by the end of the first hour. When she dismounted to water Cow, the sand that sifted through her sandal straps was so hot she yelped and hastened to shake it out.

By the time Cow started the long scramble up the rocky slope that led to the plateau, she had a pounding headache and would have killed for a cool shower. But none of it mattered. She had the cure for GED in her hands.

They reached the forest several hours before noon. The memory of pain and terror rippled up Irene's spine, but she wasn't going to stay long enough for the kongs to care. Soon a pillar of smoke rose to meet the sun. *There's more than one way to send a signal.*

Irene fed the fire patiently, dry wood to keep it burning, green boughs for the smoke. It might take a while, but even a flitter pilot couldn't ignore her for-ever. In fact it was just after noon when the nasal whine interrupted her yawns, and half a dozen flitters swooped in to settle in the clearing beside her fire.

They pounded her back, which hurt her aching head, and clasped her hands with their gloved ones. Their muffled voices cracked with delight at finding her alive. They wanted to take her straight to the ship, immediately, and didn't in the least understand why she insisted on riding a *camel* back, even if, with their guidance, it was only half a day's ride.

It grew harder and harder for Irene to return their smiles.

Chapter 11

She reached the settlement at dusk. Cow had been wary of the scentless, enviro-suited figures at first, but she'd accepted Irene's assurance that they weren't a threat. Irene prayed she could make good on her word.

In truth, the suited people awaiting her in the clearing between the settlement's empty buildings seemed almost as alien to her as they must have to Cow—until she saw the tears on Myrna's face inside the helmet.

"Drat you. I hate crying in these things," she muttered, hugging Irene so fiercely that Irene's eyes filled as well. "You look like Lawrence of Arabia, except not as sexy."

"That," said Willard, "is a matter of opinion." He hugged her too, in public no less, the knobs on his suit front digging into her skin. Over his shoulder she saw delight in Khalil's face, and fury in Astrid's. Had she been making progress with Willard once Irene was presumed dead?

"My dear." Willard's voice was eloquent with compassion, even through the distortion of the suit's speaker. "I'm so sorry about Mark."

"You needn't be." Irene took a deep, quivering breath. This was what she'd come here for. The moment she'd prayed to reach when she set out on the *Stanley* over fifteen months ago. The beginning of life for thousands of kids who otherwise would die. So why was her stomach trembling?

Willard pulled back to look at her, puzzled by the tension in her voice. She met his eyes. "Mark is alive. Alive and walking and getting stronger every day. There's a cure for GED here. But there are a few prob—"

He'd stopped listening, and the others' cheers would be loud enough in his helmet's pickup to drown her voice, though to her they sounded tinny and distant. The joy blazing in Willard's eyes made his happiness at her return pale in comparison.

Irene fought down a shiver and went to pull her gear off Cow.

They settled in the bio-divided conference room, so that none of them would have to wear a suit. Willard had allowed three others to join him—the rest of the crew would be glued to the com. Dr. Dahl, the ship's physician, smiled at her gravely, his eyes taking in the fine pink lines of healing scratches—the residue of the kongs' attack. Louise Yassir was a naturalist, and her bright black eyes were intent as a hunting terrier's. Ezra's steady gaze was searching—he'd reached out to her when she first came in, but then his hands dropped, thwarted by the plastic wall.

Seeing her colleagues in their sleek suit liners, Irene wondered what the soft, loose clothes Ravi had made for her looked like to them. Primitive? Exotic? Was that what she'd thought when she first saw the colonists? The sheet of Plexiglas between them made her feel like a zoo exhibit, though she knew the architects who'd designed the room had tried to avoid that by dividing the space evenly, and running the biocontainment wall through the center of the big, oval table.

"All right, Irene, talk to us." For once even Willard had been too impatient to change clothes or comb his hair. His rumpled informality would have been disarming if his gaze hadn't been so intense.

Irene plugged her analyzer into the table port, typed

commands, and the image of anomaly 1 flooded the clear plastic between them. "This is it, people. . . ."

She'd rehearsed this presentation all through the long ride across the desert—the facts were so deeply imbedded in her mind that she could have recited them in her sleep, so now she could watch their expressions change. Deep interest for the science; joy battling a persistent fear that she'd made some mistake, that it wouldn't, couldn't possibly, do all she claimed. It was Nola's notes, forty years of painstaking case studies, that drove out the fear, letting triumph simmer to the surface.

Then she explained about the camels, and curiosity and incredulity turned to disbelief. Reserve and pity on Ryan Dahl's dark face. Willard looked worried, about her, damn the condescending prick, and Ezra's wrinkled, dignified face assumed a professional nonexpression that Irene found downright chilling.

She went on to express her doubts about the camels' ability to maintain the organisms off Navohar, and the difficulty of keeping them alive outside the life pools.

"So you see, gentlemen, we have several serious problems to overcome before we can take this back to Earth. But I'm confident that with time, and the proper equipment, we can induce this organism to reproduce itself, either in the lab or in the human body, and then we can take it home."

Irene discovered that her hands were trembling and folded them in her lap, trying to look professional and confident.

There was a long pause, then Louise Yassir shifted in her seat. "It seems to me that the first step toward finding out what goes on in those camel-creatures' bodies is to dissect one. An exact knowledge of the chemical environment in their intestines at every stage of the digestive process is only the first—"

"I told you." Irene's voice sounded, even to her own ears, as if it had been chipped from a glacier.

"The camels are sentient. To kill them would be murder. To take them against their will—"

"Irene," said Willard gently, "I know you've had a hard time." His eyes swept over her grimy clothes, his expression torn between pity and distaste. "But you admitted that they have no language, use no tools, and when you tried to test their intelligence, frankly, they failed."

"They didn't fail, they refused to take the test!"

"My dear, how can you tell the difference? How do you know they understood what you wanted?"

"I told you, the camel dumped me into the blue tub—"

"Coincidence," said Louise shortly. "And many animals on Earth were clever about stealing food, but that didn't make racoons, for instance, intelligent."

Irene took a deep breath—if she started yelling they'd never listen. "The colonists, who have dealt with them for four decades, are convinced that they are a sentient species."

"But you said all the intelligence tests they tried failed too," said Willard reasonably. "And given that intelligence evolves only in tool-using animals . . ."

Nothing can move faster than the speed of light, Gus's voice echoed in Irene's memory. *The sun revolves around the earth.*

". . . and that there is no empirical evidence of their intelligence, I think we have to proceed on the basis of that evidence." He smiled, gently soothing. "Once we've discovered the factor or factors which cause the anomaly primes to reproduce, we can start back to Earth. The sooner the better. We can—"

Irene drew a breath to argue, but Ezra cut in first.

"A moment, Willard. If Irene is right, and these creatures are sentient, to use them as lab specimens would be . . . a grave wrong. Perhaps we should consider some alternatives."

"There are frozen samples of their dung available," Irene began. "All we need—"

"But we have to dissect at least one of them," Louise said urgently. "If we don't, it might take months, even years, to learn—"

Willard held up a hand to cut her off, but the look he turned on Ezra was less gentle than the one he'd given Irene. "Dr. Markhov, every day we delay may be costing another life. Frankly, even if they *were* proved to be sentient, I would sacrifice the few we'll need, to test and for breeding, to save the thousands of *human* lives that this disease threatens."

He means it. No wonder he's not listening—he doesn't even want *to hear . . . Dear God, what have I done? What have I . . .*

"Then you'd be wrong," said Ezra firmly. "Let me propose a compromise. It's going to take a while to track down and capture enough of the creatures, right?"

"Not too long," said Willard. "The flitter pilots have spotted several herds of wild camels in the desert. It shouldn't take long to locate one, and all we'll need then is a tranquilizer gun and some way to transport . . ."

"But the wild ones are intelligent, too!" Irene fought to keep her voice steady. "You're saying that if the Vrell had a medical need for us, then what they did would have been OK?"

Ezra winced, but Willard only frowned. "You're hysterical, my dear. Trust us. It will be all right in time."

"But . . ." Irene looked across at their closed faces. Ezra was the only one even listening to her. She had to stop this, but how? Her nails dug into her palms. "Every life-form on this planet is crawling with its microbiology." Maybe this was an argument they'd listen to. "You don't have a biocontainment chamber large enough to hold even one camel."

"Hmm." Willard's expression was thoughtful, but he wiped his hands against his thighs. "We'll have to empty one of the storage bays and convert it. Seal the walls. Air and water filters . . . I'll get Myrna and her people right on it."

Any delay was better than none. If she had time to convince—

"That will take several days," Ezra persisted. "Let me use them to try some of my intelligence tests on the camel Goodnight brought in. With all due respect to her and the colonists"—he flashed her a grin—"they don't have any training in this kind of thing. And if I prove they're intelligent, we can rethink the matter, agreed?"

Louise leaned forward. "We need to dissec—"

Willard smiled at Irene. "I'm always willing to consider new data," he said gravely.

He had not, Irene noticed, promised to act on that data, and she already knew what Cow would do with an intelligence test. Would even Ezra recognize that the tests he was probably considering wouldn't work if the subject wasn't interested in playing along? Irene took a deep breath. "I'd like to help with those tests. If nothing else, Cow won't let you get close without me. And if we *can* prove they're intelligent, you'll reconsider?"

"I'll consider any data you present to me," Willard repeated. "In any case, there'll be no need to harm your pet. The wild camels, if they carry the organism, can provide all the specimens we need. But are you sure you don't want to rest first? You've obviously had a very hard time."

"No," said Irene. "I don't want to rest." In fact her sleepless day was catching up with her, but she had far too much to do. And before anything else, she had to get Cow safely out of their hands. She met Willard's eyes and smiled. "Don't worry, I'll manage."

*   *   *

She'd hiked the trail over the ridge and down to the settlement often enough that it seemed familiar—more familiar than the *Stanley*'s civilized corridors, now that she thought about it. When she stopped at the ridge top to look over the moonlit desert, she was amused to see that even after all these weeks, Ezra stopped with her. The guard who carried the electro-rifle stopped too, but he didn't amuse her at all.

After over a year on the *Stanley*, everyone knew everyone else, at least by name. Hal Kesterman was one of the crew's military contingent. In fact, he was one of the flitter pilots who'd found her this morning. She'd wondered when he joined her, waiting outside the decon hatch, if he minded having to scramble in his suit again so soon—if he did, he didn't show it. He even smiled when she glared at the gun he carried.

"Be reasonable, Dr. Olsen, we've had some trouble with those kong creatures. And let's face it, that thing you ride is *big*."

"What kind of trouble with the kongs?" Irene felt a stab of alarm. "You haven't killed any of them, have you?"

"No, we've been driving them off with shot. But they've attacked the ship a couple of times, pounding on the hull with rocks and clubs. They can't do any damage, of course, and so far they've only bothered the teams in the daytime, but it pays to be careful."

Irene's objections to the electro-rifle lessened slightly, but . . . "What kind of load do you have in there—shot or singles?"

"Singles," he admitted. "Though if I want to warn them off, I can change the load in seconds. So don't worry." He smiled again, reassuringly.

Right. And if you've been using shot on the kongs, why is your first load a single rail-shot now? But she didn't need to ask aloud; only a rail-shot could stop a fleeing camel.

Ezra had hurried out of the lock then, still checking

the telltales on his suit cuff, a welcome diversion. Now he stood companionably beside Irene, gazing out over the silver filigree of the dunes.

"Did you like it, out there?" His voice was gentle. And he had lent her a shoulder to cry on, when the knowledge that Mark was dying became too much to bear.

"Yes. Yes, I did. Ezra, What the hell is going on here? They're not even listening to me."

Ezra's perceptive gaze searched her face. "Bluntly, they think you're suffering from Stockholm syndrome."

"What? You mean that thing where hostages start to identify with the people who capture them? That's ridiculous!"

"It does happen," he said calmly. "And you admitted that they held you prisoner. Besides, they don't want you to be right."

"That's the real problem, isn't it?" said Irene slowly. "The Stockholm syndrome theory just gives them an excuse. Ezra, do you think there's any chance Willard will change his mind if you prove the camels are intelligent?"

Ezra sighed. "His daughter died. I can remind you of that without revealing any professional confidences. As for the rest . . . Well, I profoundly hope you're wrong about them. It is possible, you know."

"Anything's possible," said Irene softly.

It had better be, because Willard and the others weren't going to believe her. Not in time.

Movement caught her eye at the edge of the settlement below—Cow, grazing. Waiting for Irene like the stubborn, loyal bitch she was. How to communicate this? How to warn her that the people Irene had just told her to accept had become the enemy? How to warn . . .

How had Cow warned her?

"Come on," said Irene briskly. "We may as well go for it."

She kept an eye on Cow when the curves of the trail brought the settlement into view, keeping track of her position relative to the trail's end, the direction they'd approach her from. Electro-rifles had an incredibly long range, but she didn't dare take a chance that Cow would fail to hear her. Fail to understand. She wished the camel really was telepathic—that would make things a lot simpler. She wished she'd listened to Gus in the first place. Wishing was a waste of time.

At least Hal didn't seem to be worried about her— his eyes were on the brush, scanning for marauding kongs, and God only knew what else. Would a kong attack make a good diversion? Was she desperate enough to hope for one, even if it would?

Yes, Irene decided coolly. She owed Cow and her kind too much to let anything happen to them. And even if she hadn't owed them Mark's life, and her own, she would have done the same.

She wasn't a Vrell.

The ground beneath their feet leveled out—twenty yards yet to go, through the dark leaves of the undergrowth. All Cow had to do was get into the trees, out of sight. If she was still grazing on this side of the settlement, off to the left . . .

They emerged from the brush, blinking in the bright moonlight, for Big Ben rode high, nearly full. Cow was closer than Irene had hoped, only a dozen yards off, watching them with forward pricked ears, her jaws moving on a mouthful of grass. When she saw Irene she started toward them, ambling without haste, but without caution; she trusted Irene.

"Listen up, my friend," she whispered. A rock, about two feet high, welled out of the grass in front of her. Irene took a long, running step and jumped on top of it, flung up her arms to make herself look bigger, and hissed.

Cow jerked to a stop and stiffened, gazing at Irene in alarm as she hissed again, trying to make it louder still, trying to make its menace clear.

Cow turned and ran like a dire cat was at her heels. "Yes! Go! Get—"

Hal took a step forward, his rifle swinging toward the fleeing camel. Irene leapt from the rock, throwing her whole weight at his shoulders and arms in a flying tackle that sent them both to the ground.

The rifle's sonic crack set her ears ringing—she no longer heard Cow's pounding feet. She could barely hear Hal's curses as he grabbed her arms and rolled out from under her. He spun her around, twisting one arm up between her shoulder blades hard enough to make her gasp. He reached for the electro-rifle and checked to be sure it was undamaged before he rose to his feet, hauling her up with him.

Ezra was gazing in the direction Cow had gone. "Clean away." His expression was professionally neutral, but something very like satisfaction gleamed in his eyes. "It'll reach the desert before we could even get a flitter up at that rate. How did you do that?"

"It's their warning signal," said Irene. She had to twist her neck to look up at him, for the grip on her arm forced her to bend forward. "Would you mind letting me go, Hal? I'm not going to do anything."

Anything else. She'd already accomplished her first objective, and she wasn't foolish enough to imagine she could outfight or outrun a trained soldier almost twenty years younger than she was. No, physical resistance would be useless at best, and painful at worst. But to out think them, now that was another matter.

Out thinking a locked door, on the other hand, was something of a challenge. Irene sat on her cot and eyed the door in question thoughtfully. It lay on the other side of a biolock, which led to a small observer's corridor, Plexiglas-walled, which led to the door, which led to a lab, which led to the house that Jack built. She could use the sealed coffin in which they'd carried her through the ship's biolock in the first place—morbid, but more cost-effective than stuffing her into an enviro-suit and then destroying it—to get through the biolock's scalding wash, but getting past the door to the lab was something else again. Her cell wasn't uncomfortable; it had originally been one of several small biolabs, connecting to a larger lab. They'd hastily stripped it of all equipment and furnished it with table, chair, and a cot that the coffin fit beneath—barely. All the biolabs contained a sink and a flash disposer, which, along with a bedpan, completed the necessary amenities.

That and the intercom, which they'd rewired so it only reached the lab outside where a guard sat. To Irene he seemed like overkill. *Who do they think I am, Houdini?*

She'd been so sure she could convince them. She'd had to win, to take the grail back to Camelot at any price. But this price was too high. She couldn't sacrifice . . . what had Gus called them? . . . a gentle, generous people like the camels of Navohar.

Not even to stop GED?

You can't save everyone, Goodnight.

Did she have to choose? Which would live and which would die? She wrapped her arms around her stomach. In a minute she'd be rocking her way into catatonia. No one could make a choice like that! Though Willard had, with frightening ease. No wonder the colonists had been so torn. No wonder they'd risked so much on the chance that she could find some way to make the primes breed.

And she was so close! The answer was there, somewhere. She might not even need the camels, with all that frozen dung in the settlement. All she needed was time.

She couldn't save everyone.

Wait a minute. Why did she have to? Why did *she* have to?

Irene was still for a long time. It wasn't a perfect solution. *A compromise; God I'm beginning to hate that word.* But it was the best she could do, and in any case, the next step was clear. *I have to get out of here.*

OK, genius, let's try logic. Could she break through the walls? No. Biocontainment walls were so well sealed a microbe couldn't slip through, and they were designed to resist any accident up to a mid-sized explosion. Floors and ceiling, ditto. She might get the cover off the light fixture or the clock and pull out a bit of wiring, but there was nothing she could do with it except electrocute herself.

The room hadn't been designed as a prison. The door on the other side of the decon-lock was sealed with a simple bolt, installed entirely for her benefit. But simple as it was, it was on the outside, and she was on the inside.

Therefore, she had to get someone on the outside to open it for her. Feign sickness? Irene snorted. They'd sealed her into quarantine—they expected her to get sick. All that would buy her was a visit from a heavily suited Dr. Dahl. Oh, Lord, if she couldn't get out of this, she'd spend *decades* in quarantine.

The fact that Myrna hadn't come to talk to her already indicated that they weren't going to let any of her friends in, and the rewired intercom cut off electronic access to help as well.

So no way to escape on her own, and no way to contact a friend to help her. So much for logic.

Irene snorted. Maybe her friends would come anyway. But if she hadn't been able to convince Willard, who thought he loved her, the odds of convincing anyone on the *Stanley* to jeopardize their career, maybe even their freedom, by helping her, were negligible.

Let's face it, Goodnight, people are not your strong suit.

So no friends. But perhaps . . . perhaps an enemy? Now *that* had possibilities . . .

She thought it over for five long minutes by the digital display, then rose to switch on the intercom. They'd had the courtesy to make it a two-way switch, so she could have privacy if she chose. And they'd promised that the guard would keep his end open, in case she needed anything. So he must have orders to bring her what she needed, right? He certainly answered promptly. "Yes, Dr. Olsen?"

The voice, thank God, was male. Roughly seventy percent of the *Stanley's* crew was male, so the odds were in her favor, but still . . .

"I . . . I'd like to speak to a woman, please. My friend Myrna Lessing. There's something I need."

Could the tension in her voice be interpreted as embarrassment?

"I'm sorry, ma'am, but I have orders not to let you talk to your friends. Just for the time being. Once we're in space, Captain Keene says you can speak to anyone you want."

"How generous of him," said Irene drily. "But that doesn't solve my problem now."

"You have a prob—oh. Can . . . can I get you something?"

"Would you know what to get? I'd really rather not talk about this at all, and especially not with you. Nothing personal, but . . ."

"No, I understand." He sounded as flustered as she could have wished, as flustered as Mark would have. For once the new prudishness was working in her favor.

"I have a legal right to assistance," she added. "Female assistance."

"Um . . ."

She let visions of sexual-harassment suits dance in

his head for just a few more seconds, then . . . "Look, if you have orders not to let me talk to my friends, how about someone else? Astrid Evenson, say? You have to know she's not going to break me out." In a community this small, everyone knew everything.

"Um, yeah. I think that'd be OK. I'll get her over here. It may take a little while, she's probably asleep."

"As soon as you can, please," said Irene, killing the circuit. According to the clock, it was just past midnight. Astrid would be furious at being hauled out of bed, but Irene *did* have a legal right to female assistance.

Convincing Astrid to do what she really wanted, now that was trickier. And assuming she pulled that off, there was the problem of keeping Willard from capturing the wild camels. The flitters were the key, but what could she do? Blow them up, like a vid hero?

Irene grimaced. *This is getting to you, Goodnight.* Even if she knew where and how to set them without blowing herself up in the process, the explosives and long-range weapons were among the few things on the ship she didn't have security access to. Only Willard, and a handful of the upper-echelon military types who knew how to use the stuff had that access, and a sensible procedure it was. Scratch explosives.

Could she disable their engines, in some way that couldn't be easily repaired? Without the foggiest idea how they worked or what would disable them? She could always smash things at random, but that would be both noisy and time-consuming. She could pull parts off and take them away with her, but the *Stanley* had been intended to stay in space for up to four years—any equipment component that couldn't be repaired had duplicates stored in the holds. So whatever damage she did, they could undo, one way or another. Scratch breaking the flitters.

Could she wipe their internal programming? Probably. All that took was an electromagnet held in the right place, which she could figure out by calling up their specs in the computer. But reprogramming them would be even easier and faster than repairing physical damage.

Destroy their fuel source? They ran on batteries.

Well, if she couldn't disable the flitters, how about the tranquilizer? The chem synthesizers could replace it. Tranq-dart guns? Stored with the rest of the larger weapons. But what else . . .

Twenty minutes passed before the com buzzed. Irene leapt to her feet, reaching for the button, then paused for several seconds—it wouldn't do to seem too lively.

"Yes?"

"Dr. Evenson is here, Dr. Olsen, and she brought some . . . some items. I'm admitting her now."

"Thank you," said Irene sincerely, shutting the com off again. She sank down on the cot and laid her hands over her abdomen, trying to look frail and wan.

The guard opened the door and glanced in to be sure she wasn't poised to bash her way out with the faucet or some such thing, though she couldn't possibly have made it through the decon-lock since she spoke to him.

Astrid came in, wearing a sweatshirt, jeans, and slippers. Her pale hair was rumpled. She looked annoyed, but this was one request no woman refused another. She carried a small, sealed, metal box.

"I didn't know what you use, so I brought both tampons and pads. I'll put them in the biolock, OK?" Her voice was crisp with dislike; no sympathy there. But Irene didn't want sympathy.

"I don't need them. Oh, put them in the lock and run it; the guard will get suspicious if you don't, but I really needed to talk to you. Do you want Willard's attention on you for the next year, or on me?"

Astrid's sleepy eyes snapped open. "That's . . . a pretty blunt question."

"I don't have time for finesse. If I stay on this ship—especially in prison—I'll occupy his attention, even if I don't try. I'll be on his conscience. He'll visit me, try to talk me around. Worry about me. You won't . . ." *Don't say 'stand a chance.' There are limits, Goodnight.* ". . . be seeing much of him," Irene finished smoothly. "But if I'm *off* the ship, if he's furious over my disloyalty . . ."

Astrid didn't look sleepy anymore. "You want me to help you escape? You're crazy. I'd end up in jail or something. Besides, he needs to catch those camel-things to get that organism you were talking about. I won't interfere with that. I've known people with GED myself."

"How could I possibly keep him from going after wild camels in the desert? I'm in here because he wants to keep me on the *Stanley*, not because he thinks I can stop him."

Astrid's eyes narrowed unpleasantly at the truth of this. "So why do you want to leave? It's not like—"

The com buzzed, and they both jumped.

"Everything going all right in there, ladies?"

"Fine," Irene replied, and killed the com once more.

Astrid put the box into the lock and spun the door closed to start the decon-cycle. "Supposing, theoretically, that I agree to do this—what's your plan?"

Irene took a deep breath; the lock had a thirty-second cycle, so she'd better make it fast. "I need you to drug the guard and open the door. There are things in my lab that'll work. The tranquilizer in the biokit can be ingested as well as injected. When you go out, tell him I need some herb tea for the cramps, and you're going to get it. Bring him back a cup of coffee when you come—you can have one, too. Whatever. When he falls asleep, you let me out. I leave the ship, and you have . . . clear hunting."

"And then I get arrested. How stupid do you think

I am? I can get Willard's attention just by telling him what you're planning. And help all those kids. And since you'll be in there . . . Thanks, Irene. I think this is just what I needed."

The lab's door opened. Astrid gave her a cheery wave and left.

"Bitch," Irene muttered. No, people weren't her best thing. So how could she get out of here?

Almost an hour of pacing later, she still had no answer. The door was still locked. But there had to be a way. There *had*—

The com buzzed. Irene turned and slapped it open. "Yes?"

"Irene?" The voice was warm, and male. Ezra! What in the world? "I've just seen Dr. Evenson," Ezra went on. "She said you were still up; I thought you might want to talk."

"I'd like that." Irene's knees went wobbly with hope. "Come in."

The door opened. "I'm glad you're willing to see me," Ezra said smoothly. "You've been through a lot lately and it will do you good to talk about it, don't you think? I'd like to help you." The door closed.

"I hope you're really here to help," said Irene grimly, "because at this point *talking* is the last thing I want to do."

Ezra laughed. "You don't beat around the bush, do you? Astrid found Khalil and me in the lounge and told us about your plan. She thought it was foolish, but Khalil and I rather liked it. Your guard is drinking his coffee now. We used the tranquilizer from the bio-kit, as you suggested. I trust I haven't just become a poisoner."

"No," said Irene. Excitement ran like fire through her nerves. Her skin tingled. "It won't even knock him out completely, unless he's very susceptible. He'll just fall asleep—you could wake him, if you had to."

"How long will it take to affect him?"

"I'm not sure. Give it an hour, to be on the safe side. Why are you doing this?"

Ezra smiled. "Let's just say that your point about the Vrell was well made, if not well received. Myself, I'd stay here and do whatever research your camels would consent to, but I'm not in charge. In fact, those who agree with me are a distinct minority."

Irene's eyes stung. "Myrna?"

"Sorry. She thinks you've been completely brainwashed. Probably raped and tortured as well. She's very upset about it. But there are enough of us to get you out of here, and you can warn the colonists to get their camels into hiding. I believe you said there were anomaly samples available?"

"In the settlement. Four freezers full."

"So there you are. I'd better go. I have to get you an enviro-suit."

"Wait. What will happen to you? Once Astrid tells her story, they'll know you drugged him."

Ezra shrugged. "What can they do to me? An impulsive decision to release a friend, who'd committed no crime, and in my professional opinion posed no threat to anyone? If we have the cure by then, they probably won't bother with anything worse than community service, which I won't mind. If we don't have the cure, they'll probably dismiss the whole thing as a pipe dream, and care even less."

Irene's heart ached with gratitude. "I hate to get you into trouble."

Ezra's laughter startled her. "Don't worry about it, Goodnight. If you're willing to be marooned here in the Stone Age for the rest of your life, a little community service is the least I can do."

He rapped on the door and the guard let him out, leaving Irene standing with her jaw dropped.

Marooned . . . on Navohar. Was that what she wanted? To stay with Mark and Cow and Gus, especially Gus, forever? Primitive food, primitive living conditions, *really* primitive sanitation, primitive equipment, dire cats, kongs, and God only knew what other dangers in the open, exquisite sweep of the desert and the rustling forest. *Do I really want to be marooned here?*

"Hell, yes." Her voice echoed in the small room.

Irene sank back on the cot, trying to settle her mind, to absorb the sudden change in her fortunes. She had a lot of thinking to do.

Because if she was going to choose Navohar, she had to earn the right to stay.

Chapter 12

Khalil slid through the lab door, a limp enviro-suit folded over one arm.

Irene, who'd been dithering herself into a state just short of panic, jumped and opened her mouth, but Khalil held up a hand for silence. She waited till the lab door closed softly behind him before she whispered, "Where's Ezra?"

"Telling Willard about your mental stability." Khalil thrust the suit into the lock and started the cycle. "Astrid went to him when she left us—he was still up, too. I don't think you've left many people on this ship sleeping soundly, Goodnight."

Irene snorted. "I'd hope their consciences would give them fits, but if they stay awake, they'll get in my way. Khalil, the anomaly samples are in the settlement, in the last building toward the west. Four industrial-size freezers, and you'd better take everything in them. Nola's notes will tell you what it is. You have Nola's and my notes, don't you?"

The lock opened on a puff of disinfectant-scented steam, and Irene snatched up the damp suit and slithered into it, not bothering to connect the plumbing, since she wouldn't be using it that long.

Khalil turned his back to let her dress—a modesty that seemed foolish to her now. "Yes, we have your notes."

Her loose clothes crumpled uncomfortably beneath the suit. Irene tucked her sandals into her belt and fastened the helmet and gloves, hissing with impatience as she did the safety checks.

"I'll move the freezers up to the ship first thing in the morning," Khalil went on, "if I'm not drafted to hunt camels. Can your people hide their herds by then?"

"I think so," Irene lied, stepping into the decon chamber. "You can turn around now. Khalil, I have to get a flitter up. Can you get me into the hangar?"

The familiar, steaming buffeting of the lock didn't make her sweat as it used to—for someone who'd learned to sleep through the desert days, this was nothing.

"Yes," Khalil told her as the door swished open. "But I'm supposed to go on enviro-watch in half an hour, so we'd better get going." He eased the lab door open, and Irene slipped out. The guard sprawled in a chair right beside her, his chest rising and falling in the soft rhythm of sleep. He probably wouldn't wake unless he fell out of his chair, and even then he'd see nothing but what he should see—an empty lab and a locked door. No, barring something unforeseeable, her escape wouldn't be discovered till her breakfast arrived. Of course the unforeseeable was always a possibility, but there was nothing she could do about that.

Irene's booted footsteps were loud in her fear-sharpened ears, but the guard slept on and her heart leapt with triumph as they stepped into the hallway and eased the lab door closed behind them.

The suit and helmet would make an excellent disguise, as long as no one got close enough to see through her faceplate. Mind, anyone who saw her was likely to wonder *why* someone was strolling about the ship in an enviro-suit at just past two in the morning. Fortunately the night shift consisted of whoever was assigned to the cleaning crew this week, and the person assigned to enviro-watch, who sat in the life-systems monitor room and played vid games unless one of the abnormal-range alerts buzzed.

"Where's the cleaning crew tonight?" Irene whispered. There was no need to keep her voice that low, but she couldn't help it. She kept expecting someone to dart out of a door at any minute, recognize her, and raise the alarm.

Khalil glanced at his watch. "They should be in Willard's office. Ezra promised to have a terrible accident with a coffeepot about ten minutes ago. They're probably teasing him right now."

A grin stretched Irene's mouth—even her facial muscles were tense. "Good for Ezra. I hope they take their time."

The warm memory of her first stint on cleaning duty surfaced—that was how she'd gotten to know Myrna—but it couldn't stop her. Nothing could be allowed to stop her, and she slipped through the *Stanley*'s familiar, twisting corridors like an armored ghost—not even the air could touch her. Only memories.

She was still surprised when they reached the hangar without incident. Thirty flitters, fifteen on either side of the shuttle bay, gleamed like cartoned eggs, each in its own lock. The lock doors were open now, and the recharge cables hooked into their sockets, their status lights glowing yellow—still charging. Not a problem—all that was necessary for Irene's plan to work was enough power to lift them a few thousand feet, and they were bound to have sufficient charge for that.

For she'd realized, waiting for Ezra back in her prison, that she didn't have to disable or destroy the flitters—all she had to do was organize their escape, just like her own. Only easier, because (a) the flitters weren't locked up, and (b) they had an autopilot.

"This is where I leave you," Khalil murmured. "Can you handle the controls?"

"Of course, I can." Irene gripped his hand with her gloved one. "Khalil . . . there are no words."

"Then don't try." His sudden smile lit his dark face.

"Just get your friends into hiding—it should be easy. Lord knows we've had no luck finding them so far. We'll convince Willard to leave as soon as we can. It'll be months, maybe years, before he can get back. By then, surely some bright soul will have found your cure."

"God, I hope so," Irene whispered, as he turned away. Nola had been working on it for over two decades already. They would come back; there was no way to prevent it. *First things first, Goodnight. You haven't gotten them to* leave *yet.*

In the dark privacy of the shuttle bay, Irene took off her gloves and helmet and set them aside. The glowing instrument panels gave her enough light to work by as she slid into the first flitter, settling herself in the pilot's padded chair. She'd been instructed in the controls, and even, under her teacher's watchful eyes, taken one up and flown in a wide circle. And if her landing hadn't been what you'd call gentle, at least they hadn't broken any teeth. *You can do this.*

Fifteen frustrating minutes later she climbed out of the cockpit, stalked into the hangar control room, and called up the flitter's instruction manual on the computer terminal. Air foils, Astrogation instruments . . . Autopilot! There were seven screens of instructions, and Irene squashed down her quivering impatience and read them carefully, especially the commands for setting the time delay.

Armed with knowledge, she went back to the enemy that had defeated her. It still took a few minutes fumbling to call up the autopilot program, but after that the prompts led her through it. She decided to send the flitter up five thousand feet then straight west over the desert. With any luck it would be over the sea when its power cells drained, but even if it wasn't, the odds of its hitting anything that mattered were negligible. And if they found what remained of it, the damage inflicted by a five-thousand-foot fall *would* be beyond the *Stanley*'s ability to repair. She hoped.

After some consideration, she set the time delay to start the autopilot program at 0400—that should give her time to set the rest of the programs. She'd spent enough afternoons with Mark and Khalil in the control room to know exactly how to open the bay doors and flitter ports, and if she set the rest of the pilots to activate every thirty seconds, that should keep them from crashing into each other on their way out.

She was actually ahead of schedule when she crossed the bay, walking around the angled wedge of the shuttle's nose. The shuttle she couldn't do anything about; unlike the flitters, which anyone could supposedly handle, the shuttle's instruments were password-keyed to a handful of qualified pilots, and Irene wasn't one of them. If Mark were here, he might have been able to hack through the lockout. Hell, if Mark were here, the whole operation would take about twenty minutes, instead of this being a step-by-step crawl through the instructions.

At least the shuttle, fast and high-flying, would make a very poor craft in which to search for something as small and well camouflaged as a camel in the dunes. And there was only one shuttle, which lowered the odds of their finding a herd still further, for Irene knew, as Ezra and Khalil could not, that there was no way the colonists could protect the wild cam—

A widening bar of light spilled across the floor. Irene, in the shelter of the shuttle, froze, listening. Someone had opened the door. Khalil was on envirowatch. Ezra? But why? A human-shaped shadow appeared in the bright rectangle, elongated by the angle of the lights in the corridor behind it. Its head turned one way, then the other. Irene held her breath, not daring to stir as much as an inch lest her accursed suit crackle and give away her presence.

Will whoever it is notice that the flitters on the left

*side of the room have one more light glaring on their
panels? Will he see my helmet and gloves in the shadowy corner where I dropped them? Will whatever
prompted him to open the damn door in the first
place—oh God, surely Khalil will have stopped them
from coming to clean in* here—

The shadow shrugged and turned away. The bright
patch grew narrower and vanished with the soft click
of the door.

Irene leaned against the shuttle, one hand pressed
over her heart—she knew it couldn't really beat its
way out of her chest, but it was trying.

Her fingers shook as she keyed on the computer in
the next flitter, but the door remained closed; by the
time she'd uncoupled the charger lines, closed all the
locks, and entered the control booth, she was calm
again.

The hatch controls worked for her just as they had
for Khalil and Mark. Irene fought down a wave of
amazement. She had thirteen minutes to wait before
the first autopilot kicked in, and she spent the first
thirty seconds skinning out of her suit and putting on
her sandals—which left twelve minutes and thirty seconds to bite her nails.

As soon as the last flitter was gone she could slide
out of the hatch herself, and into the woods and away.
She wasn't going to risk the public corridors again
tonight. With any luck, they'd think she'd taken one
of the flitters. She might have, despite her reservations
about flying the wretched things, but she knew the
shuttle's radar would track it straight to the stiltie
grove. No, she was better off on the ground—a thorn
whipping was less lethal than crashing several thousand feet.

The first flitter's boosters hummed, then the lock
vibrated and began to shake as the thrusters kicked
in. Irene put her hands over her ears as it shot into
the sky. She hadn't remembered how *loud* they were.

The next flitter was already humming. They launched themselves one after the other, with the fine precision of marching soldiers. No one came to check on the noise, so perhaps it wasn't as loud as it seemed.

She dragged one of the charging units out and scrambled on top of it to reach the open lock—even then its edge was breast high. The outside air smelled damp, clean and alive. Big Ben had set, but the Seer's serene eye gazed down on her, and Grandfather was creeping over the horizon. The thought of returning to the *Stanley*'s sterile corridors was suddenly intolerable, and Irene bent her legs and leapt. The charger tipped and fell, leaving her feet dangling. Hell, maybe they'd assume the flitter's launch had tipped it over. It took some squirming to hook her leg over the hatch, but soon she was sitting on the *Stanley*'s curved hull, gazing at the ground some twenty feet below.

It's just like a slide, she told herself firmly. A long, steep slide. She started down, using the friction of her palms to move slowly. The last ten feet were too steep for that, and she slithered down and landed with a bruising thump, but she wasted only a moment rubbing her knees. The night was glorious, she was free, and she wanted to put some distance between herself and the ship by sunrise.

Despite the need for haste, Irene stopped on her way through the deserted settlement and picked up half a dozen water jugs, a tight-woven plastic tarp, and a carryall to put them in. The bad news was that there was no food—the colonists had taken all their imperishable foodstuffs with them when they abandoned the place, and there was no reason to restock it. But she had water, and a way to rig shelter from the sun if it became necessary; she'd had several meals aboard the *Stanley*, and Sondi and Ayanna had pointed out quite a bit of edible flora. She should be able to make it to the encampment.

Where the colonists would probably throw her out the moment they set eyes on her. *Burned a lot of bridges lately, haven't you, Goodnight?*

No matter how angry they were, she had to warn them. Assuming she could even find their camp in the first place.

Irene scowled, worrying at the problem with the small part of her mind not taken up with moving through the shadowy underbrush. She was certain she could find the life pool, just by following the forest edge north. During the days she'd spent there with Cow, she'd become quite familiar with the area—she'd recognize it when she got there. From there she could see the rock ridge where she'd left Nola sleeping, and she was pretty sure she could make her way over the dunes to it. The encampment at the stiltie grove was more or less northwest of there, but could she locate it in the dune's trackless maze? *You can, by God, try.* She owed them that.

It took longer than she'd hoped to navigate through the dark forest, but by the time the sun rose Irene was far enough from the settlement that a search team wasn't likely to stumble over her. Frankly, she was too tired to care if they did catch her; she'd gone two nights and a day without sleep, and the carryall of water jugs weighed more with every step.

Irene found a clump of brush that would shield her from sight, crawled into it, and lay down, using the tarp for a pillow. She doubted she could walk another foot. Her eyes were closing when something small with many legs scurried over her calf. Irene twitched and brushed it away. Only a bug. A few seconds later another tickled its way across her ankle. She soon found that she was lying in the middle of an insect thoroughfare, and while they weren't inclined to fight for the turf—perhaps they couldn't bite or sting—Irene discovered she wasn't as tired as she'd thought.

The second clump of bushes she chose wasn't quite

as sheltered, or as comfortable, but at least it was unoccupied. Irene slept through the day; when she finally woke the forest was dark and still, and the sky was full of moonlight.

She didn't know how far into the night she'd slept, but since the *Stanley*'s crew had probably done their searching during the day, she felt free to start hiking at the edge of the forest, where the ground was more open.

She was making better time, despite the hollow growls of her empty stomach—she might have underestimated her need for food a bit—so when she came across a sourfruit bush, she took a few minutes to strip it of any fruit even close to ripe. Grimacing over the taste as she walked on (even insects left sourfruit alone) Irene cursed herself for not stealing some food from the *Stanley*'s kitchen when she was there. She'd been concentrating on escaping, but still . . .

Was that rock clump that looked like a hooded monk the same one that looked like a misshapen mushroom from the life pool? It might be! After all, the settlement was only half a day's camel ride from the pool, and she'd been walking for two nights. If it was, she'd spend the rest of the night gathering what food she could, sleep through the day by the pool, and set—

Moist velvet brushed the back of her neck and Irene leapt away, spun, tripped, and sat down hard, gazing up in growing delight at the furry face looming over her.

"Cow!" She climbed to her feet and reached to hug the camel's neck. "I'm so glad you're—"

A bony nose butted her in the stomach, knocking her onto her ass again. The ground was rocky. Irene rose more slowly this time, but she was too glad to see her friend alive and free to protest. Much.

"Hey, you don't have to—"

Cow's head swung around and shoved her again. Her buttocks were beginning to bruise.

"Look, I'm sorry I had to—"

This time she tried to avoid Cow's thrust, but the rough terrain was on the camel's side, and she hit the ground again, skinning her elbow in the process.

The next time she rose her fists were clenched, and she shook one in Cow's face. "Try that again, you hairy menace, and I'll slug you! Right on the nose, you hear me? I'll do it!"

Cow gazed at her for a long moment, snorted, turned in place, lifted her ropy tail, and farted, hugely.

"Ugh!" Irene backed off, trying not to breathe; Cow ambled off, evidently feeling no further comment was necessary.

"Consider yourself rebuked." Sondi's voice, behind her, very cold.

Irene spun and stared down the barrel of Sondi's fléchette gun.

"Sondi . . ." Her throat tightened at the icy fury in the girl's eyes.

"Don't. Don't say one word, or I'll forget that Mark loves you and solve all our problems right now."

"Shooting me won't solve anything." Irene's scalp prickled. She was careful to make no sudden moves. "It's too late for that. I need to talk to the others."

"Yes," said Sondi. Her smile was more frightening than the gun muzzle. "Yes, I think they'd like to talk to you."

Irene was intensely aware of the fléchette gun, trained on the center of her spine, all the way to the colonists' camp.

They'd hidden themselves just inside the woods— kong territory unfortunately, but safe from passing flitters. At least that was no longer a danger.

"Why is everyone here?" Irene whispered to Mark. The meeting had convened in a clearing at the forest edge, which gave a magnificent view over the shadowed dunes. For the first time, no one had objected to Irene's presence, but she didn't take it as a good sign. The colonists' anger was like a physical force in the air around her. The remoteness in Gus's eyes as he turned away from her was like a blow. Mark was the only one who sat near Irene, but most of the other colonists she'd been traveling with were present, along with quite a few camels. They hadn't all come; the kid flock was notably absent, but all Irene's friends were there—though perhaps they weren't friends, anymore. Even Maureen Greville was with them.

"Cow brought us." Mark returned the others' glares, defiant, protective. "They weren't sure what to do when Nola came back and told us you'd . . . that she'd lost you."

Irene looked around the crowd and flinched when she met Nola's bitter stare. The vet's lips tightened, and Irene's gaze slid away. She owed Nola, and the guard kid, one hell of an apology, but that was for later.

"Anyway," Mark went on. "When Cow came dashing into camp and did a really remarkable Lassie imitation, they figured they'd better follow her."

"All right, my friends," Gus's quiet voice called the meeting to order. "Let's find out what we're dealing with first. Dr. Olsen says she has something to tell us."

Irene winced at the coolness of his voice, but she knew she deserved it. The story was hard to tell, but she took it methodically, like a math proof. No one seemed surprised by Willard's intransigence, though Nola's mouth twisted in disappointment. Eyebrows lifted around the circle when she explained how she got rid of the flitters. "I would have done the same to the shuttle, but it has a security lockout to keep unqualified people from flying it. So he still has a chance to go out and find some camels. I'm sorry." It was hard to keep her voice steady.

The silence stretched painfully.

Then Juana Kobiche, her plump, motherly face taut with anger, rose to her feet and Gus sat down, in what looked to Irene like a formal yielding of the floor. No one had asked her to stand when she spoke—what did that mean? That she was only present as a witness and had no rights, no citizenship, in this circle?

"I'd like to make several motions," Juana said, "for immediate hand vote. This situation is urgent, and we need to make some decisions fast." She paused, but no one objected. "Very well. My first motion is to question our leadership. I like Gus, and I respect him—most of the time—but I believe his judgment has been influenced by . . . personal considerations, with disastrous consequences. I don't want him making any important decisions for *us* until that damn ship is off our planet. I move that Gus be replaced by Nola as First Councilor for the duration of this travel season."

A ripple of consternation arose, and Irene stiffened—surely Gus couldn't lose his position so—

"Second!" someone called loudly, and Gus rose smoothly to his feet.

"The motion has been made and seconded. Does anyone insist on discussion? Very well, I call for a vote. In favor?"

"Wait a minute!" Nola yelped, suddenly recovering her wits. "I don't . . ."

But hands were rising all through the crowd, far too many hands, even— Irene's jaw dropped. Gus was voting *against* himself?

"The motion carries," he said firmly. "I yield the Council to Nola." He walked over and seated himself beside Irene, who stared at him in astonishment.

"What the hell do you think—"

"Hush," said Gus shortly. "This is important." But he smiled at her, despite the reserve that still lingered in his eyes.

Irene blinked back tears and clamped down on her self-control. Gus was right; this was too important for her to disintegrate.

Nola rose to her feet, glowering at the determined faces around her. "Oh, all right. But someday, Sardakowski, I'm going to get you for this."

Gus shrugged, ceding her the right to try. His grin looked tired, but sincere, and Irene fought the desire to reach out to him. She needed an arm about her shoulders rather badly just then.

"I have another motion." Juana Kobiche had been watching the interplay between them, and her mouth twisted with contempt. "I move we dump that treacherous bitch back with her friends, where she can do no further harm. She made her choice when she betrayed us—let her live with the consequences!"

"I'd like to respond to that." Gus stood swiftly. "If I may?"

"You're in love with the bitch!" Juana snapped. "You're so biased it's pathetic. And that's what got us into—"

"But I'm not the First Councilor anymore," said Gus. "So it doesn't matter if I'm biased or not. I can say anything I want, unless Nola puts a time limit on it, and then she has to put one on everybody else as well."

"No," said Nola, looking harassed. "No time limits. But keep it short, OK? And sit down, Juana; you've made a motion, Gus has a right to address it."

"My first point," said Gus hastily, as Juana sat reluctantly beside her husband, "is that Irene hasn't betrayed us—she never offered us her loyalty in the first place. From the moment she arrived, searching for her nephew, whom *we* kidnapped, she made her loyalty and intentions crystal-clear—to find the source of Mark's cure and return it to Earth. We held her prisoner! We were polite about it, but that's the truth. The only people she's 'betrayed' are the crew of the

Stanley, and she did that for us, or more accurately, for our friends here." He gestured to the camels, most of whom looked bored. Several, including Cow, had already wandered away.

"In destroying their flitters," Gus went on passionately, "she chose to come over to *our* side. If they can use Nola's frozen samples to replicate the life pools, it not only saves them, it will solve our long-term problem as well. Which, if you recall, was part of the reason I wanted to let her try *before* I ever got to know her. And finally"—he gestured to the watching camels—"*you* can't throw her out. It's Cow's decision whether or not to remain with this herd, and with Irene. We can usually persuade a camel to take someone off to one of the other herds—sometimes they do it on their own—but that won't solve or change anything in this case. And if we return her to the *Stanley* and Cow goes with her, we'll be putting a camel into their hands, which is just what we're trying to avoid!"

He looked around at them for a moment, then sank down beside Irene, and this time he did put an arm round her shoulders as a storm of debate erupted.

"Quiet!" Nola bellowed, and her camel bugled, reinforcing the order. "Thank you," she said, taking her hands off her ears. "Look, we could debate this for days, and it would never go anywhere. I'm furious about the whole mess myself, but I have to admit that in Dr. Olsen's shoes I might have done the same thing. More importantly, Gus is right; it doesn't matter a damn how he, or I, or any of us feel, it's the camels who decide who's part of their herd. Unless Cow repudiates Irene, talking about throwing her out is irrelevant. If you want to try to make her uncomfortable enough that Cow takes her to another herd, that's your decision. Mine is that she stays, so unless you want to replace me as First Councilor . . . please? . . . anyone? . . . rats. Well, as First Councilor, I choose to table this issue. We will now discuss the only thing that really matters, which is: What are we going to do next?"

As it turned out, there wasn't much they could do.

"You already did it," Gus told Irene, "when you took out their flitters."

The colonists had scattered through the trees, in small, tense groups. Many of them still glared angrily at Irene, but both Nola and Ravi had come over to speak with her after the meeting, and Cicero, deep in animated argument, had broken off to wave and wink at her.

"We'll warn the others to watch out for the shuttle," Gus went on. "And if Captain Keene should find a wild herd, it will be tragic, but there's nothing we can do to prevent it . . . unless you smuggled a few surface-to-air missiles off the *Stanley* in your underwear?"

"I thought about it." Irene's shoulders sagged. "But the security lockout on the heavy weapons is even tighter than the one on the shuttle."

There was a small, startled silence.

"My dear," said Gus. "I was joking." He put his arm around her, and Irene's weary heart lifted. "I think you did remarkably well, under the circumstances."

"But suppose Willard comes back from Earth with troops, equipped to search?"

"Then he does," said Gus. "We'll deal with that when, and if, it happens. Frankly, I'm not too concerned—I'm betting someone else will use the samples to find a cure. You're not the only competent microbiologist, you know? In any case, there's nothing more you, or anyone else, can do now."

The iron-tense muscles in Irene's neck loosened. "I finally figured that out," she said. "But I can't help but feel that there's something else I could have done—to sabotage the shuttle, or better yet *convince* them the camels are intelligent. If I could bring that off, even now, we might . . ."

Gus and Mark were staring at her, incredulous.

"I wasn't going to go back," she protested. "I wasn't even thinking . . . Well, I was, but if I *could* think of a way . . ."

Gus's body began to quiver, his face alight with suppressed laughter.

Mark shook head. "You're a good knight, Auntie, but it's time to lay down the lance. You can't win this one."

"Hear, hear," said Gus emphatically. "But tell me, love, why didn't you agree with Captain Keene? Many would think that a few alien lives, even intelligent aliens, would be a cheap price to pay to save thousands of humans."

Love? Had Juana been right when she said Gus loved her? "It would be wrong," said Irene absently. Then her brain caught up with the conversation. "It would have been wrong," she said more soberly. "This is their planet, their . . . miracle. We have no more right to enslave and destroy them to serve our needs than the Vrell had the right to do it to us—no matter how great that need might be. If nothing else, we should have learned that from them."

To consider not only the price of victory, but who pays.

"In that case, I'll stop worrying about you going back," said Gus. "And thank God for it. When you first returned, I was afraid I'd have to put a guard on you for the next few weeks. And confiscate your bio-kit. And chain you to a stiltie root. And knowing you, it still wouldn't have been enough."

His eyes were laughing again, with a warmth beneath the laughter that eased the shadows in Irene's heart.

"I'm sorry," she said. "About you not being First Councilor anymore. I didn't mean—"

"You're sorry?" Gus's brows lifted. "And here I thought you liked me. For God's sake, Goodnight, you *saw* what it's like. Besides, it was the only way I could speak for you—First Councilors are supposed to be neutral. Nola's due for a turn at it."

But Irene still worried.

The next evening, when the camp woke, Maureen Greville was gone.

"Straight to the *Stanley*, of course," said Gus with resignation. "I should have anticipated it; she's always hated Navohar."

Nola was trying to cope with a dozen colonists' furious and impractical demands for pursuit, revenge, *something* to be done. Irene began to understand why Gus was glad to be rid of the job.

"Can't you go after her?" Irene asked. "On camels you'd be much faster than she is on foot."

"Several people tried," said Gus. "Their camels weren't interested. Which is fascinating, because when we're tracking down a lost child they're very helpful."

"How frustrating," said Irene. "If we could catch her . . . Wait. Did the camels refuse to follow me when I escaped?"

"You should have heard Nola's comments." Gus's eyes lit with suppressed laughter. "You probably will, someday. Frustrated doesn't begin to cover it."

Irene nodded slowly. She was beginning to understand how much influence the camels exercised in this strange society. "So Maureen is going to make it."

"But she'll be in quarantine for years," Mark protested. "Doesn't she know that?"

"She probably doesn't care," said Gus. "And as far as I'm concerned, that's her choice and her problem."

"When she reaches them, she'll tell them where we are," Irene fretted.

"Which is why Nola's already told us to pack," Gus replied. "Stop looking like that, Goodnight." He touched the frown lines between her brows. "I'm still not worried."

But Nola was sufficiently concerned to send Eric Hoffman to the stiltie grove to tell the others to move camp, too, since Eric's Nightflyer was the fleetest camel present. Unfortunately there was only one satellite link for each group, and Ravi had brought it with him—which at least enabled them to warn the other groups to avoid any campsites Maureen might know. They set up their tents in the desert that day, avoiding the rock ridge, and departed soon after sunset.

"We'll find the others in a few days, wherever they go," said Gus, swaying gracefully to Kirk's easy stride. "You can't separate a camel herd; they always find each other. We've never figured out how."

As they moved farther into the desert and nothing dreadful happened, Irene's nerves settled, but she still had a hard time believing it could end so easily.

The colonists' hostility wasn't as bad as she expected. Many, even some like Sondi, who'd been friendly before, shunned her, but paradoxically, some of those who'd regarded her with suspicion seemed willing to be friends—now that she'd already done all the harm she could.

The camels, to her relief, acted as if she'd never been gone. Perhaps they didn't understand what she'd done. Irene had no idea at this point how much they might or might not comprehend, though she apologized to Cow, and ended up weeping her remorse into the coarse fur in a way she'd never have felt free to do with the human Navoharans. Cow accepted this with more patience than Irene would have expected, and she felt better for it.

But two nights later, standing in the dinner line, she still sensed something.... unfinished about the situation. When she saw the look on Nola's face, nerves tensed throughout her body. Ravi walked beside the vet, carrying the satellite link.

"Gus, this is addressed to you, so you'd better see it," Nola said. Ravi held the screen for Gus to read, and Irene peered over his shoulder.

> DR. SARDAKOWSKI AND COLONISTS OF NAVOHAR, WE HAVE TAKEN POSSESSION OF YOUR GENE BANK. WE WILL RETURN IT TO YOU ONLY IN EXCHANGE FOR EIGHT OF YOUR CAMELS, MALE AND FEMALE, WHOSE BLOOD CARRIES THE ORGANISM, ANOMALY 1. RETURN TO THE SETTLEMENT WITH THE CAMELS, WITHIN SEVEN DAYS, OR WE WILL LEAVE ORBIT, TAKING THE GENE BANK WITH US. CAPTAIN WILLARD KEENE, U.E.F. *STANLEY*, COMMANDING.

"Maureen must have told them we use the links to communicate," said Ravi grimly.

Other colonists had seen the message; their voices rose in a babble of protest and fear.

"The gene banks," said Mark softly. "They're the one thing you can't do without, aren't they?"

Gus's eyes were on the screen, his face stark. Irene plucked up her courage and laid a hand on his arm. "In the short run it wouldn't make much difference," she said. "The sterilization procedure could be reversed. But the population here is far too small to form a viable gene pool. Even if anomaly 1 repairs some genetic problems, and neither Nola or I are certain it does, a few generations down the line . . ."

But Gus knew that. He was a man who thought in the long term. He met Nola's gaze, and understanding seemed to pass between them. One by one the colonists fell silent.

Then Gus turned to Irene, laid his hand over hers, and smiled. "Now."

"Now? Now what?"

"Now I'm worried," he said.

Nola nodded grimly. "Worried is the least of it. Because now"—she looked at the intent crowd around them—"we have to fight."

Chapter 13

The worst of it, for Irene, was the waiting.

"This isn't easy," said Mark, brows drawn down in concentration as he leaned over the portable computer Maureen had used for teaching. "This piece of . . . hardware doesn't have enough RAM to fill a teaspoon."

"I thought you said creating the virus would be easy," said Irene snappishly.

"It is," Mark told her. "I had the virus worked out in a few hours. But making it invisible to someone doing a code check is harder, safeing it against the virus sweeps is a lot harder, and enabling it to travel through the interface between the net and the Vrell computers is effing impossible, especially on a . . ." He caught her eyes and his face softened. "Hey, I can do it. It's just going to take a while, OK?"

"Sure," she said. "It's fine. Take all the time you need."

But they didn't have all the time he might need. In the dim, low-oven heat of their tent, she listened to the keys clicking far into the day.

They'd argued, via the link, but Willard was adamant. He didn't want samples, especially when the anomaly in those samples had failed to reproduce, despite twenty years of effort. He wanted eight live camels, or . . .

Irene had volunteered to be one of the negotiation team the moment the plan was proposed. "Willard will never believe I'd let Mark do this by himself," she told them. "Besides, refusing to let me aboard will give him a feeling of control, and make it more likely that he'll allow Mark to go in. You need me." What she didn't say was that *she* needed to go. To do something, however minor, to amend her errors. Even if the danger involved for Mark, Gus, and herself made her stomach cramp tighter with every passing hour.

Gus said he didn't mind the delay, it gave them time to refine their plans. And plan for any possible contingency. And then plan for the impossible contingencies. And then . . .

"Relax love," said Gus, massaging her shoulders. "It's a simple plan, really. We get the drop on them, get our gene banks back, and then they leave. The worst that can happen is that they'll get the drop on us, take off with the gene banks after all, and we'll have to bargain with the next wave."

"No," said Irene. "The worst that could happen is that they'll shoot the lot of us, take the camels by force, and then come back for the rest of the herds in two years and enslave them all."

"OK, you're right, that's the worst."

But it wasn't—the worst was that whatever happened would be Irene's fault. She'd managed not to blame herself, much, for assisting the genetics team that had created GED, but this mess really was of her making. And in a plan based on the reading of a person's character, even one as boringly predictable as Willard, all kinds of things could go wrong.

It took Mark five grueling nights to finish the program to his satisfaction. But when he said it would work, Irene knew it would.

"All I need now," Mark assured them, "is five minutes' access to any terminal on the ship. And that's your department, Nola."

"No," said Nola. "That part of this fiasco belongs

to Gus. I believe I mentioned that I'd get you, Sardakowski."

"So you did," said Gus mildly.

He'd been doing maintenance on the fléchette guns over the last few days; moonlight gleamed on the plasticine barrel he was polishing. It was a sensible idea, to clean the guns and check their mechanisms. But they had only eighteen guns among them, and by Irene's count he'd worked on at least thirty. She wondered how many times he'd had this one apart as Nola went on, "Ravi, send this message up to the satellite—Captain Keene. We have no choice but to accede to your request. We will meet you in the settlement tomorrow night. Mind if I put your name on that, Gus?"

They'd all agreed they shouldn't alarm Willard by switching leaders midstream, so Gus was assigned the task of negotiating for the colony.

"Not at all."

"Then sign it Gus Sardakowski."

"You're not going to meet him today?" Mark had been too busy to find out about the refinements they'd discussed. "If anything goes wrong, we won't have much time to fix it."

"If we meet during the day," said Nola, "he'll be alert and we'll be sleepy. And the darkness will give us better cover. And we can all"—she tactfully avoided looking at the dark shadows beneath Mark's eyes—"use a good day's sleep."

"I thought you were going to ask him not to come armed," said Sondi curiously.

Since Irene had volunteered, Sondi's antipathy had eased. She hadn't forgiven Irene, but the possibility was there.

"He'd just ignore it if we did," said Gus. "Let him think he has us beaten. The longer he thinks it, the better off we are."

Irene said nothing, but her hands felt cold, despite the balmy warmth of the night. Willard did have them beaten; he had the gene bank the colony needed to survive, and he had them outgunned. All the colonists had was brains and determination. *But brains and determination can beat guns any day, right?*

Irene slept badly.

They decided to approach the settlement through the woods, for all it was harder walking for Mark, because "the longer before they realize we don't have any camels with us, the better," said Gus.

Mark continued his slow, determined march around a particularly thorny clump of brush. "Unless they decide we've broken our end of the dealing and shoot us on the spot. What happens then?"

Gus grinned. "Then the whole mess becomes Nola's problem."

"No one is going to get shot," said Irene firmly, wishing she felt as certain as she sounded. "Anyway, it'll all be decided by . . . Lord, they do have the place staked out, don't they?"

Suited, helmeted figures, bearing electro-rifles, surrounded the clearing between the buildings. Three others stood in the empty square, body language revealing their impatience.

Irene, Mark, and Gus stopped for a moment, hiding in the shadows; the moonlit clearing was bright as a stage.

The same comparison must have struck Gus. "Come along, my friends, we're on."

Every head turned toward them as they stepped out of the bushes, and rifle barrels tracked their owners' gazes. Irene's steps faltered, and Mark caught her arm and steadied her. She smiled a quick thanks and turned to face Willard.

He was looking at Mark. Mark, walking, looking vital and healthy, if still a bit thin. Even in the concealing helmet, Willard's face was incandescent with joy and grief, triumph and hunger. Angry as he must be at her escape, he didn't even glance at Irene, and a chill touched her spine. He hadn't really believed in anomaly 1 before—oh, intellectually perhaps, but not in his gut, his heart. Now he *knew*, and he'd fight to the last ditch to take its power home with him.

From what you've told us, he's a rational man, Gus had said when they made their plan. *He should make a rational decision when the time comes.*

Irene was no longer sure of that, and the knot of tension in her stomach twisted tighter.

He'd brought Louise Yassir with him, and Irene's lips tightened at the sight, for the weapon she carried was a tranquilizer gun. She couldn't have a *clue* how the camels' alien physiology would react to her drugs. She might poison the lot of them. *All the better to dissect you, my dear.* Irene fought down a flash of pure hatred.

The other woman, lurking behind Willard, was Maureen Greville.

"Captain Keene," said Gus politely, dragging Willard's avid gaze from Mark at last. He glared at Gus and Irene, his eyes lingering at their belts, noting that they carried no weapons. Then his eyes swept the clearing and the woods behind them.

"Where are the camels?" he demanded.

"Where you won't be able to find them without our help," said Gus calmly. "Surely you didn't expect us to give them up without some assurance that our gene banks—which I see *you* haven't brought either— would be restored to us."

Willard shrugged impatiently. "What would I want with them, once I have the camels?"

"I neither know nor care," said Gus. "But those gene banks are vital to the survival of my colony, and you're not getting any camels until they're in our hands."

"In that case, Dr. Sardakowski—" Willard looked at Mark again. "I'm told you *are* Dr. Sardakowski, by the way. The real . . . that is . . ." His eyes were alight with wonder, and Irene remembered how she felt when she discovered that particular truth.

"Yes." Gus gestured impatiently. "The one and only. You're about to tell me that we have a standoff, because you're not giving up the gene banks until you have the camels, right?"

"That's right. Are you going to propose a solution?"

"Well, I've got one, but if *you* have a suggestion . . . ?"

"No, no, Doctor. After you."

Gus shrugged. "All right. My suggestion is that you put the gene banks in your shuttle and bring it down here. Mark and two of my people will check to be sure the gene banks are intact and fly it off. Once they've had time to get out of the *Stanley*'s missile range, you can take Goodnight and me as hostages and we'll take you to the camels, where you'll exchange us for them."

Willard's eyes narrowed, but before he could speak Maureen clutched his arm. "Don't believe him, Willard. He'd never give up the camels. Not that easily. He's planning something."

Willard's eyes never left Gus's face, but he patted her hand soothingly, and Irene's brows lifted. Did Astrid have competition? Astrid and Maureen—Irene almost felt sorry for him. But not quite.

"And how do you propose to return our shuttle?" Willard asked.

"I don't. I consider it part of your payment for the transportation you'll be depriving us of. Besides"—Gus waved vaguely toward the ridge that separated them from the *Stanley*—"the empty shuttle bay will give you a large, easily accessible, biosealed room to put camels in. They're too big to fit through your corridors, you know. Not to mention your decon-locks. You'd have to abandon the shuttle anyway."

"Don't believe him," said Maureen. "I told you, the camels are more than just transportation to them."

Willard nodded. "Do you have any other requests?"

"Yes." Irene stepped forward. "Mark and I are going to stay here, so I want to go back to the *Stanley* and get some things from our quarters. Personal items. Mark wants to send a letter to his parents, too, and I want to copy some files from the microbiology library—even with anomaly 1, this planet is full of—"

Willard held up a hand and she stopped. "Given the . . . inventiveness you displayed the last time you were on the *Stanley*, I'm not about to let you back on board."

Irene opened her mouth to protest, and he went on hastily, "But your request to retrieve your personal effects isn't unreasonable, so I'll permit young Mark to go aboard, suited and under escort at all times, write his letter, and gather up your gear. As to the files you want . . . No."

"But there may be things that anomaly 1 can't handle! I'll need—"

"You may, but you're the one who has chosen to stay; I'm not letting either of you near any part of the *Stanley*'s data net except the message system."

"But we could—"

"No." And that's an order, his tone added.

Irene fell silent, trying to look sulky instead of triumphant, and probably botching it. It was a good thing that Willard turned to Gus.

"As to the shuttle, you're right—we'd already decided to abandon it and use the bay to house camels. And *we'll* need some large samples of the native vegetation they eat, so we can fabricate a healthy diet for them."

Fiber pellets no doubt, containing all the camel's nutritional requirements, but nothing with taste or variety. Prison food. Animal food. Irene shivered.

"That can be arranged." Gus's voice was harsh, for

all his effort to keep it level. "We'd also like to have some large, deep-cell—"

"Before you present me with a shopping list," said Willard, "explain why you're willing to do this. Ms. Greville assured me you'd fight to the last ditch for these creatures of yours. Was she lying?"

"No." The muscles of Gus's jaw stood out as his teeth clenched. "If you'd tried any other method to take them, we'd have fought to the last of our ability. But this . . . you're holding our children hostage. If it's a choice between our survival as a colony and a few of their lives, then we have to save our own kind. But it wasn't an easy choice, or one we'll be able to forgive ourselves for anytime soon." He paused a moment, then his shoulders sagged. "Forget everything else. Just give us the shuttle, let Mark and Goodnight get their things, and we'll get this over with."

"Agreed." Willard tried to keep the triumph out of his expression—there was even a flicker of pity in his eyes—but Gus's logic justified his own. *It's the same choice he made*, Gus had said. *He has to believe we'd make it, too.* And Gus had made selling a gentle and intelligent race into slavery sound like such a reasonable thing to do. Irene remembered the Vrell and winced.

"Willard, they won't!" Maureen's gloved hand tugged at his sleeve. "I tell you, they're up to something."

But the arrangements went forward. Mark and Louise Yassir climbed the ridge to the ships, planning to return with the shuttle, Mark and Irene's things, and the precious gene banks. Once the gene banks were in their hands, the dangerous part of the game began—for the final twist of the plan, to which they'd all agreed, was that no matter what happened, no camels would leave Navohar.

Irene wrapped her arms around herself and Gus put his arm around her shoulders, warm and reassuring.

Maureen took one look at Willard's face and pulled

him away, arguing, gesturing. Armored in their suits, even the simple comfort of touch was beyond them. No, Irene had made the right choice in the end, even if some of the choices leading up to it had been bad.

Gus's arm tightened, but he didn't speak—there was no need.

The shuttle returned quickly—there was only time for Irene to imagine forty or fifty things that might have gone wrong, instead of hundreds.

Mark was the first off. He'd had to suit up to board the *Stanley*, and when he removed it he'd evidently chosen to change clothes, for he now wore the T-shirt with the skeleton knight in black armor. The caption beneath it read, *I always win.*

Irene's heart began to pound. He saw her looking at the dark warrior and nodded, so faintly that no one who wasn't looking for it could possibly catch it. Irene's knees went wobbly with relief. The virus was planted—in the message system, true, but the locks that separated it from the net at large were, according to Mark, the simplest problem he'd had to overcome. *A devious eight-year-old could break them.*

Khalil climbed out of the shuttle behind him, his eyes dark with worry.

Gus put two fingers to his lips and whistled, and Irene clapped a hand over her left ear. "*Warn* me when you're going to do that, OK?"

"Sorry." A shadow of his imp grin ghosted over Gus's face, but most of his attention was on Ravi and Nola as they emerged from the jungle where they'd been waiting.

Willard's face was sharp with suspicion, but Gus waved the others to the shuttle without even trying to speak to them, and his expression relaxed a bit as he gestured for Irene and Gus to join him.

Mark went with Khalil, to show Ravi the controls,

and Louise was no doubt keeping a sharp eye on Nola as she checked the gene banks.

"I don't want you having private conversations with any of your people," Willard told Gus, with the unconscious arrogance of a man who has the guns on his side. "You can say anything you need to in front of me."

Gus's shoulders sagged further. "Very well." He was giving the best impression of defeat with dignity Irene had ever seen, but tension flowed through the hand that still lay on her arm; she wished she could send him calm and reassurance in return, instead of more tension.

About fifteen minutes dragged past before Nola came down the steps. "The gene banks are all there." She started talking a dozen feet away. "They're all alive, properly stored, and the seals on the individual containers are unbroken. Of course, they might have replaced them, but the only reason for that would be to tamper with each sample on a cellular level, and that takes time—I doubt they'd have had a chance to alter more than a few hundred, a thousand or so tops. And Ravi's pretty sure he and Mark between them can fly this thing, so it's a go."

"Good," said Gus. "You know where to—"

"Not so fast," said Willard. "I want Mark as a hostage."

"No!" said Irene. Gus's hand clenched hard on her arm and she subsided.

"Ravi has never flown this type of craft," said Gus slowly. "We were counting on Mark to explain anything unfamiliar."

"Then leave the shuttle here," said Willard. "I won't try to take it back. I don't need it. And I do need Mark, to keep the impetuous Dr. Olsen from doing anything foolish. She might take risks with her own life—she won't with Mark's."

"Then why not send them both off in the shuttle,"

said Gus. "And just keep me as a hostage. I promise you"—his lips twitched—"I'm not at all impetuous."

Willard smiled. "I'm going to leave you here as . . . insurance? I've already set it up with the guards who'll stay here—by com." He touched the button at the neck of his helmet that let him communicate with different suit-coms. "They'll call me every five minutes— if I don't answer within fifteen seconds, you die. If at any time I call them and say the prearranged code word, you die. Conversely, if you try anything here, one of them will contact me, and Dr. Olsen and Mark will pay the price. I'm not a fool, Dr. Sardakowski; I'm sure you have something planned. But whatever it is, separating you into two groups should neutralize it. I don't want to make this a shooting war. Don't make me. These creatures aren't worth dying for, but the lives, human lives, the organism in their blood will save are worth both dying and killing for. Dr. Olsen will tell you that I mean that. I'll do it."

Irene nodded slowly. "He does. He will."

Her voice sounded brittle. They'd discussed this contingency, too. Gus hadn't said anything as melodramatic as, 'I'm expendable.' But what he had said meant the same thing—*No matter what happens, no camels will leave Navohar.*

"I'm sure you mean it." Gus sounded weary and disgusted, not at all like a man whose plans had just acquired a potentially lethal crimp. "At this point, all I want is to get the lot of you out of here." He gave Irene's arm a final squeeze and stepped away, releasing her, freeing her to take whatever action she needed to. Resolve crystallized in Irene's heart, hard and sure.

No camels would leave Navohar. But no one was going to die today, either. Except maybe Willard, who she'd kill with her bare hands if he fucked things up any further.

Willard has the guns, Goodnight. Don't get carried

away. How could she get to him? He didn't care about anything except wiping out GED.

The guards had lifted their rifles when Willard made his dramatic speech; they tracked Irene as she made her way to the shuttle to explain the change of plan to Mark and the others, under Louise and Khalil's watchful eyes. Louise nodded approval when she heard, but Khalil looked even more worried. Nola's face was white; she had wanted to be the negotiator, but she was also the only colonist with medical experience, so the others overruled her. She and Ravi had the colony's future in their keeping.

"*Can* you fly this thing without Mark?" Irene asked Ravi. "Crashing this cargo would be a very bad idea."

"Not just for the cargo, either," he murmured. "Yes, I can fly it. There are a few new buttons, but the basic controls are the same."

"You know what those new buttons do?"

"No," said Ravi serenely. "So I won't push them. Don't worry, Goodnight, Nola and I can handle our part."

"I'm not worried," said Irene. Ravi gave her a strange look, and Nola snorted.

"Come on," said Louise. "You've said all you need to."

Irene turned without another word, her hand on Mark's shoulder pushing him ahead.

Willard didn't care about Mark, or her, or anyone else—not really.

Khalil was behind her on the stairs.

"You have the samples?" she asked.

Khalil nodded. "Safe on the *Stanley*. Irene, I . . . I was watching Mark on the ship." His eyes were darkly troubled.

Irene's heart froze, as if it had been flooded with liquid helium. He might be willing to spare the camels as long as access to the cure was still available, but would he be willing to sever all connection? If he said anything to Willard . . . "Yes?"

Khalil took a deep breath. "I'm trusting you, Goodnight. A lot of us are."

"You can," said Irene, her panic easing. But to do what? How could she reach through Willard's obsession?

Half a dozen guards held Gus on the far side of the clearing as the shuttle lifted, his face was bright with relief as he watched it go.

"Now the camels," said Willard firmly.

"No," said Irene, even more firmly. "Not till they're safely out of missile range. As you agreed, remember?"

Willard's brows rose at her tone, but he opened his hands and stepped back. He had all the advantages. He could afford to be generous.

It only took five minutes for the shuttle to put a mountain between it and the *Stanley*'s launchers—and their missiles, designed for deep-space combat, had no ability to change course except to follow a target they'd already locked on to, or so Mark assured them. Willard announced that Maureen, the most suspicious, would stay with the guards who watched Gus, and Louise, who carried the tranq gun, would accompany them. Irene didn't care.

How do you threaten someone who doesn't even care if he lives or dies, as long as his mission is accomplished?

"All right," she said abruptly. "It's time."

Irene tried not to look back at Gus as they left the clearing, but her gaze was drawn to him as if he'd been magnetized. He gave her an imp grin and sketched a thumbs-up, seemingly oblivious to the rifles pointed at him, and a lump of fear choked her breath away. That was the danger point, all those rifles aimed at Gus, where she couldn't control them, couldn't do a damn thing to stop their loads from tearing him apart. Gus, who, unlike Willard, cared about everything—or at least a lot. And most of those things cared back. Willard was a fool. With all the guns, all the advantages.

No, Willard wasn't a fool. And he was as angry, as determined, as motivated as she was. Maybe more.

What do you care about, Goodnight? What do you care about more than anything?

She cared about Gus, yes, very much. And Mark, of course. And all the kids back on Earth whom anomaly 1 might save. But she cared about Cow and her friends, too. Even the mysterious, dangerous forest, with the life pools nestling in its skirts, and the camel song rising over the sculpted, moonlit dunes had become precious to her. She cared about all of it.

You can't save everyone. Irene thrust the thought away. She couldn't sacrifice the camels, especially when the samples that could take their place were already aboard. Willard's choices were easy—he only cared about one thing.

Can I use that against him?

He thought he was safe, with his armor and his guns. He hadn't learned that safety could be a prison, that you had to step into the air and embrace it. Could she lock him in that prison, and walk away?

The jungle enclosed them in rustling darkness. The sharp, focused beams of the guards' hand lights only made the shadows around them denser. Irene was so worried about their plan that there was no room for fear of the kongs. Willard's obsession was his weakness. She would use it. She would take that obsession and twist him into knots. She would—

"Stop looking so worried," Mark murmured beside her. "People might think you're hiding something."

"I'm not worried," Irene told him.

Mark snorted. "You can fool some of the people all of the time, and all of the people, some of the time, but you can fool yourself anytime you need to badly enough."

"What?"

"So I'm psychologizing. Sue me."

"I'd prefer that you didn't talk anymore." Willard's politeness was almost insulting, considering the threat that underlay it.

So they didn't talk, on that long march through the tangled scrub. After they'd walked about twenty minutes, Willard looked at this watch. After fifteen more minutes, he looked again. Irene observed him, more interested in timing out the five-minute intervals in which the guards who held Gus contacted him than his impatience.

By the time an hour had passed, he was looking at his watch every few steps, his patience stretched to snapping. He answered the distant guard's prompt, and turned to Irene to demand action, but she forestalled him.

"We're here."

Unless you knew their shape, the camels' ragged silhouettes were indistinguishable from the brush around them. It was only when the humans stepped into the clearing, and the stark, white beams touched them that Willard and the others saw they were there.

The camels' eyes narrowed against the light. Cow, Kirk, Ent, and five others who'd been willing to work for turnip root. They looked hostile, for once, but they didn't move except to shuffle a few feet. The colonists had hung loops of rope around their necks, to encourage the delusion that someone could just lead them away, but how had they gotten them to stand so submissively?

Willard made a soft sound of satisfaction and waved the guards forward. "They are male and female pairs, aren't—" His suit-com beeped. "Yes, we're fine here. We've reached the camels. Keene out." He turned back to Irene. "They are male and—"

She had five minutes, starting now. Irene stepped forward and lifted a hand, and the hiss-click of fléchette guns being pumped sounded all around the clearing.

Willard's hand shot for his pistol, and Irene was horribly aware of the guards' rifles lifting—most pointed into the forest, seeking the invisible source of the threat. They'd find nothing to shoot at, for Sondi was in charge of setting up the ambush. But some of the guns pointed at her, and some—*God, I wish he'd gone with the shuttle*—pointed at Mark.

Willard's other hand reached for the com button on his suit, and that was the hand she grabbed, seizing his wrist, pulling it down even as the pistol muzzle came to rest against her diaphragm.

"If you kill Gus, the cure for GED will never reach Earth." That caught his attention as no personal threat could. He stopped trying to reach the com button, but his muscles were rigid.

"Those guns are loaded with fléchettes," said Irene. "They won't kill anyone, not even Mark and me, but they'll tear your suits to rags. Open, bleeding wounds, for almost two hours hiking back to the *Stanley*. You'll be contaminated, the lot of you, and so will the guard around Gus, for we have people there, too. There aren't enough quarantine facilities for you all. How many will be left here, to die of infection? Unless the kongs kill them first. You can't have the camels."

Willard looked down at her, something almost like apology in his eyes. "I'm sorry, my dear. I'm afraid we can."

"They will fire, Willard. They'll let you shoot all three of us if they have to."

Would he shoot? If he did, at least she wouldn't have to see Mark and Gus die. Her throat was dry.

"I expect they would fire." Willard used one hand to spin the dial that amplified his voice, loud enough to be heard by the colonists lurking in the trees. His free arm settled Irene more firmly against him, the electro-pistol snug against her ribs. "But it would be quite futile. Do you really think I didn't consider this possibility? We checked out the engineering specs on your fléchette guns in the colonists' log." His eyes roved over the silent, watching woods. "They haven't enough power to penetrate our enviro-suits, except at point-blank range. So if anyone comes near us—if anyone even shows themselves nearer than thirty feet—*we* will open fire upon *them*. And rail-shot," he went on, "will blow right through tree trunks at this range. Even if your body is concealed, we can kill you. And take the camels anyway. So please, no foolish heroics."

His com beeped. Irene stopped breathing. "Base to Captain Keene." Irene was close enough to hear the tinny voice in Willard's helmet. "This is Safety Net, clear there?"

Willard scrolled the volume back down. "This is Keene," he said slowly, scanning the quiet brush. The seconds beating past were a glacial eternity. Gus . . .

"Everything under control," said Willard, making up his mind. "Continue checks. Keene out."

"Yes, sir." The guard's voice was perfectly calm—not that of someone who'd just received a coded order to shoot a man. Irene's knees weakened—she had to clutch at Willard to stay upright.

Willard snapped off the com, released Irene, and removed her hand from his sleeve with his fingertips, as if it were a creature he didn't want to touch any more than he had to.

Mark came up and put a steadying arm around her, but it wasn't much help, for he was trembling almost as hard as she was.

"You know"—Willard's smile was almost smug—"I'm quite relieved to see the other shoe drop, so to speak. I knew you were planning something. And don't try to spook the beasts as you did last time—we're good enough shots to take out a leg, or two, without killing them. Now, perhaps, we can get on with the job without these . . . distractions. A and D groups, take those lead ropes. Those who have rifles . . .

They were taking the camels. What could she do? If Sondi and the others opened fire, Willard would kill them. If she warned the camels, he would cripple them. And if she tried anything that looked like it might succeed, he'd have Gus shot.

Maybe guns did beat brains and determination.

You can't save everyone. Nausea stirred at the thought of what might happen if she even tried. She couldn't save anyone, it seemed. Wait a minute. Maybe *she* couldn't, but . . .

Irene opened her eyes and looked at Cow. "If you've got any bright ideas, camel, now would be a really good time."

She wasn't sure what she expected. A practical joke perhaps? Something that would distract Willard and his troops sufficiently for the camels to escape? But the camels walked docilely forward, as if they'd been trained to the lead rope from birth. So much for letting other people do the rescuing.

Willard took her arm, gesturing for his men to lead the camels after him. Louise escorted Mark, and the rest of the guards formed a protective circle around them, facing out, alert for anything Sondi and the others might try.

There had to be some way out of this, there *had* to. Irene no longer cared who rescued whom, but she couldn't think of anything anyone could do to save the camels now.

"Shit!" she whispered. No wonder she'd never been able to accept defeat—it hurt.

Cow's head lifted slowly. The guard she was following let the lead rope slacken and raised his pistol.

"*Nah-wooooooon.*" The melodious call echoed, unsoftened by the surrounding trees. The others took up the call immediately. At close range it was deafening.

The helmeted troopers reached as one to turn down their audio pickups. Irene clapped her hands over her ears, tears blurring her sight. She needed an escape plan, not a concert! If only there was some way to make Cow understand . . .

But the camel strolled on, warbling away, the other camels' voices twining around hers in endless, effortless harmony. Even with her hands over her ears, the sound was almost loud enough to stop thought. Irene wished *she* had a helmet. She wouldn't have thought that just eight camels . . . surely there were more than eight voices weaving all those threads. Were the others out there, singing too?

Keeping her eyes on the shifting forest, Irene thought she could see them, moving shadows, barely visible. But not out of earshot. Irene's hearing was fading, shutting down in self-defense despite her tight-clasped hands, but the song still rang in the bones of her skull and vibrated in the pit of her stomach.

A dead branch crashed to the ground and half a dozen guards trained their guns on it before they saw what it was. Willard motioned the others to pick up their pace, worry eating at the irritation his face had displayed till then.

Irene thought the volume was growing less, but somehow the resonance grew stronger. Another branch crashed down, and another. If she didn't know better, she'd have sworn the earth itself shook beneath her feet.

The camels were trying something, but what?

The same thought evidently occurred to Willard, for he gestured for the others to run. But now the camels refused the tug on their lead ropes, striding along at their easy pace, yodeling away like strolling carolers in camel fur.

Irene's giggle died as Willard lifted his pistol and pointed it at Kirk's front leg. She couldn't hear what he said, if anything, but the meaning was perfectly clear. To her. Would the camel—

Kirk inflated his lungs, bellowing out his part in the chorus, and Willard pulled the trigger.

Irene started to leap, to knock the gun aside, *too late*—

The pistol didn't fire.

Willard pointed it at the sky and tried again, and again, but no recoil kicked at his wrist.

Irene's jaw dropped. The others came to a standstill as well, watching Willard. Several guards tried their guns to no avail.

Subharmonics, Irene realized dazedly, *and electronic equipment. But how would the camels know . . . ?*

Louise Yassir dropped her useless tranq gun and sprinted for the settlement, but the military contingent was made of sterner stuff. They led the howling camels on, their rifles held like clubs, and Irene went with them, her laughter inaudible even to herself in the battering maelstrom of sound. Her former crewmates didn't break until the first of the faceplates fractured, a spreading crack that shot across the man's horrified expression as if his face itself had broken.

His mouth opened in a scream no one could hear. He turned and ran, and the others followed, even Willard, hurtling through the brush, trying to outrun the avalanche of sound before they, too, were exposed.

Cow knelt for Irene to mount, and she managed to scramble on without taking her hands off her ears. As Mark climbed onto Ent's back, the camel reached around and licked his face with a tongue as long as an anteater's.

They burst from the forest and into the settlement. Gus crouched on his knees, doubled over. For a heart-stopping moment, Irene thought he'd been shot; then he lifted a face alight with laughter.

Kirk knelt for him, but the others were already pressing on, scrambling up the hillside at the fleeing humans' heels, and it seemed to Irene that even the rocks shattered as they passed.

They crested the ridge and started down the slope to the ships. Louise Yassir was already halfway up the ladder, and Irene watched the others follow with the deepest satisfaction she'd ever known. Who cared if she was deaf for the rest of her life?

Then the last of them crammed themselves into the lock, and the *Stanley*'s door snapped shut.

The cessation of sound was like a blow. Like gravity had suddenly vanished.

Irene could hear nothing but the ringing in her ears. Gus said something, but only a few of the stronger consonants got through. "What?"

"Other side of the ridge," Gus shouted, turning toward the trail. "Boosters."

The *Stanley*'s boosters, which would incinerate them when the ship lifted off. Irene turned Cow and urged her up the path—fast. The rest of the camels trailed them like shadows.

They crested the ridge and plunged down the other side, without pausing to look at the view.

"We can slow down now, can't we?" Irene could at least hear her own voice now.

"Well, we're safe from the *Stanley*'s takeoff." She could hear Gus's voice, too, though he sounded a bit distant. "But it occurs to me—"

The thunder of the engines' ignition drowned him out. The *Stanley* rose slowly on the other side of the ridge, a fire-breathing leviathan blotting out the sky. Irene felt the heat on her face, even at this distance. She paused to watch it go, but Gus was urging Kirk onward.

"It occurs to me," he continued, "that Captain Keene doesn't know he can't come back here. In fact, he's probably counting on it."

"So what?" The thunder was fading—the *Stanley* only a white-gold streak against the darkness.

"So it may occur to him that *we* might leave. *Henrietta* is still spaceworthy, and she could hold a lot of camels. And he has enough missiles to prevent that possibility quite effectively."

Irene's breath caught. "Is there anything you need on the *Henrietta*?"

"No. Everything of importance except the gene banks was moved down to the settlement long ago. We left them there because they were the one thing we *had* to keep safe."

"Then what's the problem?" Mark panted. "Even if they . . . blow *Henrietta* . . . ridge between us . . ."

"Yes, but he's feeling miffed. Suppose while he's firing off missiles, he decides to take out the settlement as well?"

The trail was too steep for the camels to run, but they hurried down it and broke into their bone-jarring lope across the cleared earth of the settlement. Then into the woods, veering toward the outskirts where they'd make better time, though the ground was still too rough to run much.

The other colonists and their camels joined them, shouting questions, but it was also too rough to talk, until they'd traveled several klicks and the camels finally slowed.

Irene turned to Gus. "Do you really think he'll—"

Gus held up his hand. "Listen."

The distant whine of a missile answered her question, growing louder and lower-pitched as it screamed in on its target.

Irene looked for shelter, despite the distance they'd gained. There wasn't much, small boulders and high scrub—not enough to shelter the humans, far less the camels.

Gus, the idiot, turned Kirk around and rose up on his knees to watch. The flash that silhouetted the ridge reached them before the cataclysmic thump of the explosion. Several camels shied, but Cow just snorted and flattened her big ears, trying to escape the rolling echoes.

Irene pulled her hands away from her head. "You and me, too, my friend."

Had they come far enough to survive if Willard destroyed the settlement? Seconds crawled past. Finally, Gus settled down on Kirk's back, satisfaction easing his tense expression.

"A reasonable man, your Willard, despite his anger. I commend him."

"Taking out the settlement wouldn't help him reach his goal," said Irene, sounding more confident than she'd actually been. "He doesn't care about anything but anomaly 1. Not even revenge." She felt sorry for Astrid and Maureen; neither of them stood a chance. Not in any way that mattered. "I tried to use that against him, in the end, but it didn't come off. Fortunately, *I* don't have to be the one who saves everybody." She felt . . . strange, laying that burden down. Light and unbalanced.

Gus smiled at her, then turned to Mark. "For the record, you *did* get your virus into their computer?"

"Yes. I just pulled the disc out of my pocket and told Khalil I had permission to send a letter to my parents. In some ways, writing that letter was tougher than designing the virus. I think Khalil was suspicious." Mark sounded shaky now that it was over. "But he didn't try to stop me."

"You're sure they won't find it later?" Gus persisted.

"Why should they? Once it's in the system it will hide itself; I programmed it not to activate until the *Stanley*'s computer links the net, so by the time it becomes noticeable it will be too late. Three or four hours after the *Stanley* hooks in, Navohar's coordinates will change to random numbers, all over the net—even in the Vrell database. And it will go onto people' discs with the next published update, so even the backups will be corrupted."

"Won't the pilots who took us here remember the course they set?" Irene had worried about that since the plan was first proposed, but since there hadn't been any way around it short of assassination . . .

Mark and Gus both gave her the pitying look reserved for techno-illiterates.

"It's not that simple, Auntie. They had to make four or five wave changes. And correct by tacking over the waves to the right place. Khalil or one of the others might be able to bring them to the right general area, but there's thousands of stars around here. Without knowing the precise coordinates . . . Well, their chances are really bad. I couldn't believe it when those pistols misfired. I didn't think they understood our technology that well. Thanks, my friend," he added, patting Ent's hump.

"Do you really think they knew what they were doing?" Sondi sounded dazed. "I can't believe . . ."

But Irene knew Cow had answered her plea—even if she couldn't prove it. "Thank you for my life," she told the camel softly. "Now that I finally have one, I'd hate to lose it."

Cow's third eye blinked smugly.

"Speaking of lives," said Gus, "mine is looking up just now. I rehearsed—I was thinking about that, with all those rifles pointed at me. Now that your Willard has kindly given us a shuttle and spared the settlement, we can move it to Oasis. Leave some people there year-round. Plant crops and camel pasturage. Expand our tech base, and population. Settle this planet, at last."

"That's fine for you," Irene grumbled. Expanding population? Children would be part of that. *Her* children? The thought was . . . terrifying, mostly. "I don't even have a real job around here."

Gus raised an eyebrow. "Our schoolteacher just

went off to spend most of her life in quarantine. How about that?"

"Me?" Irene's jaw sagged. "The kid flock? Thank you, but no."

"Why not?" asked Mark, who was listening with considerable interest. "You certainly kept us in line."

"Yes, but—"

"Try it for a while," said Gus. "See how you like it." He hesitated, looking almost shy. "Those terms apply to any other offer you might receive, as well. Because speaking of lives, I was wondering if you'd consider sharing one? With me. You don't have to ans—"

"Yes," said Irene, and watched his evil imp grin grow to impossible proportions.

Some chances, some people, you seized with both hands.

Mark was crowing, and Sondi shushed him, but Irene didn't mind. The future lay before her, and if the changes and challenges were intimidating, she'd have Gus and Mark and Cow, and all her new friends, to help her meet them—good company.

Even the fascinating, unsolved puzzle of anomaly 1 remained to her, for if she and Nola could induce the anomaly primes to breed before her colleagues back home managed it, they still had the message buoys.

Big Ben was rising over the forest, Seer, Rosebud, and Pipsqueak dancing before it. Irene's own grin stretched her face, but it wasn't enough—she threw back her head, and howled.